STARGATE
ATLANTIS ™

ALLEGIANCE

Book three of the LEGACY series

MELISSA SCOTT & AMY GRISWOLD

FANDEMONIUM BOOKS

An original publication of Fandemonium Ltd, produced under license from MGM Consumer Products.

Fandemonium Books
United Kingdom
Visit our website: www.stargatenovels.com

S T A R G A T E
A T L Å N T I S ™

METRO-GOLDWYN-MAYER Presents
STARGATE ATLANTIS™
JOE FLANIGAN   RACHEL LUTTRELL   JASON MOMOA   JEWEL STAITE
ROBERT PICARDO and DAVID HEWLETT as Dr. McKay
Executive Producers BRAD WRIGHT & ROBERT C. COOPER
Created by BRAD WRIGHT & ROBERT C. COOPER

STARGATE ATLANTIS is a trademark of Metro-Goldwyn-Mayer Studios Inc.
© 2004-2020 MGM Global Holdings Inc. All Rights Reserved.
METRO-GOLDWYN-MAYER is a trademark of Metro-Goldwyn-Mayer Lion Corp.
© 2020 Metro-Goldwyn-Mayer Studios Inc. All Rights Reserved.
© 2020Metro-Goldwyn-Mayer. All Rights Reserved. Photography and cover art:
© 2004-2020 MGM Global Holdings Inc. All Rights Reserved.

WWW.MGM.COM

No part of this publication may be reproduced, stored in or introduced into a retrieval system, or transmitted, in any form, or by any means (electronic, mechanical, photocopying, recording or otherwise) without the prior written consent of the publisher. Any person who does any unauthorised act in relation to this publication may be liable to criminal prosecution and civil claims for damages. If you purchase this book without a cover, you should be aware that this book is stolen property. It was reported as "unsold and destroyed" to the publisher and neither the author nor the publisher has received any payment for this "stripped book".
Print ISBN: 978-1-905586-56-1 Ebook ISBN: 978-1-80070-002-4

We'd like to thank the early readers — especially Mary Day, Katerina Niklova, Anna Kiwiel, Rachel Barenblat, Gretchen Brinckerhoff, Anna Lindstrom, Jennifer Roberson, Lina Sheng, Lena Strid and Gabrielle Lyons — whose comments, questions, translations and support helped us enormously. If errors or infelicities remain, it's because we didn't take their advice.

PROLOGUE
Previously, in Legacy...

THE WRAITH invasion of Earth has been defeated, and the city of
Atlantis has settled to the surface of the Pacific just off San Francisco.
The team assumes that this is a temporary respite before the city
returns to Pegasus, but it becomes clear that the IOA and its member
governments would like to keep the city on Earth. Woolsey recruits
Teyla to be "the face" for the people of Pegasus, and she and the rest of
the team throw themselves into the unfamiliar political arena. Despite
their best efforts, the IOA's decision goes against them: Atlantis is to
remain on Earth, to be slowly dismantled for its technology.

This hits the team hard, but there seems to be nothing left that
they can do about it. Rodney McKay resigns in a temper, and takes a
job at Area 51; Jennifer Keller goes with him, and they begin to build
their new life together. Colonel Carter, now in command of the *George
Hammond*, begins siphoning off the cream of Atlantis's military personnel for her new ship; she also invites both Ronan and Teyla to join
her team, as advisors. John Sheppard is left in limbo. There's no place
for him on the *Hammond*, and neither Woolsey nor Jack O'Neill will
accept his resignation. The only good thing about still being on the
city is that he is able to thwart the IOA's attempt to take Guide, the
captive Wraith known as Todd, for medical experimentation. Instead,
John and Carson Beckett succeed in putting him into stasis, but that
is only a temporary solution.

O'Neill, however, has one last card to play. As Atlantis has landed
in US territorial waters, he claims the city for the United States, and
in the ensuing uproar, the IOA agrees to send Atlantis back rather
than see it fall into the sole possession of any one country. Woolsey
resumes command, and the team reassembles to prepare the city for
departure before the IOA can change its mind.

Atlantis lifts from Earth, and begins the long trip to Pegasus.
Despite the shortened preparations, everything seems to be going
well—until a hyperdrive emitter fails, throwing them out of hyperspace and using up nearly all of the power in their ZPM. There is a
single planet close enough to reach at slower-than-light speeds. It's a

cold world without a Stargate, but it's their only choice. After a difficult flight, John successfully lands the city, but there's not enough power left in the ZPM to move the city or gate back to Earth.

The crew reestablishes contact with their old allies in Pegasus, only to discover that things have not been going well in their absence. The Wraith have united under a new queen who calls herself Death, and they have destroyed a number of human worlds. As the team investigates the devastation on one such planet, Todd manages to escape, only to discover that he has lost control of his alliance and has only a single hive under his command. In a bid to weaken Queen Death and regain his former power, Todd informs Atlantis of the location of the queen's next great attack.

Trusting Todd is always a gamble, but John sees this as a chance to stop Queen Death in her tracks. The team travels to the planet Levanna, where they join with the local ruler and a detachment of Genii to wait for Queen Death's attack. The Wraith arrive in force, Darts and drone infantry backed by a hiveship in orbit. The battle is close and hard fought, but at last the Wraith retreat. For the first time, Queen Death has been defeated, and even it if it's only temporary, it's a boost for humans throughout Pegasus.

However, Queen Death's response is rapid and devastating. Atlantis receives a distress call from New Athos, warning of a Culling. John leads the team through, only to find—nothing. There has been no attack; everything is perfectly normal in the settlement. As they try to figure out what happened, the Wraith attack in truth—and the Darts target Rodney. Before the others realize what's going on, the attackers have snatched up Rodney and have vanished back through the gate.

Their first desperate searches turn up nothing, and the team splits up to pursue two sets of leads with two sets of reluctant allies.

John, Teyla and Carson Beckett meet with the Genii leader Ladon Radim, who promises them the aid of his spies all over the galaxy if they will help him with a project of his own. The Genii have found an Ancient warship that had crashed on a remote planet. Genii salvage teams have been repairing it but they need someone with the ATA gene to fly it back to the Genii homeworld. John agrees that they will accompany Radim's sister Dahlia and bring the warship back to the Genii in exchange for their help. Unfortunately, the Wraith ambush them, forcing them to make a long hike across a hostile desert to reach the warship. An attack by carnivorous lizards leaves Teyla and Carson injured, and John questioning his own judgment about his rash decision to do this without consulting Atlantis or getting additional personnel — this is too much like the mission in Afghanistan that cost the life of his friend Holland many years ago.

Meanwhile, Ronon and Jennifer have been sent to meet with Todd on a world controlled by Wraith Worshippers. Despite Todd's assurances that the Wraith consider this world neutral ground, all bets are off when Queen Death's people arrive and Ronon and Jennifer are forced to hide in a tomb. One of the Wraith Worshippers double crosses Todd and tries to kill them, thwarted only by Jennifer's quick thinking. Ronon blames Todd, but he assures them he is no fonder of Queen Death than they are, and says that he will let them know if he finds out anything about Rodney's fate. They must be satisfied with that, desperate as they are to save Rodney.

At the same time, Rodney is in a situation that's far more horrific than his friends have imagined. Queen Death's men have reverse engineered the retrovirus created by Dr. Beckett that turned a Wraith into the human the Atlantis expedition called Michael, and Rodney is now a Wraith! Known as Quicksilver, and believing himself to be fully part of Queen Death's court, he is now bending all his attention to helping the Wraith conquer Atlantis.

After a dangerous flight home, John returns to Atlantis with his team and the badly damaged Ancient warship. Shortly thereafter Sam Carter arrives in Atlantis with the *George Hammond*. When Todd contacts Atlantis and tells them where Queen Death's ship will be powered down briefly for repairs, it seems like a good time to attack and retrieve Rodney. However, the mission goes wrong when Rodney, believing he's a Wraith, resists the attempts of the team to rescue him. He stuns John and as the hive ship powers up, Sam beams off John and the rest of the team before they can be captured. But Rodney is still in the hands of the Wraith, and now Atlantis faces a more dangerous foe than ever before — their own man, turned against them.

CHAPTER ONE
Moving On

"LET'S take stock," Dick Woolsey said, looking across the conference table at the weary team. No one looked very happy, but then they didn't have much reason to. He wasn't expecting much good news.

Everyone at the table had believed that the raid to recapture Dr. McKay from the Wraith would succeed. Instead, not only had the mission failed, with the *Hammond* sustaining serious damage in the process, but Colonel Sheppard's team had come face to face with McKay, and made the grim discovery that he had somehow been transformed beyond recognition.

"What's our present situation?" he prompted when no one seemed eager to speak up.

Dr. Zelenka, Colonel Sheppard, and Colonel Carter exchanged glances. He didn't think any of them were dying for the chance to report first.

"Not great," Sheppard said finally. He looked like he'd recovered fully from the series of stun blasts that had left him confined to the infirmary the day before, although he hadn't apparently managed to shave. "Rodney's still in the hands of the enemy. We're not sure what they did to him, but he looks like a Wraith, and he wasn't acting like he remembered he was on our side."

"We have some theories," Dr. Keller said, glancing at Dr. Beckett beside her. If so, they'd been up early developing them. Dick had called the meeting as early in the morning as he'd thought was reasonable, given that people did need to eat and sleep.

He wasn't sure Dr. Beckett had taken the opportunity to do either. "Aye," he said without enthusiasm. "Go on and tell them all about it."

"We've been working for some time on a retrovirus we originally hoped could physically transform Wraith into humans," Dr. Keller said. "That didn't exactly work out as well as we hoped. We've since moved on to trying to find a way to give the Wraith a more human-like metabolism that would allow adult Wraith to survive on normal food rather than feeding on humans."

"We know that," Teyla said, with a smile that was encouraging but not particularly patient.

"Sorry," Dr. Keller said. "Just trying to get everyone up to speed, here."

"Which those of us who haven't been here for a while appreciate," Carter said.

Jennifer nodded and went on quickly. "It seems pretty likely that the Wraith have found a way to reverse engineer one of the versions of the retrovirus that we tested on live subjects. They've created a way to transform humans into Wraith."

"As Michael did with his hybrids," Teyla said.

"Something like that," Jennifer said. "But he was trying to create an intermediate form between humans and Wraith. Here…" She looked across the table at Sheppard and his team. "From everything everyone's said, Rodney didn't look much like any of the hybrids."

"He was Wraith," Teyla said. "If I had not known his face, I would not have believed he was anything else."

"He had a Wraith feeding hand," Ronon said.

"That would be necessary for a complete transformation," Dr. Keller said. "Of course, it could be cosmetic. We've faked that ourselves. It would be nice if it is."

Dick frowned. "And if it's not?"

"Then he probably has the ability to feed on humans. And he may not remember why that would be bad."

Sheppard broke the silence that settled around the table. "But that's not going to happen, because we're going to get him back. Right?"

"That's the idea," Dick said. He was on his third cup of coffee, but it wasn't making up for not having had much sleep. "The problem is, he doesn't remember that we're trying to rescue him."

"That could be a side effect of whatever process they used on him," Dr. Keller said. "Our first version of the retrovirus produced complete amnesia as long as the dose was kept at a high enough level. Which, when you think about it, may actually be a good thing for us."

Ronon gave her a look. "How is that good?"

Dr. Keller shrugged. "If he was afraid of you when you tried to rescue him because he didn't remember who you were, then he might not remember his access codes for the computer."

"Or where this planet is located," Sheppard said. "Or the location of Earth. Or how ships using Ancient technology can penetrate our shields. Or—"

"I get the picture," Dick said.

"We are already working on securing the computer system," Zelenka said. "There are many ways Rodney could access the system officially, and we have already found numerous back doors. We will keep working."

"I'd be happy to help if you could use another pair of eyes," Carter said. "We dealt with a lot of security problems when I was at the SGC."

"Yes, please," Zelenka said before Dick could say that they were grateful for the offer and would take it under consideration. It probably didn't matter at this point. Any tension between himself and Carter over her help being needed in Atlantis would be beside the point if McKay effectively handed Atlantis over to the Wraith.

"Sure," Carter said. "After the meeting, why don't you show me what you've been doing?"

Zelenka nodded. "It would help if you could also read Rodney's mind."

"I don't know about that," Carter said. "But I'll see what I can do."

"As we are speaking of reading Rodney's mind," Teyla said, a little reluctantly. "Things happened very quickly, but I believe I was able to sense Rodney's presence as if he were a Wraith. I might be able to make contact with him if I were close enough."

"Something to keep in mind when we're at a point where another rescue attempt is practical," Dick said. "At the moment, though, we have no idea where Death's hive ship went after the *Hammond* entered hyperspace."

"We have no clue," Carter said. "I don't expect they're still sitting around at the repair facility waiting for us to come back, though."

"I think that's a little much to hope for," Sheppard said. "We can check back with the Genii, see if they've come up with anything."

"I'll get in contact with Radim," Dick said. "In the meantime, I want our first priority to be securing the computer system. If the Wraith can lower our shields, or lower the iris, there's nothing to keep them from dropping a nuclear bomb on us at any time."

Carter and Sheppard exchanged glances.

"They probably won't do that," Carter said.

"We've got a ZPM," Sheppard said, in answer to Dick's questioning look. "And lots of tasty people for them to snack on. Blowing us up is probably plan B."

"I don't think I like plan A any better," he said. "Assuming it's invading Atlantis and taking us all prisoner to feed on later."

Radek shifted restlessly in his seat. "You know, the longer we are sitting here talking, the longer we are not working on computer security."

"Go," Dick said. "Colonel Carter, any assistance you can provide would be appreciated."

"It's my pleasure," she said. "I've got time right now while we're repairing the damage to the *Hammond's* shield emitters. By the time that's done and I can take the *Hammond* back out, Jeannie Miller will be here to assist Dr. Zelenka."

"She is coming out aboard *Daedalus*," Zelenka said. "I wish she could have come through the Stargate, but apparently that was not possible to arrange."

As Dick was the one who hadn't been able to arrange it, he felt it was worth pointing out why. "Since the Wraith destroyed the ZPM installed in the weapons chair at Area 51, Earth's only ZPM is aboard *Odyssey*," Dick said. "The *Odyssey* is on a deep-space mission, and even if it had been possible to recall it, it would take nearly as long to reach Earth as *Daedalus* will to reach Atlantis."

"You can't ever get a cab when you need one," Sheppard said.

"Well, let us hope that the delay is not critical to preventing Atlantis from being invaded," Zelenka said. "That would be nice to think."

Dick let the door close behind Zelenka and Carter before he raised his eyebrows. "He doesn't seem optimistic."

"We are all worried about Rodney," Teyla said.

"Of course," Dick said. He suspected that his decision to assign Zelenka to Sheppard's gate team might also have something to do with Zelenka's mood, but he still didn't see any alternative. They couldn't go on as though McKay might walk through the gate at any minute. "I'd like you to think about the best tactics for another rescue attempt, should we be in that position."

"I'll do that," Sheppard said. "And also get some extra security teams to keep an eye on critical areas of the city, just in case."

Dick turned to Dr. Keller. "Assuming for a moment that we do get Dr. McKay back, what happens then?"

"We don't know," Dr. Beckett said before Dr. Keller could answer. "If the process they used is based on our original retrovirus, it should simply wear off once the virus is no longer being administered," she said.

"Yes, but we don't know that it is," Dr. Beckett said. "It could just as easily be based on the process I developed for Michael, or they could have designed it from scratch after we gave them the idea."

"Whatever they based it on, I think we should go back to your original work as a starting place," Dr. Keller said. "It's the best chance of figuring out what they did and making sure it's fully reversible."

"Please keep me posted," Dick said.

"I will," she said. "If that's all…"

"One more thing," he said. "I hate to have to be the one to say so, but we can't put all our energies into this. I am not saying that we should stop trying to recover Dr. McKay. That has to be a priority, and not just because of the obvious security risk of having his knowledge in the hands of the Wraith. He's a member of our team, and it's important to all of us that we find him. But we came out here to do any number of important things, and the hard truth is that we can't stop doing them just because one person is missing."

"I think we all understand that," Teyla said after a moment's pause. He hoped it was just that she was the quickest to speak, and not that she was the only one at the table who agreed with him.

"All right," Dick said. He stood as people began to push back their chairs. "Colonel Sheppard, if you've got time this morning, I'd like to discuss your team's schedule for the rest of the week."

"I'm not exactly booked up," Sheppard said as the others made their way out. "I'd like to have a word with Lorne about security first."

"Of course," Dick said. "There's also plenty of time for you to go shave."

"I expect there is," Sheppard said after a moment.

"We can't act as though we're in a state of crisis all the time," Dick said. "I just think we need to send the message that things are getting back to normal."

He could see Sheppard bite back whatever sharp reply had first come to mind. He might not like it, but he knew it was true. "Yeah, but what if we *are* in a state of crisis all the time?" he said instead.

"We still act like we have things under control," Dick said. "At least, I always understood that to be part of my job description."

"Which is why I'm glad you have the job and not me," Sheppard said.

Dick was tempted to point out that it was a good question whether that would still be true once he heard from the IOA about his most recent set of reports. That problem could wait, though. He thought they had enough to keep everyone busy for the day.

They'd lost their usual outdoor table to their new home's freezing weather, but John and Teyla were already camped out at a table inside when Ronon got through the mess hall line. They were sitting very close together, as if they intended to defend the table against possible attack. Teyla looked up as he approached and smiled. John didn't exactly smile, but he relaxed a little and nudged a chair toward Ronon with his foot.

"Are we expecting to get shot at over lunch?" Ronon said, sitting down and spearing a bite of meat on his fork.

"Maybe," John said with his mouth full of sandwich.

"No," Teyla said. "We are expecting to be shot at eventually."

"So what else is new?" Ronon said.

John snorted. "Not so much." He stood up, glancing down at Teyla with what looked very close to a smile, and picked up his tray. "See you when you get back."

"Where are you going?" Ronon asked as John made his way out.

"New Athos," Teyla said. "I said I would pick up Torren this afternoon, and I have goods to take for trade. Mr. Woolsey says we may trade some of the packaged food for fresh, as well as the medical supplies and equipment brought out on the *Hammond*. We owe a certain amount already for the milk." She swirled her coffee in her cup pointedly.

"We could trade more manufactured stuff than we do," Ronon said. "It's not like there's not a market."

Teyla shook her head. "I thought so when I first came to Atlantis, but there would be no profit in it," she said. "It is so expensive to transport anything aboard one of the ships. The cost is in the generation of so much power."

Ronon shrugged agreement, although he wondered sometimes why they didn't make an effort to use some of the city's machines to produce something that would be in demand outside the city. "Want me to come along?"

Teyla looked tempted, but like she wanted him to talk her into it.

"I hate to go among my own people with armed backup."

"You're going to be armed," Ronon said.

"Yes," she said, her expression sharpening. He didn't think she'd ever be as easy on New Athos as she'd been before the time she and Keller found it overrun by the Bola Kai, her people gone.

"So, I'm a friend. Who happens to be armed."

"You are," she said, smiling. "Very well, if you have the time."

It might have been better to wait for someone who could fly a jumper, Ronon thought when he saw the boxes she'd stacked onto a cart in the gate room, but he gave it an experimental shove and found it easy enough to push.

"I can't cover you if I've got this," he pointed out.

"I am not really expecting an ambush," Teyla said. "It is just as well these days to have…"

"Friends who happen to be armed," Ronon finished. "Yes."

"Give my regards to the Athosians," Woolsey said from the rail above.

Teyla smiled. "We will."

On the other side, it was actually warm, a light breeze moving the tall grasses of the gate field. Teyla reached for one side of the cart's handle, and Ronon shook his head. "Keep your hands free," he said.

She shook her head. "We are so jumpy these days."

Ronon shrugged. "It's what McKay would say."

Teyla smiled. "I never thought I would hear you standing in for Rodney. Besides, if he were here he would keep his hands free to cover us both so that he did none of the work."

"Yep," Ronon said. He wrestled with the cart for a minute, Teyla eventually lending a hand to tug it free of a rut in the too-soft dirt.

"It is too quiet without him," she said when they had the cart freed.

"There wasn't anything else to do," Ronon said.

"I am not blaming you," Teyla said. "I hope you do not blame yourself."

"It was my decision," he said. "I made the call I had to make. How it went down is my responsibility."

"Then if we had all been captured, that would have been your responsibility as well. That would not have been better." Teyla sounded a little frustrated.

"I'm not saying it would be," Ronon said. "Sheppard, though…"

"He blames himself," Teyla said. "Not you. And he would not truly be happier if we were all in the hands of the Wraith now."

"If he'd been in charge, do you think he would have pulled us out?"

Teyla looked like she was considering her answer carefully. "It is terribly hard for him to leave a man behind," she said. "I think—"

"Teyla!" Halling called from ahead, and Teyla lifted her head.

"Halling!" she called in greeting, her face lighting. Although she couldn't spend much time on New Athos these days, at least she could visit. Surely she must appreciate that even more keenly after months of thinking all her people lost, and more months spent a galaxy away from them.

He and Kanaan were waiting at the outskirts of the camp, Torren in Kanaan's arms, and once they drew close Teyla went swiftly to take her son. She and Kanaan exchanged awkward smiles, although when he would have pressed his forehead to hers, she ducked her head to Torren's hair instead.

Ronon turned away, suspecting that her next move would be to draw him into the conversation to make a buffer between them, and not intending to let her. "Halling," he said.

"Ronon, my friend," Halling said. "What news from Atlantis?"

"No news," Ronon said. "The Wraith still have McKay."

"I am sorry for that," Halling said.

"We all are," Kanaan said. "It makes Atlantis a dangerous place."

"There is no safe place," Teyla said, her arms tightening around Torren. If Ronon could see it, he thought Kanaan could as well. "We have all seen that."

"We have," Halling said. "All the same…" He glanced at Kanaan, as if unsure he wanted to continue.

"All the same, it is something we must consider," Kanaan said. "We would like the people of Atlantis to come here for the milk we trade them, so that we are not sending our young men and women to the city of the Ancestors when it may at any time come under attack."

"That has always been the case," Teyla said. "Surely Jinto has not said he is afraid to come."

"We are too few, and we will be two fewer when you leave today," Kanaan said. "We spoke of this in council for a long time, and it was agreed that no one can take the risk for trade goods, no matter how comfortable they make us."

Teyla's face was sharp, her body tensing as if for a fight. Torren frowned, sensing her mood. "You did not ask me to be a part of this council. It is usual for all to be asked if they wish to speak."

"You were not here," Halling said. "You were not here, and you were not in the city when we called. Decisions must be made when there is something to decide, not at your pleasure."

"Halling," Teyla said, looking for the first time more hurt than angry.

"You are not a child, for me to scold you," Halling said. "I know you were looking for your friend, and I would have done the same. But we could not wait for you."

Teyla took a deep breath. "I will speak to Mr. Woolsey," she said. "We can certainly send someone here to trade, although I will not always be able to come myself."

"It might be better if you were not the one to come," Halling said.

"And what do you mean by that?"

"Who are you representing when you come to us to trade?" Kanaan asked. "The Lanteans, or the Athosians? We are hardly trade partners if you speak for us both, and stand always between us."

"I have brought goods from the expedition here for more than five years," Teyla said. "And I have brought them your work in trade, and no one has complained that I have made a poor bargain for them."

"Our work," Kanaan said. "Not the work of your hands. The things made here are not yours to trade, Teyla. Not anymore."

Teyla looked at him as though he'd struck her. "I did not think you were so angry at me," she said.

"I am not angry at you," Kanaan said, and he sounded like that might be true. "But if you come back to us again to trade with goods from Atlantis, we will expect to bargain with you as with any trading partner, and you must not also be part of the council to choose our terms."

"Must I not?" Teyla said, her voice dangerous.

"I wish that you would not," Kanaan said. "The truth is I cannot stop you. I expect you could persuade people to your point of view, if you were here to speak on your behalf. But what then? You will go back to Atlantis, and then what? Now that you are gone, the people look to me to warn them of the Wraith, to protect them. That is not a thing I have ever wanted, Teyla, believe me. I would much rather you were here to do it instead."

"I am sorry," Teyla said. "I thought you understood why I must stay in Atlantis, must help defend us all from the Wraith."

"I do," Kanaan said. "It would be easier if I did not." He turned away abruptly, and Halling cleared his throat.

"Thank you for bringing us these goods in trade," he said. "We will look for your man to come to us three days from now for the milk, and we can talk then of any other changes to the trade agreement."

"I will ask Mr. Woolsey when it would be possible for him to meet with you," Teyla said, the words too pleasant, as if talking to a stranger.

"That is well." Halling embraced her, touching his forehead to hers, and after a moment's stiffness she returned the embrace. "We will look for your coming as well," he said. "You are always welcome among us."

"I never thought you would need to say so," Teyla said, and Ronon looked away; he didn't think she'd want him to see if she cried.

She talked cheerfully enough to Torren on the way back to the Stargate, but it was the kind of relentless good cheer that mothers everywhere used in an attempt to convince children that nothing was wrong.

"Ride!" Torren demanded, struggling to clamber down and onto the cart, now empty of all but Torren's traveling bag.

"Can't hurt," Ronon said, and Teyla let him climb down to the cart, where he sprawled happily. He risked a glance at Teyla. Her eyes were clear, but her jaw was set hard. "You okay?"

"I would never cheat my own people in a trade," Teyla said hotly. "I cannot imagine that anyone would think I would do such a thing."

"You could try to get back to New Athos more," Ronon said.

"Back," Teyla said, shaking her head more ruefully. He waited for her to say more, catching Torren when he seemed about to topple to the ground. "I lived on New Athos for a few weeks, not even for a whole season. I helped build the settlement, but this season I have not put crops in the ground, or hunted, or cared for anyone else's children."

"They're your people," Ronon said. "That still matters."

"Of course it does," Teyla said. "But it is Miko who I will help with her work in return for her watching my child. No one in Atlantis grew the food we eat, but I will earn my share of it guarding the city of the Ancestors. For the Athosians, all I have been for seasons is a trader, and now even that…"

"You did rescue them all from Michael," Ronon said. "That was kind of important."

"The people of Atlantis rescued them," Teyla said. "I was in no position at the time to rescue anyone, including myself."

"You would have," Ronon said.

"But I did not."

"That's not your fault," Ronon said.

Teyla smiled faintly. "It is my responsibility."

"Maybe they'll get over it."

"It is possible," Teyla said, in a tone that suggested she thought he was missing the point. "Come up now, Torren. You may not ride on the cart through the Stargate."

Torren made a noise of protest and clung tighter to the cart as Ronon dialed the gate, leaving Teyla to pry him loose and gather him up. "Ride," Torren demanded in what sounded like an imitation of Teyla's most dangerous voice, although he didn't expect she would let him follow it up by hitting anybody with sticks if they didn't agree.

"Up for a minute," she said, wrestling him onto her hip and catching at his bag when its contents nearly spilled out onto the grass. "We will be home very soon."

Ronon wasn't sure if she'd noticed what she'd said, but Torren nodded decisively and said, "Home."

CHAPTER TWO
Aboard the Hive

THE COMMANDER'S quarters aboard the hive ship Just Fortune were pleasant, even luxurious, as befitted a hive whose queen was currently absent on business of her own. Except that that was a lie, as much of a bluff as anything else the commander had managed to achieve since he had escaped from Atlantis, as much a lie as the ridiculous name John Sheppard had given him. He was Guide, commander and Consort, and if the Lanteans called him "Todd" that was not his concern. His concern was his ship, his men, and the Lanteans' unaccountable failure to rescue Rodney McKay.

They failed. Guide was unable to hide his anger, but Bonewhite faced him squarely.

Did you honestly expect otherwise?

I thought if I handed them Death's hive powered down and feeding, they would be able to recover McKay and destroy it. They've been extremely efficient at such things before. Guide took a breath, made himself relax, his hands uncurl. *Which makes our position even more awkward.*

There was a flash of something, bitter amusement, from Bonewhite, but when Guide rounded on him, the other had mastered his thoughts.

And what are we to do about it?

We are summoned to our queen's assistance, Guide said, without inflection. *We can respond or we can flee. I see no choice there.*

No. Bonewhite met his gaze. *We must do as she demands.*

Guide bared teeth, a general complaint. He could no longer sit still, paced the length of his outer chamber, coat swirling at his ankles. Their repairs, at least, were finished; the hive was a strong as it would be, the hull healthy, systems fed… And how Sheppard had failed to destroy Bright Venture when it lay helpless, failed to rescue McKay — Bonewhite was watching, head tipped to one side in silent question, and Guide made himself stop, stand still again in the center of the oval room.

What do our people make of this?

Bonewhite laughed. *That we are trussed for feeding.*

Guide smiled reluctantly. *Besides that. What do they think of Queen Death?*

Ah. Bonewhite shrugged. *The clevermen are loyal to Steelflower, to a man. Ember's influence is strong there, and he — doesn't love her. Not after their first meeting.*

Guide nodded, remembering the ritual submission, Ember's face thinning as the queen fed, claiming his hive as her own. He had thought they were beyond such things, did not need to revert to the ways of their ancestors…

The blades, however… Bonewhite showed teeth. *There have been quarrels in commons and in the game rooms, though for now the majority holds for Steelflower.* He paused, gauging his moment. *We can't keep up the pretense much longer.*

I know, Guide said. *But the alternative is no better.*

We could agree that she was missing long enough that we could assume her dead, Bonewhite said, but his tone was less confident than the words. *Accept Death provisionally.*

She'd never permit that, Guide answered. *And it gains us nothing, anyway.*

And then there is McKay, Bonewhite said, after a moment, and Guide snarled.

*McKay — *

Is a danger to us all, Bonewhite said. *Frankly, I don't know why Death hasn't turned her fleet on us, or declared us outlawed and fair game. I can't understand how he could have resisted her this long.*

The Lanteans are stronger than we think, Guide said, but Bonewhite had given voice to his nightmare. McKay might be strong, despite his erratic nature, but Death was stronger by far. She was the strongest queen Guide had seen in generations; he didn't know himself if he could stand against her for very long. More likely he would be on his knees in an instant, as he had knelt to her mother-in-lineage Coldamber, when the Ancients still ruled in Atlantis… He shook his head, shook away the memory. *She has requested aid, clevermen and help with the repairs. I intend to send her Ember.*

Bonewhite looked up at that, and Guide glared at him.

Well? He was your man first, your choice.

*He is," Bonewhite agreed. *And a good one. I trust him.*

Good. Guide intended his tone to end the conversation, but

Bonewhite didn't move.

You haven't always fared well with ambitious clevermen, he said.

I want him to find out what is happening with McKay, Guide said. *Nothing more.*

Guide had not expected Ember to return so quickly from the Bright Venture, felt his back tighten with fear as the drone announced him. The door spiraled open, and Ember spoke even before it closed behind him.

I have news.

He was trembling, Guide saw, and felt the tang of fear beneath the words. It was contagious, a spark to tinder, and he controlled himself with an effort.

Within. This was not the place for this discussion, not the public room, but the inner chamber, the most private place on this queenless hive. He pointed to the shadowed door, and Ember obeyed. It was warm inside, the lights soft and pleasing, the walls curved to hold the sleeping niche and a comfortable seat, where he could curl into the hive's embrace, and he saw Ember relax and draw a shuddering breath, soothed by the surroundings.

What are you doing here? Guide asked, and the cleverman dipped his head.

I told them I needed diagnostics — that we had some to spare, and it would make the work go faster. They won't miss me for an hour yet.

Good. Guide nodded. *And your news?*

McKay — he's told them nothing.

There was a note in Ember's voice that made Guide lift his own head sharply. *And how can that be?* Humans were not that strong, to stand against a queen —

The queen's chief cleverman, Dust, Ember said. *It was his plan to take McKay. He's done much work on human DNA, and on the retrovirus that the Lanteans used on the blade who became Michael. He's used something like that on McKay. He's made him Wraith.*

Guide stood frozen. Impossible, he wanted to say, but clearly it was not. Disastrous? Yes, very possibly. If McKay were Wraith, were a cleverman loyal to his queen — he knew too much of Guide's dealings with the humans, with Sheppard and Teyla Emmagan. Guide closed his eyes to block out the images, the hive shredded, his own death assured. It had not happened, so clearly McKay had not volunteered everything he knew. *Why, then — *

Because in transforming him, they've made him believe he's one of us — he believes he's Dust's brother, a lord among the clevermen. Ember paused. *Or believes he was Dust's brother. Dust was killed when the Lanteans tried to rescue McKay.*

And they did not try to kill McKay, Guide said.

They would not, Ember said, practically. The trembling had stopped, soothed by the warmth and the pale shiplight. *They knew him, even if he didn't know them.*

Guide growled at that, but he could hardly blame them. They had been taken by surprise— he had not known to warn them—and he would not have killed a man of his own under the circumstances. But he wished it had been otherwise. *Why didn't he know them?*

Because — I think because of the nature of the virus. Ember's fear was fading fast, replaced by a cleverman's interest. *I believe that Dust wished to make him a willing party to this, to make him believe he was Wraith in truth. I spoke to one of the assistants, and he said McKay could be Dust's brother, at least in looks. His hair is cropped and he bears no tattoos, but he is a man and whole.* He held up his feeding hand. *He feeds.*

It was possible. Michael had become human, or close to it, had lost the ability, the need to feed on the humans' lifeforce. Guide himself had once accepted a similar transformation, the gift of another retrovirus, felt his body change and alter, becoming a child again — though that had ended badly. He had still not entirely decided if that had been deliberate betrayal, though if it had been, he did not think Sheppard had known. Or Keller, and if they had not, he could not think who to blame. His thoughts had chased themselves around that circle a hundred times before: old business, long past. He looked instead at Ember, young and eager in the gentle light.

And he does not remember.

No more than we are told Michael did, Ember answered. *Which is logical if one wishes him to cooperate. They have told him that he was captured and tortured by the Lanteans — and it worked well enough, Commander, that he fought back when the Consort would have rescued him.*

So, Guide thought. That explained much. And it gave him a little breathing room. *What do they plan now that Dust is dead?* With any luck, they would kill McKay as unmanageable, and that would keep him safe a little longer —

The queen wants to destroy Atlantis, Ember said.

I knew that.

Ember allowed himself a demure smile, acknowledging the joke. *She believes McKay—Quicksilver—holds the key, if he can be made to remember so much without also remembering who he is.*

Guide nodded. *Who now commands the project?*

No one, as yet. Ember lifted his head. *Propose me, lord, and I will assure that McKay does not betray you.*

Guide looked at him for a long moment: a young man, a clever-man, handsome and quick and ambitious. The last time he'd trusted such a one, he'd lost a cruiser and the man himself—but there was little choice.

Very well, he said. *I'll put you forward. But, Ember. If McKay remembers too much—kill him.*

Ember bowed. *That was my intent, Commander.*

The lords of Queen Death's zenana were well fed. That was clear in the instant Guide stepped past the waiting drones, clear in the lazy smiles and the full-fleshed faces. He felt instantly at a disadvantage, sharp and dusty in his plain leathers, while the zenana's lords gleamed with dark jewels and silver glittered in hair and beards. Death reclined in her throne, sitting casually askew, her head resting against one of the great bone wings that curved above the center.

Guide, she said, and her voice was a caress. *Good. There is a matter for discussion.*

As my queen wishes, he answered, bowing, and glanced quickly at the others. Farseer was there, looking sleek, his braid bound with silver and the dark blossom of a new tattoo on his scalp. Sky, the youngest of the blades, leaned against Death's throne, his hair and coat in art-ful disarray, while the Old One rested his back against the chamber wall, watching with an air of sardonic detachment. It had been a long time since Guide had moved in such company, and then he had stood in Sky's place, Consort and companion, but he felt himself respond anyway, his body shifting to meet the rhythm of the once-familiar dance. He swept the others with a look, respect balanced against his own worth, and saw heads tip in grudging answer.

My queen. That was the cleverman who stood at the foot of Death's throne, head bowed. He was not a man Guide knew, his mind pale and thin as sunlight in winter. *Forgive me if I press you, but I believe we must make a decision soon.*

And so we shall, Death said. She looked at Guide. *We speak of the one called Quicksilver.*

Rodney McKay, Guide said, and Farseer bared teeth.

You know this?

Clearly. Guide did not look at him, his attention focused instead on Death, watching carefully for signs of anger. *And I have heard, too, that you are considering abandoning the — project.*

I am not Dust, Wintersun said. *I cannot pretend that this — this creature, this creation — that it is a man and my brother, as Dust did. Better to end this farce, and take what information we can from him.*

Dust said he could acquire McKay's cooperation. That was the Old One, his tone as stiff as unoiled metal. *That was the purpose of this charade. Not mere information.*

But he cannot remember, Death said. *No matter how willing he is to aid us, if he cannot remember Atlantis's systems, he's of little use to us.*

Dust did say the drug could be changed. That was another blade, voice sharp as a hook. *Wintersun could do more.*

I am not Dust, Wintersun said again. *And I can promise nothing.*

If I may, my queen. Guide bowed. It was a risk, he knew, but less of one than letting Death's blades carve information indiscriminately from the human's mind.

Death lifted a hand. *Say on.* She looked more amused than anything, as though she enjoyed the clash of words as much as any other combat.

I have a cleverman of my own, the chief of my hive, Guide said. *He is a master of sciences biological, wise beyond his years. And he is not so squeamish as some. Let him take over the project.*

A stranger, Wintersun said.

An ally's man, Farseer corrected, but without emphasis.

Death tipped her head to one side, her hair gleaming in the ship-light. *And your cleverman is — clever?* She smiled.

He is the best I have. Guide bowed again, hiding the hope that rose in him. If he could get away with this, if he could place Ember in command, then he would have achieved at least some temporary safety.

To take Atlantis from within, the Old One said thoughtfully. *That would be a feat, indeed.*

Dust's work was promising, Death said. *Very well. Let your man take his place, and you, Wintersun, will not need to work with the changeling. Let it be done.*

Guide lowered his head still further, aware of the envy at the edges of the chamber. *It shall be as you command, my queen.*

CHAPTER THREE
Back Doors

IT WAS a quiet afternoon, a steady snow falling beyond the gateroom windows, the kind of snow that made the younger airmen grin at each other and talk of Christmas, for all it was August by their calendar. It made Radek think of pastries in coffee houses and regrettable student love affairs, snow dotting his glasses on the walk back to his apartment, lamplight golden under the heavy sky, not hurrying because the anticipation was part of the pleasure. He sighed, remembering coffee rich with real cream, napoleons and little neapolitan biscuits. The cream was the thing he missed most, if he were honest with himself, and it was also the thing least likely to be supplied. Pegasus didn't seem to run to dairy cattle.

He glanced at the boards below him, lovely monotonous rows of green lights and nominal readings. He had spent most of the morning closing one of Rodney's back doors — a nice piece of code, designed to restore itself after deletion, but only after he had run certain checks — and he thought he'd earned a quiet afternoon. On the board below, Salawi had her laptop open and was looking at one of the tutorials, frowning over a set of diagrams. Taggert and another former SGC tech — Mcmillan, Radek remembered — were talking quietly, Taggert leaning over Mcmillan's shoulder to look at something on his screen.

Radek's attention sharpened abruptly. Something had changed, some miniscule shift in posture that meant they were no longer talking about baseball or football or whatever, and he had started down the steps even before Taggert looked over her shoulder.

"We've got — something — doc."

"Something?" Radek repeated. He stopped behind Mcmillan, and Taggert edged away, giving him room. "Let me see."

"It's gone," Mcmillan said. He was older, another sergeant, with graying hair cut close to his scalp and a constant wary look that seemed to have developed at Cheyenne Mountain and hadn't improved since he'd joined Atlantis.

"What is gone?" Radek asked. The readings all looked normal, even perfect — Mcmillan was monitoring the external sensors, and they rarely showed small anomalies. Except for the pigeons, of course, and a minor issue with falling ice…

"There," Taggert said, and Mcmillan hit keys to freeze the image. He dragged the result to a secondary screen, revealing readings once again reset to nominal.

"OK," Radek said. He slid into the seat next to Mcmillan's console. "What does it say that was?"

"It doesn't even say it happened," Mcmillan said.

"That is not a good sign," Radek murmured. He tipped his head to one side, studying the screen. It claimed to have picked up an anomaly on the sensors below the old North Pier, something small and dense and close. Like a bomb, he thought, with a jolt of adrenaline, and then common sense reasserted itself. A bomb was not on the face of it impossible, but it was impossible for one to simply appear beneath the city, not without triggering sensors designed to watch for those very things. "Salawi, run a diagnostic on the North Pier underwater array, please — the old North Pier, I mean. Sergeant Taggert, is there anything on your arrays?"

Taggert was already back at her workstation, paging rapidly through screens. "No, nothing. I show everything nominal."

"North Pier array is nominal, too," Salawi said. "Sir, could it be one of those squids?"

They seemed to have caught everyone's attention, Radek thought, along with the pigeons. "Too dense," he said, absently. Not a real reading, not something actually out there, but not a normal malfunction, either. A power issue? Some kind of fluctuation that triggered a ghost signal when the current hit a crucial point? He looked at Mcmillan's screens, and nodded as he saw the other man already typing in the query.

"Power's steady, doc," Mcmillan said, and Radek sighed.

"OK." He looked at the other boards again, the reassuring green lights, the steady pulse of data. At least it was not an immediate crisis — and perhaps not even a crisis at all, but he knew better than to make that assumption. "OK," he said again. "We are going to decouple the outgoing comm array from the main city system. Salawi, you'll handle communications manually until I say otherwise. And when it's done, get me Mr. Woolsey, please."

"OK, Dr. Zelenka," Salawi said, and shifted to the new position.

Taggert's hands were already busy on her keys, and Mcmillan came around the front of the consoles to flip the last switches.

"Done," he said, and Taggert nodded.

"Confirmed." She gave him a sideways glance. "Are we in trouble?"

"I have no idea," Radek answered. "Better to be safe."

"Amen," Taggert said, and Salawi cleared her throat.

"Mr. Woolsey's on his way, Doctor."

"Thank you." Radek saw the door open, Woolsey bustling out with a wary look on his face, and made himself focus on the consoles. There was no real reason to think that someone — say it, he told himself, that *Rodney* had been forced to write a program that would make the city broadcast its location, no reason except that it had been done before, and it was better to be safe…

"Is there a problem?" Woolsey asked.

"I don't know," Radek answered. "We picked up an errant sensor reading, which I am not sure is actually a sensor issue, but more likely to be a code issue."

"One of Dr. McKay's back doors?" Woolsey sounded pained.

"Possibly. Possibly someone using one of them. And quite possibly nothing." Radek took a breath. "I've disconnected our communications from the city's main systems as a precaution."

"That's quite a precaution," Woolsey said. "Can we manage this way?"

"Oh, yes, yes, that's not a problem," Radek said. "It's just — I need to look at this code more carefully—"

"Please," Woolsey said. "Go right ahead."

Radek settled himself in front of his screen, shoving his glasses to a more comfortable position, frowned as the code for the sensor array began to scroll slowly past. There wasn't much an intruder could do from here, he thought — well, Rodney could do something, and he himself could probably find a way to promote himself into more critical systems, but it wasn't the place he would have chosen to start. Something in the Ancient code caught his eye, a break in the hypnotic pattern, and he touched keys to stop the scrolling. Yes, there it was, a line, ten lines, that shouldn't be there, that weren't Ancient but definitely their own. Except that they had not recorded a modification to this section of the system. Perhaps in the early days, when they'd been struggling just to stay alive? But the underwater sensors had hardly been a priority then. He stared at the screen, trying to make sense of the neat, elliptical code. It was Rodney's style, for sure — it was amazing how terse his code was, for such a talkative man — and a voice spoke behind him.

"Problems?"

And that, of course, was Colonel Carter, though how she had heard that something was happening was outside Radek's ability to guess. "A very good question," he said loud, and she came down to the second tier of consoles to look over his shoulder.

"What have you got?"

"This," Radek said. "This is Rodney's work, I think." He highlighted the lines of code, expanded them so that they filled the screen. "But we did not record him working on this part of the city's programming, and I do not see —" He stopped, exhaled sharply. "Except now I do."

"What?" Woolsey asked.

Carter leaned closer, peering at the screen. "A back door?"

"Of a kind." Radek glared at the symbols. "I have spent six hours already today removing one problematic routine from our systems, and now — this is what results. It is not progress."

It was Woolsey who spoke first. "So this is definitely something of McKay's."

"Yes. Well, I am nearly certain. But yes. This is another iteration of the program I removed earlier, set to pop up again after a certain amount of time." Radek pushed his glasses up again. "And it is now caught and contained, so —"

"No harm, no foul?" Carter said. The words had a distinctly dubious tone.

"Yes. But there will be more. There are more." Radek shrugged. "And I am running out of places that I think Rodney would think to look."

"Mrs. Miller will be here on *Daedalus*," Woolsey said. "In five days. That will help."

Radek took a deep breath, and then another. He despaired sometimes of explaining anything technical to Woolsey — though perhaps the question was intended to remind the rest of the gateroom crew that help was on the way. That would be almost Machiavellian enough for Woolsey.

"We hope Mrs. Miller will be able to speed up the process," he compromised. "And of course Colonel Carter's help has been invaluable —"

"Then we will carry on," Woolsey said, firmly, and turned away.

Radek said something in Czech that he sincerely hoped no one would repeat and thrust his hands into his hair.

William Lynn found an empty table in the corner of the *Daedalus's* messroom, and opened his laptop like a shield. The room was crowded, even after the hot food service had ended, airmen and officers gathering for a snack or a cold meal or quick cup of coffee as they went on and off duty, and the volume of conversation was not going to be overcome by the music he had on his computer. But it was better than the narrow cabin he shared with three other men. At least his age and seniority had gotten him a lower bunk—that and being both quick and politely determined—but the poor reservist who had the bunk above him snored, and the meteorologist opposite was an insomniac who lay awake for hours reading from his phone. The fourth man—a wormhole physicist—hadn't said much of anything since offering to take the upper bunk, just lay there listening to his iPod with his forearm thrown across his eyes. Having second thoughts, William guessed: he was willing to bet all the civilians had signed their contracts before things started to go wrong in Pegasus.

Not that second thoughts were all that unreasonable; he'd had second thoughts himself. Any sane person would, confronted with a posting not to a well-defended Ancient city, nestled pleasantly into tropical seas, but a city newly vulnerable, and a climate that resembled a North Sea oil rig. Though at least on a rig, you were likely to be spared attacks by life-sucking aliens… He smiled to himself then. He'd thought he was pretty tough, able to cope with just about anything—after all, he'd grown up on dig sites all across the Middle East, and spent most of his working life either in the field or playing with the artifacts brought back by the SG teams, both of which had a rather high risk of unpleasant if unintended consequences. But being eaten by aliens was definitely in a different class from the risks he was used to. It had taken him a full twenty-four hours to decide that, when you came down to it, dead was dead.

And the crisis meant that his project was that much more valuable. His original proposal had been a survey of contemporary Pegasus-galaxy technologies with an eye to helping their allies take the next steps in their development. With the Wraith on the offensive, it was already clear that he'd be expected to dive straight into what had been Phase 2. Which was all right, it was a manageable task, but, as usual, scholarship would go by the board…

"Mind if I join you?"

He looked up at the voice, an automatic smile on his face. The speaker was one of the *Daedalus's* officers, a good-looking, red-haired lieutenant colonel, and he shook his head. "Not at all, colonel. Please, make free."

"Thanks." She returned the smile. "Mel Hocken. I have the *Daedalus's* 302 wing."

"William Lynn." There was no room to shake hands without risking everything on the little table, and her hands were busy with her tray in any case. William compromised with a wider smile and a nod, and shifted his laptop to make more room.

"Thanks, Dr. Lynn," she said again, and settled herself in the opposite chair. "Physicist?"

"Archeologist, actually," he answered, and her smile widened.

"Ah. Atlantis's version of Dr. Jackson."

"God, I hope not," William said, and she laughed aloud.

"I mean, I'd rather not end up dead quite so many times," William said. "Or Ascended. Or many of the things that have happened to him."

"I can understand that," Hocken said, and turned her attention to constructing a sandwich from the contents of her tray. She'd selected quite a lot of the pale orange 'cheese' that seemed to be a favorite of the *Daedalus's* crew, and Lynn looked hastily back at his screen, touching the pad to call up the reports he'd uploaded in the last hours before he left Earth.

The trouble was, Jackson had been right the first time they'd discussed this mission. No one had ever done anything approaching a systematic survey of the cultures the Atlantis expedition had encountered. There were some solid facts — for example, it was a good bet that the Wraith were preferentially feeding on the more technologically advanced cultures — and some plausible theories, like the correlation between proximity to the Stargate and strategies for dealing with the Wraith, but there was so much more he would like to have known before he started making suggestions. And a part of him still felt guilty about that, too; he was supposed to study the dead past, not meddle with the living.

"Excuse me."

William looked up again to see a tired-looking blonde in civilian clothes standing beside the remaining chair. He recognized her at once — *Daedalus* was too small for a story like hers not to have spread — and saw the same flash of sympathy on Hocken's face.

"Is this seat taken?" Jeannie Miller asked.

"No," William began, and in the same instant, Hocken said, "Help yourself."

"Thanks." Jeannie seated herself, set her mug carefully on the table in front of her. A tag dangled over the lip, yellow and green letters proclaiming it to be chamomile and caffeine free. Jeannie frowned at it, and began to dunk the bag up and down as though that would hasten the steeping process.

William looked at Hocken, saw the same embarrassed uncertainty in her face. You couldn't pretend everything was normal, that Jeannie Miller was just another civilian contractor heading to Atlantis, not when everyone knew that her brother was Rodney McKay, and everyone also knew that McKay had been captured by the Wraith and was probably dead, and she was going to Atlantis to try to help protect the city from anything her brother might have betrayed. But at the same time, it was obvious from her stare, from the tilt of her head and the way she avoided their eyes, that she did not want a conversation. He cleared his throat nervously, and Jeannie looked up, her lips curving in something that wasn't a smile.

"Please don't," she said. "I know — I appreciate it, but…"

Her voice trailed off, and William felt himself blush. "No, no, of course not." He sounded more English than ever, the Hooray-Henry voice of his childhood coming back at the worst possible time. But at least it was something to hide behind, along with the laptop screen. Across the table, Hocken was staring intently at her sandwich, a touch of color on her cheeks as well. William cleared his throat again, and tugged the laptop toward him, pretending to study the report. The last thing he wanted to do was add to her troubles.

"Sorry," Jeannie said, to no one in particular, and pushed herself away from the table. For a second, William thought she was going to leave the tea, but she turned back to snag it, before working her way to the door.

"Well," Hocken said, after a moment. "That was awkward."

"Very," William agreed, and looked back at the laptop.

Quicksilver did not know how long he had lain in his nest, wrapped in sorrow and the aching loss, the absence that left his mind empty. Long enough for the hive to be underway again, long enough for strangers to come, and go again when he would not respond, long enough that he felt empty, as dry as the touch of his brother's mind. He should move, he knew, rise and be about his work, but that was lost to him, too, and so he waited, too drained to do more than wait for what would come next.

Quicksilver?

The voice in his mind was banked fire, a coal still warm at the core; not a man he knew, and Quicksilver rolled over, untangling himself from the quilts that filled his nest. It should have been Dust, standing there, and the sorrow broke over him like a wave, so that he ducked his head, covering his face with his off hand until he had mastered himself.

I honor your grief, Ember said, and there was compassion in his mind.

Quicksilver peered from between his fingers, seeing a blade standing there — no, a cleverman, but a cleverman in blade's clothes, his long leather coat dulled and dark. He was fair, and passably handsome, his hair pulled up and back in a style Quicksilver hadn't seen before. A stranger, then, not of the hive, and he lowered his hand, lips parting in a reflexive snarl.

Who are you?

Ember ducked his head. *I am chief cleverman of the Just Fortune — Queen Steelflower's hive.*

That name was familiar in a way few things had been lately, and Quicksilver frowned. Where had he heard it — when had he seen her, small and fierce and young, hands closed on a weapon, her head barely topping his shoulder? But, no, that was wrong. Dust had mentioned her, that was it, and Quicksilver looked up. *She is missing, your queen.*

She is. Ember's tone was even, betraying nothing. *Her consort speaks in her absence — Guide. He has made alliance in her name with Queen Death, and we were summoned to her aid.*

There was more to it than that, Quicksilver thought, but he couldn't recall. Dust had been so patient, explaining everything that he needed to know—what would he do without that gentle guidance? He remembered the human sprawled on the floor of the lab, wished again that he had killed him, him and the others who had killed his brother. *How fares the hive?* he asked, shoving memory away. Ironic, that he should want to be free of the only thing he could remember clearly.

Healing cleanly, Ember answered. *Our queen has summoned the clevermen of half a dozen hives to help with the work, and it proceeds well.* He paused, showing teeth in something like a smile. *She believes it was a ruse to cover their attempt to steal you back. They must truly fear what you learned in Atlantis.*

If I could just remember! Quicksilver covered his face again. *And Dust is dead.*

Ember dipped his head. *I am sorry.*

Quicksilver did not answer, staring blindly at the chamber wall. He could not imagine his future any more than he could see his past; he was useless to his queen, and lost…

The queen has need of you, Ember said, after what seemed a very long time. *There is still much to be done, and you may— You must hold the key, if the Lanteans would try to kidnap you. And we must answer this attack as soon as we may.*

Avenge Dust, Quicksilver said, his voice bleak. Vengeance was hollow, would not repair his loss or ease his mind, but at least Dust would be remembered that little while longer.

Yes.

I should go to my lab, Quicksilver said. He looked at himself, at the disarray of his quarters, and shook his head, not knowing where to begin.

I will help you, Ember said. *If you wish.*

Why you? You're not even of our hive. Quicksilver glared at him, though it wasn't his fault.

I can be spared, Ember said, with wry amusement. *And I volunteered. My commander also has a score to settle with Atlantis.*

That, at least, Quicksilver understood. He looked around the chamber again, newly aware that some of Dust's things were missing, his clothes and his games and the case of his jewelry. *They could have left me that much,* he thought, and Ember tipped his head to one side.

I think they wished to spare you, he said.

Quicksilver didn't answer, closing his thoughts, and Ember sighed.

Shall I help you make ready?

I suppose. Quicksilver followed listlessly as Ember rummaged among the stores, choosing shirt and coat from among the clothing that remained. He pulled them on, allowed Ember to tug them into place and brush his hair. That last was kindness rather than necessity; there was still too little to dress properly, and he sighed, looking at Ember's hair with envy.

Your nails, Ember said, and Quicksilver extended his hands, palms politely down. *They'll do. Though we must tend them tomorrow.*

Quicksilver glanced down, saw chips in the flat blue glaze.

Mine are worse, Ember said, and showed his own off hand. Sure enough, the blood-black color had worn away at the tips, showing the dark horn beneath. *But for the labs, it will suffice.*

Quicksilver bared teeth in agreement — he really didn't care, except that he would not disgrace his brother — and Ember reached into the pocket of his coat.

And one thing more.

He held out a physician's dart, the short needle gleaming, and Quicksilver recoiled.

What is that?

Ember paused. *It's your medicine.*

What medicine? Quicksilver lifted his feeding hand, flexing the claws. He had no stunner, not even a ceremonial dagger — and why he had reacted so, he could not have said. Except that Ember was a stranger, man of another hive, a cleverman in blade's leather. It was only right to be cautious.

*For — * Ember blinked. *Didn't Dust tell you?*

My brother gave me no injections, Quicksilver said. *Nor spoke of any.*

Ember lowered the dart, frowning slightly. *I don't understand. His records say — He said that whatever was done to you left you hyperplastic. This was to control the cell division. From his notes, it was working well.*

Quicksilver stared at him. There had been no injections, he was sure of that, no drugs. But hyperplasty was real enough, frightening, a malfunction of the body's normal healing ability, when the body went on remaking itself unnecessarily. It was treatable, controllable, but incurable —

Why didn't he tell me? he asked, and Ember gave him a look of compassion.

You'd been through so much, he said. *Perhaps he wished to spare you this, one thing too many.*

Dust had been protective, Quicksilver thought. That was certainly true — and how he missed that steady, supportive mind — but it seemed unlike him to have kept something so important a secret. Maybe he had been waiting until more memory returned? Quicksilver had always been sickly anyway, that much he was sure he remembered. He started to push up his sleeve, searching for the marks of past injections, and stopped. Of course there would be none, and why had he bothered to look at all? Those pinpricks would heal in a breath, a heartbeat, and leave no sign.

If you'd prefer, Ember said. *It won't hurt you to miss a dose. Then you can review Dust's notes and see what he prescribed.*

No. The offer was reassuring, and Quicksilver shook his head, pushing back the loose sleeve. *No, it's all right.*

Ember stepped closer, cupping his feeding hand to steady the other man's arm without the mouth touching his skin, and with the other hand drove home the dart. Quicksilver hissed — not the little stick he had somehow been expecting, but a jolt of pain, a thick needle driven deep into muscle — but there was not even a drop of blood, the skin closing almost as the needle was withdrawn.

Done, Ember said, and folded the dart back into its case. "Let us go.*

CHAPTER FOUR
New Arrivals

JOHN looked out at the *Daedalus* nestled onto the South Pier — they'd pretty much given up worrying about the city's actual orientation, went with the names everyone was used to. If Rodney was here, it would drive him crazy, and John winced, deflecting that thought with what was becoming practiced ease. When they got him back, he told himself, it would give him something to bitch about. He tried not to think about guys he'd seen who'd survived capture, survived the Taliban, made himself look back at *Daedalus*, her hatches open now to disgorge the latest batch of scientists. This wasn't its usual spot, but that was taken by the *Hammond*, still under repair. And that was something that would annoy Colonel Caldwell, and John was still trying to work up a response that would convey just how much he didn't care...

Except that this was also a distraction, one more way of putting off thinking about what he had to say to Jeannie Miller, and in what order he could say it that would be most reassuring when there wasn't much reassurance to be had. He could see her now in the open hatch, a bright red hat covering her blonde hair — a red hat with a pompom and matching red mittens, just another Canadian housewife off to rescue her brother from life-sucking aliens — and he bit down hard on his lip, knowing the flippancy was just another form of avoidance.

Caldwell was with her, hand ready at her elbow in case she stumbled on the ice, but Jeannie moved as though she didn't see him, striding across the pier toward the nearest tower. At his side, Woolsey squared his shoulders, one hand rising briefly as though he wanted to adjust the tie he wasn't wearing, and John plastered a smile on his own face as the doors slid open. He exchanged salutes with Caldwell, seeing in memory Rodney's outraged stare when he and Caldwell and Carter had greeted each other formally. *Seriously*? he'd said, looking from colonel to colonel, and John bit his lip to keep from flinching.

"Mrs. Miller," Woolsey said. "We are very grateful you are here."

She was looking tired, John thought, tired and a little pale. That might be the twelve days in hyperspace, or it might be because she knew the chances of finding Rodney alive were dwindling by the hour.

"Is there any news?" she asked, and John saw Woolsey flinch.

Jeannie saw it, too, and her face changed. "Is he dead? You have to tell me—"

"He's alive," John said, quickly, and she looked from him to Woolsey and back.

"What's the catch?"

"It's not entirely good news," Woolsey said. "There have been— developments—since you left Earth." His look included Caldwell, whose mouth tightened. "I know it's been a long trip, but I assumed you would want to hear the news immediately."

Jeannie managed a wry smile. "Mr. Woolsey, I've had nothing to do for the last two weeks but sit in a metal box and worry. It'll be a relief to know what I'm worrying about."

Caldwell looked momentarily annoyed by the 'metal box' comment, but he had more sense than to say anything. "I'm assuming that has something to do with why we don't have our usual landing spot? And *Hammond* being under repairs?"

"Yes," Woolsey said, shortly. "The *Hammond* was damaged in combat with the Wraith. I'll have all the details for you—"

John hung back to be sure that someone had taken charge of Jeannie's bag, and found himself at her side as they made their way down the corridor. "Thanks for coming," he said, and she reached out impulsively to squeeze his arm.

"It's good to see you. I feel like I can finally do something."

"Radek thinks you can be a big help," John said.

"God, I hope so," Jeannie said. "Is it—really bad?"

"We'll get him back," John said, and knew he sounded grim.

Woolsey had chosen to hold the meeting in a different room, one with a view of the city's north side, where they could see the crews working on the *Hammond* in the thickening light and the soft chains of light that draped the towers. Predictably, Caldwell went to the window to look down at the other ship, assessing the visible damage, and John saw him raise an eyebrow. Probably at the missing shield emitter, he thought, it was the most obvious problem, and carefully didn't look himself. Instead, he poured himself a cup of coffee—Jeannie shook her head at his offer, found tea instead—and took his place at the big table. Keller and Beckett were both there, and Zelenka, and a moment later the door slid open to admit Sam Carter.

"Sorry," she said, to the table at large, and seated herself next to Zelenka.

"Very well," Woolsey said. "As I said earlier, there have been — developments — since *Daedalus* left Earth. We have positive information that Rodney McKay is still alive. We received intelligence pinpointing his location, and incidentally giving us the chance to ambush Queen Death's primary hive, and mounted a rescue operation. Our team was successful in surprising Death, and in doing significant damage to her ship, but unfortunately our information was incomplete, and the team was confronted with an unexpected development. Dr. McKay was alive, but uncooperative. He — he had been transformed into a Wraith."

"What?" Jeannie's voice rose sharply.

"I'm sorry," Woolsey said.

"It's impossible," Jeannie said. She looked around the table, settled on John. "Isn't it?"

John shook his head. "I'm afraid not."

"Dr. Keller and Dr. Becket have a possible explanation," Woolsey said. "If you would, Dr. Keller?"

And that wasn't fair, either, John thought. It wasn't fair to make Rodney's girlfriend explain to Rodney's sister just what had happened to someone they both loved — it was Beckett's retrovirus, probably; let him do it.

Keller took a breath. "Yes. I'm afraid it is possible. At least in theory." She looked down at her notes. "Four years ago, Dr. Beckett developed a retrovirus that was intended to deactivate the Iratus bug DNA that we believe makes the Wraith what they are. It was partially successful, but the transformed patient — we call him Michael because it doesn't seem as though the Wraith have individual names — escaped and was in contact with a number of different hives before he was killed. We think it's very possible that some hive could have gotten the idea to try a similar procedure on humans."

That was a pretty narrow summary, John thought. It left out a whole lot of awkward parts, like some disastrous deals with the Wraith, and Michael trying to create his own new species when the Wraith rejected him as tainted. It left out kidnapping Teyla when she was pregnant with Torren, and the horrible possible future that only Rodney's stubbornness managed to avert, not to mention the last terrifying attack on Atlantis —

Caldwell said, "You mean the Wraith can actually turn a human being into one of them?"

"It's not that unlikely," Keller said. "The Wraith are actually related to humans — their genetic material is a mix of human DNA and DNA from the Iratus bug. And they are very skilled biologists. Essentially, all they would need to do is introduce the Iratus bug DNA into Rodney's system." To her credit, her voice didn't shake at all on the last words.

Beckett cleared his throat. "We've already seen the result of Iratus bug DNA on Colonel Sheppard."

I knew somebody would mention that, John thought. Caldwell gave him a look, and he met the other man's stare guilelessly. "It turned me blue. And scaly."

"What would be the point of this experiment on McKay?" Caldwell asked, after a moment.

"We believe that the Wraith want Dr. McKay's cooperation," Woolsey said. "Our intelligence suggests that Queen Death wants to claim the Milky Way as her new feeding ground."

"That's not exactly new information," Caldwell said.

"No," Carter said, "but the method is new. And if McKay does cooperate — he's very good. And he knows Atlantis's systems inside and out."

"Excuse me," Jeannie said. "What — what *exactly* do you want me to do here?"

There was a note in her voice that made John wince and bite his lip, but Woolsey regarded her gravely. "I asked for your help finding the places where Dr. McKay has rewritten our codes to give him unauthorized access to our systems here. And to help rewrite our current programs to make sure he cannot gain access in any other way. That has not changed."

"Dammit!" Jeannie looked like she wanted to throw something. She glared at each of them in turn, fixing finally on John. "And while I'm doing this, is there some kind of plan to find Meredith? To get him back? Do any of you people know whether or not he can be changed back — if he's even really himself any more? If that's even what they've done? Or will I have some weird alien — monster — instead of a brother? Or are you just planning to kill him the next time you find him?"

"We'll get him back," John said.

"How?" Jeannie's hands were white-knuckled on her mug.

"I don't know," John said. "But we don't leave our people behind."

"Right." For a second, Jeannie looked as though she wanted to spit, but then, with an effort, she uncurled her fingers. "All right, then, I'll do it. But — you'll keep me informed."

That was directed at Keller, who nodded. "Of course."

Woolsey cleared his throat. "Thank you. Colonel Caldwell, I assume you have seen the damage to the *General Hammond*, and I'm sure Colonel Carter will want to fill you in on the details."

Carter nodded helpfully, though John suspected that was the last thing she actually wanted to do.

"Dr. Zelenka, did you have anything you wanted to add?" Woolsey went on.

"Nothing that cannot wait until Mrs. Miller is settled," Zelenka said. "Except to say that I am sorry to have you here under these circumstances."

"Thank you," Jeannie said, in a muffled voice.

"I'm sure we all share those sentiments," Woolsey said. He tapped his papers together. "You all have copies of the detailed reports on the attempted rescue, and we will meet later to go over any questions. But for now, I believe we should concentrate on getting Mrs. Miller and the rest of our new personnel squared away."

That was as abrupt as dismissal as John had ever heard from Woolsey, but he doubted the little bureaucrat was any more eager than the rest of them to sit around and go over the details of precisely how they had failed. He stood aside to let Woolsey escort Jeannie out, followed by Carter and Zelenka, and then by the doctors, Keller looking even less pleased than before. He started to follow them, but Caldwell said, "Sheppard."

"Sir?" John paused in the doorway, trying to look respectful.

"Don't make promises you can't keep," Caldwell said. "She deserves better than that."

"We'll get him back," John said, and there was something in his voice that made Caldwell look away.

"So, you and Meredith," Jeannie said. Jennifer wished she had some idea whether that was *welcome to the family* or *what are your intentions toward my brother* and wasn't sure what to do with either one.

They'd wound up the last people at the dinner table, after Teyla, Ronon, and Sheppard had all exchanged awkwardly obvious *let's let them talk* looks and taken themselves off—Teyla to put Torren to bed, Sheppard apparently to help, and Ronon to do whatever it was Ronon did with his evenings. Find someone to inflict bodily harm on in the gym, probably.

She was sure they meant well, but she'd been strongly tempted to make her own excuses at the same time. Only the fact that she would have felt guilty leaving Jeannie alone at the table under the circumstances kept her in her seat, poking at the remains of her salad. The mess hall was getting quiet, the cooks starting to close down the serving line to leave packaged sandwiches and fruit the only options for late-comers.

"We've been dating," Jennifer said.

"He told me," Jeannie said. "I'm lucky I knew that much, he's not much with the personal news. It was months before I figured out that he'd stopped dating, what was her name, Katie?"

"Katie Brown," Jennifer said. "They just didn't... I mean, she was a perfectly nice person, it just wasn't working out."

"Believe me, I'm not surprised," Jeannie said. "Meredith can be a little hard to take."

"I don't find him—we've always gotten along surprisingly well, considering that Rodney is... a little intense."

"Intense," Jeannie said, shaking her head and smiling. "That would be my brother." Her eyes were sharp, and it dawned on Jennifer that her smile was not necessarily a friendly one. "I wish you'd told me that you were seeing each other when I was here before."

"We weren't," Jennifer said. "We were just friends. It was after that that we..." She hesitated, not finding the words to describe hearing Rodney tell her how he felt at the same time that she was watching his painful decline, wondering what it meant that he was saying it now. Probably that he wasn't worried about the suspense of wondering what her reaction would be, because it hadn't seemed like it was going to matter. She wasn't sure he even remembered what he'd said the next day.

"Oh," Jeannie said. "So when you were being all... that was just being friends."

"He was my patient," Jennifer said.

"And he's my brother," Jeannie said. "But it seemed like you would have been happier if I hadn't been around to have opinions."

"I really didn't mean it to seem that way," Jennifer said. "I was… pretty upset at the time."

Jeannie seemed to be considering her for a while, and then her smile softened. "I can see that you would be. I don't think I could deal with your job. Be a doctor and have to treat all my friends when they got hurt, or taken over by little alien robots, or infected by weird brain parasites."

"It's not always like that," Jennifer said. "Sometimes it's just headaches and sprained ankles all day. It does get stressful, though. We lose a lot of people."

She could see Jeannie's expression change at the words, her eyes shadowing in a way that was all too familiar to Jennifer, and she wished she'd thought before she spoke them.

"So," Jeannie said in the tone of someone determined to change the subject. "You and Meredith. Is this serious, or what? Because I really think Meredith needs to be thinking about moving toward… I'm not saying you need to get married right away, but I think it would be good for him at this point in his life to get that settled."

"Umm. Wow." Jennifer glanced around the mess hall as if it were likely that she'd spot a medical emergency that required her immediate attention. "I think we're, you know, taking steps that lead in a certain direction."

"Are you living together? I'm not trying to be a prude or anything. I'm just wondering if you've survived living in close quarters with Meredith for long enough to know what it's like."

"We were, on Earth," Jennifer said. "And we've been sharing quarters here, although that's more… you know, it's kind of more like being roommates in a dorm than anything else. It's not like you can really spend a lot of time alone together, unless you want to eat all your meals out of the microwave and never leave your quarters."

"It is kind of like that," Jeannie said. "I think Meredith's achieved his dream of going back to grad school and staying there."

"You think that's his dream?"

"I really don't know," Jeannie said. "He didn't speak to me for several years, so maybe I'm not the best authority here. I know he liked college and hated living at home. And I don't just mean high school.

I mean, okay, who doesn't hate high school, but if you could move away from home when you were ten years old, Meredith would have."

"It doesn't seem like he was a very happy kid."

Jeannie breathed a laugh. "I think that's the understatement of the century. Mom and Dad were kind of seriously dysfunctional, and Meredith always took that very hard. He's a lot more sensitive than you'd think."

"I'm not sure sensitive is the word I'd apply to Rodney."

"I mean, not in the sense that he knows what to say to people, or that he notices how they feel unless they're right up in his face. But he cares about things more than he likes people to think."

"I know that," Jennifer said.

"Good," Jeannie said. "Because I know how hard it is for him to actually try dating someone. He apparently thinks the idea of winding up in a house in the suburbs and coming home every evening to a wife and kids is some kind of horrible fate. You should have heard him on how I was wasting my life and was going to end up drinking all day and leave Madison with permanent emotional scars because of my resentment of her. Which is really not about me, needless to say."

"We were more at the getting an apartment stage," Jennifer said. "Although I wouldn't rule out a house in the suburbs." Not the way she'd had to rule out small towns, unless you counted a military base, which she didn't. But teaching hospitals and secret military research facilities both required living somewhere convenient, and ignoring the little part of her that said she'd like to live somewhere where the sky wasn't broken up with buildings and where the neighbors all knew her parents' names.

"The suburbs might be good for him. You know, taking part in normal life more. But it's good that if he never actually gets that far, that he's got someplace like this that makes him happy."

"It's an interesting place to live," Jennifer said. "I don't regret coming out here. But it is sort of like being in college forever. In kind of unfortunate ways, sometimes."

"It's a nice place to visit," Jeannie said. "It would also be nice to see Meredith when something isn't horribly wrong."

"We were going to come to see you when we were on Earth," Jennifer said. "It's just we got caught up in moving, and everything was in boxes—"

"I know. He told me. I figure at least I got to talk to him on the phone." She looked dangerously like she was going to cry.

"It's going to be all right," Jennifer said quickly.

Jeannie looked at her like she saw through her. "Do you really believe that?"

"I know his team would do anything to get him back. They kind of define stubborn."

Jeannie smiled ruefully. "It's good that you're an optimist. Meredith is enough of a pessimist for any two people."

"He is," Jennifer said, wishing she felt more like she was holding up her end of that bargain right now.

CHAPTER FIVE
Recall

DICK waited until it seemed remotely possible that he might have a few moments of peace and quiet before he retreated to his office to open the email from the head of the IOA that had arrived in the databurst. He certainly felt retreat was the word for it. He tried not to think of himself as defeated before he even opened the email, but there was no way this boded well. He didn't think they'd dropped him a friendly message to ask how the weather was in Atlantis.

He opened the file and read it quickly, braced for the worst. It wasn't, in fact, the worst. The IOA requested his attendance at a hearing to review his decisions while in command of Atlantis. He wasn't fooled for a minute by the *requested* into believing it was optional, but on the other hand, if they were calling a hearing, it meant they hadn't already made a decision. Or that whatever decision they'd made was unpopular enough with one or another IOA member that the majority wanted more evidence on their side.

He closed the file and sat for a moment considering the blank screen. The next thing to do was tell Sheppard. Instead, he hesitated, not yet activating his radio. He walked outside, ducking quickly out onto the balcony before anyone could find him and raise whatever their next problem was.

The sun was shining brightly for a change, although the piers still glittered white with accumulated snow. It was warm enough with the sun shining that he wasn't uncomfortable even without having put on a heavy coat. The water stretched out to the horizon, a deep and unbroken blue.

He walked to the end of the balcony where he could see the city. The towers rose against the sky, blue and silver, catching the afternoon sun. It was truly a magnificent sight. He hadn't spent much time appreciating it. There had always been something to do that would keep him at his desk. There always was, if you looked hard enough.

When they'd been on Earth, he'd kept busy, too, scheming and playing politics, pulling every string he could find that might get Atlantis back to the Pegasus Galaxy. He'd made impassioned speeches about what it would mean for the residents of Pegasus if they never returned, without ever having time to think about what it would mean for him. Ultimately that wasn't what was important. Atlantis and the Pegasus Galaxy would both get along without him.

He would get along without Atlantis, if it came to that, but the words rang hollow even as he thought them. He couldn't think of anything on Earth that had actually made him feel a sense of... It made him feel overdramatic to say it, even in his head, but a sense of wonder. And if it was overdramatic to say that the legendary city of the Ancients inspired wonder, then he wasn't entirely sure what the word was for.

He'd seen it. That was something. He'd been in some small part responsible for preserving it, and in larger part responsible for returning it to where it belonged. It probably wasn't very reasonable to ask for a bigger role in history, but he couldn't help feeling like a chance to do something that mattered was slipping away from him, and might never come again.

He shook his head. He could indulge in maudlin thoughts later, when he was back on Earth, but there were all too many things to be arranged first. Starting with informing Colonel Sheppard.

Sheppard arrived in his office not long after he called, looking like he had a headache. Dick couldn't say he was surprised. It had been that kind of day all around. "What's up?"

"Come in and shut the door," Dick said.

Sheppard did, frowning. "That's never good."

"No," Dick said, trying to smile but not sure how well he succeeded. "The IOA has requested my presence on Earth at my earliest convenience. They would like to discuss my recent decisions."

"Ouch," Sheppard said. "That doesn't sound like fun." He paused, his eyes searching Dick's face, probably trying to judge how worried he was. "They made Elizabeth go 'discuss her decisions' a couple of times, but she always came out of it all right."

"I sincerely hope I can manage the same," Dick said. "But it won't help to start by making them wait. I'm leaving you in charge of Atlantis while I'm gone. I trust that you'll make every effort to continue securing the city."

"Believe me, it's at the top of my list," Sheppard said. "We were scheduled to go check out some new planets in the next couple of days, but we can call those missions off."

"That might not be the best thing to do," Dick said. "I think it would be better not to suspend all our regular operations while you wait for me to get back."

"Right," Sheppard said. "Just how long are you expecting to be gone?"

"In the best-case scenario, General O'Neill will agree to recall *Odyssey* to Earth as soon as I go through. We'll have a couple of days of fairly unpleasant hearings, and then when *Odyssey* arrives with her ZPM, I can come back through the Stargate. If that happened, I would think I'd be back in no more than a week."

"That sounds a lot like 'we'll be home for Christmas'," Sheppard said.

"Something like that."

"Realistically speaking."

"Realistically speaking, it could take significantly longer than that, and if I have to wait to return on *Daedalus* or *Hammond*…"

"They're both here," Sheppard finished. "Which means it'll be at least a month before either of them can make the round trip." He was beginning to look distinctly unhappy. "I'd really rather not be in charge here for a month."

"I'm sure you'll do just fine," Dick said. "Until such time as I get back, or…"

"Let's pretend there's not an 'or'," Sheppard said.

"Thank you for the vote of confidence," Dick said after a moment. It was a rather unexpected one, and it made him feel the tiniest bit better.

Sheppard shrugged. "I like dealing with known quantities."

"And yet you enjoy working in Atlantis."

"Our people are a known quantity," Sheppard said. "Everything else, I'm not so sure about."

Dick nodded agreement. There didn't seem to be much more to say. "I'll give the IOA your regards."

"You know, between that and staying here where we might get invaded by the Wraith…"

"Try to avoid that if you can," Dick said. "I'd like there to still be a city for me to come back to."

"We can handle the Wraith," Sheppard said, with a smile that didn't reach his eyes. "Trust us. We won't have wild parties while you're gone, either."

"Just as long as they're not parties that the IOA ever hears about."

"We won't tell anyone," Sheppard said. He hesitated, and then extended his hand. Dick stood to shake it. "Good luck," Sheppard said.

"Thank you," Dick said. "Good luck to you, too. If you'd find it convenient to use the office while I'm gone…"

"I don't know," Sheppard said. "I'm never very comfortable in the big chair."

"It's adjustable."

"That's not what I meant."

"I know what you meant," Dick said. "But you're going to have to make yourself as comfortable as you can for at least the next few weeks."

"Right," Sheppard said. He looked like he thought that would be a tall order.

"You want to take a break?" Jennifer asked. Carson looked up at her, realizing that he'd been staring at his computer screen for the last whoever knew how long rather than reading the words on it. "We've got a lot of notes to go through here."

"No, let's go on," Carson said. "I'd rather get it over with."

"It's your work, so you may not really need to look over it," Jennifer said, turning her lab stool so that she was talking to him and not to her own screen. "It's just been a while since I started back at the beginning and approached this fresh."

"It's my work, and then again it isn't, given that I'm a clone of the man who did it," Carson said. He hadn't worried about that as much when he was out in the field, but lately he was beginning to feel like a nice long chat with their new psychiatrist Dr. Robinson might be in order. "I remember doing these experiments. I even remember why it seemed like such a good idea. I don't expect that the original Carson Beckett ever changed his mind about that before he died."

"You haven't changed your mind, have you?" Jennifer said. "I know we've had a lot of trouble figuring out how to make your original concept of a retrovirus stable, but it's been less than four years. It takes longer than that back on Earth to develop a new drug for athlete's foot."

"I think that's my point," Carson said. "I thought I knew what I was doing when I tested the retrovirus on Michael. It would either work or it wouldn't, and either way we'd learn something. I never imagined that it would work well enough for everyone to accept the man as a human being, and then…"

"If we can ever get the new version to work permanently, I think it'll be worth it," Jennifer said. "Given that the alternative is either going on the way we have been, with whole societies being wiped out, or exterminating the Wraith as a species."

"I think we may be the only ones in this city who have a problem with that idea," Carson said.

Jennifer gave him a stubborn look that he rather liked. "That doesn't make us wrong."

"It doesn't," he said. "That's why I did it, for whatever that's worth. We were all a lot more sure of ourselves once, talking about winning the war with the Wraith for good as if we had any idea how to do that. And then there was Ellia, poor soul. You've seen the reports?"

"The immature Wraith queen who had been raised as a human," Jennifer said. "The retrovirus backfired in her, activating more traits that must have come from the Iratus bug."

"That's a nice tidy way of summing up a terrible thing," Carson said. A nice dry scientific explanation that wouldn't trouble anyone's sleep. "She was a little girl, a little shy thing who served us tea. Her father had been letting her feed off him so that she could survive, sacrificing years of his life. Because he loved his little girl. And we turned her into a monster, and then we killed her."

"She was killing people," Jennifer said.

"I know that," Carson said. "It was wrong, but she wasn't some creature we could say we had to put down like an animal. She was a child who had been forced to do terrible things to survive. And after that when we sat around the table and talked about all our newest ideas for how to wipe out the Wraith threat—" He turned up his hands. "We were talking about genocide. No one wanted to hear it, because it was easier to think of our enemies as things rather than as people. I expect it usually is."

"That was the whole idea of the retrovirus," Jennifer said. "To remove their need to feed on us without killing them all."

"Don't have too many illusions about our purity of purpose at the time," Carson said. "Dr. Weir and Colonel Sheppard came around to the idea because by that point, we were starting to get some idea of how hard it would be to defeat the Wraith by shooting at them. If I'd had a way to kill all the Wraith, I expect they'd have preferred that."

"I don't know. Dr. Weir never struck me as exactly trigger-happy, and Colonel Sheppard… he doesn't act like he thinks Todd is an animal."

"Maybe not. But they'd both lost a lot of people, and seeing what was going on out there — they thought if there was any way to put an end to it, it would be worth it. And you see how that worked out."

"We just need more time," Jennifer said. "We've gotten so close. If we can get it right, we could save millions of lives, prevent entire civilizations from being wiped out. Human and Wraith."

"Aye, we could. Hypothetically, if we ever get it right. And in the mean time, we've certainly been paying for it. Ask Teyla about that, and she's one of the ones you can ask, because Michael didn't actually kill her."

"Carson —"

He couldn't make himself stop. "How many people are dead because Michael decimated whole planets with the Hoffan drug? Or because of his hybrids? Both of which I actually helped him to perfect. And that was *me* who helped him, not the Carson Beckett who was here in Atlantis writing letters home to his mum. I was spending two years locked in a prison cell at the time, waiting for a rescue attempt that was never going to come and watching a lot of people die. So if you'll excuse me, I think I get to have a say in whether it was worth it."

Jennifer looked more than a little surprised, maybe all the way to alarmed. Carson regretted the outburst already, but it was harder than he'd expected to pretend to any kind of objectivity about this research.

"I think maybe you should talk to someone about what happened to you," she said. "It can't be easy working on something that's so much like helping Michael create his hybrids."

"I have and I will," Carson said. "But just because I expect I'll be dealing with this for a long time doesn't mean I'm not right. I wish I'd never tested the retrovirus without a better idea of what it would do, and frankly I wish I'd never heard of the bloody thing."

"That's not going to help Rodney," Jennifer said.

"If I didn't care about Rodney, I wouldn't have agreed to do this. But he's a good friend, and a good man, and I'm going to do everything I can —" He broke off, wishing he was sure he could trust his voice.

"We still have your turtles," Jennifer said, as if that weren't a total non sequitur. "I mean, now that we have a cat, I don't know if Rodney's still quite as attached…"

"Well, don't give them to me now," Carson said. "How do you expect him to like it if he comes back and finds out that you've given his turtles away? He'll be impossible to live with."

"They're your turtles."

"I never actually bought the things," Carson said.

"I suppose that was the other one of you," Jennifer said. "I always forget."

"Everyone does."

"I'm really sorry," she said, sounding like she really was. "I just want to figure this out, so that we can be sure that if we do get him back, we're actually going to be able to get him back to… you know, our regular Rodney."

"Frightening as that is," Carson said, giving her as much of a smile as he could. "Well, unless they've come up with something immensely clever, and there's no way of anticipating that, the process should start wearing off once they're no longer administering their retrovirus on a regular basis. What we need is to be able to predict how his body will react to that."

"It doesn't seem that Michael ever entirely regained his Wraith form completely," Jennifer said, as if reluctant to speak the words. "Of course, it's hard to tell, once he began manipulating his own genetic structure, but…"

"We may be able to help the reversion process along," Carson said. "You did a fine job of that with the hybrids. I wouldn't give up hope that we'll get our Rodney back with his body and his memory intact." He intended to just leave it there, but Jennifer's sharp eyes must have caught something in his expression.

"What?"

"Don't expect this to be easy for him to put behind him. Especially if he's actually had to feed on a human being."

"I don't think that's going to happen."

"We have no reason whatsoever to think that it won't. Except that we don't like to think about it, but if we don't think about it, who will? You heard Colonel Sheppard on the subject. It's not something he can let himself imagine. But it's part of being a doctor to face the hard truths."

"I know that," Jennifer said. "Believe me, I get to do enough of that in this job."

"I know you do," Carson said. "And I shouldn't take my bad temper out on you. I probably should take myself to Dr. Robinson about some of this, although I've been trying to give her time to get settled in before making her deal with a story that begins 'to start with, I still have some complicated feelings about being a clone'."

"She used to work for the SGC back on Earth. It's probably not the weirdest thing she's ever heard," Jennifer said.

Carson shook his head. "It won't be for long if she keeps working here."

Quicksilver dreamed he was pursued, and then pursuing, changing roles with a fluency that told him he was asleep, even though he could not seem to wake. Sometimes it was the Lanteans who pursued him, the one he had stunned, the big barbarian who had guarded the door, the tiny dangerous one, and then again it was his lab assistants, ringing him in, feeding hands outstretched, while Ember turned his back and Dust laughed. He fled from his brother in a fever of fear, through the corridors of the hive, and metal halls, down stairs that gleamed bronze in the light that fell from tall and narrow windows.

And then quite suddenly he came through metal doors — metal doors familiar in a way that seemed different, as though he had once known them well — ugly heavy things painted with numbers half as tall as he was that lifted away to reveal a room filled with screens and consoles. Beyond a huge window stood a Stargate, quiescent, all its symbols dark. He needed to dial the ship, needed to dial home, and he went unerringly to a keyboard. It was not a proper device, not the Ancients' work, but he knew it would do the job.

"Rodney."

He looked over his shoulder, startled, to see the dark-haired queen behind him, her arms folded across her chest.

"You don't want to do that," she said.

"I have to," he answered. "I have to go home."

"No," she said.

"But I do." He looked down at the screen again, frowning, feeling his way into a system that wasn't the gate after all. "It's vital."

"It's a very bad idea."

He could hear something like sorrow in her voice, but didn't turn to see. On the screen, the numbers shifted, changing like a flower unfolding —

"Are you sure this is what you want?" she asked.

"Of course I am," he answered. "Why wouldn't I? I need to go home."

"Then come with me."

Quicksilver looked up, startled, and they were suddenly in front of the gate, on the metal ramp that led up to its opening. His feet echoed, clumsy, but hers made no sound.

"I believe I should say something cryptic," she said, "but it seems — pointless. Are you sure you want this?"

"Yes! Of course!" Quicksilver glared at her, looked up at the gate and its darkened symbols. "Of course I do."

"Very well."

She gave him a tight, unfriendly smile, and turned away. Abruptly, there were shapes behind the glass, figures moving, a fair-haired woman bent over the control console, and the gate ground into motion, the first symbol lighting. Quicksilver started to take a step back, to get out of the way of the expanding wormhole, but his feet wouldn't move. He looked down, saw that he was wearing magnetic boots.

"Hey! Hey, I'm down here—"

He pulled harder, rocked his right foot from side to side the way he'd been taught, but the connection was too strong. A second symbol lit and locked, and a third.

"Hey! Stop!"

The people in the control room ignored him utterly, as though he didn't exist for them at all. He bent down, fumbling for the catch that closed the boots—the fourth symbol was locked now—and found nothing but smooth plastic. The gate turned, lighting the fifth symbol, moved smoothly toward the sixth. He flung himself forward with all his strength, trying to break the seal, but he remained locked in place. The sixth symbol lit.

"Oh, no," he said. "No, no, no—"

The seventh symbol locked. He closed his eyes tightly, but the light engulfed him anyway, scalding cold, consuming him—

He woke, mouth open, suspecting that he had screamed. Sure enough, Ember was bending over him, half dressed, hair in wild disarray. His pupils were huge in the dim light, and he looked almost afraid himself.

Quicksilver, he said. *Are you all right?*

No, I— Quicksilver stopped, the dream memories slotting into place, driving back the terror. *Yes. Oh, yes! We have to go to the labs.*
He swung himself out of the nest, reaching for the tunic he had left on

the floor. *I remember — I remember many things, Ember.*

Do you indeed? There was an odd note in Ember's mind, gone before Quicksilver could define it. *It's the middle-night watch, Quicksilver. Only the most junior clevermen will be there.*

Quicksilver waved his hand in dismissal. *I don't need them. I just need a computer.* He glared at the other cleverman, for the first time in many days feeling almost himself. *Will you hurry? No one's going to care about your hair.*

Ember blinked, showed teeth, but then controlled himself. *I will come,* he said.

CHAPTER SIX
Meetings

THE SUN was actually out, sending long shadows through the mess hall. If the day followed the usual pattern, the clouds would build back in by noon, and it would probably snow again toward evening, but John was unreasonably heartened by the slanting light. With Woolsey already on his way to Earth, it was nice to have something cheerful to look at. He added another of the orange egg-things to his tray — he'd pretty much decided he liked them, especially with a side of the spicy chopped vegetables that Pollard optimistically labeled "salsa" and turned away from the line, looking for a table in the sun. It looked as though half of Atlantis and most of *Daedalus's* crew had had the same idea, and it took him a minute to find an empty spot. It was tucked in a corner, half in shadow, but that would change, and he lengthened his stride to get there before anyone else could claim it.

"John!"

That was a voice he hadn't heard in years, but it was still unmistakable. "Mel?"

He set his tray down, turned to see Mel Hocken coming toward him, the *Daedalus* flight suit explaining her presence. He swallowed his first question, said instead, "Wow. It's great to see you."

"You, too." The sun was gleaming in her red hair, her shadow falling long and straight away from the window, and her smile was as dazzling as ever. His eyes slid across the patches, and his eyebrows rose. "302s? Nice."

"I'm in command of *Daedalus's* wing," she answered, and the pride in her voice was almost thick enough to touch.

"Congratulations," John said, and meant it.

"To you, too," she said. "Mind if I join you?"

"Be my guest," John said, and they settled together at the table. It was, of course, one of the ones that wobbled badly. He swore, and Mel put her foot firmly on one of its feet, pinning it in place.

"Hell of a place this is," she said.

"That's not Ancient technology," John answered.

"I wasn't talking about the table." She took a careful sip of her coffee, decided it was real, and took a longer drink. "I mean all of this. What a sight!"

"Yeah," John said. He remembered his own first days on Atlantis, the shock of coming around corners, down stairs, to find another gorgeous vista, the towers gleaming against the sky, metal curved and cut to frame yet another perfect view. "It's — something else."

He wished he'd thought of something better as soon as the words were out of his mouth, but she nodded in agreement. "Yeah. It really is. A girl could get used to a place like this."

There was a faintly smug note in her voice that made John look up sharply. "You've got the gene."

"Yep." Her smile was definitely smug, and John couldn't stop his own delighted grin.

"Damn! That's excellent!"

"It's recessive, not naturally expressed," she said. "I took the treatment a while back, right after I got assigned to the SGC. But I've never been much of anywhere that it mattered."

"It matters here, all right," John said. "We should get you checked out in the puddlejumpers, and try you in the chair — " He stopped abruptly, remembering that she was with *Daedalus*, had her own responsibilities, and she nodded more seriously.

"I'd like that."

"There have been some times when we've needed everyone with the gene to lend a hand," John said. "The first time we flew the city, we ended up in the edge of an asteroid field, and we literally got everybody here who had the gene to take up a jumper and blast a path for us. It was a little hairy, especially for the folks who hadn't ever flown one and used the weapons at the same time, but it worked."

Mel shook her head. "Man, playing *Star Wars* never gets old."

John laughed. "I'm serious, and I'm serious about the chair. We've only got two people who can fly the city, and if there's any chance that you're a third…"

"I've only got the recessive," Mel said, but her face was eager.

"It's not a 302," John said, "but it's — " He shook his head. "It's like nothing else."

"I'd like it," Mel said again.

She looked past him, her eyes fixing for a moment, and John glanced sideways, curious to see what had caught her eye. Teyla had just left the breakfast line, was coming toward them with a smile of greeting, and this time John knew his smile was the smug one. "Yes. She is."

"Hmm?" Mel's innocence was a little forced, and John's smile widened.

"Hot. Very."

Mel's eyebrows flicked up. "Good to see your taste has improved."

"While yours — " Teyla was in earshot now, and John finished, "Remains exactly the same. Teyla, I'd like you to meet a very old friend of mine, Mel Hocken. She's in command of *Daedalus's* 302 wing."

"A pleasure," Mel said, and John could see the laughter in her eyes.

"Any friend of Colonel Sheppard's is a friend of mine," Teyla answered, and they shifted their trays to make room for her.

Lorne looked up as someone leaned in the door of his office. "Hi, Major."

"Cadman," Lorne said, pleased to see her still in one piece after spending the last couple of years back at the SGC. She looked both unscathed and cheerful, wearing the jumpsuit of the *Hammond's* crew rather than the Atlantis uniform he remembered her in. "And I hear it's Captain now," he said. "Congrats. How's Earth?"

"Still there, but not as interesting as space," she said, coming in, a tablet computer tucked under her arm. "And thanks. How's Atlantis?"

"Never a dull moment," Lorne said. "The *Hammond's* a pretty ship."

"Isn't she? Colonel Carter's pretty unhappy about having scratched the finish already. You know, you can repair it but it never gets that new-car smell back, I guess."

"I think the new-car smell wore off in Atlantis a few thousand years ago, so at least we don't have to worry about that."

Cadman grinned. "I remember now. This was a weird place to work."

Lorne raised an eyebrow at her. "You mean compared to a spaceship?"

"Definitely weirder," Cadman said. "I ran into Carson Beckett on my way up here. That was awkward."

"You mean the whole working with your ex thing, or…"

"The whole working with my ex's clone thing, actually. At least we split up before he was cloned." She shook her head. "And I can't believe that sentence just came out of my mouth."

"I get that a lot," Lorne said.

"It was kind of freaky, though," Cadman said. "I mean, more than usual Atlantis levels of freaky. Because… we did split up, but we had this whole thing, and when I heard he died I was pretty upset. And this is kind of like finding out that, no, he was a prisoner of war for a year while we thought he was dead, only it's not actually *him*, right? He remembers when we were going out, but we never actually…" She turned up her hands unhappily.

"We've all gotten used to treating him like he's Dr. Beckett, only with about six months he can't remember," Lorne said. "It's just easier than worrying all the time about what the whole clone thing really means."

"That being the six months between when he was cloned and when he died." Cadman shook her head. "I mean, General O'Neill was cloned once, and now there's him *and* his clone, so his clone can't really be him, right?"

"Maybe it would be easier to just think of it as if this were Dr. Beckett from an alternate universe."

Cadman looked at him, her head to one side. "I am going to pretend you didn't just say that like that would be more normal."

"Okay, maybe not," Lorne said. "But you get used to it. He doesn't talk much about the year he wasn't here."

"Yeah. I think if I'd been the prisoner of a crazy Wraith for a year, I wouldn't talk about it much either." She shrugged. "I guess… well, I hope he's okay, whoever he is."

"He's okay, I think," Lorne said. "Probably a little stressed out right now about what's happened to Dr. McKay, given that 'captured by the Wraith' is probably an issue for him."

"I was sorry to hear about McKay," Cadman said. "He wasn't so bad, really."

"Don't write him off yet," Lorne said. "He's surprisingly hard to kill, and I wouldn't bet against Colonel Sheppard when it comes to rescuing a member of his team. Knowing Dr. McKay, he could be working on a way to escape right now."

Quicksilver had been in the Queen's audience room before, but still her nearness struck fear in his heart. And this was at his own request, not at her summons, an importunity even for a cleverman of his status. Ember seemed nervous as well, his mind closed like a fist even as he gave them both a last assessing glance.

You'll do, he said, and Quicksilver bared teeth as the drones came to attention.

Enter.

Ember straightened his back, lifting his head to show his profile to best advantage, and the doors opened before them.

Death sat straight in her throne, its bone wings rising above her shoulders, off hand and feeding hand resting lightly on its arms. The lords of her zenana accompanied her, blades in leather and silver, and a coterie of masked drones lined the long walls. Ember dipped his head, his long hair falling forward, and Quicksilver copied him, aware again of his own shorn head. Of the many things the Lanteans had done to him, it was among the smallest, but it galled him unreasonably.

So, clevermen, Death said. *Quicksilver, I rejoice to see you so recovered. And, you, Ember. I commend you for your care of him.*

Thank you, my queen, Ember answered, his tone tightly controlled, but Quicksilver smiled in spite of himself. She was radiant, his queen, young and beautiful and strong, and he rejoiced at the gift he was bringing her.

Her smile widened, and she lifted her off hand, beckoning them forward. *And what is it that is so important, then?*

I have two things for you, my queen, Quicksilver said. He did not quite dare look at her directly, glanced up under his lashes to see her smiling.

Say on.

My queen, the Lanteans have defeated us more than once because they have energy shields that can take far more damage than a hive ship's hull. Quicksilver glanced up again, aware that she and all the zenana were listening intently. *I have worked out a way to install such a shield on our own ships, so that we can stand as much damage, perhaps more, than the Lanteans' ships can. And it will never be possible for the Lanteans to invade our hives as they have done in the past.*

This has been proposed before, the oldest blade said. *And always the power required was too great to make it practical.*

I have solved that problem, Quicksilver said. *It's just a matter of adjusting some minor parameters—*

Death lifted her hand. *Skilldark. Is such a thing possible?*

The cleverman who stood to the back of the chamber bowed his head.

It has never been before. But Quicksilver may have found something.

Of course I have, Quicksilver began, and Ember touched his hand in warning.

My queen, he said. * I also believe it will work.*

Death stared at them for a long moment, then, slowly, nodded. *See to it, then. Two things, you said, Quicksilver. What is the second?*

I have found a way into Atlantis, Quicksilver said.

Several of the lords lifted their heads at that, and Quicksilver felt their attention sharpen, thoughts focusing on him. He did not know them, and Ember offered him no clue, his mind closed tight, so he pushed them to the periphery of his thoughts, concentrating on his queen.

Have you, now, she murmured. *Tell me more, cleverman.*

Their gate address is known, Quicksilver said.

Which avails us nothing. That was the very young blade who stood to the queen's left, the touch of his mind the vivid blue of a cloudless sky. *The gate is well shielded.*

Of course it is, Quicksilver said. *And I know how to lower that shield.*

A ripple of emotion crossed the chamber, shock, pleased surprise, and Death said, *How?*

While I was a prisoner, I managed to find a code that will give me entrance to their computers, Quicksilver said. *We dial the gate, and I will transmit the code — the shield won't stop it.*

How did you get this code? That was the oldest of the blades, and Quicksilver shot him an annoyed look.

I don't actually remember, but it doesn't matter. The point is, I can get in, and I can leverage that access to lower Atlantis's shield.

I think it does matter, Sky said. Death reached up without looking, laid her hand on his where it touched her throne, and he was silent.

If it can be done, another blade began, and shook his head. His mind was a planet's surface seen from a great height. *It is a risk, my queen.*

It's hardly a risk, Quicksilver said. *The worst that could happen is that we fail to breach the computers.* At his side, Ember hissed softly, a warning, and Quicksilver suppressed the rest of what he would have said.

Farseer's right, another blade said. He hesitated, as though he were choosing his words with great care. *The risk...*

Ember lifted his head. *I believe that can be mitigated. There are precautions we can take that I believe will be sufficient.*

Very well, Death said. She looked again at Quicksilver, her head tipped to one side. *And you will lower Atlantis's shield for me.*

Yes, Quicksilver said. *I will.* For you, he wanted to add, but that was a blade's boldness, to court a queen, and he had just enough sense not to speak so before the lords of the zenana.

Then we should attack, Sky said, with a shrug of his shoulders. *My queen, we'll never have a better chance.*

It will need more men than we can spare — maybe more than we have — to take the city, Farseer said. *The Lanteans will resist, and they are well armed.*

It would be worth it if Atlantis is destroyed, the Old One said.

My queen. Quicksilver spoke without thinking, blinked at the scowls turned in his direction. *I don't think we have to capture the city. I know a way to cripple it, and at the same time gain an advantage that will make us unstoppable.*

Death looked at him, a long, level stare from golden eyes that made him want to duck his head in submission. Instead, he met her gaze, offering wordless service, and, slowly, she smiled.

If this is true, she said, and looked at the blades surrounding her. *If this is true, we will most certainly act. Speak, cleverman.*

Quicksilver took a breath. *My queen. There is a thing the Lanteans call a ZPM.*

CHAPTER SEVEN
Invasion

THE FOOD line had closed a couple of hours ago, and the mess hall was quiet, just a few of the cooks tidying away the last leftovers and refilling the giant coffee urns. Someone would be on duty all night to keep them filled, William knew, and to make more sandwiches if there was a rush, but otherwise the huge room was almost empty. A young airman was filling a cardboard carrier — six coffees and six of the giant cookies that had appeared with *Daedalus* — and a couple of scientists were playing chess at a corner table. He was finding it hard to settle into a routine when no one was quite sure what to do with their new archeologist yet, and he'd hoped for conversation as well as coffee, so it was with relief that he spotted Eva Robinson making her way toward the tray of cookies. He had known her at the SGC, at least slightly, and besides, it was her job to provide support for Atlantis's crew.

"Dr. Robinson."

Her broad face lightened, and she set her cookie onto a small plate. She was drinking herbal tea, he saw, and thought again that he probably should have poured himself decaf.

"Dr. Lynn. Nice to see you."

"And you," William said. "I wondered where you'd gone after Colorado Springs."

"Someplace even more interesting," she answered with a smile. "Care to join me?"

"Thanks."

They found a table toward the window, where they could see the pale aurora, but far enough back that the cold didn't radiate. It was surprising that the sound didn't echo more in such a large and empty space, and William found himself scanning the ceiling to see if he could spot the sound baffles.

"I wonder — "

"The current theory is that it's the shape of the room," Eva said. "In fact, there's a pool running, if you're interested."

"Why doesn't that surprise me?" William said. "What's your position, Doctor?"

"My dollar is on 'otherwise unspecified weird Ancient thing,'" Eva answered. "OUWAT, with an emphasis on the 'oooh'. Actually, I bet that in all the pools."

"Not much of a gambler, then," William said.

"I prefer as close to a sure thing as I can get." Eva took a sip of her tea, her eyes traveling to something over William's shoulder. "Oh, hello, Dr. Zelenka."

"You are not in the right place for sure things," Radek said. He had a sandwich on his plate, as well as a large mug of coffee.

"So I'm beginning to see," Eva said.

"Do you mind if I join you?" Radek asked, and Eva shook her head. William copied her, though he wasn't entirely sure he didn't mind. He had been avoiding Zelenka since he arrived on Atlantis, though he'd hoped it hadn't been obvious. Apparently, though, he'd been less subtle than he'd thought, and he gave the other man what he hoped was a conciliatory smile.

"It's been a while."

"Since Cambridge, yes," Radek answered, with a show of teeth that wasn't entirely a smile.

Oh, dear, William thought. He hadn't really thought that Radek would have forgotten the things he said when Radek had gone to work for the US military, but he'd hoped they might at least be ignored. He said, to Eva, "Dr. Zelenka and I were in graduate school together."

She made a non-committal noise in answer, and Radek settled himself at the table. "Which is partly why I did not expect to see you here, William. In fact, you are probably the last person I was expecting. I am astonished your father allowed it."

Not fair. Especially when Radek knew perfectly well how his father would feel about his going to work for the American government, not to mention working directly for the unspeakable Nicholas Ballard's equally unsound grandson. William sat up straighter, eyes narrowing, the apology he'd been groping for forgotten. "It is, of course, possible to change one's mind. About politics as much as anything."

"Dr. Lynn did not approve of US policy, as I remember," Radek said, to Eva. "Nor did he believe that one should aid it in any way."

"I still don't think—" William began, and Eva lifted her hands.

"Hold it. I am not going to let you argue through me. I can leave, if you'd like to continue—"

"No, no," William said, and Radek gave him a look of triumph.

"Please," he said. "I am sorry, Eva. These would be what you call unresolved issues?"

"Which I would be happy to help you resolve," Eva said, with a smile that didn't quite reach her eyes. "During office hours."

"Of course," Radek said.

William took a breath. It really had been his fault, and he did owe Radek an apology. It was just hard to find the words. "I really didn't know you were here," he said. "I— I would still have come, but I would at least have dropped you an email. Let you know."

"It has been a week for awkward meetings," Radek said, and reached for his sandwich.

"How is Mrs. Miller doing?" Eva asked. "Is there any word on Dr. McKay?"

Radek sighed. His hair was thinner, William thought, with what he hoped was dispassionate assessment, and what had been a somewhat disheveled look had become distinct disarray. And he still couldn't keep his glasses in place...

"Nothing," Radek said, softly, and William grimaced at the sorrow in his voice. "We have had nothing but bad news—"

He stopped abruptly, his hand going to the receiver he wore in his ear, his face sharpening. "Yes? Yes. Yes, I am on my way—" He was pushing back his chair before he finished speaking, before William could think to ask what was going on, and was gone. William looked at Eva, knowing his eyes were wide.

"That didn't sound good," she said.

"No." William looked over his shoulder, wondering if this was the sort of emergency that needed more caffeine, or the kind that wanted the pistol he'd been issued on arrival. "That didn't sound good at all.

"So what have we got?" Lorne said as he came up the last of the stairs from the transport chamber into the back of the control room. An unscheduled offworld activation could be anything, from Radim wanting to chat, to somebody trying to dial a gate address close to theirs and getting a wrong number, but Salawi looked alarmed.

"Sir, we're still not getting an IDC."

"Any transmission?"

"I'm not picking up a transmission, but maybe…" She glanced at Taggert, who looked up from her own keyboard nervously.

"Let me see," Lorne said. He leaned over her shoulder, checking to see that she had activated the sensors that would pick up a radio transmission, or anything else coming through the gate. "It could be a misdial, or somebody trying out gate addresses." The screen flickered suddenly. "Or not. What was that?"

"I don't know," Salawi said, in a tone that made it clear she expected him to expect her to know. "I called Dr. Zelenka—"

"Yes, what is the trouble?" Zelenka said, breathing hard as he came up the stairs. He'd clearly had a brisk walk from wherever he'd been, or maybe run was more like it. As far as Lorne could tell, he'd been spending as many of his waking hours in close proximity to a computer terminal as possible.

"Salawi keeps getting this flicker on her monitor, and my computer keeps—look, there it goes again," Taggert said as her display shifted. Zelenka bent forward to look over her shoulder, and his eyes went wide.

"Oh, no, no," he said. "No, that is not good. Here, let me—" He shooed Taggert out of the way to take her place at the console, and she obligingly slid over to the next workstation. "Look at this," he said. Lorne looked, although he wasn't surprised to see lines of incomprehensible code mixed with even more incomprehensible Ancient code. "Now what is this supposed to be doing?"

"If we don't know, maybe we should shut it down," Lorne said.

"Yes, I am trying. These programs should not be running. What were you doing?"

"Nothing. The alert went off for an unscheduled offworld activation, I started monitoring for radio transmissions—"

"That might do it," Zelenka said. "Some kind of trigger—"

"There wasn't a transmission," Salawi said. "Look."

"The computer says that there was not," Zelenka said. "Yes, that is either another sensor malfunction or very bad."

"Just what are we dealing with here?" Lorne said.

"There are programs running in the security subsystems that should not be there. I am trying to shut them down, but they are triggering more subroutines—this could be a serious problem." Zelenka looked up sharply over his glasses. "I think we are under attack."

Lorne was reaching for his radio headset before Zelenka finished talking. "Colonel Sheppard?" With Woolsey out of the city, he didn't have to worry about whether technically he should have been calling Woolsey first.

"This is Sheppard. What's the problem?"

"We have a situation. You'd better get up to the control room. It seems someone's activated some programs in our computer system that Dr. Zelenka is having trouble shutting down."

"I'm on my way," Sheppard said, and then before he cut off his radio, "They've got problems upstairs." Lorne didn't think that last was addressed to him. He refrained from speculating about who it might in fact have been addressed to, on the grounds that refraining from speculating about things like that was part of his job.

"Oh, not good," Zelenka said, and followed it in Czech with what sounded like something heartfelt. "We have systems shutting down — internal sensors, power to the weapons chair —"

"Get that thing shut down," Lorne said.

"Yes, I am trying —"

"What the hell is going on?" Sheppard said, tearing up the stairs into the control room, wearing sweatpants tucked into the tops of his boots and a flannel shirt he hadn't bothered to tuck in at all.

"This is Rodney's work," Zelenka said. "His programs are shutting down our security systems, and I cannot stop it. I am afraid we are going to lose the iris."

"Security teams to the gateroom," Sheppard said into his radio. "Sound a citywide alarm." Salawi's hands moved uncertainly over her keyboard, but it was only seconds before the alarm sounded. "Put me on citywide," Sheppard said, and waited for Salawi's quick nod before he went on. "This is Colonel Sheppard. Assume that as of now we are facing an attack by unknown hostiles who are trying to get through the Stargate. I want security teams on full alert —"

Zelenka breathed a curse in Czech, all the more alarming because his tone was hushed rather than heated. "The iris is shutting down," he said. "I am trying, but —"

"God damn it," Sheppard said, heading back down the rear stairs and drawing his pistol in one motion. Lorne was already moving in the same direction. Rear stairs instead of main ones, because they weren't in body armor, and that sweeping marble staircase gave anyone coming through the Stargate a lovely clear shot—

He could hear the electric crackle of the iris collapsing, see the Stargate rippling blue and unobstructed as he came down the stairs. Below in the gate room, two Marine teams were already in position, leveling weapons on the Stargate. One of the Marines handed a P90 up to Sheppard, who holstered his pistol and cradled the rifle without taking his eyes off the gate.

The room lit with bolts of stunner fire, spitting through the gate like a lightning storm, and the Marines opened up, the first of the attackers—Wraith, they were definitely Wraith—crumpling under the barrage. There were more coming behind them, though, charging forward over the bodies and leaping to the sides, masked drones heading straight for the Marine teams.

Their bodies jerked as the bullets hit them, but too many of them staggered without falling and kept on walking. Lorne could feel his blood run cold with the same crawling sense of wrongness it always gave him, watching them take more damage than anyone should be able to and keep moving, heads whipping around inhumanly fast at each new burst of gunfire.

"We have Wraith inside the city," Sheppard said over the radio. "All teams—" The thunder of gunfire drowned out his words. The gate was still open, more and more Wraith stepping through. Lorne caught a glimpse of another security team taking up position at the entrance to the gateroom, but he wasn't sure how long they could possibly hold.

"Radek!" Sheppard yelled between bursts of fire. "We need that iris!" Lorne couldn't hear Zelenka's answer, but he didn't think Sheppard liked it.

Stunner fire crackled against the wall, too close, and Lorne moved out of the way fast, still firing, taking careful aim before each shot. He was very aware that he only had one spare clip on him. It would have been nice for the Wraith to give them a little warning before they invaded. He would have packed differently—

A series of distant metallic clangs rose over the thunder of weapons fire. Zelenka must have put the city into a full lockdown, shutting all the security doors. Good for keeping the Wraith confined to the area around the gateroom. Not so great for getting more reinforcements.

Lorne scrambled forward, ducking to the side of the main staircase, using it for what cover it could provide. He leaned out for a moment, just long enough to see that there were male Wraith coming in behind the drones, their faces unmasked, hanging back in tight groups. He was about to duck back under cover when he glanced over at Sheppard and saw his expression, his eyes wide with shock and the muzzle of his weapon lowering a bare few inches.

"Rodney!" Sheppard called out. "Rodney, damn it —"

He was dressed like a Wraith, all in black in a dark coat that swept to his knees, and his hair was stark white, but Lorne still recognized him as soon as he saw him. Rodney was pointing with one clawed hand, snapping some instruction, and then Lorne was distracted by one of the Marines falling almost at his feet. He crouched, grabbing the man's rifle and swinging it up as one of the drones reached for him, feeding hand outstretched, and then all he could do was fire.

Radek ducked as another stun bolt crashed against the console behind him, hunching his shoulders as though that could somehow protect him. New lines of code were scrolling past, and on Salawi's screen alarms glared yellow and red. The shield was down, the chair was offline, power was fluctuating as a program tried to override the jury-rigged controls of the naquadah generators; he'd managed to get the internal sensors back up, but he didn't know how long he could hold them.

"Lockdown complete," Salawi said, her voice a little higher than normal, but amazingly steady under the circumstances. "Except — the transport chambers are still working."

"Damn it," Radek said, and hit keys, calling up another screen. The P90s fired below him in the gateroom, the concussion splitting the air, and he ducked his head further, not daring to look.

Radek shook his head in dismay and glanced back at the screen. Yes, some of the transport chambers were still working, and he was getting contradictory readings on the lockdown, too, as though maybe some of the doors hadn't properly sealed themselves...

He found the screen he wanted, entered the override code he and Sam had devised, and launched a program that he hoped would kill at least some of Rodney's subroutines. Another bolt crackled against the consoles behind him, and then another, and he repressed the desire to cover his head. In a minute, in less than a minute, he told himself, in seconds only you will dive under the console and be safe, but now there is this program to run, and that one, and power to cut here if you can—

"Dr. Zelenka!" Salawi slammed against him, knocking him out of his chair, fell on top of him as they tumbled beneath the console. Radek grabbed for his glasses—thank God, intact—and she rolled away. Behind where he had been sitting, the console shimmered with the fading blast of a stunner.

"Radek!" That was Sheppard, a voice in his ear, and Radek pulled himself upright.

"Yes."

"The shield! Can you get it back?"

"No. I'm sorry." He risked a glance at the screen anyway, on his knees peering over the edge of the console like a child playing peek-a-boo. "No."

"Damn it—" Sheppard's words were cut off in a burst of machine gun fire. "Get your people out of there, we can't hold them—"

"Yes," Radek said. He was missing something, he knew, but in the chaos he couldn't see it. He looked around quickly, seeing who was still there, grateful it was the night shift and fewer people on duty. Salawi and Taggert and Mcmillan and Neumeier and Martinez, only there was no sign of Mcmillan, and he thought Martinez had grabbed a P90 as soon as the shooting started—

He risked a look over the edge of the console, ducked back down again, swearing. The gate room was full of Wraith, the gate shimmering blue, rippling as still more Wraith emerged from it and headed for the stairs. And that meant it was time to go, there was nothing they could do, no weapon they had, that would stop the Wraith. He reached across, tapped Salawi's shoulder. "We must get out of here. Colonel Sheppard's orders."

She blinked, then nodded, and plucked at Neumeier's sleeve. "Which way, doctor?"

Am I in charge? Radek bit back the words, knowing that, in fact, he was, and pointed toward the rear of the control room, toward the transport chamber that was their best hope of safety. "The back doors. Keep low."

"That's supposed to seal," Neumeier said. "When we're in lock-down—"

"It did not," Radek said. For which we should be grateful, he added silently. "Go!"

Neumeier moved, crouching low, scrambling awkwardly between the rows of consoles. Salawi followed, glancing over her shoulder as she went, face screwed up in determination and fear.

"Radek!" Sheppard again, shouting, painful in the earpiece. "Radek, pull the ZPM!"

"What—" Radek began, then shook himself. "Yes, yes, I will do that." Of course; if they couldn't get the shield working again, there was no point in leaving the ZPM in place and vulnerable.

"Doc!" That was Taggert. She'd gotten a pistol from somewhere, though Radek didn't remember her carrying one—most of the control room staff didn't, they relied on the shield and the Marines—and she crouched now in the shelter of the lower console, pistol braced on the nearest board. Martinez was beside her, P90 in hand, slotting a new magazine into place. "Get moving, the Wraith are on the stairs—"

A stun bolt knocked her backwards, sprawling bonelessly against the base of the upper consoles.

"Jesus, Mary—" Radek started to reach for her, but another stunner blast slammed against the consoles.

"Go!" Martinez yelled, and fired a long burst.

Radek obeyed, scrambling without grace between the consoles, breath catching in his chest. He heard the sound of Martinez's P90, found the door at last and laid his hand on the lock plate, praying it was still open, and to his relief it slid back a few inches. P90s faced him, and he fell back, lifting his hands, but someone grabbed his shirt and pulled him through. Martinez followed a second later, and the door slid shut again, locking solidly into place.

"Will it hold?" Radek blinked in startlement as he saw that it was Captain Cadman, P90 flat against her body, wearing the dark jumpsuit of the *Hammond's* crew rather than an Atlantis uniform. She must have been already in the city when the raid began, perhaps catching up with friends from the days when she was stationed here. Possibly now she regretted it. Radek shrugged in answer to her question.

"Maybe. It is Rodney who is attacking us, so—" He shook himself, looked around, counting heads. Salawi, Neumeier, Martinez—and yes, Mcmillan, but Taggert was left behind. He shook that thought away, too, knowing she was dead, fed upon by now, made himself focus on Sheppard's last order. "We must pull the ZPM, Lieutenant.

Rodney knows where it is, what it is. We must pull it first."

Cadman hesitated for a heartbeat, then nodded. "Okay. Blais, take four men, go with Dr. Zelenka. There's a team already at the ZPM room, rendezvous with them, tell them what's happening. Go!"

"Yes," Radek said. He turned on his heel, heading for the transport chamber. He only hoped they would get there in time.

CHAPTER EIGHT
Quicksilver in Atlantis

RONON flattened himself against the wall of his transport chamber as the door opened, to be faced with the barrels of lowered P90s. "Don't shoot!"

One of the young Marines he was facing waved the others back from the door, and they took up position tensely on either side of the hallway. PFC Washington, the man's name patch said, one of the new ones. No officers or noncoms in sight, so he'd taken charge the way he should, but he wasn't much more than a kid. "Why are the transport chambers still working?"

"Don't know," Ronon said. "Everything else is locked down."

"Not on this level," Washington said. "The security doors on this corridor aren't closing. There's still access to two stairwells."

That made it possible to actually reach the gateroom, but also meant that if the Wraith came through them they'd be into the lower levels of the tower, including the infirmary. "Anybody know how to get the doors to close?"

Washington looked at the rest of the security team, and got nothing but shaking heads. "I'm thinking no."

"Then we'd better stop the Wraith," Ronon said. "They're up the stairs."

"Right," Washington said, a little too loud, like he was trying to steel himself into motion.

"Then move." Ronon made for the stairway, hoping they were behind him, wishing he had something to work with besides green soldiers who'd never faced the Wraith before. He felt for his radio. "Teyla, you want to get up here?" He flattened himself against the stairwell wall at the sound of pounding feet coming down the stairs. "We're about to have Wraith on the mess hall level."

"I cannot," Teyla said in his ear in frustration. "The security doors in the residential areas have sealed. Colonel Carter says that all the exterior doors near the pier are sealed as well."

"Can't she beam people into the city?"

"She and Colonel Caldwell are trying," Teyla said. "But some device within the city is now transmitting the Wraith jamming frequencies, and so far she has been unable to do so."

"All right," Ronon said. That wasn't their problem to solve. "Try the transport chamber."

"I will," Teyla said.

"We'll be here," Ronon said. He thumbed his pistol to stun and fired up the stairs before he could see who was rounding the landing above him. If it was a Marine team, he'd apologize later.

He heard the pistol shots from beside him ricochet off the wall, started to call for the Marines to hold their fire, and then saw the sweep of a leather trenchcoat, high boots with no laces. He thumbed the setting over to kill instead and caught the Wraith in the legs, fired again as the Wraith tumbled down the stairs, rolling to try to get its balance, the leg wound already healing.

He could see the drones coming down behind the male, and ducked under the spitting stunner fire. "Get down!" he yelled, yanking the Marine next to him to one knee and grabbing the muzzle of the young man's P90 to point it up the stairs instead of at them. "Don't let them get close!"

"I hear you," the man said, firing in quick bursts. The Wraith drones staggered, one of them falling heavily and fouling the shots of the ones around him. Ronon kept his own pistol trained on the male Wraith, shooting him again and then yet again until he went still at their feet.

"Is he — ?" the Marine next to Ronon began, looking just on this side of panic.

"If he moves, shoot him," Ronon said, and raised his pistol to cover the stairs. Eventually they'd get another Wraith captain up there who'd tell the drones to do something smarter than walk down the stairs into P90 fire. He hoped it wouldn't be soon.

One of them screamed and launched himself off the stairs, whether trying to dodge or in a purposeful leap, Ronon couldn't tell. Ronon scrambled back, slapped the shoulder of the young Marine next to him, grabbed his jacket and yanked when he wasn't moving fast enough. The Wraith landed mostly on top of the Marine, rolling him over and clawing at his shirt. Ronon fired, aimed a vicious kick at the side of the Wraith's head, and fired again when it came up fighting.

"We have to fall back!" Washington yelled from the other side of the stairs. "They're still coming—"

Ronon fired again, and the Wraith finally jerked and went limp. Ronon hauled him up and shoved him toward the stairs, one more obstacle for the ones on the stairs above to have to scramble over.

"Down. Go!" he yelled. "Take the next landing down!"

If the Wraith didn't try to shoot their way down another flight of stairs, took the corridor on this level to the next landing, they'd be able to work their way around the defenders — but he just had to hope they didn't know the city that well. "Any security teams who can hear me, we need someone to cover the south tower stairs on the infirmary level."

"Ronon, that you?" Sheppard said over the radio.

"We've got about a hundred Wraith trying to come down these stairs," Ronon said, putting his back to the wall of the landing and firing steadily, the Marines doing better this time at getting into position on either side of the staircase. "And we just gave up the mess hall level." He hoped the kitchen staff had gotten off that floor, or at least put the heavy door of one of the walk-in freezers between them and any Wraith who got through.

"Copy that," Sheppard said, his voice drowned out by P90 fire on his end of the radio. He didn't sound like he was really in a position to talk. "Just hang on."

"What do we do?" Washington yelled over the gunfire.

"Keep shooting!" Ronon yelled back. If it wasn't a great plan, at least it was simple enough that he thought they'd have no problem following along.

John flung himself into the shelter of the doorway, flattening his back against the wall as he slammed a fresh magazine into his P90. Wraith in the gate room, Wraith on the stairs that led to the mess hall level — no, on the mess hall level — worst of all Rodney with a Wraith's face, a Wraith's hand and mind commanding drones as though he'd been born to it —

He shoved that thought aside, risked another glance around the corner. Most of the Wraith were still there, drones covering the approaches while the males moved into operations. If they'd been spectacularly lucky, Radek would have gotten the consoles locked down, but given that Rodney was in control of the security systems, that didn't seem very likely. So the Wraith would be busy consolidating their control of the shield and the gate, making sure they could keep getting reinforcements… He closed his eyes for an instant, visualizing the situation. Wraith on the stairs — Wraith in the gate room and ops and then the stairs, heading down into the vulnerable parts of the city. On the mess hall floor already, and moving down — except that it made more sense to keep bringing in troops, make sure there was no way they could get control back again, and that had to mean that the stairway attack was meant to draw attention. But away from what? Rodney was up in operations — wasn't he?

John braced himself, took another quick look around the edge of the doorway. He got one good look at the consoles, a trio of males working at the boards, before a drone spotted him and fired. He ducked back, the stun bolt splashing harmlessly on the far wall, a tight knot of fear in the pit of his stomach. All of them had had long hair, and there was no way he could convince himself that any of them was Rodney. He touched his earpiece.

"Lorne!"

"Sir?"

"Do you have a visual of ops?"

"Yes, sir."

"See if you can spot McKay up there." John pressed himself harder against the wall as another stunner bolt slammed past. He nodded to the nearest Marine, who returned fire briefly before ducking back into shelter. Words sounded in his ear, but they were drowned by the noise of the P90s. "Say again?"

"He's not up there," Lorne said. "Just Wraith. Regular Wraith."

"Right." It all fit, suddenly, the pieces coming together in his mind: the way the lockdown had been interrupted, the transport chambers that still worked, the way the diversionary attack had gone, the fact that Rodney was involved… He touched the radio again. "Radek! Radek, can you hear me?"

There was a little silence, and he could feel his heart kicking against his ribs. Too long, it had taken him too long to work this out, Rodney could be there by now—

"I hear you, John," Radek said. "We are in the ZPM room—"

"Rodney is headed your way," John interrupted. "Lock yourselves in and stay alert. I'm coming to you."

There was a pause, but Radek's voice was steady. "OK. We will be ready."

John took a breath. "Lorne. Rodney's heading for the ZPM room. I'm taking a team and going after him. Cover the approaches and make damn sure he doesn't get back in."

"Copy that," Lorne answered, his voice matter-of-fact for all that they both knew what he'd just been asked to do. "Good luck, sir."

"To you, too," John answered. He looked at the people gathered in the corridor, Marines and airmen, pointed quickly to half a dozen. "You, come with me. Degan, take over here."

"Yessir," the sergeant said, and John turned away. He only hoped they'd be in time.

Quicksilver glanced at the laptop he had taken from the operations room, checking the specifications of the tower against the maps in his mind. It was almost painfully bizarre to be here in the Ancients' city, under the soaring windows that had haunted his dreams, and once or twice he had to shake himself away from some memory, some image, that rose unbidden and irrelevant. It was worth it, he told himself, worth a little disorientation to see the rout in the gate room, to see the humans fall, to punish them for what they had done to him—to him, to Dust, and to so many more.

He found the hall he wanted, the one that led to the next transport chamber that he had carefully excluded from the lockdown. It was all working perfectly, all the pieces meshing just as he had known they would, and he pointed left at the next intersection.

This way.

You're sure? That was Ardent, the younger of the two blades he had been given to manage the drones, and Quicksilver rolled his eyes.

Yes, of course I'm sure.

Ardent glared at him, not quite daring to show teeth, but the other blade, Wakeful, waved his drones ahead without a word.

Be careful, Ember said softly, at his back, but Quicksilver ignored him, all his attention on the plan.

The transport chamber was unguarded, as he'd planned—as he'd arranged, certain doors sealing too quickly to allow the defenders to reach this hall, this chamber. He stepped forward, ready to enter their destination, but Ember caught his sleeve.

Send Ardent first.

The queen's brother did snarl at that, but Wakeful nodded. *Go.*

The door slid shut, and when it opened again, Ardent and his drones were gone. Wakeful cocked his head to one side, then waved another group of drones into the chamber, and paused to listen again.

They have secured the hall. There were human soldiers, and more in this power room, and they are fighting hard. Are you sure this is worth it, Quicksilver?

Quicksilver was already in the chamber, turned to glare at him, and something in the movement, in the fall of light from the windows and the sleek bronze walls and the pattern of the carvings, caught at his heart. This was — something was terribly wrong here, and for an instant the faces of his friends became like monsters, so that he flung up his arm to shield himself from the sight.

Quicksilver?

Ember's voice brought him back to himself, and he shook his head, hard, scowling.

Are you all right?

If he is — unwell, Wakeful began, in the same moment, and Quicksilver shook himself. The queen was depending on him. They would never reach the Milky Way without more power, and this was the greatest source of power available to them.

I'm fine, he said, and willed it to be true. *Let's go.*

Radek made himself take two slow deep breaths before he looked at the young lieutenant in command of the ZPM room team. He was all too aware of how badly young lieutenants had fared on Atlantis, hoped this wouldn't be another one. "You heard?"

"Yes."

Radek squinted at his name badge — Sabine — and recognized the sergeant behind him with relief. Hector had been on Atlantis from the beginning, knew how to fight the Wraith.

"Permission to take a team and secure the transport chamber?" Hector asked, and the lieutenant nodded.

"Go."

They left in a flurry of purposeful movement, and Radek looked around the chamber, automatically checking the displays. "I am to pull the ZPM," he said. "We think that is what they want—"

Sabine nodded, waving his men into position. "Do it quick, doc.

There's only one way out."

"Yes, yes, I am well aware of that." Radek moved to the first console, touched keys to begin transferring the crucial systems over to the naquadah generators. That was supposed to happen automatically if the ZPM went off-line, but he didn't trust those subroutines, not with Rodney's programs loose in the system. The shield was out of his control, shut down as though there was no power for it; he spared it a single glance and typed a second set of commands, watching as the city's subsystems switched reluctantly to the new power source. The process usually seemed almost ridiculously fast, but today—

He brushed that thought aside, and shoved his glasses into a better position as he turned to the board the controlled the ZPMs. Only one of the three slots was filled, the one at the closest point of the triangular console. He entered the password that unlocked the system, and froze as P90s fired in the hallway.

"We've got company," Sabine said, over his shoulder, and held out a P90. "Can you use this, doc?"

"Yes," Radek said. He'd fired one four or five times in practice, Ronon had made sure of that since he'd been assigned to the gate team. He took it—it felt heavier—but focused on the controls a moment more, just long enough to erase his password and back out of the access screens. Sabine ducked out to join the others, keeping low.

Then there were shouts from the hall, machine gun fire and the heavy snap of the Wraith stunners, and he tucked the P90 awkwardly into firing position. He would have been better with the pistol, maybe, though he'd never really expected to have to use either one—

"Fall back!" That was Hector, he thought, and instinctively Radek stepped backward, into the shelter of one of the elaborate sculptures that protruded from the wall behind the control consoles. They'd argued, he and Rodney, about whether they were decorative or functional in some as-yet-unidentified but probably dangerous way, and he hoped he wasn't about to have that question answered the hard way.

A body tumbled in the door, one of the Marines, and the sound of the P90s ceased abruptly. A stunner fired again, and Radek flattened himself into the shadows, wondering what the hell he was supposed to do now. He could hear footsteps, but didn't dare look: two people, he thought, and then one set of footsteps retreated. Only one of them, he told himself, and eased carefully forward.

A figure in black was bent over the controls, familiar and not familiar, Rodney and not Rodney, the familiar high forehead and bony nose, the same set shoulders and the same quick hands, but all that made literally alien, snow-white hair and green-toned skin, deep sensor pits carved into his cheeks, the clever hands that moved so deftly on the controls now tipped with heavy black claws. He bared sharp teeth at some recalcitrant piece of code.

And that was not so very different from Rodney at the best of times, Radek thought, and lifted the P90. "Rodney," he said. "Step away from the console."

The white head whipped up, too fast, too sure, and the lips parted in a snarl.

"Keep quiet," Radek said. "Quiet, or I will shoot." Whether he would or not, he didn't know, prayed he wouldn't find out.

Rodney snarled again. "Are you completely stupid?" His voice was the same and different, the inflection, the pitch the same as it had always been, the timbre Wraith.

"Step back," Radek said. "There are enough bullets in this clip that you will not regenerate." If in fact he could. If he was truly Wraith. There was so much they didn't know.

"And then the rest of my men will hear the shots, and come and kill you," Rodney said. "That's a brilliant plan!"

Nonetheless, he stepped away from the controls, moving away from the door. Radek took a step forward himself, not wanting to risk missing him even at this range. He was no longer completely in cover, had his back half to the door, but it didn't seem to matter.

"Jesus, Rodney," he said, and stumbled to a stop. What was there to say to this Wraith that looked like Rodney, that gave him Rodney's furious glare from slitted pupils? "If you come with me — we can help you. Dr. Keller — Jennifer — she will take care of you —"

"Please," Rodney said. "This is a waste of time. I've been taken care of here before. Put the gun down, and I'm prepared to see that you're not harmed."

"And you are criticizing my tactics?" Radek snapped. Maybe he could make Rodney come with him, though that was being optimistic about the hordes of Wraith outside — but maybe he could use Rodney as a hostage? He saw Rodney's eyes shift, turned a second too late, to take the stunner's bolt full in the chest.

Quicksilver flinched as the stunner's blast knocked the human backward, the weapon clattering from his hands.

That was close, Ember said, and slipped the stunner back into its holster.

Yes, too close, Quicksilver snapped. *You should have checked better in here.*

And how was I to do that when you rushed in first? Ember asked. *We hold the hall for now, and the transport chamber, but some of this group got away, and Greyblood reports that the Lanteans are regrouping.*

Ember's eyes fixed on the body sprawled at the base of the sculpture. There were holes in the arm of his coat and across one hip, and he reached greedily for the human, dragging him into a more accessible position. A jolt of something remarkably like panic shot through Quicksilver.

No —

Ember glanced over his shoulder, frowning slightly. *I must feed*

There's no time, Quicksilver said. *I need your help.*

Ember gave the human a last hungry look, but came obediently to his feet. *What must I do?*

Watch this, Quicksilver said, and waved at a screen. *Watch if it spikes — if it goes over this line. Why they didn't give me a master of sciences physical —*

Because none would agree to it, Ember said. *And what do I do if it does?*

Just tell me, Quicksilver said. He frowned at the board, remembering the pattern: here, and here, and a code, and then here again, and another password —

With a soft click, the ZPM rose from its socket, glowing orange, wound with veins as dark as his own, shot here and there with shades of red and rusty green. He smiled, and stepped around the console, lifted it carefully from its socket. The light faded and died, and he felt a twinge of inappropriate sorrow. *All right. Where's the case?*

Here.

Ember held it out, open to reveal the heavy padding, roughly shaped to fit the tapering cylinder. Quicksilver laid it in place and closed the case over it, cinching the clasps tight. That should protect the ZPM against almost anything, including direct machine gun fire —

Quicksilver! That was Wakeful, his tone urgent. *Time to go.*

Coming, Quicksilver answered, and together they started for the door.

John waved his team to a halt as they reached the transport chamber, not much liking the idea of what had to come next. They'd never make it down through the maze of corridors blocked by security doors, even if Rodney had left a single path through the maze as an alternate means of escape for himself. That meant this was their way down. The only problem was, the Wraith knew that, too.

It would be nice to be able to send a grenade down ahead of them. All they needed was someone who could hotwire the transport chamber to activate from outside without someone having to touch the map on its back wall. John was pretty sure he'd watched Rodney do that once, but all he could call up was a vivid memory of covering the corridor, saying "Hurry *up*, McKay," while Rodney said "Believe me, no one is as committed to our survival here as me."

It wasn't going to get better the longer he thought about it. "Let's do this," he said, waiting until the airmen and Marines had flattened themselves against the sides of the transport chamber walls before he tagged the screen at the back of the chamber, whipping his P90 around toward the doors in the same movement.

Nothing happened. "Oh, come on," he said.

"Maybe they shut it down," one of the Marines volunteered.

"It's showing as active, and so is the one near the ZPM chamber, but nothing's happening." Internal sensors were offline, but the transport chamber map was still obligingly showing him which transport chambers were functional. The maps were just glorified elevator maps, not part of the internal security system, and it looked like Rodney had overlooked shutting them down. Good, John thought; it wasn't like they'd gotten a lot of other breaks.

The map was showing a transport chamber on the floor above the ZPM room. He nearly punched it, and hesitated, his fingers hovering over the map. He just didn't buy it. Rodney would have wanted an easy escape route. He wouldn't have shut down the nearest transport chamber, but he also wouldn't have wanted security teams transporting in from all over the city.

"Look at that," he said. "These two transport chambers way down below the ZPM level. "There's nothing down there Rodney would want."

"So?"

"So, I'm betting that to get to where we want to go, we have to take a detour. Watch yourselves." He tapped one of the two transport chambers. Nothing happened, so he tapped the other, and was rewarded by the bright flash of the transporter activating. He swung the muzzle of his P90 up as the doors opened, but the long corridor was empty.

"Now what, sir?" one of the Marines said from behind him.

"Now, I'm betting that the other transport chamber on this level will take us to the one outside the ZPM room."

"Unless this whole thing is just designed to waste our time," a young airman said from his other side as they advanced.

"Unless it is," John said, in a tone that he hoped would discourage further useless speculation on all the ways they could be screwed at the moment. "Trust me, I'm pretty sure I know how Rodney's mind works." He reached for his radio. "Radek, what's your situation?" There was no answer. "Dr. Zelenka, come in." There was nothing but silence. His hand clenched on the grip of his P90.

They were rounding a corner toward the second transport chamber when John heard the whine of the transport chamber activating. *Too slow,* he snarled at himself, at the same time that he was diving back behind the corner, trying to get the team behind what little cover there was.

The Wraith wouldn't be expecting them here, or at least he hoped not, because the element of surprise was about their only advantage. If they came around the corner firing—he could see it all too clearly, rounding the corner already firing, Rodney's head turning, his body jerking back as the P90 fire tore into him.

"Flashbang," he mouthed, and someone pressed a stun grenade into his hand. He pulled the pin and tossed it, turning his head away into the crook of his arm, feeling the thunderclap through the soles of his feet and stabbing through his ears. He swung around the corner to see the Wraith staggering back, one of them stumbling to his knees and hopefully getting in the way of the others.

John fired at one of the drones and dodged bolts of blindly aimed stunner fire, marking his targets. Three males, a handful of drones, and there was Rodney, arm thrown over his eyes, holding the ZPM case. "Try to take the rest of them out!" John yelled.

Rodney swung his stunner around, apparently toward the sound of John's voice, and John dodged again. The drones still seemed dazed, but the other male Wraith were recovering fast, too fast. One of them was firing purposely, though his eyes were streaming, and one of the Marines went down under stunner fire, the smartass airman dragging him back around the corner.

"Rodney!" John shouted. "Damn it, I *will* shoot you!"

Rodney snarled, baring teeth, his own eyes watering as well, though John thought he was starting to focus on his face. "Don't you start!"

It sounded like Rodney, too much like Rodney as John aimed. He'd try a leg shot, but he remembered all too well that he hadn't been able to drop Ford that way, and Rodney looked fully Wraith. If he had to shoot him in the chest...

"Hey, I know you," Rodney said, squinting at him, and John hesitated. Maybe, just maybe, Rodney was snapping out of it.

"That's right," John said. "It's me."

"You killed my brother," Rodney said. "You are going to be *so* sorry you did that." He fired, and as John dodged the stunner blast, he saw that the drones were moving again, lunging around the corner toward him. Toward him in particular, apparently. Great. He backed up, firing, trying not to trip over anybody.

One of the drones grabbed the airman who was covering the downed Marine and shook him like a ragdoll, shoving him back against the wall with his hand clawing the man's chest even as John was firing. Another Marine was down, the Wraith drones piling onto them, trying to force them back against the wall.

The young airman screamed, and John knew he wasn't going to take the drone down in time. The other Marine still standing grabbed at the drone, pulling it back, and John shot it in the head.

"Sir!" the other airman yelled. The first of the Wraith had reached the transport chamber at the other end of the hall.

"Shoot them!" John yelled back.

"But Dr. McKay—"

"That's an order!" The man fired, but he didn't have a clear shot. He hit one of the other male Wraith, who screamed and shoved Rodney into the transport chamber, throwing himself in after him. One of the males was down, unmoving. The other two made it into the transport chamber as John watched, the doors closing with two drones still on their feet in the hallway.

They went down under a hail of gunfire, and John turned, dropping to one knee beside the fallen airman. He looked like he was years dead, like something you'd find if you dug up a desert grave. Grieg, his name patch said, and John would probably still be thinking of him as *that smartass* when he had to write the letter home.

"Ah, Jesus," the other airman said, going to his knees beside Grieg. He'd probably never seen this before. John had seen it plenty of times, enough that his eyes didn't linger on the man's face.

"Fall back, into the transport chamber." The stunned Marine was staggering to his feet, the other Marine helping him up. John reached for his radio as he moved. "Lorne, come in," he said. "We've got a problem."

"You mean another one?" Lorne said. He sounded harried, which from Lorne suggested they still had a hell of a fight on their hands up there.

"Rodney just got past us with the ZPM," he said. "I'm guessing he's on his way back up to the Stargate."

"We've just taken back the control room," Lorne said. "We're trying to get someone up here who can get back into the computer —"

"Zelenka's not responding to his radio," John said. "Just don't let Rodney get to the gate. I'm on my way back up."

"Copy that," Lorne said, tightly, and John hit the button and let everything dissolve in the transporter's light.

"Everybody down there in the gateroom, we have incoming Wraith in the transport chamber," Lorne said over the intercom down to the gateroom. "They've got the ZPM and Dr. McKay. You are authorized to use whatever force is necessary to —"

There was a rattle of gunfire and then Colonel Sheppard's voice yelling "Jesus, hold your fire!"

That meant Rodney hadn't transported to the chamber on the gateroom level. All right, if he'd heard that they'd taken back the gateroom, that made sense, but going anywhere else wouldn't get him out of the city—

"The jumper bay," Lorne said. "We need a security team up to the jumper bay!" He was already moving for the stairs, activating his radio as he ran. "If anybody can get find a way to get back into the computer and keep them from dialing out, now would be a really good time."

He was the first one up to the jumper bay, although he could hear the sound of pounding feet behind him. He saw them across the bay coming out of the transport chamber, and ducked behind one of the jumpers that was partly disassembled for repair. He didn't have a good shot, and he didn't want to draw their fire for no purpose. If he could get close enough to shoot at the ZPM case that he could see Rodney carrying, that ought to at least provide a distraction.

"Lorne, this is Sheppard," Sheppard said over the radio. "I've got teams on their way up to you now—"

"That would be nice," Lorne said.

"I'm right behind them. See if you can get one of the jumpers in the air, try and cut them off."

He started moving toward one of the jumpers, but that didn't mean he liked the idea. "Sir, if we start fighting it out right above the gateroom—"

"I know," Sheppard said. "But we can't let them take the ZPM."

There were Marines coming up behind him, now, and two of the male Wraith turned at the sound, firing stunner bolts toward them. A couple of drones started running toward the Marine team, taking heavy fire but being effectively distracting. Lorne kept his eyes on Rodney.

He aimed for the ZPM case, and fired a tight burst. The case jerked in Rodney's hands, sparks flying, but whatever they'd done to Rodney must have given him Wraith strength; he held onto the case, clutching it to his chest with one arm as he punched at the door controls of the jumper.

One of the male Wraith was behind Rodney now, in the way, and Lorne shot him. He hissed, staggering back, but the jumper door was opening, and Rodney and the male Wraith piled inside. One of the Wraith drones was down, the other one staggering to one knee.

None of them were looking at him. He made a dash out from cover toward the nearest jumper, diving in as the door opened. He reached for the controls and started powering up. All he needed was a couple of seconds for the shields and inertial dampeners to kick in and they just might be in business.

He didn't get them. He caught the movement out of the corner of his eye at the same time that the jumper sounded a warning, both audible and seemingly shrieking directly into his brain: *collision alert.*

He saw the other jumper bearing down on him, felt the impact, and then the second impact as the jumper smashed back into the one behind it. There was no pain, just a metallic crashing noise that seemed to go on for a very long time as the world around him went black.

John was on his way up from the control room to the gateroom, taking the stairs two at a time, when someone called from behind him, "The incoming wormhole's cutting off!"

He had a moment's hope that meant they'd gotten the computers back before he heard the heavy grind of the gate dialing. It was followed by an echoing crash from above their heads.

He took the rest of the stairs at a dead run, skidding out into the jumper bay to see one of the jumpers hovering above the door down into the gateroom, which was already sliding open. Another jumper had clearly skidded halfway across the gateroom floor; it was on its side, and looked like it had taken some pretty heavy damage.

John made a dash for one of the other jumpers, but he knew there was no time. He powered it up anyway, urging it under its breath to power up faster — come on, baby, hurry — and was still working on getting weapons initialized as the guidance system kicked in, sweeping it out toward the jumper bay door and down into the gateroom.

The other jumper was already sliding through the event horizon, and as the weapons finally came online, it disappeared through, the wormhole shimmering for another few heartbeats before it vanished.

John let the jumper lower to the gateroom floor and climbed out. The gateroom suddenly seemed very quiet. "Major Lorne, what's your status?"

It took a moment for anyone to respond. "Lorne's down," someone said over the radio. "We're trying to get a medical team up here."

"Copy that," he said. He waved the Marines in the gateroom who were still on their feet into position to guard the gate. He could see too many people down, stunned or worse, and they must have more casualties in the rest of the city.

Up in the control room, Salawi was just sliding back behind her console. She looked up when he came up the stairs. "They said this level was clear, so I thought I should—"

"You thought right," John said. "Can we dial out?"

She glanced at her screen. "I think so," she said. "The main gate controls were never locked out."

"Dial the alpha site, now," he said. "And when the wormhole goes down in thirty-eight minutes, dial it again unless you hear otherwise. I don't want anyone dialing in while we don't have control of the security system." He reached for his radio. "Dr. Zelenka, this is Colonel Sheppard. Please respond."

He wasn't really hoping for a response from Zelenka, and was caught short in surprise when he got one.

"I am here," Radek said shakily. "They have taken the ZPM, I am sorry—"

"Don't be," John said. "Just see if you can get us full computer access back."

"I am already working on it," Radek said. "I have been able to patch into the computer systems here, and I think I may have something."

"We need those security doors down," John said. "I've got a lot of men down, and Dr. Keller says she's stuck on the level her quarters are on, along with most of her staff."

"I am working as fast as I can," Radek said. "You do not have to inspire me to action by explaining how dire is the emergency. It will not really help me work."

"Right," John said. "Security teams, report in. We may still have some Wraith in the city, and internal sensors are still down. I'm going to see if I can get Teyla to give us some idea whether we still have company, but until then, watch yourselves." He leaned against the wall, adrenaline-fueled energy beginning to ebb. "Teyla, what's your status?"

"I am still on a residential level," she said, the frustration in her voice nearly crackling over the radio. "We are safe, but cut off here. John, what is happening?"

"Rodney took the ZPM," John said. "We're in a lot of trouble."

CHAPTER NINE
Aftermath

JOHN carried his cup of coffee to the head of the table, taking a certain morbid pleasure in seeing how many people looked just as bad as he felt. Radek looked worse, but that didn't really count. He doubted the engineer had slept more than a few hours since the attack, and he'd been pretty heavily stunned into the bargain. Keller looked like death warmed over, too, though these days that metaphor didn't work the way it used to. Ronon didn't look as though he'd gotten any rest, either, sprawled sideways in his chair with a stare that suggested he was actually sleeping with his eyes open. Caldwell and Carter both looked better — as though they'd had a chance to get some sleep and a decent shower — and Teyla was as sharp as ever, but Beckett clearly hadn't shaved since the attack. John ran his own hand over his chin, hoping that Woolsey was right and cleanliness was next to leadership, and took a last long swallow of the coffee.

"OK," he said, and was still a little startled when everyone looked at him expectantly. "So where are we? Keller?"

"Anders died last night," the doctor answered.

John bit his lip. That wasn't unexpected, the guy had been fed on pretty badly before his buddies managed to kill the drone, but he'd still hoped maybe they could do something.

"But I think everyone else is going to pull through," Keller went on. "That makes ten dead, and twenty-four injured. Most of those are fairly minor — people who were stunned and fell down stairs, a couple of sprains and some bad bruises from the hand-to-hand fighting." She glanced at her notes. "Also Dr. Meyers got trapped in a room with something that he's allergic to, and had a bad asthma attack, but he's pulling out of that nicely. We have three people more seriously hurt, enough to keep them out of action for a while, but I expect all of them to make a full recovery."

John nodded. That was about what you'd expect with the Wraith: if they didn't get close enough to feed on you, their main weapons weren't lethal. "How's Lorne?"

"Still unconscious. He has a concussion on top of the broken leg. We set the leg last night, put in pins, and I'm waiting to see how it holds before I consider more surgery."

That wasn't all that surprising either, considering the way the jumper had looked. He was mostly just glad Lorne hadn't been hurt worse. What was surprising was how confident Keller sounded. Usually she was stopping and starting, as though she was double-thinking every word. "What about Rizkala and Jovell?"

"Rizkala is doing much better than expected," Keller answered. "To the point where I'm not planning to do surgery just yet. If he continues the way he's been going, it's not going to be needed. Jovell —" She hesitated then, shook her head. "His wrist was pretty well shattered. He'll need at least one more surgery here, and then —" She stopped abruptly, as though she'd just remembered that they wouldn't be able to evacuate him through the gate. "But none of these are life-threatening."

Just career-threatening, John thought, if they couldn't get the gate open.

Keller folded her own hands on the table's gleaming surface, fingers carefully interlaced. "I'd like — If Colonel Caldwell's medical officer has the room, I'd like to discuss transferring Jovell over to *Daedalus*. Even if *Daedalus* isn't leaving this minute, it's still the fastest way we have right now to evacuate anyone who needs treatment on Earth."

"Whatever you need, Doctor," Caldwell said, and John nodded. "Go ahead."

"Then that's everything," Keller said. "As far as casualties go."

She was handling it well, John thought. It had to have hit her harder than anyone, knowing that Rodney had returned, a Wraith and an enemy. "Thanks, Doctor," he said aloud, and took a careful breath. "Dr. Zelenka?"

Radek gave a mirthless smile. "Rodney took the ZPM. Which has some fairly bad implications for what he can do with it, but I am concentrating for now on what it does to us. Which is also fairly bad. We cannot run the shield or power the weapons chair, and we cannot dial the Milky Way. With naquadah generators, we can dial destinations in Pegasus, but we are effectively cut off from home. Without a shield."

"What's the good news?" Caldwell said, under his breath, and Radek looked at him.

"That was the good news. The bad news is that we still have no way to stop Rodney from accessing the city systems. Mrs. Miller has helped us find a number of his back doors, but I doubt we have found them all. We are successfully maintaining an open wormhole, currently dialed through to our alpha site, but we do not have enough power to do this forever. Not to mention that we may want to communicate with the rest of the galaxy at some point."

That was laying it out with a vengeance, John thought. "How long can we hold the wormhole open?"

"Dialing every thirty-eight minutes—" Radek shrugged. "Days, certainly. Perhaps weeks."

"If I might interject here?" Carter said, and both John and Radek nodded. "We should probably cut the wormhole a little before the actual thirty-eight-minute limit—some random and varying number of seconds before, so Rodney can't predict when the wormhole might go down."

"That is a good thought," Radek said, and reached for his radio. "Excuse me." He turned away from the table, speaking quietly into his headset, and John looked around the table again.

"There's one other thing that we need to consider," Beckett said. He had been very quiet until now. "Rodney flew the jumper."

There was a little silence, and John frowned. "So? We know Rodney has the ATA gene—" He stopped abruptly, and Beckett nodded.

"Aye. Whatever they've done to him hasn't changed that. He can still use the Ancient technology."

"This just gets better and better," Caldwell muttered.

"Hold on," Keller said. "This—I mean, it's not good news, but it's also—we can maybe tell something about how the Wraith transformed him. We've got some actual data to work with, here."

Beckett nodded slowly. "That's true."

"OK," John said. "Let's hold that for later. Right now, our main concern has to be keeping the city safe. Ideas?"

There was a discouraging silence, and then at last Radek shrugged one shoulder. "Well, there is the obvious solution. Build a mechanical iris, like the one on Earth."

"Out of what?" Caldwell asked. He looked at Carter. "That thing's made of what, titanium alloy? It's not like we've got a whole lot of it just lying around."

Radek shrugged again. "We have no shield. Even if we had another

ZPM, we cannot trust that Rodney would not be able to access the city systems again. A mechanical iris is the safest thing I can think of."

"Radek's right," Carter said. "It's a logical solution. So the next question is, do we have — or can we get — the amount of titanium we're going to need?"

"There is none in the city," Radek said. "Not that we brought with us, anyway. Perhaps there are a few pieces of plate left over from the last time *Daedalus* was repaired here."

"I've used most of my spares already," Carter said. "And frankly I'm not keen to give up all my repair options."

"Me, neither," Caldwell said.

"Are you sure there's nothing in the city?" Ronon asked. "You said you haven't really looked at most of it."

"It's possible there is something in the parts we have not explored thoroughly," Radek said. "We can certainly set teams looking."

"Do that," John said, and looked from Ronon to Teyla. "What about our allies? Is there anyone out there we could get it from?"

Teyla shook her head. "There are not so many peoples who can make such a metal. And Death has attacked most of them already."

"The Genii," Ronon said.

"Perhaps," Teyla said. She sounded doubtful, and John couldn't help agreeing. After they'd nearly had a serious misunderstanding over the Ancient warship, he wasn't eager to go asking them for more help. "The Manarians dealt in metal ores, but…"

Manaria had been devastated only a few weeks before, in one of Queen Death's aggressive Cullings. John winced, and pulled himself upright in his chair. "First things first," he said. "Radek. Can we build and install a mechanical iris? Assuming we have the materials, I mean."

Radek nodded. "Yes. Yes, I think we can. We know the design, and how it works. It's only a matter of fitting it to our own gate."

"Our people can help with that," Carter said, and Caldwell nodded, face grim.

"OK," John said. "So what we need is the material." That, at least, he understood, and he looked around the table. "Radek, get your people searching the city, see what we have that we can use. Ronon, Teyla, I'd like you to compile a list of our allies and anybody else who might have suitable alloys we can trade for. Colonel Carter, Colonel Caldwell, if there is anything on either of your ships that you can spare, we'd be grateful for it." He looked around the table a final time. "Let's go with Plan B."

John caught Carter's eye before she left the conference room. "Have you got a minute?"

"Sure," she said, sitting back down. "What's up?"

"Now we're even more understaffed than we were to start with. You know we couldn't get back all the personnel who were transferred. There wasn't even time to get everybody back from the SGC, let alone people who got sent to Iraq or Afghanistan."

"I'm happy to lend you personnel if I can, but we still have repairs ongoing," Carter said, sounding like she was sympathetic but being careful not to commit herself before she heard what he wanted.

"I was actually wondering if I could borrow Captain Cadman for a while."

Carter's eyebrows went up. "Seriously?"

"Lorne's down for the count," John said. "Even if he pulls through this okay — which he will — he's going to be out of the action for weeks. I have a bunch of kids who've never even been through a Stargate yet and some lieutenants who think they know everything. I need somebody with a brain to take charge of Lorne's team."

"You have Marine lieutenants," Carter said.

"You're right, I do." He couldn't exactly say *I need a Marine with a brain*, but he could see from Carter's amused expression that he didn't have to. "But Cadman did a whole tour here as a lieutenant and didn't get shot, fed on by the Wraith, injured in some even weirder way, or sent home for being a pain in the ass. I can't say that about a lot of people, unfortunately. And you know perfectly well that when we need the backup team, we really need it."

"All right," Carter said. "I'll temporarily detach her. But you can't keep her."

John smiled. "Would I try to poach your crew?"

"You would if you're as smart as I think you are," Carter said.

The Queen had been pleased. Quicksilver could still feel the caress of her mind as he presented her with the ZPM, her delight, unguarded and unfeigned, as she unlatched the case and lifted the glowing cylinder from its padding.

Cleverest of clevermen, she had said, and behind her the lords of the zenana had bared teeth and bowed heads in varying acknowledgement of her praise.

We're not there yet, he had said. *There's a lot of work to do before we can use it — modifications to the hyperdrive, to all our systems — but it will help us with the new energy shields —*

I have every confidence in you, Death had said, and rested her off hand on his arm. He could still feel the touch of her fingers, cool and soft and yet burning like a brand. Perhaps he should have their shape tattooed on him, etched into his skin while he could still remember each fractional point of contact —

Are you well? Ember's thought broke the pleasant memory, and Quicksilver bared teeth in automatic reproof.

Yes, of course, he began, and realized abruptly that he was not. He felt odd, hollow, his legs at once weak and distant, as though they were no longer connected to his body. His feeding hand hurt, a slow pulse of pain in the palm of his hand. He stumbled, and Ember caught his arm.

When did you last feed?

For some reason, the question sent a jolt of pure terror racing through him, snapping him upright. He controlled himself with an effort, scowling at the other cleverman. *I have no idea.*

Then it is past time, Ember said. *Come.*

Another pang shot through him, and his hand throbbed sharply. He shook his head, unable to explain his reluctance. *I'm — I don't have time.*

If you don't feed, you won't be able to work, Ember said.

Later, Quicksilver said. The idea of feeding made him feel weak and ill, and at the same time, his hand, his heart throbbed with sudden need. A strange and nameless fear filled him: he could not remember having fed, could not remember how, what to do.

There is plenty of time, Ember said. His patience was fading palpably. *If you do not waste it. Come.*

I have better things to do —

Ember bared teeth in a full snarl. *For a cleverman, you compound folly!*

I —

No more! Ember controlled himself with a visible effort *This is foolish, Quicksilver. You must feed now.*

I must not. The words trembled in the forefront of his mind, but he did not press them forward, aware of how ridiculous they were. Of course he must feed. Of course he needed to revive himself, he could feel it now that Ember had given this weakness a name. This reluctance, this fear, had no logic behind it. He would not give in to folly.

He followed Ember along the main corridor, forward out of the clevermen's lairs toward the domains of blades and drones. They took the left hand fork where the corridor split, and Quicksilver was sure that was propriety, the proper way for clevermen, but even so, he was aware of odd looks and bared teeth, and Ember's mind was tightly held, giving him no sense of the cause.

Then they had reached the holding pens, and he checked in the entrance, fear sweeping over him like a wave. He had stood in such a place before, he was sure of that as he had been sure of nothing since his rescue, stood with weapon in hand and terror like copper in his throat, darkness folding in on him like a great cloak... Perhaps it had been a raid? An attack on some other hive, when they were desperate to Cull? All that he was sure of was the dark and the fear.

Quicksilver? Ember looked over his shoulder, frowning, and Quicksilver made himself take a step forward, and then another, advancing slowly through the haze of memory.

The pen was low-ceilinged, each cell sealed with a thick corded webbing that held the contents upright, only their faces visible. Most hung with eyes closed; here and there, one watched with fear or anger, or wept silently. Quicksilver shivered, hot and cold as though with fever. They were aware, watching, waiting his choice... Of course they were, he told himself. They were human, not completely animal. They would provide no nourishment otherwise. That knowledge was hollow, set against the living eyes.

Ember moved along the row of cells, eyes flicking over the faces. He stopped at least perhaps a third of the way down, and tugged the webbing away from the human's chest. It was a male, middle-aged, pale with fear. He made a soft sound, a whimper of a plea, and Ember sank claws into his chest, draining him in a heartbeat. Someone, somewhere in the row of cells, cried out, a single note of fear and sorrow. Ember flexed his fingers in satisfaction.

Have you chosen?

I — Quicksilver froze, made himself point at random. *There.*

He found himself pointing at a young woman who sagged half conscious in her webbing. He swallowed hard, lifted his hand, feeling the mouth stretch and open. It burned, he burned, but he could not bring himself to tear the webbing away from her. He stood shaking, unable to understand what was wrong with him, what was happening to him. The woman opened blue eyes, wide and uncomprehending, and Ember looked from one to the other, irritation fading to something like understanding. He caught Quicksilver's arm in his own off hand and bore it gently down.

I'm sorry, he said. *I ask too much of you. I knew Dust had fed you himself, when you were first returned, but I did not realize —*

I don't — Quicksilver stopped, not sure what he would have said. I don't understand, I don't want this, I don't know what's wrong with me: all true, but he had enough shreds of self-preservation left that he would not say them.

It has happened before, Ember said. *Men so badly hurt they could not feed themselves, not for months and sometimes years. This is not unknown, Quicksilver.*

I was not hurt, Quicksilver said, bitterly.

Injuries of the mind are no less real. Ember reached out, ripped the webbing free, and sank his claws into the woman's chest. She withered silently, with only the murmur of the hive to mark her death. Quicksilver shuddered again, knowing that something was terribly wrong, and Ember glanced quickly over his shoulder.

We must keep this secret. But you must feed, and if you cannot — Permit me to help you.

He extended his feeding hand. The mouth was open still, swollen at the edges, the feeding membrane dark within. Quicksilver stared, caught like a human in the cleverman's stare, and Ember bent his head.

Your brother did this for you, he said. *Allow me to act as he would.*

Quicksilver could not move, and Ember took his silence for assent. He stepped closer, close enough to slide his feeding hand under Quicksilver's shirt, claws cold against bare skin. Quicksilver caught his breath, the terror returning, and Ember flexed his hands, setting his claws. The feeding mouth touched him, sharp as fire, hot as fear, and pain seared through him, radiating from Ember's hand to the tips of his fingers, the soles of his feet. As abruptly as it had begun, the pain eased, was replaced by warmth, tingling, a strange pleasure and a new strength. He straightened in spite of himself, and Ember drew his hand away.

Better?

Quicksilver shook himself, but could not deny that he was restored. He snarled, groping for the right words, for anger to cover emotions he did not dare name, and Ember gave a rueful smile.

I see you are.

CHAPTER TEN
Necessary Measures

"DR. KELLER, do you have a moment?" Teyla said, coming in the door of the infirmary with Torren balanced on her hip.

"Sure," Jennifer said. "As much as I'm likely to today."

"I am sure you are busy," she said. Torren hid his face in Teyla's shirt, peering out with a frown; Jennifer didn't think she was one of his favorite people. "I am taking Torren back to New Athos, and I wondered if you could make sure that all is well with him first. If there are immunizations he will need soon, it might be better if he could have them now."

"Okay," Jennifer said. "I can take a look, but he's a pretty healthy kid, so I don't expect I've got much work here." She busied herself with the exam, which gave her time to figure out what to say. Teyla smiled at Torren as she tried to coax him to let Jennifer look in his ears, but she didn't exactly look happy. "How long do you think he'll be staying there with Kanaan?"

Teyla smoothed Torren's hair. "At least until we have an iris again," she said. "It has not ever been perfectly safe in the city, but when we do not even have the iris…" She met Jennifer's eyes over Torren's head. "And I would have him have every benefit of this city's medicine before he goes."

You mean *in case the Wraith nuke Atlantis and he never comes back*, Jennifer thought. *That's cheery.* She wouldn't say it in front of Torren, though, and she supposed that Teyla had to think that way; she'd grown up with the knowledge that any community, no matter how strong, could be wiped out by the Wraith.

Jennifer wasn't sure how anyone could stand to have kids in the face of that knowledge. She was starting to feel pretty guilty herself about having brought the kitten, although at least the Wraith didn't eat cats—

She cleared her throat, aware that she'd taken too long to reply. "I can go ahead and give him his MMR booster early, and the Varicella—that's chicken pox. He's current on everything that's specific to the Pegasus galaxy."

"That is good," Teyla said, her hand curled protectively over the top of Torren's head again.

Colonel Sheppard came into the infirmary as she was giving Torren the second injection. "What's the matter with him?"

"He's getting a measles shot," Jennifer said. "I gave you one before we left Earth, but you didn't scream."

"I thought about it," Sheppard said. "I came to see if I could talk to Lorne."

Jennifer frowned at him. "Is that talk as in bother, or talk as in cheer up?"

"Talk as in see how he's doing and tell him everything's okay," Sheppard said as if he thought that should have been obvious. He glanced at Teyla. "For a certain value of okay."

"All right," Jennifer said. "He's conscious, but he has a concussion, okay? Don't make his head hurt even worse than it does."

"I'll use my inside voice," Sheppard said.

"Speaking of which, could you take Torren for a moment?" Teyla said. "I would like to ask Dr. Keller about Rodney."

Sheppard grimaced, as if acknowledging that the subject was probably not toddler-appropriate, at least not for a toddler who didn't need to hear the words 'Wraith' and 'Uncle Rodney' in the same sentence. "Up you go," he said, hoisting Torren off Teyla's lap. "Let's go see Major Lorne."

Teyla met Jennifer's eyes once John had gone around the corner with Torren. "I am sure you may not know anything yet."

"Carson and I ran some computer models based on our best guess at the structure of their retrovirus," Jennifer said reluctantly. "We know that whatever they did didn't affect the ATA gene. That narrows down the possibilities. Still, I want to stress that at this point we have very little actual data —"

"What did you find?" Teyla's voice was gentle but insistent.

"Our best computer models right now have Rodney not returning completely to human form, even after he's no longer receiving doses of the retrovirus. In the best-case scenarios, the lasting effects are essentially cosmetic."

"Rodney would not like it if his hair were permanently white, but I think we would all learn to live with it," Teyla said. "But if he remained much more like the Wraith in appearance… it would be a difficult thing for him, and I am sure for you."

"Right now, I'm not even worried about that," Jennifer said, although she wasn't entirely sure Teyla believed her. "If he ends up staying green, we'll… you know, we'll cross that bridge when we come to it." She wasn't sure what it would mean for him ever being able to go back to Earth, even to visit, but that wasn't something she was ready to think about at the moment.

"Then…?"

Jennifer began peeling off her exam gloves to give her something to do with her hands. "The big problem is that the worst-case scenario shows him not regaining the ability to survive on human food. That's… obviously, we'll figure out how to avoid that, but it's not a possibility we wanted to see coming up at all."

"I am sure you and Carson will do everything you can," Teyla said.

"We all want to fix this," Jennifer said. "I'll keep working with Carson and see if we can get a better model. We may be able to use some version of our own retrovirus to complete the transformation from Wraith back to human."

She was kind of hoping Teyla wouldn't see the catch there, but she frowned and said, "And when you stopped administering your drug?"

"Let's cross that bridge when we come to it, too," Jennifer said. "Even if he ended up having to take doses of our retrovirus on a regular basis, that's a result we could live with."

"Mr. Woolsey would not want Rodney to be sent back to Earth, even if he were dependent on the retrovirus," Teyla said, as if it were a comforting thought. It probably was, to her and Sheppard.

"No, I imagine he wouldn't," Jennifer said. "What would we do without Rodney in Atlantis performing technological miracles?"

"We will have him back to perform miracles again soon," Teyla said firmly, her eyes on something behind Jennifer. Jennifer wasn't surprised to see that Sheppard had returned, carrying Torren against his shoulder.

"I think he's going to sleep," Sheppard said. "Either you wore him out, or I'm just really boring today."

"He had an exciting night," Teyla said. Jennifer wondered what Torren had made of the alarm in the middle of the night. He seemed fine now, content to take a nap on Sheppard's chest. "I must take him, John. The wormhole to the alpha site will disengage soon, and they will be dialing New Athos for me."

"I've got some medical supplies that it would be great if you could take with you," Jennifer said. "I was going to go over there myself once we got settled, but since it might be a little while, I'd at least like to send a couple of boxes of antibiotics."

"I can carry Torren on the way upstairs if you want to get the boxes," Sheppard said. "I'm headed that way anyway, since I get to sit in the big office now. But if you'd rather take him—" He sounded like he was trying very hard to sound casual. It hadn't occurred to Jennifer before that he'd probably miss Torren too, as much time as he'd been spending with him.

Teyla met Sheppard's eyes for a moment, a wordless exchange that Jennifer couldn't read and wasn't sure she was meant to. "It would be a help for you to carry him," Teyla said gently. "As far as the gate-room. I will take the boxes."

"It won't be for long," Sheppard said. Jennifer hoped he was right.

Dick tried to look like repacking his briefcase was a complicated task, giving the assembled IOA members time to leave the room. He didn't want to look like he was running away from them, as tempting as that thought was at the moment. Finally he straightened up in the empty room.

"I think that went well," he said. It didn't sound convincing even to him.

He stepped outside to the unwelcome sight of General O'Neill waiting in the hallway. It had been an entire day of explaining himself, at great length and repeatedly, and he had hoped that the next few hours would involve nothing but his hotel room and the chance to take his shoes off.

"General O'Neill," he said, trying to sound more pleased than he felt.

"Woolsey," O'Neill said. "Having fun?"

"The committee is going to recommend a more thorough review by the full IOA," Dick said. "In the mean time, they'd like to go over our full inventory list."

"Exciting."

Dick wasn't sure what O'Neill's agenda here was, and the fact that he was making smart remarks told him nothing except that this was O'Neill. He squared his shoulders. "What can I do for you, General?"

"I think the question is what I can do for you," O'Neill said. "Or, more to the point, what I'm prepared to do."

Dick looked back at the conference room wearily. "I suppose we should…"

"After you," O'Neill said. He pulled the door shut after him. "All right. What the hell's going on in Pegasus?"

"I'm sure you've read my latest report," Woolsey said.

"I have. I'm just hoping I haven't read it right. You seriously gave the Genii an Ancient battlecruiser? Why would you do that?"

It was tempting to say, 'No, Colonel Sheppard gave the Genii an Ancient battlecruiser, and it seemed like a bad idea to take it back.' That wouldn't win him any points with O'Neill, though, and it wasn't fair, either. He'd known Sheppard wasn't exactly a diplomat, and he'd sent him anyway, because the Genii were reluctant to negotiate with civilians.

"If you've read my report, you know that we were hoping to obtain intelligence about the location of Dr. McKay. Although we didn't get that information from the Genii, we did preserve our tentative alliance with them."

"Preserving alliances means sending a fruit basket, not a warship."

"I don't think Ladon Radim is very interested in fruit baskets."

"Ladon Radim is a tinpot dictator with ambitions to take over the Pegasus Galaxy," O'Neill said. "Are we going to help?"

"He probably can't even get the thing to work," Dick said. The moment the words were out of his mouth, he suspected that had been a mistake.

"And according to your reports, we could have!" O'Neill said. "With our engineers and a pilot with the ATA gene, we'd have a functional Ancient battle cruiser. Our only one, since you people got the *Orion* blown up."

"That was a year and a half before I took command of the expedition," Dick said, but it didn't seem to slow O'Neill down.

"Now, the best case scenario is that it's a great big paperweight. If we're not so lucky, Radim will paste the thing together, find a pilot with the gene, and start knocking over the neighbors. What the hell were you thinking, writing Sheppard a blank check like that? I don't expect him to be sensible when it's a member of his team who's missing, but I expect you to be."

"As long as he's in the hands of the enemy, Dr. McKay poses a threat to the security of Atlantis—and Earth—that is difficult to overestimate," Dick said. "More than that, he's a valued member of the expedition, and I don't think it's unreasonable to make every effort to find him." After the silence dragged out for a moment, Dick couldn't help asking, "What?"

"I'm just wondering," O'Neill said. "Because I remember sitting—well, not right here, but at a table a lot like this one only not as nice—while you explained that it hadn't been cost-effective for us to rescue one of our teams. And so now I'm wondering, just because I'm curious, how much do you think an Ancient battlecruiser is worth? More, or less, than the one person you're looking for?"

"Are you suggesting that if it were a trade, it would be reasonable to sacrifice McKay for the ship?"

"I'm just asking for a simple opinion. A cost-benefit analysis. That's what all these decisions boil down to, right?"

He wanted to defend himself against the anger in O'Neill's voice, but he didn't think there was an answer O'Neill wanted to hear, other than the value of a human life is priceless. And there was a sense in which that was true, and a sense in which it wasn't, and neither one was the most important point at the moment.

"The real benefit of letting them have the ship is something more important than whether we find Dr. McKay or not," Dick said. "It's perfectly clear to me that Homeworld Security has no intention of sending us the kind of firepower we would need to conduct a successful war against the Wraith on our own."

"I haven't got it," O'Neill said frankly. "And if I get it, you can't have it. The Ori may be out of the picture, but if there's one thing I know, it's that there's always going to be another bad guy. You can have what I can spare, but it says 'Homeworld Security' on my door for a reason."

"I don't think any of the other member governments of the IOA are any more eager to provide us with what we'd need to win the war singlehandedly, assuming that's even possible. We need allies in the Pegasus Galaxy, and the Genii are the strongest and most organized force fighting the Wraith."

"Go on," O'Neill said, a little more patiently.

"The Genii found the ship in the first place. I think it's reasonable to say that they had salvage rights. Sheppard did them the favor of flying it in hopes of gaining valuable information, which I will grant you that they turned out not to have. But the ship was never ours."

"That's a reasonable argument," O'Neill said. "I'm not sure the IOA's going to buy it."

"Neither am I," Dick said.

"Nechayev agrees with you about making friends with the Genii," O'Neill said. "He's an old soldier, and he's been around the block too many times to think it's a good idea to piss off the locals."

"He may be the only one," Dick said.

"Dixon-Smythe's got a stick up her ass. She doesn't care what happens in Pegasus, because nobody there is British. Shen's after your job, so you'll get no love there. Desai might be worth working on. The President hasn't decided who the new American representative is supposed to be, so that should be interesting."

"You expect they'll want you to testify?"

"I expect they will. And you know I just love testifying."

"What are you planning to say?"

O'Neill ran a hand through his hair. "I would have backed you up all the way on the rescue if it had actually worked," he said. "Did you have to get the *Hammond* shot up while the paint was still new? Carter likes that ship."

"Carter and Sheppard both felt that the mission had a strong chance of succeeding, and that it was the best chance we were likely to get," Dick said. "You know I'm no tactician. I took their advice."

"Tell Sheppard not to blow the mission next time," O'Neill said. "If you'd tried to blame the screw-up with the Genii on him, I'd have said you could go hang, but he's the one who's supposed to do the impossible in the field."

"Doing the impossible isn't actually a job requirement, is it?"

O'Neill gave him a long look. "Not technically," he said. "In actual practice, you'd be surprised."

"Maybe not all that surprised," Dick said.

"Things look a little different from the other side of that table, don't they?"

"They do," Dick said. "For what it's worth, I wish I'd understood then what it felt like to have to make these decisions. And at the same time, I am still very aware that we don't have unlimited resources to put into anything. We have to make choices."

"I have to make choices," O'Neill said. "They're not always ones I like. Funny thing, you defeat the Ori, and suddenly people start talking about peacetime dividends and budget cuts. You'd think they'd want to get us something nice."

"Maybe a fruit basket," Dick said.

"That would be nice."

"Backing me up to the IOA is free."

"You know better than that," O'Neill said. "But I think you had the right general idea. Some of the details could have maybe used some work."

"I'll keep that in mind."

"So what are you planning to do now?" O'Neill said.

"I was thinking I'd just go back to my hotel and order room service," Dick said. "It's been a long day."

O'Neill just looked at him. "I mean about McKay."

"Yes, right. Well, obviously we need to find him. Again."

"Why don't you think about coming up with some more specific plans?"

"For when I go back to Atlantis?" He couldn't keep the skepticism out of his voice.

"You never know," O'Neill said. "They haven't made any decisions yet. This party's just getting started."

"You know, I'm beginning to understand why they call it an exhaustive review," Dick said.

O'Neill snorted. "Tell me about it."

CHAPTER ELEVEN
Down Time

RADEK looked down at his empty plate, all too aware that this was the first time since the attack that he had had anything approaching a normal day. A day that began with a shower and a shave, and ended with dinner — admittedly one that included tava beans, but that counted as ordinary now — and in which no one had actually shot at anyone. He was still dead tired, and, more to the point, despite spending the day directing teams to search the city, they were no closer to finding enough titanium to make a workable mechanical iris, but at least no one had died.

And it would not help to worry about that tonight. Keeping the gate open was working, would prevent a Wraith attack until they could get an iris built. It would be enough. He sighed, unable to convince himself that it would be that simple, and took off his glasses to rub the bridge of his nose. Without them, the mess hall was a blur, oddly comforting, and he closed his eyes, imagining that his fears were a small bundle, one he could hold in both hands, compress and mold until they were a little ball that he could lock away, seal up tight in a special box with a special key —

It wasn't really working. He sighed, and slipped his glasses back on. He had felt this way often enough the first year, but then there had been Peter Grodin to keep him company, to talk him out of these moods, or stay awake with him when they were both too tired to sleep.

"Dr. Zelenka?"

He didn't recognize the voice, looked up to see an Air Force sergeant, a stocky dark-skinned woman with a cardboard box tucked under her arm. For a second, he hoped she had found something useful, but common sense reasserted itself. That news would have been broadcast all over the city, not brought to him personally. "Yes?"

"I'm Clea Dockery. I was a friend of Taggert's."

Radek winced in spite of himself, but she pretended not to notice.

"Tag and I had a little — we've been doing some off-duty experimentation down under the south pier? Strictly under the radar, doc, I know you understand, but —" Dockery reached into the box, and produced what looked like a specimen jar half-filled with a colorless liquid. "I wanted to share out the first run with her friends."

"A still," Radek said.

Dockery looked hastily over her shoulder. "Yeah. But, you know, we have to keep it quiet —"

"Yes. I understand." Radek looked from the jar to Dockery and away again. "I did not know her so well," he said, quietly. "Perhaps you should save it for those who were closer. I did not even know her first name."

Dockery grinned. "That's 'cause she didn't tell anybody. It's — it was Debbi, two Bs and an I, and her mama would've put a little heart over the I if they'd let her do it on the birth certificate."

Radek smiled back — no, that did not suit Taggert at all — and Dockery set the jar on the table.

"She liked Atlantis, liked working for you, liked being on your shift. She'd want you to have it."

"Thank you, then," Radek said. He unscrewed the lid, took a cautious sip, blinking as the stuff burned its way down his throat. It tasted like nothing he'd ever had — well, perhaps home-brewed grappa he'd had once, and this had to be even stronger, though it was not the alcohol that brought the tears to his eyes. "She was good," he said. "I'll miss her."

Teyla sat next to John on the couch in her quarters with her feet tucked sideways under her and her cheek resting on the back of the couch, as if she were going to fall asleep sitting up. Sleep was probably a good idea, John thought. He just wasn't sure how that was going to happen at the moment.

"How is Major Lorne?" Teyla asked.

"He's okay. Keller gave him some stuff to help him sleep. She says it was a pretty clean fracture. Which is a good thing, I guess, because it's not like we can dial Earth and send anybody home right now."

"We should all try to rest," Teyla said.

"I know," John said. He leaned back, looking up at the ceiling. "It's just knowing that the Wraith could send a nuclear bomb or another strike team through the gate at any moment isn't really relaxing."

He could feel his heart still pounding, his breathing too fast. He couldn't stay wound up like this forever, and he couldn't afford to crash hard later when something bad really was happening. Thinking about that just wound him tighter, though. He shifted restlessly, unable to get even momentarily comfortable.

Teyla nodded. "I know how you feel. I think we are not the only ones. Ronon said he did not plan to sleep in his quarters tonight."

"Where is he planning to sleep, then?"

"In his hidden lair."

"His…"

Teyla shrugged. "I think it is up in the superstructure somewhere. He keeps weapons and supplies there in case of an emergency. Have you nothing similar?"

"I don't have a *lair*," John said. "I might maybe have a stash of weapons up there, but it's not someplace I'd want to camp out."

"Might?"

"Okay, do. I don't think I'm the only one, though. I think Lorne has some stuff put by in case of emergencies."

"Radek, too," Teyla said. "Once when we were looking for water damage in the sublevels of the city, I found a spare laptop and a supply of food in one of the crawl spaces, along with quite a variety of other things."

"Just in case," John said. He shook his head. "We're all a little screwed up, you know? Dr. Robinson would probably have a field day."

"It is only practical," Teyla said. "There are many reasons why it might be necessary to hide within the city."

"If we sit here and list them, I'm never going to get to sleep."

Teyla's hand was on his shoulder, as much measuring the tension in his muscles as making an attempt to ease it. "I have a lair," she said after a moment.

He looked over at her. "A lair."

"Yes," she said, the corner of her mouth turning up. "Do you want to see it?"

It wasn't like they were sleeping anyway. "Sure," he said. "Let's go see your lair."

They took the transport chamber to a hallway that Teyla said was floors below her hiding place, in what looked like it had been an old residential area of the city. There were still plenty of buildings they'd never really explored, especially the ones that looked at first glance to be apartments rather than laboratories. He wasn't sure if they'd ever been in this one at all, or if one of Rodney's teams had tramped through and deemed it a useless waste of time.

"Basement, or catwalk?" he asked when they reached a flight of stairs, their risers chased with bronze plates in a repeating design that looked like a cross between a sine wave and a bird's wing.

"Neither, but up from here," Teyla said. He followed her up seven flights of stairs until she took the door out of the stairwell.

"Why seven flights?"

She shrugged. "It seemed an unlikely number for anyone to guess." She led him down the corridor, around to the right, and then left again. "Here," she said, swiping her hand to open a door that looked identical to all the other doors.

"You didn't get Rodney to key this door for you, did you?" John said.

"I did not," Teyla said. "I have the security clearance to key doors for myself, and have known how for some time. John, I have worked in the control room. I am not so unused to computers."

"I forget," he said. "Hey, wow."

The room was easily the size of the sitting room in Teyla's quarters, with a broad window that looked out over the ocean. From near the doorway, he couldn't see the pier below, and there weren't any other buildings to block the view from this angle, only sea and sky.

There was a bed, piled high with blankets, a second nest of cushions and blankets that he thought looked Torren-sized, and a set of shelves against one wall well-stocked with MREs, bottled water, a medical kit, and what looked like a stack of coloring books and a basket of soft toys. On the top shelf sat a Wraith stunner and a pistol case.

"No P90?" he said. He'd brought his with him; he'd half-expected her to comment on that, but she hadn't seemed to mind.

"It is above one of the ceiling panels," she said. "Not so convenient to hand, but I did not have a case with a lock for it, and I was thinking of what would happen if I had to bring Torren here." She watched him check the place out some more. "What?"

"Just looking for the kitchen sink," he said.

"There is one," she said. "This whole side of the building is connected, nine rooms with a kitchen and two bathrooms. The only problem is that if someone were really looking for us, they would be able to see that we are using the city's water."

"This is a vacation condo, not a lair," John said.

"No one is using the space," Teyla said a little defensively. "It seemed worth the time to make it comfortable."

"I'm not complaining," he said. "I was just expecting something more like camping."

"I could put up a tent, if you would like."

"You've got a tent in here?"

"Not yet," she said, with the barest hint of a smile.

Only Teyla, he thought. It was unreasonable to feel the tension in his chest ease just because no one knew where they were, but he couldn't deny that he felt better. "Okay, this is cool."

"We could sleep here tonight if you want," she said. "We have our radios if anyone needs to reach us."

He smiled and tried to keep his voice light. "You'd share your lair with me?"

"I would," she said. "I am happy for you to share my tent."

"Not exactly a tent."

"It does not literally have to be a tent," she said, sounding just a little exasperated.

"I know," he said, stepping in, putting his arms around her waist, still feeling awkward about it. It was easier when he bent his head to hers in a now-familiar gesture of affection, when she put her arm around his waist tightly, as if for him to throw his arm around her shoulders and let her take some of his weight. "I know what you mean."

The antechamber was well occupied, as it always was, the lords of the zenana eager to put themselves foremost in the queen's memory. Guide made his appearances there, too, not wanting to stint his respect, though in the safety of his own hive, his own chamber at the heart of the ship, the risks he ran sometimes made him tremble. Those moments, that release, made him stronger now, and he lounged against the chamber wall, pretending to watch a group of younger blades playing at towers. It was a game he had not seen played since his own youth, and it seemed the rules had changed: his agemates would have not have allowed him to place that gray blade in opposition to the vizier —

He felt someone's gaze on him, looked up to see the Old One watching from his seat beside the inner door. He seemed to be one of Death's particular favorites, though Guide doubted he shared her bed, and he dipped his head in polite acknowledgement.

Come and sit by me, the Old One said, and Guide moved reluctantly to join him. He would have preferred to keep his distance — he had not gotten the measure of the Old One's strength of mind — but he did not wish to make an enemy of him. Instead, he gathered the skirts of his coat and sat, a careful hand's-breadth away.

You're no young blade, the Old One said, after a while.

I am not, Guide agreed, and the Old One made a sound of creaking laughter.

And you are thinking I am older still, and you would be right. But I have a reason for asking.

Guide waited, and the Old One sighed, resting his head against the chamber wall. He was very old indeed, Guide thought, vigorous enough, but so old that he had not been bred to any of the familiar types. Even young, his face had not been as strongly modeled as most blades; it had an archaic look, like the foremost mothers of Snow's hive.

*You fought against the Ancients," the Old One said.

I did.

And before that?

Guide shook his head. *I was born at the beginning of that war, for that war. I came of age not long before our victory.*

Our war with the Ancients is far older than that, the Old One said sharply. *From our first beginnings, we were at war. But no matter. You saw Atlantis fall.*

Yes. Guide paused. *And I have seen it risen again.*

To our grave discredit, the Old One said. *It must be destroyed completely this time, so that it can never threaten us again.*

Guide hesitated, choosing his words with care. *Granting that it can be done — because I do not see it as an easy or inevitable thing — what then? We will still be hungry.*

The Old One nodded. *We need new feeding grounds. Even if we sleep, turn and turn about, and no one breaks our queen's law, still it will be too long before the kine rebound. If they can.* He paused, his eyes on the game, watching as the counters collapsed under an injudicious move. *That is why I have supported this plan of Dust's, for all that the abomination makes my very bones ache. We must have a way to leave this galaxy.*

And if we find it, Guide said, *if all goes as we hope, and the humans there are more easily cowed than they have been here, on strange ground—what then? You will remember as well as I what happened once the Ancients were defeated. There were too many of us, drones and even blades bred in anticipation of loss, and no queen then living would be first to sacrifice even her drones. That will happen again, and if there is another galaxy beyond this one, still it will happen each time. We cannot go on like this.*

No. The Old One did not look at him, the touch of his mind soft and fading. *That is why we need one queen over us all, one queen to hold us safe under her rule, so that no one starves. Death will do that for us, Guide. And the bones of the Ancients will be ground to dust beneath our feet.*

The Ancients are dust already, Guide said. *They were dust ten thousand years ago.*

Their city remains.

But not its builders.

Their children live, the Old One answered, and there was a bitterness in his tone that struck Guide silent.

CHAPTER TWELVE
Sateda

IT WAS their usual morning meeting, but it was still strange for John to sit down at what he thought of as Woolsey's end of the table. Teyla, Ronon, and Radek were already waiting when he came in, Teyla and Radek holding steaming cups of coffee.

"This is still a little weird," John admitted after a moment. He felt he probably ought to put a better face on it than that, but there wasn't anyone there but the team.

"You are telling me," Radek said.

"How are we doing on the iris?" John asked.

"With Colonel Carter's assistance, I think we have a workable design," Radek said. "Our current plan is for essentially manual operation."

"I take it you don't mean the Marines will have to get out there and push it open and shut," John said.

"Not quite, but almost. The process of opening and closing the iris will be powered by a generator, but we are talking about wiring the iris directly to the generator, and to nothing else. No computer control."

"Someone's going to have to stand there and push a button?" Ronon said skeptically.

"Or pull a lever, or — that part is not important. But, yes, it will require that someone operate the control mechanism by hand. If we build any automatic control system that is connected to the DHD or the city's computers —"

"Then we're right back where we started," John said. "All right, that's not a problem. We're posting a security detail in the gateroom around the clock anyway."

"The problem is the materials," Radek said. "The towers in Atlantis contain mainly steel, with small amounts of other metals used for decorative purposes. That would be better than nothing, but would still leave the iris extremely vulnerable to explosives. The iris on Earth uses a trinium-titanium alloy, but for now I would be satisfied with titanium."

"There is none in the city?" Teyla asked.

"There are some titanium components in the city's hyperdrive.

Removing them will render the hyperdrive temporarily inoperable, although since we have no ZPM, that may not matter. The big problem is that it would not be nearly enough material for the iris. We could use titanium plating over steel and hope for the best."

"I have a problem with any plan that involves the words 'hope for the best' when we're talking about explosives," John said.

Radek shrugged. "So did Colonel Carter."

"I think Sam's right on this one," John said. "What about finding the titanium somewhere else in Pegasus?"

"We have tried to contact the Travellers, but we have had no success so far," Teyla said. "It is likely to take some time for us to get a message to them, and even then, they are likely to charge a high price for the material we need."

"I think right now we'd be willing to pay, but we can't do much if they won't pick up the phone. What about the Genii? Not that we're likely to be their favorite people right now, since Dahlia Radim probably told her brother we're scary people who tried to steal his ship."

"As far as we can tell, titanium is very rare on the Genii homeworld, even more so than it is on Earth," Radek said. "They have been using steel alloys in their experiments in aviation. Their most likely source of the material we need would be their salvaged Ancient warship, but…"

"But they're not exactly about to take it apart for us. Great." John ran a hand through his hair. "We may be back to 'hope for the best'. At least then we'd have an anti-personnel shield."

"I know where you can get the titanium," Ronon said. He looked as if he didn't like his own idea much.

"Where?" John asked, after it became clear he was going to have to.

"It wasn't that rare on Sateda. They used it in buildings, and in a bunch of different kinds of machines. There must be tons of the stuff still there. It's not valuable enough to most people to be worth salvaging."

Teyla raised her eyebrows. "The idea of taking it from the ruins of Sateda does not bother you?" Her people had left their own ruined cities on Athos alone, although in Teyla's encampment when he'd first seen it, they'd certainly been using scrap metal that must have come from at least the outskirts of the city.

"Yeah, it bothers me," Ronon said shortly. "But it's better than letting the Wraith blow up Atlantis."

"You've been there before since the Wraith trashed the place," John said. "I know you brought some things back."

"Some books, that painting," Ronon said. "Small things. I didn't think anybody would have a problem with that."

John was getting the feeling that *anybody* here meant *dead people*, and he wasn't sure where to even start with the question of whether dead Satedans would have minded them taking their stuff. "You think they'd have a problem with us taking the titanium?"

"I said let's do it," Ronon said. "The gate's in the middle of a city. If you look around, you can find what we need?"

"I think so," Radek said. "We would want a team of engineers."

"We need to check it out first," John said. "As far as we know, there's nobody living there now, but we don't want any surprises."

"It would make a useful base for the Wraith," Teyla pointed out.

"And that's the kind of surprise we don't want. So let's —" John stopped himself in mid-sentence. *Let's go check it out.* And leave who in command of Atlantis? *Colonel Carter*, he thought rebelliously, *who actually wanted this job*, but it didn't work that way and he knew it. Anyway, Caldwell was senior to Sam, and the idea of leaving the city in Caldwell's hands wasn't nearly as attractive.

He started over. "Ronon, why don't you take Teyla and Radek and go check it out." Teyla had seniority as team leader, but given that it was Ronon's home planet, it seemed reasonable for him to run the show this time.

"All right," Ronon said after a moment. He looked at Teyla and Radek. "So… gear up, and let's go check it out."

"Let us do that," Teyla said, standing up.

"Yes, great," Radek said, without a lot of visible enthusiasm. "Time to 'gear up'."

"The sooner we go, the sooner you can be back in Atlantis building the defense we need against the Wraith," Teyla pointed out.

"You know, Rodney learned to like offworld missions," John said as Ronon and Teyla went out. "At least the ones where nobody tries to kill us."

"Rodney is a crazy person," Radek said. "And people try to kill you all the time."

"Only some of the time," John said. "And some of them are trying to kill Rodney in particular."

"That is sort of comforting," Radek said. "I will try to keep that in mind."

Teyla shouldered her pack and gave Radek an encouraging smile. She and Ronon had wordlessly moved to put the scientist between them, so that they could watch out for him if there was any danger. Teyla privately felt that was unlikely in the extreme, and thought she might have done better to stay at Ronon's side. It could not be easy for him to have to face again what the years were making of Sateda.

It had not been easy for her to face, and it had never been her home. It was one thing to walk into a village that had been Culled and see the familiar aftermath, buildings burned and crops ruined by dart fire, families grieving the missing. It was another to walk into a city that was bigger than any she had seen before it and see the ruin the Wraith had made of it.

It made her imagine unwillingly what it must have been like when the Wraith had destroyed the cities of Athos. She knew the pain of Cullings well enough, but she had not imagined before what it must have been to leave the dead lying unburned in the streets because there were not enough hands to build pyres for them. She had never walked in the streets of her own ruined cities with broken glass crunching under her feet like snow.

Teyla had seen Sateda twice. The first time was when the Wraith had recaptured Ronon and brought him there to hunt him, like the entertainments on some worlds where wild animals were brought into town to be killed for sport. The second time would not have happened were it not for Rodney.

It was later the same year that they had rescued Ronon from Sateda, on a quiet enough day that there was time for idle curiosity. Rodney was examining Ronon's pistol, more carefully than he usually examined things because Ronon had told Rodney that he would break his limbs if Rodney broke the pistol.

"I'm not going to break it," Rodney said. "I'm not sure where I'd even start with trying to build you a replacement ray gun. I don't suppose there are a lot of these just lying around somewhere on Sateda? Because Sheppard for one would be happy about that."

"No," Ronon said. He held out his hand, and Rodney reluctantly

returned his pistol.

"It is unlikely that anything so valuable would still be 'lying around'," Teyla said.

Ronon nodded. "People had eight years to scavenge things before the Wraith blew up the Stargate."

Rodney's brow furrowed. "Before the Wraith did what?"

"I saw the explosion," Ronon said. "Before the rest of you guys showed up. You can't dial in now."

"Huh," Rodney said. "They probably just knocked the gate over, or maybe a building fell on it or something. If there's enough junk inside the ring, it won't dial."

Teyla glanced sideways at Ronon. She knew it had troubled him that Sateda's Stargate was gone, and that to ever reach his home planet again he would have to depend on Colonel Caldwell to be willing to take him on Daedalus.

She did not think the people from Earth understood how disturbing the idea was, even if Ronon had no intention of ever actually going there again. The first thing children learned about the Stargates was how to dial their home. She remembered her own father allowing her to touch the symbols on the dialing device for the first time, after she had proved she knew them by heart, his hand over hers. He had told her the Ring of the Ancestors would always bring her home.

"You do not think it was destroyed?" she asked Rodney.

"The Stargates are basically indestructible by anything short of a massive nuclear explosion," Rodney said, in what for him was a relatively patient tone.

"It looked like a pretty big explosion," Ronon said.

"And yet you weren't instantly vaporized. Look, a Mark IX naquadriah-enhanced warhead can take out a Stargate. It has a blast radius of a hundred miles. You'd be a smear of ash in a city-sized crater."

Ronon nodded slowly. "So you think we can fix the gate."

"Probably," Rodney said. "But it's not like we're running there every ten minutes. There's no reason we can't get there on the Daedalus if we ever need to."

"Even so," Teyla said. "We know there are other Satedan survivors. Someone will try dialing Sateda again someday. If the gate will not even open…" She shook her head, not sure how to explain and sure that Ronon would be no better at finding the words. "It will be another *blow for people who have already suffered a great deal."*

Rodney shrugged. *"So tell Sheppard that. He'll take looking for ray guns as enough of an excuse to go back."*

"He's not going to find one," Ronon said.

"Thus the word 'excuse'," Rodney said, *and after a moment Ronon nodded in return, thanks he would not say; the two men were little enough alike, but she thought this time they understood each other well enough.*

It had been a quick trip, that time. It had not taken long for Rodney to get the gate operational again, and none of them had wanted to linger after that. Ronon had said little, clearly far away in some other time, and John had looked at the city with the pained expression he usually wore when confronted with the aftermath of war. This time they were likely to be there longer.

"Will it be winter there as well?" she asked Ronon, more for something to say to break the tension than because the answer mattered. She wished she had not spoken the moment after she had, because she thought she could read his expression well enough: he had forgotten after so long, and was trying to work out how his calendar fit with the Earth one they had grown used to.

"I think so," Ronon said after a minute. "You ready?"

"We are," Radek said.

"Then let's go do this."

It was warm as they stepped through the gate, too warm for winter, with a light breeze blowing and the sun shining bright. Teyla saw Ronon's look of startlement, and for a moment she took it for a reaction to the weather until she realized that the square surrounding the Stargate was not just as they left it.

Much of the rubble that had filled the square and the streets leading out from it was gone, the pavement swept bare of glass. There were canvas tents set up on one side of the square, with lines strung between a few of them where someone had hung out clothes to dry. Many of the windows that faced on the square had been boarded up, and others that still had glass looked clean. Smoke was rising behind one of the buildings, not the smell of burning buildings but the smell of cooking.

She raised her P90 as she was taking it all in. If there were scavengers living here, they were not likely to be much of a threat, but it was rare for scavenging parties to make this much of a camp. Most of those who made their living hunting through the ruins of Culled worlds were the very young or the very desperate, those who had no trade they could follow that would make them welcome in a settlement.

"It appears that someone is living here," she said.

"I see that," Ronon said.

"Is that good or bad?" Radek asked.

Ronon shrugged. "Doesn't look like Wraith, at least."

"No," Teyla said. The Wraith rarely camped on planets except at utmost need, and they had no need for cooking fires.

Ronon brought his pistol up at movement in one of the doorways. An older man with white hair stepped out into the sunlight, followed by two younger men with rifles slung over their shoulders. Teyla thought the rifles were not the ones the Genii used. They might be Satedan, although it had been years since the Satedans had offered such things in trade on Athos.

The older man was dressed in a dark coat and patterned waistcoat over dark trousers, his white shirt open at the neck. His boots were good but worn, and the trousers were mended at the knee. He looked at them as if sizing them up, curiously but without alarm, his gaze coming to rest on Ronon.

"You're Satedan," Ronon said.

"We are," the older man said. Teyla could see Ronon beginning to smile, looking suddenly younger. She was pleased to see it, but she kept her eyes on the men with the rifles, not yet ready to relax. "Have you come to trade? Or to join us?"

"I'm Ronon Dex," he said. "This is Teyla Emmagan and Radek Zelenka."

"Ushan Cai," the man said, clasping Ronon's forearm with a smile. "You are from Atlantis, then. We have heard many stories of you."

"I hope you have heard well of us," Teyla said.

"You've killed a lot of Wraith," Cai said. "But we heard that the City of the Ancestors had been destroyed."

"It's still here," Ronon said. "We had some problems for a while." He glanced at Teyla as if expecting her to speak; negotiating was normally her task, but these were his own people. She gave him an encouraging look, and he went on. "We came to see if we could find some titanium. We didn't think anyone was here."

"We've been here the better part of a year," Cai said. "I would say we should talk terms for it, but as you're Satedan yourself, and you'll have to do the work of finding what you want and hauling it out... Well, come inside and have a drink while we talk. I'm the provisional governor of Sateda, or so everyone says. I'm not sure how much that means, but it makes people feel better."

He turned back toward the building, and after a moment, Ronon said, "We should go hear what he has to say."

"I agree," Teyla said. She lowered her weapon, but kept it at the ready. She meant no disrespect for Ronon's people, but it was best to be cautious with strangers, and the Satedans were not like the Athosians. If she had come home to find some of her people still on Athos, they would be people she knew, lost friends or relatives whose arms she would have readily rushed into.

This man was a stranger to Ronon, for all that he was one of Ronon's people, and her time on Earth had taught her just how little being of the same people could mean to those who lived in great cities. She caught Radek's eye, intending to tell him to stay watchful, but she saw that he was watching Cai's guards carefully himself.

Radek was not a trusting person by nature, Teyla thought, and was glad of it.

The building Cai showed them into had once been a hotel. Ronon remembered it full of wealthy travelers, in the city to make business deals or to spend the night before making a trip through the Ring. It had been a place for people from offworld to stay, too, if they weren't guests of someone important.

He had never stayed there, but had been inside a few times, to have a drink or on some errand. He remembered laughing with Tyre about a huddled knot of offworlders in the bar, their clothes severe and their backs straight, who were scowling as if the courting couples listening to music over glasses of beer might as well have been taking their clothes off in a brothel.

The place was empty now, the soft carpet waterstained and the electric lights gone dark, part of the staircase up to the second floor crumbled away and the rest braced with a frame of timbers. The tables in the bar were scrubbed clean, though, and there were oil lamps lit on the sills of boarded-up windows. A radio set still stood in the corner, and he had the weird desire to turn it on, even though he knew it wouldn't make any sound.

"We got the coal boiler working, but we haven't got all the coal in the world, so we don't run it in good weather," Cai said. "By next winter we'll have hauled in more." He waved them to a table and poured drinks for them himself, not beer but strong grain spirits that should have been mixed with something. "Nobody's brewing beer, and what we can get in trade goes fast, so if you don't mind drinking what's lasted—"

"Not at all," Teyla said, although he saw her exchange a look with Radek when she tasted hers. Ronon hoped both of them had sense not to drain their cups fast, or they'd end up reeling, as small as they both were. He drank thirstily himself, letting the strong drink take the edge off the weirdness of being here.

"What are you doing here?" Ronon said after he'd drunk.

Cai put his own cup down. "It's been ten years," he said. "Going on eleven, now, but it was reaching ten years that got a few of us thinking maybe we'd risk it." He shrugged. "I had warehouses full of trade goods that had been sitting here ten years, not to mention what other people left behind. It seemed like that was worth coming back for. And besides, it's our home."

"Not much left of it," Ronon said.

Cai nodded. "Not much compared to what was. And not enough people to farm or mine coal or do the things we'd need to bring back what was. But there's enough here that we can sell offworld that we don't need to farm. We're no better than scavengers right now, it's true. But at least we're home, and by the time what we can salvage begins to run low, we may be able to manage light industry again. It seems like a better bet than trying to start again as farmers and trappers. Not that there's anything wrong with that," he said quickly to Teyla.

"On Athos we chose not to risk attracting the attention of the Wraith again by rebuilding our cities," Teyla said. "But they still returned, and drove us from our homes."

"You've made them pay dearly for that," Cai said. "Or so I hear."

Teyla inclined her head, taking that as the compliment it was. "We have."

"We've killed a lot of Wraith," Ronon said. "I've fought beside

Teyla for nearly five years. And Zelenka is one of our best scientists. They're both friends."

He felt that was worth saying. They'd never been particular allies of the Athosians, who hadn't had much that Sateda had wanted, and the people from Earth were an unknown. The best he could do to make this go smoothly was make it clear that these were friends, people he was willing to speak for.

"Your friends are welcome on Sateda," Cai said. "And we would be pleased to trade with the Lanteans."

"We are looking for titanium," Radek said, finally speaking up. "As pure as we can find, although the shape does not matter."

"What for?" Cai asked, with a businessman's easy smile. Ronon glanced at Teyla, who gave him a warning look.

"An extra defense for the city," Ronon said. He expected what she didn't want him to say was *because we don't have a shield at the moment.* "A metal shield for the gate that can be opened and closed."

"We have a similar device on our home world," Radek said. "The titanium is strong enough to defend against a nuclear explosion." He turned up his hands. "You may not have seen such weapons."

"I have heard that the Genii are testing great bombs they say are nuclear, weapons that can destroy a city," Cai said. "I expect that part is boasting."

Ronon shook his head. "It's not."

Cai frowned. "Wonderful."

"We are less concerned with the Genii than with the Wraith," Teyla said. "They have been very active of late."

"So can we look around and see if we can find the titanium?"

"I can probably find it for you," Cai said. "There's a metalworking plant that manufactured train cars, among other things. They used titanium, or at least an alloy. But you have to understand, right now the right to salvage what's left here is pretty much all the Satedan people have."

"We're willing to trade for what we need," Ronon said, glancing at Teyla again.

Teyla nodded. "We are. I cannot offer weapons, but we can certainly trade stores of food and medicine. And our scientists may be able to help you repair some of your machines."

"I'm sure we can work something out," Cai said. He waved one of the guards over from where they'd been leaning against the wall by the door. Not soldiers, Ronon thought, but young men who looked barely old enough to be out of school. They must have been children when Sateda fell, and he wondered how they'd made it off-world. "Vin, can you take them to the old Kusada plant, the one down by the tracks? And maybe one of you can stay and talk terms in the meantime."

Ronon wasn't sure about leaving Teyla alone, although he thought she'd make a better bargain than he would, even not being Satedan. "It's not that we don't trust you," he said slowly.

Cai gave him a measuring look. "But?"

Ronon hesitated. He hated to speak of how Tyre and Rakai and Ara had been broken and given their service to the Wraith, to spread the news of their dishonor any further. "I've met Satedans who worked for the Wraith," he said.

"And you would be valuable if we held you hostage," Cai said. "I know. And you don't know me. You probably never knew anyone I ever spoke to. Except Kell—"

"I wouldn't use him to speak for your trustworthiness."

"He can't speak for anything, since I hear that he's dead," Cai said. "All I can do is ask you to trust that I'm not the kind of man who would sell anyone to the Wraith, and that I'm a sensible enough man to know that I wouldn't live long if I tried it."

"You wouldn't," Ronon said.

"I will be fine," Teyla said. She put her P90 pointedly on the table between her and Cai, one hand resting on it while the other curled around her cup. "I am happy to stay here and negotiate."

Cai smiled a little. "Are you sure you're not Genii?"

"I am Athosian," Teyla said serenely.

The Kusada plant had been badly damaged, but Cai's people had shored up the weakest beams, and reinforced the main entrance with new timber. Ronon eyed it warily, and glanced at Radek to see if he thought it was safe. To his surprise, the scientist was nodding in approval, and followed Vin into the building without hesitation. Ronon came after them a little more slowly, hunching his shoulders in spite of himself.

"This is good work," Radek said. He was blinking hard behind his glasses, as though that would make his eyes adjust faster to the relatively dim light, and Vin paused.

"Thanks. It's mostly Martei's doing, he's — he used to be an architect, and he told us where to place the supports. Cai recruited him after we nearly lost Pollar in the old Manbael Building. We thought we'd shored up the stairway enough, but we hadn't. Martei can tell us just where to put the props."

Ronon looked around, letting his own eyes adjust. He didn't know this part of the city well, never had reason to be there — soldiers and factory hands didn't mix much — but even he could see how the massive working frames were bent and broken. They had made train cars here, Cai had said, and he could sort of picture it. There were the tracks, running in and out of what had been massive doors, and overhead were the ruins of the power supply, wheels and shafts that ran the length of the factory. He had been to such a plant once or twice, vaguely remembered the screech of metal and the whine of the enormous leather belts that took power from the driveshafts to the individual machines. Now the machines were dead, thrown from their platforms, and the floor was covered with a thick layer of debris.

"The storage areas are back here," Vin said.

"How do you know all this?" Ronon asked. It seemed suddenly too easy, and his hand twitched on the butt of his blaster.

Vin glanced over his shoulder. "I was an engineer-apprentice — not here, with Tolland Sons, but it's pretty much the same layout." He shook his head, turned back to the path that had been cleared through the rubble. "It's funny, Kusada was our biggest rival, but Tolland's factory burned and theirs didn't, so —" He shrugged. "Here we are."

They had reached a sliding door, now permanently bent out of true. Radek reached for his flashlight, shone it through the gap into the greater darkness. He said something in Czech as the light struck the slabs of metal, and ducked past both of them into the storage area. Ronon clicked on his own light and followed, and a moment later Vin came after him, carrying an oil lantern. In the combined light, Ronon could see what had been the neatly stacked raw materials for the train cars, now tumbled into ugly heaps. It would be impossible to move most of it without heavy equipment, and he hoped no one had been in here when the Wraith attacked. There was pig iron, showing rust-red in the light, and what looked like a roll of something silvery, and then Radek's light swung and steadied, and Ronon tipped his head to one side.

"That it?"

"Oh, yes," Radek said, almost reverently. "Yes, this should be exactly—" He stopped, as though he'd suddenly remembered they were supposed to be driving a bargain, and Ronon shrugged.

"We'll see." Out of the corner of his eye, he could see Vin grinning, and didn't think they'd fooled him one bit.

"Yes," Radek said, and moved forward to examine the plates more closely.

"Careful—" Ronon began, and bit back the rest of what he might have said. Human strength alone wasn't going to move these piles of metal.

"Yes, yes," Radek said, and edged into the gap between what looked like two different kinds of plating. "This may take a while."

It took, in fact, the better part of an hour, Vin trailing Radek with the lamp, the two of them sharing a huddled conversation, and then moving on again. After twenty minutes, Ronon was bored, and convinced that Vin, at least, was honest; after forty-five minutes, he stopped the ex-apprentice as he darted after Radek.

"Is there a way to the roof?"

Vin blinked. "Yes—yes, actually. Through there. We've shored them up, and the roof, too, it's perfectly safe—"

"Thanks," Ronon said, and turned away. He couldn't have said quite what he was looking for, if he was even looking for anything, and not just trying to distract himself. The factory smelled old and dry, not even dead, and he needed air and light.

He ducked through the doorway that Vin had indicated, and started up the stairs, body tensed just in case the next step was the one that wouldn't take his weight. He could see the paler wood of the repairs, and it wasn't that he didn't believe Vin when he said it would hold—well, his mind believed, but his body did not. The occasional crack and groan didn't improve matters.

Then at last he came out onto the roof, and stood for a moment, staring. Most of the biggest buildings were still there, their shells intact, roofless, broken, but recognizable. Somehow that seemed worse than if they had been missing altogether, and he shook his head, wishing he had the words. It was like looking at the skeleton of something so long dead that half the bones were missing. The eye filled in the gaps even as it noted them, shapes made as familiar as they were strange. There was the old guildhall, converted before he was born to a commercial exchange: the long windows were empty, carved frames broken out, but the line of the roof was intact. The Panopticon's roof had fallen in, but its narrow towers still flanked the gap, scorched and blackened against the pale sky. In the far distance, sunlight glinted from the dome of the City Museum. Somehow most of the gilding had survived, and it had not been worth anyone's while to pull it down for salvage. Or at least, not worth it yet. Cai was bound to get there, in the end.

Beyond that was the gap that had been Centenary Park, once dark with trees, now bleak and empty, a few twisted stumps thrusting out of the rubble. He and Melena had never gone there much, preferred the livelier amusement of Gateside, where there were band concerts three nights a week, and you could buy cakes and tea from a dozen vendors, and bring a flask of your own if you were reasonably discreet...

He looked back at the Museum, the afternoon sun bright on the gilded dome. If there'd been no looting there, no salvage — it had had what was supposed to be an important collection of Ancient artifacts. He remembered being taken there on school trips, walking through the echoing halls, boys in one long line, girls in the other, giggling and shoving each other when the teachers weren't looking. There was much more in the catacombs beneath the museum: he definitely remembered one young teacher explaining that there was far too much to display, as well as things that were too fragile, and things that were too dangerous. Maybe that would be worth investigating, too, if Teyla'd managed to strike a deal.

They walked back to the hotel through lengthening shadows, Radek vainly trying to suppress his excitement. Teyla met them in the doorway, calm as ever, P90 still clipped to her chest.

"We — there is quite a bit of what we need," Radek began, trying to be cautious, and Teyla nodded.

"We have come to some provisional arrangements," she said, and smiled. Cai was smiling, too, Ronon saw, so the deal seemed fair to him. "We must return to Atlantis and confer with our superiors, of course, but I believe this will do well for both of us."

Cai bowed. "I sincerely hope so."

CHAPTER THIRTEEN
The City Museum

THE DEBRIEFING didn't take long — in fact, the longest part was Radek waxing rhapsodic about the titanium plates he had found. Though mostly, Ronon thought, it was quick because they didn't have much choice. They could pay what Cai wanted, or look somewhere else. And Sheppard was not the kind of man who'd send a raiding party to steal something he could afford to pay for. Ronon allowed himself a crooked smile. And besides, the plates were too big and heavy to move if somebody was shooting at them. Sheppard was making wrap-it-up noises, and Ronon pulled himself upright.

"Sheppard. There's one more thing."

Everyone looked at him, Teyla with her head to one side, and he licked his lips.

"While Zelenka was doing his thing, I went up on the roof to take a look around. The City Museum looks pretty much intact. When I was a kid, they said there was a big collection of Ancient artifacts there. I'm thinking we should take a look."

Sheppard nodded. "Sounds interesting. Teyla, do you think Cai would go for that?"

She paused, considering. "We might have to offer a little more, but, yes, I think he would agree. The Ancient gene is so rare here that there is little use any of us, Satedans, Athosians, Genii, or any other people, can make of their devices."

"OK," Sheppard said. "See what you can do. Ronon, you'll be in charge if we get clearance, and, Radek, I'd like you to be part of that group."

Radek nodded, took a deep breath. "We should also bring Dr. Lynn." He paused, gave a rueful smile. "After all, is this not exactly what we have archeologists for?"

"OK," Sheppard said again. "Then tomorrow we send the engineers — and I appreciate the loan of *Hammond's* people, Colonel Carter — and Ronon and his team will check out this museum collection. But remember. Don't touch the glowing things."

William was the last to arrive in the gate room. He wasn't actually late, but he was carrying a travel mug, which would have merited remark, Radek thought, if he hadn't been carrying one himself. They had to wait for the control room team to disengage and redial the gate, a team of Marines with P90s at the ready just in case the Wraith picked that moment to try to dial in. The odds of that were vanishingly small, but it was not a chance anyone wanted to take.

Nonetheless, it was a relief to see the gate light again, the burst of blue steadying to the shimmer of the event horizon, filing the circle of the gate. The Marine detail formed up sharply, the engineers following with less conscious swagger, and Ronon and Teyla moved forward, ready to be first through the gate. Radek took a deep breath — this was really not what he'd signed up for — and followed. At the edge of the event horizon, he glanced over his shoulder, saw Sheppard watching from the rail of the control room, his face so expressionless it was clear how much he wanted to go in their place. *I wish you could*, Radek thought, and stepped through the gate.

He emerged into the chill of a spring morning, the light gold and new, the shadows long across the square. Smoke rose from the tents, and a bonfire was burning in a cleared spot at the center of the square. His breath left a trail of fog, but it was the kind of chill that promised a warm day to follow.

"Dex!" Ushan Cai emerged from the best-repaired of the buildings, a stocky woman at his side, and Ronon lifted his hand in greeting.

"Cai."

"And Teyla and Dr. Zelenka," Cai went on. "Welcome. I'm glad we've been able to come to an agreement."

"As are we," Teyla said.

"I assume there are more coming?" Cai asked, and Ronon nodded.

"Right behind us."

Even as he spoke, the event horizon rippled again, and the first of the Marines emerged, hauling the crated trade goods. Cai nodded, nodded again as the engineers followed them, and there was the usual milling around as the Marines looked for the right place to leave the crates and the engineers looked for their orders. Ronon got them sorted out quickly enough, and Teyla smiled at Cai.

"There was another matter we were interested in discussing. Perhaps I might have a word?"

"Of course," Cai answered, and they moved out of earshot.

"Zelenka!" Ronon called. "Help Vin get Captain Corvasc set up at the factory. Then come back and we'll see what Teyla's come up with."

"Yes, of course," Radek said, and hurried to help.

It didn't take long to show the engineers the plates, and to get them started. They'd brought plasma torches and an Ancient skid that seemed have some kind of antigravity, as well as props and blocks, and Vin was happy to help, particularly when the detail sergeant proved willing to explain the torch. Radek waited a few minutes to be sure it was all in order, then started back to the square.

He was expecting a call to tell him to hurry up, but the radio stayed silent the whole way. Instead, there was birdsong and sunlight, a sense of spring that felt impossibly good after the weeks of cold and snow. There was new growth in what had obviously been household gardens, tucked in between ruined houses, and he guessed that Cai's people would be able to eat well for the summer, at least. They didn't lack courage, coming back here, particularly with Death gathering the Wraith behind her, but if she could be stopped — From the look of things, they could do well.

William was standing by the dying bonfire, talking to the stocky woman who had been with Cai — in fact, they were trading tastes of each other's drinks, nodding seriously. That was also something Radek remembered, the way William had always used food and drink to make connections, talking as easily to grandmothers as to street vendors, and he made himself smile as he moved to join them. William's greeting was equally reserved, and Radek was glad to see movement in the doorway of Cai's headquarters. Ronon emerged, followed by Teyla, still talking over her shoulder to Cai, who stooped slightly to listen.

"Zelenka," Ronon said. "We're good to go."

"Very well," Radek answered. "The engineers are settled to work, and I think that will go well."

"How far is it to this museum?" William asked.

Ronon paused, obviously calculating. "About — three kilometers, I'd say. A little less than that."

"Not bad," William said, and tucked the now-empty travel mug into his pack.

Radek looked at Teyla. "So we have a deal?"

"Yes." Her smile was serene. "I have agreed that we will share information on what is still in the museum, in exchange for first choice of what is found. I think it is fair."

"Good enough for me," Ronon said. He wasn't looking good, Radek thought, as though the first pleasure of seeing his fellow Satedans had worn off and he was seeing the ruined city all the more clearly for having been happy. "Let's go."

Cai's people had done some clearing of the streets around the gate square, but once they'd gone a kilometer or so, the damage was more impressive. Buildings had collapsed into the street, spilling bricks across what had been a broad roadway, so that they had to scramble over and around the piles of debris. Glass glittered between the paving stones, spread in swaths across the bricks. The birds seemed more distant now, driven off by the sound of their footsteps.

Walking would have been bearable, but the uneven footing, the detours and the occasional climb, was making Radek's leg begin to ache. He felt himself lagging, gritted his teeth, not wanting to say anything, and was only mildly embarrassed when Teyla called a halt at the next open square. He sat on the edge of the now-dry fountain — otherwise almost untouched; winged nymphs lifted wreaths to a central pillar, their bodies chipped but intact — and discreetly massaged the cramped muscle while the others took long drinks from their water bottles. The sun was definitely hot now, and Radek loosened his own jacket.

William turned on his heel, surveying the square. "Residential?" he asked, and Ronon glared at him.

"Yeah."

"A nice neighborhood," William said, almost to himself, looking over the top of his glasses at the lines of the roofs.

"It used to be," Ronon said, and his voice was grim.

"I believe I was here once," Teyla began, and looked at Ronon.

"But no matter."

Radek looked up at them, the pain in his leg forgotten. There was a baffled anger in Ronon's face that made him wince in sympathy. "When I was a little boy," he said, groping for the words. "The town I grew up in had been bombed in the war. There had been a German manufacturing plant there, and the center of the city was destroyed with it. I was not yet born, of course, but I heard the stories. Three nights of raids, with a bomber's moon high in the sky, and everyone huddling in their cellars not knowing what they wished except to survive."

William nodded, familiar quick sympathy, but Radek was watching Ronon, saw the hint of curiosity. Behind the Satedan, Teyla nodded gravely, and Radek wondered what stories Sheppard had told her, while they were trapped on Earth.

"We had been conquered by our enemy," he said, his eyes on Ronon. "So we wished to see them beaten, and yet the cost..." He shrugged. "The new town, the center that everyone was so proud of, it was gone. The Old Town was shattered, and the people were gone, and there were streets filled to the second floors of the houses with broken stone. But by the time I was born... When I was very little, there were empty cellars, wrecked houses, and we were told never to play in them, or we would drown or be buried alive. By the time I was in school, the cellars were filled in, and my grandmother had a garden again. My uncle built his house where there had been a drygoods shop." He hesitated, shrugged again. "It is possible to rebuild. And Cai is making a good beginning, I think."

"It won't be the same," Ronon said.

"No," Radek agreed. "But it will exist."

Ronon turned away, the heavy dreadlocks flying. Radek sighed, and took a long drink from his water bottle. His leg was feeling better, and he couldn't help thinking perhaps he should not have said anything.

"Let us move on," Teyla said, after a moment.

Radek tucked his bottle back into the pack and began to haul himself to his feet, but to his surprise Ronon turned and held out his hand. Radek took it, grateful for the support as he got his knee working again, and Ronon said, "Thanks."

I meant it, Radek wanted to say, but they both knew that. He nodded instead, and settled the P90 more comfortably against his chest.

They came up to the Museum by the back way, or so Ronon said — the street that had been the intended approach was still blocked by a collapsed building, and this was easier, if a little longer. Even from the back, the building was impressive: a long stretch of once-pale stone, fire-streaked now in places, the severe line of windows gaping empty. Everything was sharp, straight lines, except for the dome that rose from the center of the building. There had been statues once at the four corners of that central portion, but only fragments remained. It looked vaguely German, Radek thought — pre-war, pre-Hitler German — except for the lines of Satedan script carved into the band of stone that marked the division between the first and second stories.

"What does that say?" William asked, and Ronon looked over his shoulder, impatient.

"It's the names of the city districts, and the suburbs. It's the Museum of the City."

"Ah." William had his camera out, was recording the facade with practiced ease.

"This door is open," Teyla said. She looked at Ronon. "Is this the best way in?"

He hesitated, frowning as though he was trying to remember — or, more likely, Radek thought, trying to match what was still here with what had been. The door was open, certainly: it was missing altogether, the frame scorched and blackened. The stone to either side was pockmarked by shrapnel. A bomb, then, rather than fire, and that was a good thing.

"Yeah." Ronon closed his eyes for a moment. "Yeah. If we go in here, we should be able to go straight to the main hall, and then the Hall of the Ancients will be to the left…"

"Let us go," Teyla said. She touched the switch that activated the P90's light, and stepped through the broken doorway. Radek took a breath, and did the same. Ronon followed, looking over his shoulder.

"Dr. Lynn!"

"Coming."

Radek swung his P90 carefully from side to side, letting the light pick out the details. They were in what looked like a service corridor, part of the museum's functional space, not any of the exhibit halls. Here, by the doorway, there was plaster down, and cracked floors; to the right, another door hung half off its hinges, and the room beyond it was half filled with debris, chunks of plaster and a fallen beam covering what looked like a desk and chairs. Not far ahead, though, the damage was considerably less, and he let the light play over the supporting walls, assessing their stability. They looked remarkably solid, considering, and he picked his way carefully over the debris.

"I think this way is safe," he said, and Teyla nodded.

"Ronon, you said we should go straight here?"

"Yeah." Ronon stepped past them, blaster loose in his hand, like an extension of his arm. Teyla shifted to let her light play ahead of him down the corridor. It ended in a dark green door — a padded door, Radek saw, as they came closer, and guessed it must lead into the exhibit area. He shifted his own light to check the stability of the wall and ceiling.

"OK," he said, and Ronon shifted his blaster to his left hand to try the latch.

To everyone's surprise, the door opened smoothly, without even a whisper of metal on metal. Sunlight poured in, blinding, and for an instant Radek could see only a riot of color. And then his sight cleared, and the colors resolved to a vividly patterned tile floor — like an Oriental carpet in stone — and the peeling remains of painting on a carved pillar. Beyond the pillars was an open atrium, and multi-colored glass from the broken skylights glittered against the patterned stone. A bird scolded, and there was a whir of wings as it launched itself from among the pillars. It was pigeon-sized, and gray-blue, and Radek couldn't help laughing at the sight.

"Not more pigeons."

To his surprise, Ronon gave a rueful smile. "Choua. They're everywhere."

"Evidently." That was William, looking with disapproval at a deposit of droppings at the base of one of the columns.

Teyla's eyes were laughing, but her voice was grave. "I believe there are symbols from the DHD on the doorway here. Perhaps it leads to the Ancient collection?"

"Right." Ronon looked around again. "Yeah. Through there."

The corridor led back into the dark. Radek flicked his light back on, looked over his shoulder to see William carefully filming the doorway and its symbols. They were the familiar markings from the DHD, all right, and Sateda's address arched above the doorway, the rest of the patterns trailing down the sides. The ones closest to the floor were damaged, the paint flaking away, but the words on the lintel had been carved too deeply to be erased in a mere decade.

"What does it say?" William asked, and Ronon looked back, impatient.

"Hall of the Ancients, Ancestors of Humanity. Come on."

William made a soft sound that might have meant anything, but put the camera aside. Radek let his light play along the corridor's walls. There had been fire here, he thought, perhaps the flash of a bomb; the paint was scorched in spots, dark and peeling, and when he checked overhead, there were only beams and emptiness where a ceiling had been.

"Here's the Stargate," William said, pointing to the wall. The circle of his flashlight caught a panel that was mostly intact, the gate standing empty in the center of a field, a few humans gathered by the DHD.

"And here also," Teyla said. She let the light of her P90 play across the opposite wall, picking out a similar scene. This time, Radek thought he recognized some of the buildings surrounding the gate.

"That is here, the gate square, yes?"

"A history — it's a history of Satedan gate use, right?" William swung his light back and forth, scanning the murals. "Oh, and that's nice. The frames are the Stargate itself."

Ronon was staring at him, and he shrugged.

"I suppose that's what the captions say? You'll have to teach me your alphabet, I hate being illiterate."

"Perhaps later," Teyla said, reluctantly. "Is that —?"

She stopped abruptly, eyes widening. Radek lifted his P90 in reflex, joining its light to hers.

The corridor ended in an arched doorway, and through its opening the lights flashed from glass and metal. Display cases, Radek thought, some broken, some intact — and then he saw it, too, the tripod of a portable lamp, a coil of rope and a woven basket, and the breath caught in his throat.

"Someone's been here."

"Did Cai mention anyone else?" Ronon asked.

Teyla shook her head. "He did not."

"This is recent," Radek said. The plaster dust had been swept off the cases, and the floor was relatively clean. He let the light play around the room again, picking out more display cases, metal and crystal glittering within, found a shuttered window. It looked as though it had been repaired, and he crossed to it, eased it back. The sunlight poured into the room in an almost solid wedge, dust dancing in its beam, and his breath caught again at the sight of the display cases. There were two ranks of them, stretching the length of the hall; on the walls to either side were more murals, scenes of what must be Ancient history alternating with stylized starscapes. At the end of the hall, part of the ceiling had fallen — nothing structural, just lathe and plaster and perhaps some light boards — and the display cases were broken but not crushed beneath it. Most of the rest were intact, and he saw what looked like a lifesigns detector laid between the panels of a lamp and the cracked crystal from a control board.

"This is Genii," William said. He crouched beside the basket, poking cautiously at its contents. "The equivalent of an MRE." He held up a box with unfamiliar lettering.

Teyla frowned. "Perhaps this has been here some time?"

William shook his head. "This says it was packed three months ago."

Ronon lifted an eyebrow. "You can read Genii and not Satedan?"

"It seemed relevant at the time," William answered. He set the box carefully back into the basket, stood up, dusting his hands on his thighs. "Food and water. I think they're planning to come back."

"That's not good," Ronon said.

"No." Teyla turned slowly, surveying the room. "I think — this all looks valuable and important, and I think we need to examine it closely. But I would also like to know what the Genii are doing here. If they are still here at all."

"I agree," Ronon said. He took a breath. "We split up. Zelenka, Dr. Lynn, take stock of what's here, collect anything that's useful. Teyla, let's you and me see if we can find any Genii."

Teyla followed Ronon back to the hall with the atrium, frowning at the tracks they had left on the dusty floor.

"If the Genii are still here," she began, and Ronon nodded.

"Yeah. I know. Let's hope they're not."

There wasn't anything to say to that, at least nothing that did not sound more critical than she meant. And she was to blame as much as anyone: she had trusted Cai — still more than half trusted him, if it came to that, and she frowned again. Everything he had said had seemed honest; she could not point to a moment when she had thought, he is concealing something, even in the details of their bargaining. That was disconcerting, and she put it aside, to be dealt with later. She would get answers from Cai on their return.

The atrium gave onto another, smaller hall, this one lined with pillars carved like kneeling men, taking the weight of the ceiling on their shoulders. The dome they had seen from outside rose overhead, a dozen round windows piercing its surface. The glass was missing, and the hall was full of leaves and the damp tracks of rain and wind. And of humans, she saw, and in the same moment Ronon pointed.

"They came in this way."

"Or someone did," Teyla said.

Ronon stooped to examine the marks. "Looks like Genii boots to me."

"Can you tell how long ago they were here?"

Ronon straightened, shaking his head. "Not more than a week ago — maybe as recently as yesterday, depending on the weather." He met her eyes. "Cai should have told us."

Teyla nodded. "Yes. And still — Ronon, I trusted him. I don't know what to think."

"Maybe we can get some answers from the Genii," Ronon said, with a sudden smile.

"Perhaps," Teyla answered. "But — we should be cautious."

"Absolutely," Ronon said. He looked around again. "This way. There's a side door we can use."

Radek walked the length of the Hall of the Ancients, glancing from case to case. He recognized perhaps half of their contents, recognized that some of the items weren't even Ancient — that odd silver sphere, half crushed, looked almost Asgard — and his fingers itched to examine them more closely.

"Don't even think of it," William said, without looking up from his camera, and Radek muttered a Czech curse under his breath. "We need to make a record first."

"We may not have time for that," Radek said. "Not if the Genii are here."

"We know they have been here," William said. "Not that they're here now."

"And that they're planning to come back," Radek pointed out. "You said that yourself."

"Yeah, OK, I did say that." William straightened, took a breath. "Priorities?"

Radek gave the Asgard sphere a last regretful look. "Undamaged Ancient objects. Things that we can maybe use on Atlantis."

"Control crystals?"

"Have you found some?" Radek moved to join the other man at a long case that had stood against the wall. It gaped open now, the shards of glass covering the long, pale blue crystals that lay on stained velvet.

"Yes —"

"No, we have plenty of those," Radek said. "And, look, see there? Most of them are cracked."

"Well, it was a start," William said. "These?" He pointed to the next case, where a scattering of smaller crystals were laid out in a spreading fan-shape, bright against a soft dark-red backing. There were gaps in the sequence, crystals replaced by plasticine models, but Radek caught his breath again.

"Yes. Oh, yes. Those we should take."

"I'll make a list," William said. "See what we have, and then we can take as much as we can carry. The most important things first."

There was a park next to the museum, where saplings were beginning to spring from the broken trunks of the old trees. At the far end of the green space, a thread of smoke was rising between two ruined buildings — clean smoke, cooking smoke, and Teyla looked at Ronon.

"I thought Cai said all his people were staying by the gate."

"He did." Ronon flicked his blaster from stun to kill and back again. "It could be somebody else. Somebody Satedan, I mean."

"It could," Teyla agreed.

"Yeah. I don't think so, either." Ronon looked around, surveying the broken ground. "If we move north along the edge of the park, we'll be in cover most of the way."

Teyla nodded. "Our main goal is to find out if the Genii are here.

Not to engage them."

"I know!" Ronon glared at her, and she met his stare squarely. He sighed, and looked away. "I know."

"And then we will have a conversation with Ushan Cai," she said.

"Yeah." Ronon looked happier at the thought, and pointed along the crumbling facade of a long low building. "That way."

The sprouting trees screened them from the distant camp for most of the way. The smell of the smoke was stronger, wood and cooking, and Teyla wished she'd had more than a power bar when they had stopped earlier. But that was pointless, a weakness, and she put it aside with the ease of long practice. She could see the tip of a canvas tent between the buildings, white in the sunlight, and Ronon came to a stop behind a broken set of stairs.

"Looks like the Genii to me," he said, softly.

Teyla reached into her pockets, pulled out a pair of the Earth people's binoculars, and eased forward to peer over the edge of the stones. The tent did look like Genii work, the odd mix of primitive and sophisticated that they now showed the rest of the galaxy — and, yes, the man stirring the kettle slung over the campfire was wearing a Genii uniform. Another man was sitting on a three-legged stool outside a second tent, working on some piece of equipment, but there was no one else in sight.

"That cannot be all their people," she said, and Ronon shook his head.

"No."

Teyla lifted the glasses to her eyes again, scanning the camp a second time. It looked as though they had been in the Museum — surely that metal crate was Ancient work — and she reached for her radio. "Radek. Radek, come in."

"I want to get a little closer," Ronon said, and slipped forward without waiting for an answer.

"Radek," Teyla said again. "This is Teyla. The Genii are here in the city, and may be coming your way." She paused, waiting for an answer, some acknowledgement, and none came.

Ronon signaled, and she moved to join him, crouching low.

"I'm guessing maybe six, ten men all told —" he began, and she lifted her hand.

"I am not getting a response from Radek."

"Damn it," Ronon muttered. He looked at the Museum, then back at the camp.

"We should go back," Teyla said.

"Yeah." Ronon didn't move, and in the same moment, the tent flap was flung aside, and a slender red-haired woman stepped out into the sunlight. Her uniform jacket was open to the waist in the warm air, showing a pale undershirt. "Is that —?"

"Yes," Teyla said. "Sora Tyrus." She touched her radio again. "Radek. Respond, please." Ronon looked at her, and she shook her head. "Nothing."

Ronon met her eyes. "Back to the Museum."

They were getting toward the end of the hall, and Radek shook his head in frustration. The list was already too long for them to take everything that was on it, and it was obvious that this end, where the ceiling had come down, was where the curators had displayed their largest pieces. He ducked under a beam, crouched to see into the next case. It was bigger than the others had been, perhaps a meter long and half a meter deep; two of its legs had broken when part of the ceiling fell on it, and the body of the case sloped down and away from him. He checked the heavy wedge of plaster, and when he was sure it was secure, worked himself further into the debris so that he could see into the case.

It was beautiful. That was his first thought, incoherent and startled. It had been lovely enough on Atlantis even burnt-out and cracked; the intact array caught the light from his flashlight, reflected it back in a cloud of multi-colored stars. It couldn't possibly be — but it was, it definitely was a hyperdrive control array, the missing crystal, the one that had blown out on them and dumped them onto an unnamed world, and he sat back on his heels, swearing in Czech.

"Was that an invitation?" William asked, working his way through the rubble after him, and stopped. "That — that looks important."

"Yes. Oh, yes." Radek pushed his glasses up onto his nose, still not quite able to believe what he was seeing. "This — whatever happens, William, this has to get back to Atlantis."

For a second, he thought the other would object, but William nodded slowly. "All right. What is it?"

"One of the major control crystals for the hyperdrive," Radek said.

He was almost afraid to say it out loud, for fear it might somehow vanish. "With this — and a ZPM, of course — we can fly the city again."

William stuffed the notebook into his pocket, pulled out his flashlight. "It's really beautiful. Very sculptural."

The doubled lights drew more colors from interior facets, thin sheets of color like the aurora playing inside the crystal. Reflections danced on the walls, on the fallen ceiling, sparks that drew bits of color from the paintings. The Satedan curators might not have known what they had, but they had taken good care of it, secured it against the padding so that even the collapse of the display hadn't jarred it loose. Reluctantly, Radek turned his beam away from the array, scanned the case and the straps that held the crystal in place. It would take some planning to get it out safely, but he thought he could do it —

"Hang on," William said. "I thought I heard something."

Radek cocked his head, listening. For a second, there was nothing, but then he heard it, too, the unmistakable sound of booted feet on the stone floors. "Crap."

"Not our people," William said nervously.

Radek said something stronger in Czech, swung his flashlight around again, looking for a way out. There was only one entrance to the hall, and if they could hear the Genii coming — because it had to be the Genii — it was too late to get out that way. His light struck the edge of a doorway, the frame picked out with DHD symbols; there was another beam down in front of it, but if the door opened away from them... He was already moving, ducking under first one beam and then another, William scrambling at his heels. There was just enough room to stand upright inside the last beam, and he quickly checked the door, praying it wasn't locked, praying it opened the right way. He worked the latch and pushed hard, and to his relief the door scraped open half a meter, loosing a shower of plaster.

"Quick, inside."

William slipped past him, pistol in one hand, flashlight in the other. "It's — not very big. Some sort of storage —"

"Be quiet," Radek said, and stepped in after him. William flattened himself against the back wall — it was covered with narrow shelves that were crammed with boxes, and Radek managed to work the door almost closed again. "Turn out your light."

William obeyed, and Radek did the same. The P90 was heavy

against his chest, and he worked it awkwardly into position, elbowing William hard in the process. The archeologist grunted, shifted so that he could aim his pistol over the shorter man's shoulder. The footsteps were coming closer, louder and more distinct. Definitely more than one person, Radek thought, craning to see through the crack he'd left in the door, and—yes, definitely Genii. There was a thump as someone dropped something, and then the rattle of someone shedding equipment.

"Well?" William's voice was barely a breath in his ear.

"Ssh."

William shifted uncomfortably. They were so close in the dark that Radek could feel the pressure of William's hip, feel him breathing, the quick movement of his chest.

"Radek." That was Teyla's voice in his ear, the radio he'd forgotten until now, and he jumped, reached hastily to shut it off, not daring to risk anyone else hearing. They would contact her later, when the Genii had left—though it sounded as though they were settling in for the day. He could hear voices now, soft conversation, though he couldn't quite make out the words. If they had to stay here for more than an hour or two—already his leg was starting to ache. It would cramp soon enough, and then he'd have trouble walking, wouldn't be able to keep up if they needed to move fast.

The unmistakable crackle of a Genii radio cut through his rising fear.

"Team one, this is base. Report." It was a woman's voice, and Radek swore again. Surely their luck couldn't be running this badly.

"Team one here," a man answered. "It looks as though the Satedans have been back here, Sora. Someone's been checking on what we're doing."

Radek felt William shift again, heard the breath of a curse, and felt like swearing himself. Of course they'd left tracks, marks in the dust; probably they hadn't put the Genii supplies back exactly the way they'd been. And of course it was Sora.

"Any damage?" the woman asked.

"No. Just looking around."

There was a little pause, and then the woman's voice said, "Right. We can't have that. Head back to camp, we need to have a talk with Cai."

"We could still get some work done," the man protested.

"Negative. We need to establish our position. Head back now. Base out."

One of the Genii said something that had to be a curse, and the man who'd been on the radio raised his voice. "Roal! Come on out of there. We're heading back to camp."

Radek closed his eyes, feeling almost faint with relief. They stood listening for what seemed like hours as the Genii team recovered their equipment and moved reluctantly away. When he was sure they were out of earshot, he risked lighting his watch, counted off ten minutes before he took a slow breath and reached for the door.

"I think we can go now," he said, and felt William nod.

"Go ahead. I'll cover you."

"This is insane," Radek said under his breath, and pulled the door open again. The hall was empty, sunlight pouring in through the half opened shutter. He worked his knee, and took a cautious step. It hurt, but the leg held his weight, and he turned back to see William playing his flashlight over the shelves of boxes. "William—"

"Hang on," William said, and Radek touched his radio.

"Teyla. Teyla, this is Radek."

"Radek!" Teyla sounded relieved. "There are Genii in this area—"

"Yes, I know. They were here, and left—they were heading back to their camp. They did not see us."

"Good," Teyla said. "We must head back to the gate. Ronon wishes to have a word with Ushan Cai."

"I am sure he does," Radek said, and was rewarded by a chuckle.

"We will meet at the square where we stopped before," Teyla said. "Can you get there?"

Radek glanced at the hyperdrive array still untouched in its case. It wasn't that heavy, wasn't much bigger than a football, and they had brought carriers that would protect it. Out of the corner of his eye, he could see William stuffing what looked like decks of playing cards into every available pocket. "Yes. We'll be there shortly."

"Be careful," Teyla said, and cut the transmission.

By the time the team made it back to the gate square, the smell of cooking was in the air there too, and there were people crossing the square, apparently going about business of their own but giving Ronon and the rest of the team frankly curious glances. Ronon stopped the first person who came near enough to speak to, a woman in work clothes with her hair pinned up at the back of her neck. "Where's Cai?"

"I think he's in the old hotel," she said. "He was talking to — talking to some people."

The line of Teyla's mouth tightened, and Ronon knew what she was thinking. If the Genii had gotten here before them, they could still wind up in a fight. He waved the woman on and looked at the scientists. Radek was cradling the case that held the hyperdrive crystal as if he didn't trust it not to fall apart at any moment, or possibly just as if he didn't trust himself not to trip and drop it.

"Lynn, dial the gate to New Athos," Ronon said. "You and Zelenka take this stuff back there and wait until you can dial in to Atlantis." He wasn't finding it easy to get used to having to wait for the brief windows when they'd arranged to be able to dial in. "We'll stay and talk to Cai."

"I should stay too, I think," Radek said evenly, handing the case to Lynn, who took it with a bemused expression. "One is not much backup, even if that one is Teyla. Of course, there are the Marine teams, but they are some distance away, and if Sora is here…" He shrugged expressively.

Ronon glanced at Teyla. He didn't think she'd find Radek that much use if it came to a fight, and he expected her to tell him so.

"You are right," Teyla said instead. "Our teams are still at the factory, and they must finish their work, especially if we are not to stay here long. We will warn them that there may be trouble, but I will not call them back to the gate yet. So, yes, stay." She nodded at Radek, who shrugged a little awkwardly.

"Then perhaps I should stay as well," Lynn said.

"We need that hyperdrive array back in Atlantis no matter what," Radek said. Lynn was holding the hyperdrive crystal case more normally by its handle, his camera still in his other hand, and Radek gave him a dark look as if suspecting that he wasn't taking proper care, although Lynn didn't strike Ronon as a careless person. "It is our best chance of ever being able to fly the city again — "

"Yes, so you already explained," Lynn said fairly mildly. "All right, then. Anything in particular you want me to say other than giving a report on what happened here?"

"Tell Colonel Sheppard that we'll check in again within the hour," Ronon said. "If he doesn't hear from us—"

"Then he'll know it's time to send in the cavalry," Lynn said. "I'll tell him." He set off across the square toward the gate.

"You and Zelenka wait out here, then," Ronon told Teyla. "I'll get more out of Cai by myself."

Teyla didn't argue, although her expression was skeptical. He didn't know if that was because she didn't trust his skill at talking, or because she suspected he intended to fight rather than talk. It was certainly tempting.

He felt a knot of unreasonable betrayal curling in his chest as he stepped into the dimly-lit hotel. He shouldn't have let himself be so glad to see his own people here rebuilding that he let himself believe in strangers. He should have known it was too good to be true, should have expected the whole thing to be some kind of dirty trick—

He set his jaw and threw open the door to the hotel bar with a clatter. Cai looked up, startled at the sound, and then met Ronon's eyes, his face closed. There'd apparently been some kind of disagreement in here recently; there were overturned tables, one of which Cai had been in the process of setting to rights, and drinks spilled across the floor.

Ronon drew his pistol and leveled it at Cai's chest. "So you're working for the Genii."

Cai set the table down squarely on its feet before he answered. "I'm not working for the Genii," he said.

"Liar," Ronon said. "We know they're here."

"They've been here for half a year," Cai said. "They have their own camps at several places in the city. At first they were mainly after weapons. They were talking about getting some of the munitions factories working again. Exploring the museum is new. That's Sora's project."

"You know Sora."

"She says she's in charge of Genii operations on Sateda."

"And you work for her?"

"I work for the Satedan people."

"Yeah, it's really going to help them to sell Sateda to the Genii."

Cai actually laughed, an unexpected bitter bark that made Ronon's finger tighten on the pistol's trigger. "Sell it? The Genii don't have to buy anything here. They've claimed the planet, Ronon. They say they're taking over."

"And you let them?"

"I'm not a soldier," Cai said. "What have the soldiers who escaped Sateda done? Found work as mercenaries? Killing people is a surprisingly marketable skill. Become heroes fighting the Wraith?"

Ronon didn't lower the pistol. "So?"

"They've built lives somewhere. They're not desperate to get back to Sateda. Any world will take in good soldiers or good farmers. Good carpenters, even. But what do you think the rest of us had to offer out there?" Cai's voice was tired. "I owned a factory. I spent most of my days sitting behind a table and the rest on the factory floor. I never fired a gun or plowed a field or dug a ditch. I had a dozen mechanical engineers working for me. What do you think they did on planets where the horse collar would be a breakthrough? Plowed fields, maybe. Dug ditches. Badly."

"Sure, but—"

Cai kept talking, like maybe he'd been wanting to say all this for a while. "I had a secretary, typists, clerks. Do you know of anywhere that needs typists now, or hairdressers, or radio operators?" He shook his head. "That's who came back, Ronon. People who'd lost everything they had. Not just their possessions and their families but their usefulness."

"Like you?"

"Like me," Cai said flatly. "It took me ten years to figure out that being able to manage people, being a good salesman... that much I still had. That's how I convinced these people to come back here. But they're ordinary people, not soldiers. The Genii sent a regiment of soldiers through the Ring. If we'd tried to fight, it would have been nothing to them to kill us all. And I couldn't let that happen to these people. I'm responsible for them. I'm not sure why they want me to be, but they do, and I am."

"You sent us to the museum," Ronon said after a moment. "You set us up."

"I didn't know they were working there today," Cai said. "We try to steer clear of their people as much as we can."

"That's not the point," Ronon said. "Why didn't you tell us about the Genii?"

Cai reached for one of the other overturned tables, ignoring the way Ronon's pistol twitched to follow him. He set it upright, squaring it with the others in the row instead of looking at Ronon. "You?" he said. "The greatest living Satedan hero, the great warrior against the Wraith? And here we sit, unable to keep the Genii from squatting in our cities and robbing our dead." He looked up, finally. "What do you think? We were too ashamed."

The words hung in the silence for a moment, and finally Ronon lowered his pistol. "You did what you could," he said. "You brought our people back to Sateda."

"I did," Cai said, raising his chin a little. "And now we can finally be rid of the Genii. Compared to the Wraith, they ought to be easy for you and the Lanteans to handle."

"Compared to the Wraith," Ronon said, "but —"

"The Genii don't own Sateda," Cai said. "The Lanteans have a reputation for being a fair people, and you call some of them friends. Surely you can bring their soldiers to help us."

"It's complicated," Ronon said.

"Not so complicated," Cai said. "We can make Sateda a world we recognize again. Our children will see the trains running again and have electric lights. Our grandchildren will have hospitals and factories and music on the radio. But none of that is going to happen if this world becomes a military outpost for the Genii. They'll take everything they can use and build their great bombs here so that if the Wraith find out, it won't be their world that gets burned to the ground."

It was all too easy to believe, especially knowing that the Genii had been poisoning their own people with their experiments with radioactive materials. They'd probably like the idea of poisoning somewhere they didn't care about that much instead.

It would be easy to promise that of course they'd help. The Genii didn't have any right to be on Sateda, and even if Woolsey might have thought it was somehow more complicated than that, Ronon didn't think that John would. But the Genii were supposed to be their allies, and it wasn't up to Ronon to decide whether the alliance was starting to be more trouble than it was worth.

"I have to talk to my commander," Ronon said. "I can't make any promises about something like this without his authority."

"That's fair," Cai said. "I know your reputation even if I don't know you, and what I've heard makes me trust that you'll do whatever it takes to help your people."

"I will," Ronon said, but he couldn't help feeling like this wasn't going to be simple at all.

CHAPTER FOURTEEN:
Michael

QUICKSILVER had not slept well since they returned from Atlantis, woke with head and hand aching as though he needed to feed, though that faded almost as soon as he came completely awake. He thought he dreamed, perhaps of the dark-haired queen who guarded his mind's gates, but he could no longer remember. Instead, he remembered human faces, fragments of places and voices. Some he recognized from the attack: the gate room in the city, the shabby little man who had tried to trick him, the warrior who had killed Dust, who had called him by a human name. Other things he could not have seen this time — the fierce and beautiful woman with the bearing of a queen, who had attacked him on the hive; the hall where the humans had their meeting; another woman with golden hair, and a smaller room with red walls where the humans' zenana gathered — and he guessed those were memories of his captivity.

He shifted on his pillows, awake again, and unsettled enough that sleep had lost its appeal. Twice they had called him by a human name, promised to help him: a terrible deception, all the worse because he could almost put a face to that name. Rodney, they had said, and in the long nights, lying silent and still so as not to disturb Ember, he had remember a second name attached to that one, in human fashion: Rodney McKay. But he knew McKay, or knew of him — no, he was sure he had known him in his captivity: a human scientist, a clever man even by his own high standards, the man he was sure had been his greatest enemy among the Lanteans. Handsome and strong, at least by human measure, and certainly brilliant — a worthy adversary, Quicksilver was sure of that. But why the other humans would call him by the same name, except in mockery...

And that they would pay for. He rolled out of his sleeping niche, saw to his surprise that Ember's door was drawn back, the narrow compartment empty. Frowning, he found clothes, dressed — that, at least, had come back to him — and slipped the communicator onto his wrist.

Ember.

There was no answer, and Quicksilver frowned. *Ember!*

I am with my commander, Ember said at last. *What is it? Is there a problem?*

I want you in the labs.

It is the middle of the late-night watch, Ember said. *Can it not wait — ?* He broke off then, as though someone else had spoken to him, and when he spoke again, his tone was resigned. *Come, then. I am in Guide's quarters, Steelflower's Consort. It is on your way.*

Quicksilver snarled, but there was really no point in objecting. He made his way through the corridors, brushed past the drones that guarded the rooms assigned to the visiting lords, and laid his hand on the door control. It opened, though not to his touch, the door sliding back to reveal Ember, his hair pulled back into a single loose tail.

Must we begin the day so early? he asked, but Quicksilver's gaze was fixed on the man behind him.

I know you, he said, startled. *We have worked together — where?*

He heard Ember draw breath sharply, but the older blade shook his head. *We have not,* he said. *And from what my chief cleverman tells me, it would have been a memorable experience.*

That's not right, Quicksilver said. He had just enough presence of mind not to call the man a liar outright, that was too great an insult from cleverman to blade — worse from cleverman to commander, he thought, realizing abruptly that this must be Guide himself, but he could not bring himself to let it go. *We worked on — replicators? A weapon against them?*

He heard the door slide shut behind him, felt a flash of something like fear from Ember. That was instantly controlled, and Guide shook his head again.

You and I have never met before now.

There was force behind the words, pressure to believe, and Quicksilver shook his head. *No. I'm sure of it. Something to do with Atlantis —*

I was a prisoner there, Guide said. *As were you.*

At the same time? That didn't seem right, and Quicksilver frowned.

I don't think so, Guide answered.

You know what was done to me, Quicksilver said. He couldn't have said how he knew it, but once the words were formed, he felt the confirmation, quickly shielded. *Tell me!*

Commander, Ember said, his tone a warning, and Guide shook his head.

No. Not now. He looked at Quicksilver, frowning slightly, the star tattoo around his eye very dark in the gentle shiplight. *I may not tell you.* He held up his hand, forestalling Quicksilver's instinctive outburst. *There are good reasons why you must find that out for yourself, it is not something you can come to by way of another's mind. But there is one thing I may share with you —*

Commander, Ember said again, and this time there was definitely fear in his tone. *You run too great a risk.*

Guide spared him a quick glance. *I know the risks I run, cleverman.* He looked back at Quicksilver. *Give me your hand.*

Quicksilver extended his off hand, wary, and Guide caught it in his own, circling the wrist with his long fingers, so that they spoke in intimate privacy. *I give you a name to conjure with. Michael.*

What?

Guide released him, turning away. *Go with him to the labs, Ember. We must not keep him from our queen's work.*

Yes, commander, Ember said, and opened the door again. *Let us go.*

But — Quicksilver found himself in the corridor again, the door sealed behind them. *How am I supposed to work after something like that?*

Perhaps we could sleep, then, Ember said, with some bitterness.

Oh, no. If I'm awake, we're going to work. In the labs. Both of us. Quicksilver took a breath. *And I will figure this out, with or without your commander's help. Wait and see.*

I most certainly shall, Ember answered, and they started together toward the labs.

Mel made her way through *Daedalus's* main corridor, tablet computer tucked under her arm. She'd heard the gossip along with everyone else in the city; the Genii were on Sateda, and getting the titanium there might be impossible after all. They'd retrieved some, but rumor said it wasn't quite enough, and that had gotten her thinking. She'd spent the morning in the 302 bay, going over specs and supplies, and the idea that had come to her in the middle of the night had started to look like something solid. It might not work — she was the first person to admit she was no technician — and it was a risk, but she'd talked it over with Dwayne Grant, her second-in-command, and he'd thought it was a pretty good idea, too. Except, of course, for the one glaring problem, but they'd agreed that getting the Stargate usable again had to be the top priority.

She paused in the engine room hatch, glancing around the spotless compartment. It still felt weird not to see an Asgard on board, to know that they were gone, that the Tau'ri were on their own with a technology they only barely understood — but, then, Dr. Novak had been working with it from the very beginning. If anyone knew what she was doing with this stuff, Novak did. At the moment, though, there was no one in sight, and Mel frowned. Surely somebody ought to be on duty, even with *Daedalus* parked on Atlantis?

"Colonel Hocken?" Novak popped up from behind one of the consoles like a skinny, disheveled jack-in-the-box.

"Got a minute?" Mel asked, with her most disarming smile, but Novak's wary expression didn't change.

"Sure…"

"I'm hearing that they're still short of titanium," Mel said. "Since the Genii turned out to be on Sateda. Our — the 302s — armor is titanium alloy, right?"

"Yes," Novak said. "But we don't have enough spares to do any good. Dr. Zelenka and I already went over the numbers."

"What if you took if off one of the 302s?" Mel asked. "The shields are our main defense, anyway, and the armor is a double layer by the tail. There's one piece that overlaps both of the under plates. Suppose you took off that redundant part?"

Novak tipped her head to one side. "I don't think I'd call that armor redundant."

"Just suppose," Mel said.

"Well…" Novak paused. "I don't know exactly how much is still missing, so I don't know…"

"Here's what I was thinking," Mel said, and held out the tablet.

Novak took it, frowned at the schematic of a 302, the plate Mel figured they could spare outlined in green. "Well," she said again. "Colonel, I see what you're saying, but I'm not comfortable removing armor. If you lose shields — and that always seems to happen — then you're depending on a single layer of armor at a very vulnerable point."

"A very small point," Mel said. "And not that vulnerable. Hard to hit even if you knew to try for it. Look, Dr. Novak, we're willing to take the risk if it means we can use the Stargate normally again."

"Let me run some numbers," Novak said, reluctantly, and set the tablet beside her laptop. She typed for a while, frowning to herself, then looked up. "It's possible," she said. "Which means that we'd harvest enough workable alloy to make it worthwhile — though I'd have to talk to Dr. Zelenka to find out what he still needs. But — Colonel, I can't recommend this. The 302s will be too vulnerable."

"That's my call, Doctor," Mel said, and softened it with a smile. "And Colonel Caldwell's."

Novak returned the smile. "I know how much trouble we'd be in if we lost Atlantis," she said. "But relying on shields alone — I think it's too big a risk."

"Without Atlantis, we don't have a base," Mel said. Novak handed her the tablet with an unhappy nod, and Mel turned away.

She caught up with Caldwell in Atlantis, on his way back from the mess hall. He was looking relatively relaxed — at least as much as Caldwell ever looked relaxed — and she cleared her throat.

"I wonder if I might have a word, sir?"

He gave her an appraising glance, and Mel tried to remember the last time a good conversation had started with those words.

"OK," he said. "What's on your mind, Hocken?"

"It's about the titanium for the iris, sir," she said, and could have sworn he looked faintly relieved. "I'm hearing that they're still a little short."

"That was the last I'd heard, too," Caldwell said. "What about it?"

"I've figured out a place we can get it," Mel said. She took a breath. "Off the 302s."

She could see him start to protest, hurried on before he could interrupt, holding out the tablet with the calculations. "And Dr. Novak says we could probably harvest enough plate to complete the job," she finished.

Caldwell looked at her for a long moment. "Did Dr. Novak sign off on this?"

"No, sir."

"Glad to hear it," Caldwell said.

"Grant and I discussed it pretty thoroughly," Mel said, stung. "We agreed that it barely makes a difference—I don't think I could hit a target like that under battle conditions."

"Shields alone aren't enough," Caldwell said. "And without 302s in top condition, *Daedalus* is at even more of a disadvantage against a hive ship. No way, Hocken."

"With respect," Mel said. "If we lose Atlantis—"

"I know," Caldwell said. "Don't think I don't, I was one of the people General O'Neill had talking to the IOA until I was blue in the face, telling them how badly we needed a base in Pegasus if we were going to keep the Wraith out here and away from Earth. But taking armor off the 302s is too big a risk. We're not doing it."

"Yes, sir," Mel said, and in spite of her best effort, she knew she sounded mulish.

Caldwell looked past her, at the long windows in their intricate frames, his face so stern that she looked with him, half expecting to see someone who had eavesdropped. But there was only the light midday snow, and the towers of the city against the pale sky, their edges softened by the swirling flakes. Lights glimmered here and there, points of gold, and the cornices of snow were sculpted into fantastic shapes. On the far pier, the *Hammond* sat parked, crewmen running pusher brooms along the path between her and the nearest tower. It was still enough to make the breath catch in her throat, and as she turned back, she caught a rueful smile on Caldwell's face.

"Be careful, Hocken," he said. "You don't want Atlantis to seduce you, too."

"Sir," she said, and he turned his back on the towers, heading determinedly for *Daedalus*.

The discussion had gone about as well as Guide had expected—which merely meant, he thought, with a wry and inward smile, that he had survived to think about it. A rift was developing among the lords of the zenana, he could feel it, a breach between those who would follow the Old One, and those who would urge the Queen to a more moderate policy. There was no agreement yet among the latter, no plan or consensus beyond the fear that finding Earth and its feeding ground would not prove a permanent solution to their problems. The time was not yet ripe, Guide judged, to make suggestions. Today it had been Noontide's day to protest, to plead to keep the agreements he had made for his former queen that had kept a human world fat and fertile in exchange for tribute. Ripe for the harvest, the Old One had said, and so Death had decided in the end. She had a fleet to feed, blade and clevermen in the thousands: Guide could not entirely blame her.

He leaned against one of the ship's pillars, feeling its life warm and strong against his shoulder; a good ship, Bright Venture, and nearly healed of all its damage. At the center table, Sky and another young blade were playing the stone-game, pieces clattering through their fingers. Farseer watched them, frowning slightly, and after a moment Guide caught the other commander's eye. He straightened then, moved toward the door, and knew without looking back that Farseer would follow. He reached the center of the empty reception chamber before he was overtaken.

I am — uneasy, Farseer said, bluntly.

This was as safe a space as any, open enough that they could see anyone approaching, and by tradition, at least, there were no recording devices here. Guide allowed himself a small smile, not untouched with malice. *Ah, for the days of our alliance…*

Farseer snarled. *Foolish — dangerous! — to say such a thing.*

But there is truth to it nonetheless, Guide answered, sweetly.

Of a sort. Farseer kept his tone low and even, did not look over his shoulder toward the drones guarding the door, and Guide silently approved his control. *This is ill-done, Guide.*

I agree. And yet we must feed.

But we need not Cull there. Farseer shook his head. *What are we if we do not keep our word?*

They are only human, Guide said.

And do we not prosper when the humans bring their tribute willingly? When we risk neither men nor Darts in the Culling? Farseer retorted. *They are intelligent enough, why not use it?*

I don't disagree, Guide said. *But that is not what our Queen decrees.*

No, Farseer said. *Nor what the Old One wishes.*

Gently, Guide said. He could hear someone coming, the shift of metal as the drones came to attention in the corridor outside, timed his words so that Farseer could not reply. *Still, a queen's favor doesn't last forever. And accidents do happen.*

Farseer gave a tight smile, and turned away as Ember entered the long room. A seed well sown, Guide thought, and waited.

Your pardon, Commanders, Ember said, bowing, and Farseer brushed past him without a word.

Well? Guide waited.

Your pardon, Ember said again.

I presume it is important, Guide said, *since you're here alone.*

Quicksilver is with Salt and Whiskey, Ember said. *It's of him I would speak.*

Guide laid his off hand on the cleverman's shoulder, a gesture exquisitely casual, easily broken, even as it allowed them to whisper skin to skin. *Well?*

Was it wise, lord, to tell him even so much as Michael's name?

Ember's face was thin and worn, and Guide wondered when he had last fed. More likely it was the effort of keeping up with McKay—a man incapable of moderation, Guide thought, and allowed his sympathy to show.

He works at the puzzle to the exclusion of all else, Ember said. *Oh, he does the queen's work, I see to that—and the energy shields are nearly complete, they'll function even without this ZPM—but he is a man obsessed. And heedless in the obsession.*

*McKay is like that," Guide said. *I did not expect otherwise.*

So closely linked, he could feel the surge of interest, the stirring train of thought, but Ember shook his head, smiling ruefully. *That is not my point.*

Let him be distracted, Guide said. *It will keep him from more clever ideas like this last attack on Atlantis.*

But if he remembers, Ember began, and stopped. *Then he dies, but not at your hands? I do not believe that will please the Lanteans any better.*

I don't want him dead, Guide answered. *As you say, that would make—other alliances—impossible. But if he remembers, even a little, he will have cause to keep quiet, and to seek allies among people he knows he has worked with before.*

Ember closed his eyes. *We are playing with fire.*

Of course. Where else are the treasures found?

Ember smiled at the old proverb, as Guide had meant, muscles easing a fraction, and Guide released him.

Watch him well, he said, and Ember reached for him, a breach of etiquette that stopped Guide in his tracks.

It is dangerous, Ember said, skin to skin, his off hand on Guide's wrist. *So dangerous, Guide. And you run too many risks already. Let me arrange an accident.*

No, Guide said, and gently freed himself. *It would do no good, and you know it.*

I do, Ember said, and bowed his head. *I will do as you command.*

CHAPTER FIFTEEN
Waiting By The Phone

JEANNIE was on her way back to her room, sandwich in hand, when she heard what sounded for all the world like a cat meowing. She was pretty sure that there weren't cats allowed in a military base in another galaxy, and yet it really sounded like a cat. She stopped before rounding the corner, hesitating. There were probably no dangerous aliens who sounded like cats, and yet she'd learned not to underestimate the weirdness of Meredith's work environment.

"Is anyone there?" she said. Not that it was probably the smartest move, because if there were meowing alien creatures around the corner who intended to have her for dinner, they probably weren't going to answer. She jumped as someone came around the corner, and then relaxed as she saw it was Ronon.

"Can you do something with this?" he said, holding out what in fact appeared to be a half-grown Siamese cat. It was hissing, its ears laid back, probably at the fact that it was being held at arm's length as if it might explode.

"Like what?" Jeannie said, reaching gingerly for the kitten. It yowled and writhed in alarm, but she managed to tuck it into a slightly less unhappy ball in her arms, and thankfully it didn't seem inclined to bite.

"It's McKay's," Ronon said. "Only it keeps getting out and attacking people."

"Attacking," Jeannie said.

"Lying in wait and then trying to bite people's ankles."

"Bite their ankles." She was trying really hard not to smile.

"Not very hard," he granted. "But it's annoying."

"Why don't I take the kitten back to Dr. Keller?" Jeannie suggested.

"That would be good," Ronon said, and left her trying to balance kitten and sandwich.

She managed by tucking the sandwich under her arm, and hoped she remembered where Jennifer had mentioned that her quarters were. The last thing she wanted at the end of a long day was to knock on some perfect stranger's door brandishing an angry kitten at them.

She pressed the door signal with her elbow and crossed her fingers as well as was possible under the circumstances. The door slid open to reveal Jennifer, who looked dismayed at the kitten.

"I'm sorry," she said, reaching for the kitten, who yowled at her plaintively and dug its claws into her sleeve. "Was he bothering you?"

"I think he scared Ronon," Jeannie said.

"Ah," Jennifer said. "Maybe not scared, but I don't think Ronon's a cat person." Jeannie stepped in to let the door close, and Jennifer detached the kitten with some difficulty and set it down on the floor. It leapt for the back of the sofa and perched there indignantly.

"Well, I can see that in a place like this, having anything jumping out at you might be a little spooky," Jeannie said.

"I can't seem to keep him in here," Jennifer said. "There's got to be some hole or crack or something that he's getting out through, but I can't find it. I think he wants to go hunt the pigeons."

"Pigeons?" Jeannie said.

"We picked up some accidental passengers back on Earth," Jennifer said. "They're probably going to wreak havoc with this planet's eco-system, assuming any of them survive, but we haven't really had time to worry about that very much."

"It's been a little busy," Jeannie said.

Jennifer nodded. "How's the security stuff coming?"

"Well, it's a process," Jeannie said. "I've found some things that Zelenka didn't think to look for, so that's a good thing. I'm just afraid we're only scratching the surface of how many things Meredith did to the computers here without telling anybody."

"He wasn't always really forthcoming about that kind of thing," Jennifer said.

"Isn't," Jeannie said pointedly.

"What?"

"Isn't always really forthcoming."

"Oh," Jennifer said, a hint of color coming into her cheeks. "Right, no, I just meant that when he was working on the computers before, he didn't tell anybody what he was doing, not that he won't —"

"Okay," Jeannie said.

"I mean, I know Ronon and Teyla are doing everything they can to find him. And Colonel Sheppard, although right now he can't exactly run around looking himself."

"And Dr. Zelenka," Jeannie pointed out.

"And Dr. Zelenka," Jennifer acknowledged, but she didn't sound like she found that particularly reassuring. "And we're still working on the retrovirus."

"And that's coming along well?"

"It's, you know, it's coming. Maybe not well. But we'll get there."

"Good," Jeannie said firmly.

"Actually, I was meaning to ask you a really big favor," Jennifer said.

Jeannie nodded encouragingly when Jennifer didn't immediately go on. It was probably just as well to try to get back onto the right foot with her future sister-in-law, or at least her future sister-in-law if Meredith managed to get up the nerve to propose and didn't screw it up again.

She wondered if she needed to point out to him that he should really get a new ring this time. Using a ring you bought to propose to your last girlfriend when you propose to your next girlfriend pretty much defined tacky.

"I don't know how long you're staying."

"Well, hopefully they'll find Meredith and I won't have to finish this incredibly irritating job, but if that doesn't happen first, I think we're going to have done everything we can think of to do in — I don't know, a few weeks? I mean, after a certain point, I've scraped the bottom of the barrel in terms of what I know about the way Meredith thinks."

"I was wondering if maybe you would be willing to take Newton back to Earth with you?" Jeannie must have looked blank, because Jennifer added, "The cat. His name is Newton. Or possibly Schrödinger, but I think we had more or less settled on Newton."

"He can't be that much trouble," Jeannie said.

"No, it's just… he's really more Rodney's cat, and I'm in the infirmary all day, when I'm not offworld, and right now with all the problems we've been having it's so dangerous here for a cat, and I feel like I can't take care of him the way that Rodney would have — "

"The way that Rodney would have *wanted*?"

Jennifer met her angry look without flinching. "The way that Rodney would have if he had been here when the Wraith invaded," she said. "It's not like I could take the kitten to the infirmary with me."

"If he'd been here, the Wraith wouldn't have invaded."

"That's my point," Jennifer said. "We had this idea that we could have a little more of a normal life out here, but it's just not working out that way."

"You don't think he's coming back," Jeannie said. There was a little curl of doubt in the pit of her own stomach, but she forced it ruthlessly back. Her brother was going to come back, and he was going to be all right, except that she was going to kill him for making her worry like this. "Or you think he's going to be, what? Stuck as some kind of monster forever?"

"That's not going to happen," Jennifer said, but her tone was too professional, the voice doctors used with dying patients. Her reassuring smile didn't reach her eyes.

"Is that what you really think, or what you think you're supposed to say?"

She thought the mask cracked just a little at that, frustration showing through. "What do you want me to say?"

"I want you to say you won't give up on my brother, no matter what," Jeannie said. "I want you to say that they're going to find him, and then you're going to fix him, and then he can take care of his own stupid cat."

"We will," Jennifer said. "I just don't know how long that's going to take. I can't keep saying 'oh, it's probably going to be tomorrow' when it's probably not going to be. Just for right now, we have to live with the situation the way it is, and I'm just not sure I'm cut out to be a single cat owner in Atlantis."

Jeannie let out a frustrated breath. "If we haven't found Meredith by the time I leave, we can talk about it, all right?"

"We'll probably have found him by then anyway," Jennifer said, but she didn't sound to Jeannie like she believed it.

Dick leaned back in the uncomfortable hotel room chair, phone to his ear, wondering if General O'Neill was going to answer his phone. Dick could have called his office, of course, and gotten a polite assistant who would tell him that the general was out and take a message. At least this way he'd get to leave voice mail.

"O'Neill," he heard finally, with a tone of resignation.

"General," Dick said, and tried not to sound relieved.

"Don't tell me they've decided something already," O'Neill said.

"They haven't," Dick said. "They're still scheduling the full set of hearings, and they've requested additional information. Right now I'm preparing a briefing on our process for documenting procedures."

"I'm impressed by how far removed that sounds from actually doing anything," O'Neill said.

"It's not what I'd call our central mission," Dick admitted.

"You didn't call me to ask about my process for documenting procedures. Which, if you're interested, consists of telling someone else they can do that crap. There are some advantages to the little stars on my uniform."

"Atlantis missed their scheduled weekly check-in," Dick said.

There was a momentary pause. "Maybe they overslept," O'Neill said.

"It's possible," Dick said. It was possible that there was some perfectly ordinary reason for the delay, but he didn't believe it, and he thought neither did O'Neill.

"What does Landry say?"

"General Landry says we should wait until they're twenty-four hours overdue before we start worrying."

"Whereas I like to worry early and avoid the rush," O'Neill said. "But I don't actually think we have a situation here yet. They've missed check-in times before."

"I know," Dick said. "It's probably some kind of technical problem on their end. Something involving the communications equipment, or a power failure."

"Probably."

"Of course, the last time we had a power failure in the main tower, it was because Michael and his hybrids were invading the city."

O'Neill sighed. "You understand there's not actually anything I can do about this, right?"

"I don't suppose you could arrange for us to be able to dial Atlantis?"

"Not a chance," O'Neill said. "Before I even think about recalling *Odyssey* and pulling her ZPM so that we can dial Pegasus, I'm going to need more than Atlantis being a few hours late checking in."

"I thought you'd say that," Dick said.

"Get some dinner," O'Neill said. "Try not to worry about Atlantis. Sheppard and Carter can handle things."

"I'm sure they're fine." He stared unhappily at the pattern the sunlight made on the hotel bedspread. "Still, I can't help thinking…"

"There's your problem."

"You think they're fine."

"I think that the best thing that you can do for your people is trust them to do their jobs, and let them trust that you're doing yours."

"Dealing with the IOA," Dick said.

"At least they're not actually going to suck the life from your body. Although it may feel like it."

"Believe me, it's not that I'm eager to have my life sucked, but... right now I'd rather be back there no matter what's going on than be sitting here a galaxy away waiting to see if they pick up the phone."

"Tell me about it," O'Neill said. "I've got to go. I'll be in touch."

The phone went quiet, and Dick slipped it back into his pocket. He went to the window, opening the curtains. The view of parking lot and mountains seemed alien, less familiar than silver towers rising against blue sea toward the sky.

He was staying in a hotel rather than SGC guest quarters because he'd wanted to be able to get away from the hearings and the round-the-clock activity that seemed to be normal operating procedure at Cheyenne Mountain. He'd had some idea of making the best of his enforced stay, eating in good restaurants and enjoying some of the things he hadn't had time to do when Atlantis was on Earth.

Instead, here he was sitting in his hotel room, thinking that he'd give anything to be back in Atlantis in his cold office eating something that came out of a plastic tray while Doctor McKay explained the latest incomprehensible technical problem that could potentially doom them all.

He'd worked with military personnel who felt that way for years, but he'd always thought he was immune to the appeal of facing constant danger in uncomfortable working conditions. Apparently not. He gazed down at the parking lot where his rental car was sitting.

After a moment, he pulled out his phone and dialed General Landry's number.

"I don't suppose you've heard anything," he said when Landry picked up.

"Not since the last time you called," Landry said. "I promise we'll let you know just as soon as we hear from your people."

Your people, Dick thought as he hung up. He was used to hearing it sound like a curse in the mouths of SGC personnel. For so many years, *your people* had meant the NID, and then the IOA, and he'd been perfectly aware that the men and women in uniform who he was overseeing viewed him as their enemy.

That wasn't what Landry and O'Neill meant now, though. The

Atlantis expedition members were his people, and he was responsible for them, at least for the moment. At least for a little while longer.

"Come on, Colonel Sheppard. Pick up the phone," he said, but his own phone stayed stubbornly silent.

CHAPTER SIXTEEN
Discoveries

WILLIAM held the last of the plates he'd recovered from the museum closet up to the light, checking for the cracks that had made a couple of them shatter when they were exposed to the heat of the lights, then slipped it into the improvised reader. He'd guessed right, they were part of the cataloging system, though it also looked as though they'd been superseded, if he was reading the dates right and if his assumption that sticking them in that closet meant that they were rarely used was actually correct. But at least they were going to be able to get some idea of the parts of the collection that weren't on display…

The airman that he'd borrowed from photo recon fiddled with the lenses, trying to get the image as clear as possible. They'd clean it up on the computer, of course, but you need to start with the best possible —

"Whoa," the airman said, and William blinked.

"Isn't that — ?"

The airman looked up at him. "That looks like a ZPM. Doesn't it, doc?"

"Yes."

It was a line drawing, like all the images, not a photograph — another reason to think this was an older listing, because it was clear from talking to Ronon that the Satedans had had fairly sophisticated photography. They'd set it wrong side up, rested it on the broad base, but the jagged shape, the veins of shading, were unmistakable. And, just like that, William thought, all their priorities changed.

"Get that onto the computer right away, please, and get it cleaned up. Forget about anything else for the moment, see if you can get the text as clear as possible." He touched his earpiece. "Dex. Ronon, are you there?"

"Lynn?" Ronon sounded wary, and William wondered belatedly what he'd interrupted. He hoped it wasn't a training session, or something else that couldn't be put off. "What's up?"

"I need your help translating one of the record plates we recovered," he said aloud.

"Now?"

"It's — rather important," William said, and crossed his fingers.

There was a little silence, and then Ronon said, "I'll be there."

William let out a breath he hadn't known he was holding, and the airman looked up from his monitor. "Shouldn't we let Dr. Zelenka know?"

"Not yet," William answered. "For all we know, the notes say something like 'if you ever find one of these, don't touch it' or 'we used to have this, but it was destroyed'. Let's be sure it's actually there first."

"OK, doc," the airman said, and reached for his mouse.

William watched him for a few minutes, seeing the Satedan letters — typed, with handwritten notes — come into focus. Ronon would be able to read what it said, would be able to tell them if they'd just found the ZPM to go with the hyperdrive crystal thing, and all of a sudden he couldn't stand still. He turned away from the console, paced the length of the room and back again, and the airman gave him a wary glance.

"Still working on it, sir."

"Sorry." William stuffed both hands in his pockets to keep from tapping his fingers. Coffee, he thought. If I go get coffee, by the time I get back, Ronon will be here and the file will be ready — "I'm going to the mess hall," he said. "Do you want coffee?"

The airman looked at his own half-full cup, and shook his head. "No, thanks, doc."

"Right."

It was far enough to the mess hall that he had to take a transport chamber, though a part of him just wanted to keep walking, burn off the nervous energy. But that would take too much time — it was a fine line he had to walk. But the airman would work better if he wasn't hovering over him the whole time.

It was mid-afternoon, and the mess hall was almost empty, just a couple of *Hammond's* crew talking over a laptop at the far table, one of the mess crew pushing a broom across the spotless floor. There were a few sandwiches left, and a wilted-looking salad; he ignored them, filled another mug of coffee. He hadn't consumed this much caffeine since his postdoc days, though then he'd been tougher about drinking it black. He added sugar and powdered creamer, and glanced out at the clouded sky. A few flakes of snow drifted by, but it was hard to tell if it was actually snowing, or if they were just blown from the buildings. Summer was supposed to be better, he reminded himself, and reached for the creamer again.

"You know that stuff explodes," Ronon said, and pointed to the jar.

William jumped in spite of himself, and gave the Satedan a narrow look. He was never entirely sure when the man was joking... "Oh, yes?"

Ronon nodded. "Sheppard showed me, on one of those how to blow things up shows he likes. They used it to shoot off a rocket."

"Really." William eyed the container for an instant, then, determinedly, added another spoonful to his coffee.

"I thought you were in a hurry," Ronon said. He had his own mug of something, William saw.

"I needed coffee," William said. "But I'm glad you're here. We may have found something."

"Something useful?"

"That depends on what you tell me it says."

They made their way back to William's lab in silence, Ronon steering them to a shortcut through what looked like a service corridor. It was the first one William had seen, and he made a note to come back and examine it later. He was pretty sure he'd find out more interesting things about the Ancients in their support areas than in the soaring public spaces.

He waved his hand at the lab's door sensor, checked abruptly as he saw Radek looking over the airman's shoulder. Ronon made an irritated noise, and dodged past him into the lab.

"I thought — " William began, and the airman gave him a guilty look.

"Dr. Zelenka called while you were gone, doc, asked what kind of progress we were making."

"And when he told me, I thought I would come down and see for myself," Radek said briskly.

"So what is it?" Ronon asked.

"There." William pointed to the screen. "We found — well, it looks a lot like microfiche, except stiffer — "

"Dataleaves," Ronon said, and William nodded.

"I expect so. Anyway, it seems to be part of the museum catalog, so we've been bringing it into the computers so we could analyze it properly. But today we found an entry that seems to describe a ZPM."

Ronon nodded, and the airman scooted out of his way so that he could scan the screen. William avoided looking at Radek, who was tapping his fingers lightly on the nearest table.

"You should have called me," Radek said, after a moment, and William sighed.

"There was no point in dragging you away from the new iris — how's that coming, by the way? — until I knew whether it was a real reference, or, I don't know, their head archeologist's wish list."

"If there is any chance that we might find a ZPM, I should be informed," Radek said.

"I wasn't sure that's what this was," William answered. "It might be anything."

"The drawing is too accurate to be guesswork," Radek said.

"Hey." Ronon looked up from the screen. "Do you want to know?"

"Yes," Radek said, and William nodded.

"What does it say?"

Ronon glanced at the screen again. "It says 'this artifact was found in the Ancestors' presumed guidepost installation on Ascretta' — do you want me to read all of this?"

"Yes," William said.

"Just the important points," Radek said. "Please."

Ronon nodded. "OK. The important points. The chief curator found this on Ascretta, he says it was glowing very faintly when found, and it's been stored in the museum ever since." He tilted his head to read the handwritten note that ran up the side of the typed entry. "Somebody else moved it to more secure storage thirty years ago, and it looks like it's still there."

Radek said something under his breath in Czech — anatomically unlikely, William thought — and Ronon nodded again.

"Sheppard's going to have to rethink what he was going to say to Cai."

John drummed his fingers on Woolsey's desk, wondering if he could justify going down to check on how the new iris was coming along. Radek had reconfigured the design to make better use of the titanium they'd gotten from Sateda, which meant they could stop racking their brains to figure out where they could get more. He wouldn't learn anything else that he couldn't find out by calling down there on the radio, and for that matter, he was pretty sure that what he'd learn by doing either one was 'we're working on it'. All the same, he was beginning to find himself sympathizing with Rodney's claustrophobia. Every morning he came in here, the office seemed smaller.

"Hey, Sheppard," Ronon said from the doorway. "Got a minute?"

"Sure," John said, standing up gratefully, and then sat back down as Radek followed Ronon in, laptop under his arm. "You don't mean 'let's have lunch', do you?"

"We need to go back to Sateda," Ronon said.

John ran a hand through his hair. "Look, I know how you feel about this," he said. "But we got what we needed, and we're just not in a position to help out right now. For one thing, the Genii are about the only people who like us these days — "

"For a value of 'like' that includes holding Carson hostage," Radek said.

"I'm not happy about that either," John pointed out. "But the other thing is, we've got our own problems right now. Even if we wanted to try to kick the Genii off Sateda by force, we can't spare any troops to do it as long as we've got the Wraith breathing down our necks. And the Genii have the best information network around, which means they're one of our best chances for finding Rodney. When Woolsey gets back, maybe he can talk to them, but for right now — "

"I do not think we can wait," Radek said. He set his laptop down on John's desk, its screen showing a sketch of a familiar shape surrounded by writing that looked Satedan.

"Is that what I think it is?"

"We believe it is a ZPM," Radek said. "It may still be in storage in the Satedan museum we visited earlier. The descriptions from when it was found suggest that it may not be entirely depleted. Of course there is no way to know how much power remains, but at this point any amount would be better than none."

"We could maybe run the shield," Ronon said. "At least in an emergency. We could power the weapons chair."

"We think we could *maybe* power the weapons chair," John said.

"That's better than knowing we can't."

John knew he'd be saying the same things if he were the one on the other side of the desk. He sincerely wished he was. He'd rather it be somebody else's job to argue that they couldn't afford to get on the bad side of the Genii. As far as John was concerned, the Genii could stand to make more of an effort not to get on the bad side of them.

"What do you think they're going to want for it?" John asked.

Ronon looked at him like he thought the answer should be obvious. "For you to kick the Genii out."

"That's a pretty steep price."

"Not for what the ZPM's worth."

John frowned. "To them, it's an interesting paperweight that used to belong to the Ancients."

"Not to us. You planning to cheat them?"

"You said yourself they didn't have any use for this stuff."

Ronon's expression was stormy. "That doesn't make it worthless and you know it. If they knew how much we needed it —"

"If we tell them how much we need it, they're going to set a price we can't pay."

"If you can get the Genii out, that'll be good enough," Ronon said.

"The Genii are stealing artifacts from the Satedans that cannot be replaced," Radek said. "If they have their way, they will take possession of the entire Satedan homeworld. Are we to say that this is acceptable behavior in our allies?"

John rubbed his forehead. "I don't think it's okay, no."

"Then do the right thing," Ronon said.

"We may well find that the Genii are willing to negotiate," Radek added.

John frowned. He'd wanted them to work as a team. It was good that they were putting up a united front. He just hadn't expected to be on the outside of that, and it stung unexpectedly much.

"All right," he said after a moment. "You're right that we need the ZPM, and you're right that we can't let the Genii screw over the Satedans without even trying to stop them. We've got Teyla for the negotiations, but the Genii have problems dealing with women as equals. Normally I'd say that's their problem, but it's not going to help Teyla get any concessions out of them. Sora's the only one who'll actually take her seriously, and Sora hates her."

"So handle the negotiations yourself," Ronon said. "You're in command of Atlantis, and you used to be military commander — "

"I am the military commander," John said. "This is temporary."

"Whatever," Ronon said. "The point is, they take you seriously. Lorne, too."

"Lorne's not even out of the infirmary yet," John said. "Keller's talking about letting him out on crutches in the next couple of days, but if we're off negotiating with the Genii, he's going to need to stay here and hold down the fort."

"We could hold the negotiations here," Radek offered.

"We've got enough problems without the Genii wandering around the city," John said. "Not that I don't trust Radim, but I'd still rather he didn't hear all about our problems with the iris."

"We may be getting ahead of ourselves," Radek said. "Let us first see whether the ZPM even exists, and whether it retains any power. If so, we will see what Cai wants in exchange."

"Take Teyla and Dr. Lynn and go check it out," John said. "If you find the ZPM and you're right about what Cai wants, you can tell him that we're willing to try to set up a meeting with the Genii to talk about the situation."

"That's not a lot," Ronon said.

"It's what we've got," John said. "The one thing we may have going for us is that Radim isn't Sora's biggest fan."

Ronon frowned. "So why is she running this operation?"

"I don't know, but I'm beginning to suspect," John said. "You were military on Sateda. What would your people have done with an officer who's too good at what she does to throw her out, but who has a problem following orders and drives her commanding officers crazy?"

"We called it 'being posted to a coal town'," Ronon said. "Somewhere out of the way where you couldn't screw anything up too badly." He smiled a little. "Like being sent to go fly scientists around in Antarctica."

"That's what I'm thinking," John said. "This way she's out of Radim's hair, and she isn't in a position to make trouble by mixing it up with us. At least, that's what Radim probably thought."

"He thought wrong," Ronon said.

John nodded. "I think he's about to figure that out."

It wasn't easy to search the hive's databases, particularly not for a human name that was hard to transliterate into proper symbols. It had taken him several days just to solve that problem — not the meaning of the word, which had seemed logical, nor had the clevermen used the usual way of transcribing human names, but a separate system, set apart, reserved for Lanteans and the Ancients — and then, of course, that search had led to the dead ends of denied access. Interestingly, though, they were all in the biological databases, and he had figured out Ember's codes long ago. They were insufficient — Ember was not of this hive, did not have the full access — but at last he had figured out a work-around, and wormed his way in.

And all for this. He stared at the screen that glowed in the corner of his quarters, baring his teeth in a silent snarl. Page after page of notes on a virus this Michael had created, a variant of the Hoffan plague that left humans tainted, deadly fodder; someone had been working on a way to reverse the changes, but had gotten nowhere, and the research seemed to have been abandoned. Perhaps it had been Dust's work, and that thought sent another pang of grief through him. One more thing he could not remember, one more thing gone wrong…

He pushed that aside, touched keys to re-sort his queries. Here was information on attacks — Michael had certainly been a thorn in their side, though it seemed he had held more malice toward Atlantis. It had been the Lanteans who had killed him in the end, hunted him down and destroyed his base — and that, he thought abruptly, wasn't right. That wasn't how it had happened. He frowned, but couldn't bring up the rest of that memory, either. There was only the nagging certainty that there had been more to the tale.

But that made no sense, any more than it made sense for Guide to have given him the name. A name to conjure with, he had said, but Quicksilver couldn't see the connection. Snarling again, he worked his way out of the database, careful to erase his tracks, launched another search on the name, excluding the virus this time. There were fewer connections, but still too many to review before Ember would return to their quarters. He hesitated, trying to decide, and finally chose the earliest reference. The data blossomed on the screen, unfolding to a cascade that settled to a slow and readable progress; it was a warning, Quicksilver saw, shared among all the hives. Michael had been Wraith, and had betrayed his hive — no, he had been changed by the Lanteans, made briefly human, and had been so warped, so twisted, that he had allied with them against the Queen who had rescued him. She was dead at his hands, and all Wraith were warned against him.

Quicksilver shuddered. Was that—could that have been what happened to him? Was that what Guide had been trying to tell him, that he had been made human in his captivity? Drained of his life, his true nature, everything that made him Wraith, recreated as one of the kine that existed only to be fed upon? Surely that could not be—it couldn't be true, or the Queen and commanders would not, could not, trust him this far, could never have allowed him to lead the attack on Atlantis, to seize the ZPM for his Queen…

Yet the Lanteans had called him by a human name, said they would help him. A trick, to lure him back? The humans had killed Michael in the end, and he had been their most bitter enemy. Surely they would not try that experiment a second time—

He shook himself, entering new codes. The Lanteans would not repeat so drastic a failure, he was certain of it. McKay was smarter than that, and he was head of sciences. It was his job to be sure such things did not happen twice. There was little more, the same warnings repeated, an analysis of the retrovirus the humans has used, and the causes of its failure. He bared teeth at the screen again, but there was no time remaining. Ember would return soon, and he would need to have erased all signs of his presence by then.

By the time the door opened to admit the other cleverman, he was well away from the console, fiddling idly with a handful of game pieces. *Ember!* he said, and hoped he sounded welcoming.

Ember gave him a wary look. *What now?*

Is that fair? Quicksilver paused. He had been driving his technicians hard; perhaps it would be politic to admit it. *Well, maybe it is, but listen, I need you to tell me something. If you know it, that is—*

Ember lowered himself onto the low seat opposite him, his eyes automatically sweeping the board. *Are you planning to play that pattern among the blades?*

What? No, probably not. Quicksilver frowned.

I would advise against it, Ember murmured, his attention still on the stones. *Yes, definitely not workable—*

Will you stop? Quicksilver glared, and only then wondered if the other had been trying to distract him. *I've been hearing about this—about someone called Michael. Do you know anything?*

What everyone does, Ember said, wary again. *It's not a pretty story, Quicksilver. It will not please you.*

Tell me anyway, Quicksilver said.

Ember picked up a pair of stones, rolling them between his fingers as though they were dice. *Death has forbidden us to speak of him.*

In general, or just to me?

Ember looked up sharply at that, as though he would deny it, and then his mouth curved into a wry smile. *If I speak, you must never say I told you.*

I wouldn't, Quicksilver said, and Ember tossed the stones aside. *Very well.*

Once before we slept — but this happened after we woke, after we were wakened and grew hungry. Once, then, there was a blade whose mind was the last flash of light at sunset, a blade with the heart of a cleverman, as they are often bred in the hives of the Stormdark queens. He was strong and brave, a leader risen to high trust over a hundred years and more. The Lanteans came to his queen's feeding ground — she was the cloud that shrouds the highest hills, dead now a year and more — and she sent Lastlight to drive them away. It was a trap, of course, and Lastlight stayed with the rearguard to see his men safe away. The Lanteans shot him, wounded him near to dying, and the cruiser was forced to leave him there. The one who told me this wept then, for they were at fault for what happened after.

For Lastlight did not die. He had been badly wounded, yes, but he had fed recently, and he began to heal. The Lanteans examined him and decided he would do to make a trial of their latest weapon. They injected him with a retrovirus that suppressed much of his genetic code, and over time and with much pain he became like them. Everything that makes us Wraith withered and failed, and he was left without memory, trapped in a body that seemed human. And the Lanteans told him he was one of them, a human warrior injured in battle, and for a time he believed them.

But they were not as skilled in the workings of our biology as they thought they were, and Lastlight was strong, and his true self haunted his dreams. He deduced what had been done, and broke free of the drug, escaping through the Stargate to find our people.

And there he was unlucky a second time, for the hive that found him was of the queen whose mind was a wind of darkness. You do not remember her, I think, but she was a power in her day. Once she had daughters bound to her by oath and blood, once a thousand blades fought in her name, but in the War her blades were decimated, and her daughters fell away, until she had only her hive and her reputation to bargain with, and she resented the diminishment. Nightwind took him in, and in his story she saw a way to regain her former standing. She tricked the Lanteans into giving her the formula for the retrovirus they used on Lastlight, and then betrayed them, taking the knowledge they had given her to seek for Earth.

But she was of the old ways, and could not bring herself to treat Lastlight as anything but broken, tainted stock, and her men followed her lead. And Lastlight had been foremost among Highcloud's blades, pallax, a man of standing in the zenana. Rather than endure such treatment, when the Lanteans came hunting them — as he had surely known they would — he allied with them, and it was his help that turned the tide in their favor. The hive was destroyed, and the queen herself was killed.

Of course the Lanteans did not keep their word. They drugged him again, along with the other survivors, and marooned them on a world without a Stargate, without any way to contact their own kind. But Lastlight was still determined — I think, perhaps, he was already a little mad by then, twice transformed against his will — and he managed to escape. He found his way back to Highcloud, to his own hive, and begged sanctuary, but he had killed Nightwind, and that was unforgivable. Highcloud banished him, branded him regicide. He became an enemy to Wraith and human alike, killing without thought or reason, and the Lanteans killed him in the end.

Quicksilver caught his breath. *Is that what was done to me, while I was captive? You have seen what Dust recorded, is that why I can't remember?*

You were not made human, Ember said. *That I do know.*

There was something in his tone that made Quicksilver believe him, and he turned away, pacing like a man caged. If he had not been made human, what then? Why would the Lanteans pretend to know him, why did he dream of Atlantis? He stopped abruptly. If he had not been made human — if the Lanteans did know him, if Michael was the key, as Guide had said—was he himself somehow human? He turned his feeding hand palm up, seeing the mouth tightly closed: real, unmistakable, and yet—if he were not truly Wraith, it would explain too many things.

No. He closed his mind tight against the thought, hoping Ember had not sensed his doubt, this new fear that consumed him. If it were true, he could not betray that he had guessed; if it wasn't, then he would be thought mad for conceiving of such a thing. There were things he could do to prove it—Dust's records, for one; if he could find his way into those files, that would give an answer. That would be the next step. And surely, surely, it would not be true. He clutched his thoughts, his fear, tighter still, looked up to see Ember watching him, head tipped to one side. For an instant, there was something monstrous about him, teeth too sharp, eyes too hard, thoughts unreadable behind the pale mask that was his face.

I said you would not like this story, Ember said.

CHAPTER SEVENTEEN
Negotiations

LADON Radim clasped his hands more tightly behind his back
as yet another militia unit made its way past the reviewing stand.
Normally, the largest caverns were cold, but today, filled with marching men and the small, happy crowd, the pace was uncomfortably
warm. He felt a trickle of sweat creep down his spine, felt his eyes
and mind wandering. He made himself focus again on the parade
of sweaty, half-trained farm boys marching eight abreast. That was
to fit the dimensions of the cavern; what other multiples were possible? He conjured up alternate formations, calculated the number
of men — standing perched impossibly on each other's shoulders,
and therefore discounting heads — that it would take to fill the cavern's volume, calculated the height of the average men and then the
dimensions of the parade ground in that unit of measurement. Still,
he was afraid his boredom would show all too clearly on the televi-
sion feed, and he composed his face to what he hoped would pass for
thoughtful interest. At least his speech was done, carefully worked
out and, he thought, well received, at least by the audience here. His
intelligence operatives would brief him soon enough on the more
general reaction, what the average Genii was saying in cavern and
farmhouse, but he didn't think he'd be surprised. He had always
been good at the balancing act, nudging people toward the outcome
he wanted while persuading them that nothing was really changing.

He glanced sideways at his sister Dahlia, tall and straight-backed
in her severe uniform, the double spiral of the Chief of Sciences at her
collar her only jewelry. There was the faintest of smiles on her face as
she looked across at the Elite Guard in their tight trousers. She might
as well enjoy the view, Ladon allowed, and stifled a yawn.

"Excuse me, Chief," Ambrus said softly at his elbow, voice almost
drowned in the tramp of feet.

That was never a good sign, and it took all of Ladon's willpower to
keep from turning toward his aide. "Yes?"

"The Sateda project has been compromised."

Ladon bit back a curse that would have made even Dahlia raise an eyebrow. "Compromised how?"

"The Lanteans know we are on Sateda," Ambrus said.

"Has anyone been shot?" Ladon asked.

"Not yet," Ambrus answered. "Apparently there's been no direct confrontation, but the Satedans weren't going to conceal our presence."

"And the current position?"

"The Lanteans have withdrawn," Ambrus said. "And Sora has been ordered to stay in camp for now."

The Lanteans wouldn't attack without provocation, Ladon thought. He was reasonably sure he could count on that. Sora was, still and always, a loose cannon, but if the Lanteans had pulled out, all the reports suggested that the remaining Satedans would go out of their way not to start a fight. Not 'remaining', the *returned* Satedans: he was going to need to remember that phrasing. Not for the first time, he directed a vague breath of gratitude toward any supernatural being that might exist for the fact that Ushan Cai had been unable to persuade any of the surviving Satedan military units to return to their homeworld.

"Reiterate to Sora that she's to keep her head down. No contact with the Lanteans — with anyone — unless it's completely unavoidable." Ladon kept his eyes fixed on the parade, mercifully drawing toward its end.

"Yes, Chief," Ambrus said, backing away, and Dahlia glanced sideways.

"Trouble?"

"Later," Ladon said, and she looked away, frowning.

They weren't able to return to the Chieftain's suite until well after dark, and by then Ladon's head was buzzing from round after round of toasts. There was no way of avoiding them, no way of faking, either, without losing respect, and he tugged at the chain that opened the surface ventilator. The cold night air spilled down, smelling of rain and dead leaves, and he stood for a moment in the draft, letting it clear his thoughts. Ambrus was already brewing tea on the spirit burner, and Dahlia loosened the neck of her formal coat.

"So," she began, and Ladon answered, "Sora."

"Not again." Dahlia had kicked off her polished shoes, and was massaging her toes, looked up with a scowl.

"I'm afraid so," Ambrus said. He poured her a small brandy — she had retired with the other ladies, had missed most of the drinking — and turned back to the tea service.

There was a silence, broken only by the hiss of the lamp and the murmur of the water as it came to a boil. Ambrus finished the cup, but Ladon waved it irritably aside.

"Yes, something has to be done," he said, and Dahlia nodded.

"It does," she agreed, and behind her Ambrus nodded in turn.

"She's too much of a liability."

Reluctantly, Ladon pulled himself away from the fall of cool air, let himself drop into the patched armchair. It was one of the few pieces of furniture that had been his own, and the cushions were worn to his shape. He leaned back, letting his head rest on the cushions. He had known Sora a long time, had served with her under Kolya, and he had always known this day would come.

"So."

"Do you remember Jennet Sarbres?" Dahlia asked.

Ladon blinked. "No — kin of Sarbres Tel?"

"Her father," Dahlia said. "He's still chief of mines in the western province, but Harkis is going to propose him as his successor."

Ladon nodded.

"Jennet is engaged to Faber," Dahlia said. "The announcement will be official tomorrow, but she was showing the bracelets to everyone in the withdrawing room."

"So," Ladon said again, and heard the weariness in his own voice. Faber Marz was the reason Sora had lived as long as she had: the colonel was a rising man in the Genii army, with connections and the skill to back them up, and a needed ally. Sora had also been his mistress for the last year — but if he was engaged to a politically important woman, he wasn't in any position to protect Sora. In fact, he'd probably be relieved to have the problem solved for him… Ladon couldn't help feeling a little sorry for her, hot-headed and obsessed with her father's death, but he buried the treacherous sympathy.

"There's plenty of cause for arrest," Ambrus said, tentatively, and Ladon shook his head. The last thing he wanted was a show trial, particularly on the kind of trumped-up charges they'd have to bring against her. He owed her that much — owed Dahlia, too, not to bring down one of the few other women who had held any official position.

"An accident," he said, and saw Dahlia's brief, rueful smile. "Arrange an accident."

"Yes, Chief," Ambrus said, and offered the tea again. This time Ladon took it, cradling the cup in both hands, and Dahlia sighed.

"I'm sorry."

"Don't be," Ladon said. "We knew it was coming."

The telephone buzzed in its alcove, and Ambrus moved to answer it. Ladon watched incuriously, lifted an eyebrow as Ambrus turned back to face him.

"It's the Lanteans, Chief. They want to talk to you."

"Of course they do," Ladon said. "Tell them it's the middle of the night here, and unless it's an emergency, you're not going to wake me. Find a mutually agreeable time — sometime when it's daylight here — and get back to me."

"Yes, Chief," Ambrus said again, and stepped back into the alcove.

"Sateda was always a gamble," Dahlia said.

"Yes." Ladon took a sip of the cooling tea, the brandy curdling in his stomach. "But — you said it yourself. We need to get our new ship battleworthy, and Sateda has the artifacts."

"I did say it." Dahlia sighed again. "And it's still true. We're making progress, but — it's slow going. Maybe Woolsey will be reasonable."

"Maybe," Ladon said, but he knew she heard the doubt.

The team from Atlantis came through the gate to Sateda on their guard this time, but there were no Genii uniforms visible in the square. It was near dark, with lights visible in some of the windows, and the smell of cooking strong in the air. Ronon lifted his head, testing the familiar odors.

"That smells good, whatever it is," Lynn said.

"We are not here for dinner," Radek said a little shortly.

"Let us find Ushan Cai," Teyla said in the tones of a children's teacher telling everyone that it was time to paint pictures of happy animals. Standing here in the familiar square, the memory was unexpectedly vivid, his old schoolroom and the chalky brightness of tempera paints wet on the paintbrush.

Ronon shook his head to clear it. "Let's," he said.

Cai was in the old hotel, eating dinner with several other men and women, but he stood at once when he saw them. "Ronon," he said. "Come, share our dinner if you will."

Teyla glanced at Ronon, ready to take her cue from him about whether the offer was meant to be taken or just polite words. Lynn did as well, which surprised Ronon a little, since in his experience most of the Earth people tended to do whatever they thought was polite without asking questions.

"We'd like that," he said, and took one of the empty chairs. The rest of the team followed him, and although he suspected Radek thought they were wasting their time, it didn't show. That made him think of Rodney, who'd have made his impatience clear enough even if he didn't say anything about it. It wasn't the same without him, even if it meant they didn't have Teyla shooting Rodney warning looks across the table.

He waited until someone had found them plates and served them stew that looked to be made with whatever from offworld would store well, sausage and root vegetables over cooked grains. Radek and Teyla were more earnest than effective in their attempts to eat with proper sticks instead of the Lanteans' forks, but Lynn managed well, although he held them strangely.

"We came to talk about making another trade," Ronon said.

Cai smiled, although it wasn't entirely an easy gesture. "And here I was hoping you'd had a chance to consider our request already."

"We can talk about that," Ronon said. "But we think there's something in the museum that we could really use." He nodded at Radek, and Radek put his laptop on the table to show Cai the picture of the ZPM. Cai looked both at the picture and at the computer.

"We found records that suggest that this device may be somewhere in storage at the museum," Radek said.

"Of course it's possible that it's not still intact," Lynn added. "It's apparently a fragile device, but I think the museum curators would have recognized that simply looking at it. They may well have taken sufficient precautions for it to have survived, especially since it doesn't seem to have been on display at the time of the Wraith attack."

"It's pretty enough," Cai said casually. "What is it?"

Radek hesitated, only for a moment, but Ronon didn't think Cai missed it. "A power source," he said. "We call it a ZPM, a zero-point module."

Cai frowned for a moment, probably trying to make the connection between the word and the phrase before recognizing that "ZPM" must be an abbreviation in someone else's alphabet. Then he nodded and said, "What kind of a power source?"

"One that can be used to power parts of the city of the Ancestors," Teyla said. "It was specially designed by them to be used in their devices."

Cai gave her a trader's smile. "You mean that it won't work for us here. I have to tell you, though, right now power is our greatest challenge. We're relying on coal, and that takes people to mine and transport. If this device could supply electric power — "

"I think there is no way for it to interface with your electrical power system," Radek said. "Please do not take offense, but it is simply not advanced enough. Neither are the systems on our own world. The Ancients had amazing technology."

"If you could connect it, though, make it power our systems," Cai said. "How much power are we talking about? How long to light the center city, or to heat it?"

Radek glanced at Ronon, looking like he was torn about how honestly to answer that.

"It may not be possible to know until we know how fully charged the ZPM is," Teyla said.

"But suppose you find it charged enough for it to be useful to you," Cai said. "Otherwise, there's no reason to talk of trading, is there?"

Radek let out a breath. "It is highly unlikely that it could be used to power your city at all," he said. "The amount of power required to light and heat this small part of the city would be very small compared to the ZPM's capacity, yes, but creating an interface that would conserve the power in transmission and not cause the ZPM to overload destructively in the process… I am not sure it can be done."

"Overload as in explode," Cai said, not sounding particularly daunted by the prospect. Steam power generation wasn't exactly risk-free, although it didn't have the potential that some of the Ancestors' stuff had to blow up large parts of cities.

"It could happen," Radek said. "I would not recommend playing around with it if you have no idea what you are doing."

"It's possible that there are improvements to your power generation that we could help you make," Lynn said. "Hydroelectric power — do you use dams for power generation?"

"You mean Avedan wheels? Water wheels? We've replaced those

in most industries with steam turbines."

"No, using water-powered turbines as a means of electrical power generation. I'm no expert, but we have experts, and there may be other improvements we could suggest as well."

"That's worth finding out more about," Cai said. "I'll see when my engineers have time for that. But I think there's only one thing we want in exchange for letting you continue to rifle through our historic treasures for things that might prove useful to you."

"I can't promise we'll fight the Genii for you," Ronon said.

Cai looked undaunted. "Then who can promise that?"

"Colonel Sheppard is willing to set up a meeting between you and the leaders of the Genii," Teyla said. "He believes we may be able to help you to come to some peaceful resolution to the situation."

"Only if they'll agree to leave without us putting up a fight," Cai said. "I don't think that's very likely."

"We might be able to make a deal," Ronon said.

"We're not willing to pay extortion to the Genii," Cai said. "If they get our artifacts and our goods without even having to work to salvage them, we're no better off than we are with them camped here robbing the dead."

"It may not be a matter of payment," Teyla said. "We may be able to persuade the Genii that it is in their interest to deal fairly with the Satedans."

Cai considered her for a moment. "You mean you've got something to hold over them."

"We can end our alliance with them," Ronon said.

"I had not heard that the Lanteans and the Genii were allies."

"Our interests have often been similar," Teyla said. "I believe the Genii would like for that to continue to be true."

"I'm not sure it'll do any good," Cai said. He shook his head, looking Ronon and the team over, and then shrugged. "But I don't see that it'll do any harm, either. Tell Colonel Sheppard that we're willing to talk to the Genii."

"We need to have the meeting here," Ronon said. "The Genii don't like having visitors, and we don't want the Genii running around the city of the Ancestors." He wasn't planning to explain the reasons behind the last, and he hoped Cai would take it as an insult to the Genii and not to him.

"Nor do we want them here, but we seem to have them already despite our wishes," Cai said. "Tell Colonel Sheppard that the Genii are welcome here to negotiate as our guests. With the understanding that guests eventually outstay their welcome."

"I'll tell him," Ronon said. "We'll leave a radio here so that we can get in touch with you once we've heard from the Genii."

"I'll be waiting to hear from you," Cai said.

Radek and Lynn both looked intensely disappointed. "I don't suppose we could just have another look around the museum, with your people along, of course?" Lynn tried.

"I think that's not a good idea," Cai said. "I wouldn't want you to run into the Genii and wind up in a situation with them that might jeopardize your alliance. Or that might end with your valuable power source in Genii hands."

Ronon felt he couldn't very well say that they'd fight the Genii if the Genii tried to take the ZPM, not when he wasn't promising to fight the Genii for trying to take over Sateda. He tried not to grit his teeth. Diplomacy was something Teyla was good at, something Dr. Weir had been good at. He'd rather be out in the field with something to shoot.

His only small comfort was that he was pretty sure that Sheppard felt exactly the same way.

Sora paced at the edge of her camp, staring at the now-familiar wreckage of the street in hopes of catching some sign of movement. Ambrus had made it abundantly clear that he intended to keep them bottled up while Radim made nice to the Lanteans, but of course if the Satedans came poking around she'd have to run them off. That might get things moving again.

It was maddening having so much to do and being unable to do any of it. She'd never been good at being idle, not since she was a child tagging along after her father, learning to work machinery and to fight like a boy when most of the other girls were playing with dolls. It was tiresome enough having to play farmer's daughter when they had visitors from offworld, weaving flowers in her hair and letting silly fools like Teyla Emmagan tell her how much she'd grown.

She tried to put both Teyla and the Lanteans out of her mind. They were here to scavenge too, as far as she could tell, and hopefully once they'd found whatever they wanted, they'd go back to Atlantis and stay there. It was hard not to dwell on what they might be making off with, though. It was like them to think that any artifact of the Ancients belonged by right to them.

She'd explained as patiently as she could to Ambrus that she couldn't afford to wait. The museum was a treasure trove of devices that they'd be able to use as soon as Radim's experiments in activating the Ancient gene paid off. Or as soon as they found someone who could use Ancient technology naturally and who could be trusted to work for them. The devices could take them years ahead in their development of weapons, or make Radim's space program more than a long-term gamble.

The problem was that Radim was too narrowly focused on his own plans to see how anyone else's ideas could fit into them. That was the problem when scientists presumed to be soldiers as well. He was more sensible than Kolya had ever been, that she would be the first to admit, but at least Kolya had never been over-cautious.

A movement caught her eye, and she drew her pistol in one smooth motion, but it was only one of the birds that seemed to be everywhere in the ruined city. She aimed and fired, and the bird dropped like a stone.

There was the sound of feet hurrying toward her, and she turned as Jan came up behind her, shouldering his rifle to cover the empty street. "No excitement," she said. "Just a little target practice."

He lowered his rifle, but didn't visibly relax. "There's a call for you on the radio."

She let out a frustrated breath. "I hope this means we can get back to work." She thought it was more likely that it would be another reminder to stay within the boundaries of their camp and do nothing. She had already pointed out that their supply of fresh water wouldn't make that practical forever, apparently to no effect.

She ducked into the tent where the radio was set up and impatiently waved the radio operator out. She adjusted the knobs to tame the old set's perpetually annoying crackle and picked up the transmitter. "Sora Tyrus reporting."

"Sora, this is Ladon Radim," said the voice on the other end, and Sora's hand clenched on the transmitter in the effort not to swear. Having the chief himself on the line couldn't mean a single thing that she was going to like.

"Chief Radim," Sora said. "What news of the Lanteans? Have they finished their business on Sateda?"

"I've just spoken with the Lanteans," Radim said. "They want us to sit down with Ushan Cai and his people and negotiate our respective interests there."

"I hope you told them no," Sora said.

"We're scheduling the meeting now," Radim said. "I'll be bringing some of my people, and of course you'll be present to explain our activities so far."

"That's —" Sora began. She took a deep breath and strove for calm. "I'm sure you're already aware that this is only going to give Cai's 'provisional government' more legitimacy. I'm just wondering why you don't seem to think that's a problem."

"I think it's unfortunate," Radim said. "But I think right now it can't be helped. We'll have plenty of opportunity to present our case that the Satedans are private individuals with no claim to anything but their own personal property."

"'Present our case'? To the Lanteans? Who made them the judge?"

"It's called diplomacy," Radim said, his tone more sharp than usual. "You may have heard of it. In any event, this is not a request. You'll remain in camp and do your best not to antagonize the Satedans until we can arrange a time for the meeting."

"Yes, of course," Sora said. She sat fuming for a moment after she'd silenced the radio set, and then told herself there was no use in expecting Radim to be reasonable.

She'd have to work out a way of getting their hands on the artifacts. And if Radim couldn't appreciate that, there were certainly other people — highly-placed people — who would. The thought made her tired, though. She didn't want to start playing that game again.

Part of the appeal of Kolya had been that it seemed like he might actually hold onto the reins for a while if he ever managed to take them. Then they could all have spent their time doing things that actually got results rather than endlessly maneuvering for power. It was a waste of time, when time was the one thing they didn't have, with the Wraith threat growing stronger and new horrors like the Replicators appearing every time it seemed they might be getting the upper hand.

But if that was the game they had to play, she didn't intend to lose.

CHAPTER EIGHTEEN
Diplomatic Mission

LORNE stretched uncomfortably in his office chair, wishing there were some way to sit that didn't make his leg hurt. Just then, there didn't seem to be any way to do anything that didn't make his leg hurt, so he figured that was a lost cause. Still, he wished the Ancients had dedicated just a little of their technological know-how to figuring out how to make really good adjustable chairs.

Somebody knocked on the door, and he called, "Come in," trying to shift into something resembling a work-like posture as the door opened. "Colonel Carter."

"Hi, Major," she said, with a smile that looked genuine. "I see you're up and around."

"More or less," he said. "Sorry, ma'am, I would…" He gestured apologetically in the direction of standing. "It'll just take me a minute."

"God, no, don't get up," Carter said. "I was on crutches once, I know what a pain that is." She glanced ruefully at his cast. "Same leg as last time, huh?"

"Yep. I should get some kind of a discount this time."

"I don't know. Janet always used to threaten to charge extra if we came in with the same injury more than once. She said she was getting awfully tired of the Colonel's knees."

"I remember that," Lorne said. "She kept everybody in line."

"She did," Carter said. Her smile was sad. She and Dr. Fraiser had been friends, Lorne remembered, until Dr. Fraiser was killed on a rescue mission gone bad. He'd been with SG-11 then, the third SG-11. The first two teams with that designation had been lost in action, killed to a man. He suspected her thoughts were running along the same lines, because she added, "Hey, any one you walk away from, right?"

"I'm not complaining," Lorne said, although he thought 'limp away from' might be more accurate at the moment. And maybe for longer than that, but he was trying very hard not to think like that. It was probably going to heal fine, although he was pretty sure this time he had the fun of physiotherapy waiting for him once the cast came off. "I just wish I could be out there doing more."

"You should take it easy," Carter said. "Under normal circumstances, you'd have earned yourself a trip home to recuperate for a while, but unfortunately that's not very practical right now."

"With all due respect, ma'am, even if we could dial Earth, there's a lot that needs to get done right here," Lorne said. "Dr. Keller cleared me for light duty."

"I know," Carter said. "It's just that we do like to give people who've been wounded in action a chance to rest up somewhere where they're not in constant danger of being attacked by aliens."

"And so you're suggesting Colorado Springs?"

She smiled. "You have a point there."

"Thanks for checking up on me," he said.

"Actually that's not the only reason I came by," she said. "Colonel Sheppard asked me to keep an eye on things in Atlantis while he and his team go mediate these negotiations between the Satedans and the Genii. I just wanted to touch base with you, since you're the acting military commander."

He thought that translated as, 'I hope you haven't got your feathers ruffled by Sheppard leaving me in charge instead of you.' He hadn't, particularly — at the moment, all he really wanted was to be lying down with some stronger painkillers than the Tylenol Keller had prescribed. And with three colonels currently on the station, he hadn't expected to be running the show.

"We'll hold down the fort," he said. He was tempted to say that he wished they could have her back in Atlantis on a permanent basis instead of Woolsey, but it wouldn't make him look good to criticize his current boss, even to his previous boss who he thought had been entirely unfairly screwed out of her job. "What about Colonel Caldwell?"

"He offered to help Colonel Sheppard with the negotiations," Carter said. "He thinks the rank might carry some weight with the Genii."

"Great," Lorne said, trying to sound like he meant it. Personally he thought that Colonel Sheppard and Colonel Caldwell working together on diplomatic negotiations really couldn't be good, but he suspected that Carter was well aware of that. So either there hadn't been any way to get out of it, or they thought it really was going to be useful enough to make up for the fact that Sheppard and Caldwell did not exactly play well together as a team.

"Should be interesting," Carter said, another one of those good all-purpose remarks that could mean anything. "Oh, and we're almost ready to put the new iris into place. I was just down in the lab, and they're testing the control mechanism now."

"I know everybody's going to feel better once that's done," Lorne said.

"I know I will," Carter said. "I would really rather not rely on Rodney not breaking into our computer system."

"Dr. Zelenka and Mrs. Miller have been working on that, right? So we're in better shape?"

"Well, better, yes," Carter said. "It's entirely possible that they've found most of Rodney's back doors into the system."

"I'm sensing a 'but'," Lorne said.

"Maybe not," Carter said. "It's just that he's been working with these computers for five years, and I have some idea how being in this kind of job makes you think."

"And?" Lorne said when she hesitated.

"I'm just saying that if I were locked out of the SGC's computers, I'm not sure what odds I'd give anybody trying to keep me from breaking back in." She shrugged. "It was always a problem. The only way to make it perfectly safe if one of us were compromised was to make sure there weren't any back doors into the system, but if there weren't any back doors, we wouldn't be able to get back in if there were a foothold situation. I'm not saying that we had unauthorized means of access into the computer system — "

"No, ma'am," Lorne said. She certainly was not saying that, in so many words.

"I'm just saying that from everything I know about Rodney, I think he worried a lot less about being compromised than about being locked out of Atlantis's computers and not being able to get back in."

"So what do we do?"

Carter shrugged again. "What we're doing. If we can even just make it more of a challenge for him to break in, it means we'll have more time to react if he tries it again. And we need to get the mechanical iris ready as soon as we can."

"I'll just be here with these supply forms," Lorne said. "If the Wraith attack, I figure you'll let me know."

"I'll be sure to do that," Carter said. "Take it easy, okay?"

"Yes, ma'am," Lorne said, but he found that somehow the conversation hadn't exactly eased his mind.

William hoisted his laptop bag higher onto his shoulder and tried to look as though he'd been ordered to join the Atlantis delegation rather than just attaching himself to it. And it wasn't as though he'd been told not to join the group. He simply hadn't asked, just shown up as though it was his business to be there, which was a skill he had honed at the SGC, when there was a lot more competition for the really interesting jobs. Besides, this was exactly the sort of mission that called for — well, it called for an anthropologist, really, but he was the closest they had. He took his place at the back of the group waiting for the control room to dial the gate, out of Sheppard's line of sight. Sheppard was busy with Lorne anyway, the latter leaning heavily on his crutches and nodding at some last minute instruction...

"I didn't know you were coming."

Of course that was Radek. He had paused to check on the progress of the mechanical iris — which was, William noted, looking almost complete, only the gearing that would let it open and close still to install — and that had brought them almost face to face.

"Team archeologist," William said.

"These people are alive," Radek said.

"And kicking, some of them," William murmured, in spite of himself, and Radek gave him the look that deserved.

"Now I am trying to remember how many times you told me you were not an anthropologist."

"I'm what you've got," William said.

To his surprise, Radek gave a crooked little smile. "There is that, too."

"Dialing!" a Marine called, and everyone took a few steps backward as the first symbol lit and locked. The gate turned, turned again, and locked, and the great plume of the unstable wormhole lanced out into the gate room. There were few things as beautiful, William thought. Even the lambent pool of the open Stargate was not as astonishing as that first burst of blue. At the head of the group, Sheppard looked over his shoulder, frowning slightly, almost unconsciously, and waved for them to follow.

They emerged into the now-familiar gate square, more crowded, though, than William had seen before. He recognized Cai, and the stocky woman, Arden, who had owned a string of tea-shops and now fed the settlement, but there was a second group, standing a little apart, who had to be un-returned Satedans. Some of those were wearing what looked like military uniform, black trousers and indigo jackets badged with knots of black and silver cord, discreet but elegant. There were four of them, standing together, subtly apart from both the returned and the expatriate, and William slanted a glance toward Ronon, wondering who they were. The big man was carefully not looking in their direction, but from that very care, William thought he was very aware of their presence. An elite unit? Some civilian authority? They carried sidearms, though, in holsters wound with silver filigree. He filed the question for later.

The Stargate lit again, and the first of the Genii delegation came through. He recognized Ladon Radim from Atlantis's files, short, dapper, neatly bearded — quite handsome, really — and guessed that the taller blond woman at his side was the sister, Dahlia, who was also Chief of Sciences. None of the others were in the files, and their drab, gray-green uniforms gave no clue even to relative rank. And that, William thought, was interesting. The uniforms proclaimed a radical equality that was entirely lacking in the society: another indication, perhaps, of intrinsic instability.

"There is trouble," Radek said under his breath, and William followed his gaze to see Sora and a couple of soldiers emerging from between two of the collapsed buildings. She had chosen an oblique approach, one that emphasized she and her people were already here, and William thought he saw the faintest of frowns cross Radim's face. Cai glared openly, and the other Satedans muttered among themselves. Sheppard bit his lip, and moved to intercept her and Radim, so that visually, at least, he was the arbiter.

"What is her problem?" William said softly, under the introductions, and Radek rolled his eyes.

"Teyla was responsible — indirectly and unintentionally, but responsible — for her father's death. She hasn't forgiven that."

"One wouldn't, I suppose," William murmured. She and Dahlia were the only women among the Genii delegation: also an interesting contrast to the Satedans, and to what he'd seen of the Athosians. "Who are the ones in blue, do you know?"

Radek shook his head. "Ronon does not talk about Sateda. We

thought they were all dead."

There were several answers to that, none of them appropriate. William peered over the top of his glasses at the open-sided pavilion that had been set up toward the far end of the square. Long narrow banners hung like streamers from the corner poles, and the canopy was a dusty burgundy; he wondered where they'd found it, and what traditions it represented. Cai gestured broadly, waving them all toward it, and William trailed behind the others, the sun warm on his back.

There weren't enough chairs at the three-sided table for everyone, of course, just for the leaders and a pair of aides apiece. Sheppard took the middle chair, flanked by Caldwell and Ronon; Cai and Arden and one of the blue-coated men took the Satedan side, and Radim was joined by an older man, bald and scowling, and a fair-haired, nondescript man with a bandaged hand. The rest of their parties clustered half in and half out of the shade, milling quietly behind their principals.

"Right," Sheppard said. "Glad everyone's here. Introductions first, for the record." He took a breath. "Lt. Col. John Sheppard, commander of Atlantis. Colonel Stephen Caldwell, of the *Daedalus*; Ronon Dex."

"Mr. Woolsey will not be joining us?" Radim said, with a lifted eyebrow.

"He had to return to Earth," Sheppard said. "This didn't seem like it could wait."

Radim's eyebrows rose even higher, but he nodded. "Ladon Radim, Chief of the Genii. Commander Carel Sar, Speaker Reiter Telez."

The commander was the one with the bandaged hand. That title was no surprise, but William wondered exactly what the Speaker's role was in their government. Sheppard nodded once, and looked at Cai.

"Ushan Cai, head of the Satedan provisional government —"

Radim leaned forward, folding his hands on the tabletop. "Surely that's part of what we're discussing here. Not a given."

"And if you're not willing to acknowledge that," Cai retorted, "there's no point in these discussions."

Out of the corner of his eye, William saw Teyla shift slightly, as though she would have liked to answer. Sheppard said, "Let's stipulate that nobody's agreeing to anything right at this point." Deliberately or not, he had used the same tone he used with Torren, and a smile flickered across Teyla's face.

Radim's expression didn't change, but he leaned back. "As long as that's clearly understood," he said.

Cai snorted, but gestured to the woman at his right. "Arden Mai, second-in-charge, and Colonel Kashek Yan, senior commander of the Satedan Band."

"And is the Band taking an official interest?" Radim asked.

"We hold a watching brief," Yan answered. "On behalf of those Satedans who wait to return."

"Then I'm not sure we can agree to your presence," Radim said.

William barely stopped himself from rolling his eyes. It was obvious what Radim was trying to do, derail the talks before they could get started, and equally obvious that these weren't serious protests. Under cover of the rising voices, he leaned forward to speak in Radek's ear.

"What's the Satedan Band?"

Radek shrugged, and to William's surprise, Teyla glanced over her shoulder. "They are a famous elite unit among the Satedans, oathbound to each other and to their service."

William lifted his own eyebrows at that, wondering if he was reading in more than was intended, and Sheppard tapped on the table.

"OK. Then Colonel Yan stays."

"This speaks to the basic question under discussion," Radim said. "Sateda was abandoned — with good cause, no world Culled as deeply as Sateda was can survive. Her people scattered and found new lives. Colonel Yan is an excellent example of this, and he himself says he's not returning. Sateda as we knew it is no more. Now we are — as Colonel Sheppard, and indeed everyone, is aware — in need of every scrap of Ancient technology that we can salvage to try to make some stand against Queen Death. A group of scavengers squatting in the wreckage — who cannot even use the technology they're denying to others — is not Sateda."

"We are Sateda," Cai said. "This is our world, our home. Neither the Genii nor anyone else have any right to our resources."

"You can't use what you have," Telez blurted.

"Then why not trade for it?" Sheppard asked. "It seems to me you've both got some opportunities here — "

"Meaning no offense," Radim said, in the tone that meant precisely the opposite, "but I see no reason we should withdraw and leave Atlantis in charge."

"We're here to trade," Sheppard said, firmly. "And no offense taken."

"That's what they all say."

William couldn't see who had said that, but there was a murmur of laughter from among the Genii. It was going to be a very long day.

CHAPTER NINETEEN
Diplomacy

THE SUN was setting behind the broken roofs, sending long shadows across the gate square. The last of the light shimmered on the top of the gate, the naquadah gleaming as though it were oiled or wet, the shadow of the ring stretching out behind it. Cai's people were setting up trestles, laying out food and drink they'd gotten from somewhere, and John frowned, trying to think what was wrong. Or, no, not wrong, but missing. Because there was an absence, something that should be there... Children, he realized abruptly. On almost every other world he'd visited, when the party began, the food came out and the torches were lit, there would be children in the background, either helping, or watching with excitement to see the latest travelers from another world. That was the thing he still couldn't get his mind around — well, yes, his mind, but not his heart, not the bone-deep certainty that any-one at all could open the Stargate and walk to another world. That Sateda might be destroyed, her cities burned, but her people could find refuge, and a way home again. Not like Afghanistan...

He shied away from that thought, and saw Teyla give him a curious look. She did not comment, however, merely held out a wide-mouthed cup. He took it, sniffing warily, but it smelled only of smoke and herbs.

"Dr. Lynn says he believes it to contain something like caffeine," Teyla said.

"Yeah?" John took a careful sip, decided it tasted a little bit like lemons and mint. And smoke, which was disconcerting. "You know, I don't remember including him in this."

Teyla smiled. "He says this is his job."

John smiled back, took another sip of the — he supposed it was a tea. "It's not going to replace coffee," he said. He looked back at the tables, where the Marines were hauling lamps into place, and Radek was tinkering with the generator: Atlantis's contribution to the party, light and pole heaters for the chill ahead. "How do you think it's going?"

Teyla's smile widened. "It is... going. This will take time, and I do not believe that Ladon Radim wishes it to be settled quickly."

"Not so much," John said. He glanced over his shoulder, checking the rest of the Atlantis team. One of the Satedans had come over to look at the generator, and he and Radek were talking now, gesturing as though they were sketching plans on the air. Ronon was talking to Cai and one of the Satedan Band — not Yan, a younger, more lightly built man with crooked teeth and a wide smile. Caldwell, stiff-backed and poker-faced, was listening to Sar and one of the other Genii officers, and Dahlia Radim was talking to Sora. Hopefully telling her to be sensible, John thought, but knew better than to believe it. "It's not exactly to his advantage."

"No…" Teyla's expression changed, and John turned, not surprised to see Radim approaching, the blond aide Ambrus at his heels.

"Chief Ladon."

"Colonel Sheppard." Radim gave a thin, unfriendly smile. "I am sorry Mr. Woolsey is unable to be with us. When will he be back, can you say?"

"I'm afraid I can't," John said, with a smile of his own. From Teyla's lifted eyebrow, he guessed it hadn't been successful. "The situation was fluid. But he left me with full authority."

"I'm sure he did," Radim said.

He thinks I killed him. John felt his mouth drop open, closed it sharply. *Son of a bitch.* That was about the last thing he'd expected, and it annoyed him more than he would have imagined. "How's it going with *Avenger*?" he asked, and Radim frowned.

"*Avenger*? Oh. We've renamed her *Pride of the Genii.*"

"Her name's *Avenger*," John said. It was unreasonable to be angry about that, but the Ancient warship he'd rescued for them had had a name, and a personality: a sweet ship, willing, glad to be awakened. He had liked her a lot. "How is the project coming?"

"We're making progress," Radim said, stiffly. "And it would be going faster if we were free to make use of the technology abandoned here."

John could see Teyla looking at him as though she would like to kick him, and forced another smile. "Well, that's what we're here to work out."

"Both your people and mine need what's here," Radim said. "You can't seriously mean to maintain that this is a viable government. Fifty people — at the most — squatting in the ruins, bringing in supplies from off-world." He shook his head. "And if the Wraith come, what happens then?"

"They will hide," Teyla said. "As we have all done before."

"And what's the chance that the Wraith would finish the destruction they started?" Radim asked. "This wasn't Queen Death. She would leave nothing behind. Surely you don't mean to risk losing everything that's here."

"And what, exactly, are you looking for?" John asked. Radim had a point, that was part of the problem.

"The same things you are, I imagine," Radim said. "Ronon will have told you that there was an important collection of Ancient artifacts in their museum, and among that collection were things that we could use on our warship. Crystals, for one thing, and tools we don't know how to make. I am sure there are things Atlantis needs as well."

Things you can't make, his tone implied. John said, "Yeah, plenty of things we can use. And we're happy to trade for them. It seems to me it would be to your advantage to do the same."

"And if we agree to trade with Cai, do we also pay extortion to the next group of returning Satedans who set up a so-called government?" Radim shook his head. "And the one after that? Because, to speak frankly, I can't see you wasting the manpower to shore up Cai's authority."

"Right now, the only people who are questioning his authority are the Genii," John said. "Really, we wouldn't want to have to break off relations over this."

"I don't think you could afford that," Radim answered. "Not given the threat we are both facing."

"I'm seriously hoping it won't come to that," John said. "Excuse me."

He turned away, Teyla at his side, and nearly ran into Caldwell beside the meeting tent.

"Any progress?" Caldwell asked.

John took a careful breath. "Well, I think I've made our position clear." He paused, but couldn't quite stop himself. "That little bastard thinks I murdered Woolsey to take his place."

To his surprise, Caldwell grinned. "Tell me you never thought about it, Sheppard."

"Not to get this job," John answered. Teyla was smirking, though, and he couldn't help smiling himself, even as he shook his head. "Diplomacy."

"Don't knock it," Caldwell said. "You might have a knack for it after all."

Sora ducked out of the meeting tent and made her way toward one of the long tables laden down with food. There was little point in staying inside at the moment. Sheppard didn't seem to be making any effort to get everybody back to the table rather than letting them gather in little groups spread across the square, and the conversation in the tent at the moment bore little relation to what was supposed to be the point.

She spotted Cai at the end of one of the tables, apparently setting out bottles of some kind of drink as if he had nothing better to do. She shook her head. As if alcohol was going to help anyone to keep their minds on business. But then that was Sateda. If they'd devoted more of their people's energies to fighting the Wraith rather than to distractions, clothing and music and games, all the absurd little luxuries she kept finding in the ruins —

"Sora Tyrus," Cai said when he saw her. She wasn't sure if his nod in her direction was meant as a courtesy or simply as an acknowledgement that he knew who she was. "Will you have a drink, then? We've found more liquor bottles than we expected intact, but it's still in scarce supply for the moment."

"I'm surprised you're not relying on the Lanteans for your supplies," Sora said. She waved away the cup he offered her.

"We haven't yet," Cai said. "You're sure you won't have a drink?"

"You're just relying on them for protection."

"Something the Genii haven't offered. So far I can't see that you've offered anything, except on entirely unacceptable terms," Cai said, fairly mildly.

"Believe me, the Lanteans' terms won't stay so pretty," Sora said. "Don't make the mistake of believing they can be trusted." She glanced across the square to where Teyla Emmagan was talking intently to Dahlia Radim with a false smile, no doubt making excuses for having taken Dahlia prisoner and tried to steal their Ancient warship. As if there were any to make other than *we wanted it, so we thought it should be ours.*

Sora wished she were close enough to make sure that Dahlia wasn't fooled. She'd had more than enough experience with Teyla's ability to spin pretty words until you found yourself losing track of your original purpose, starting to have doubts —

"The Lanteans defeated the Replicators," Cai said. "And they've done much to fight the Wraith in the last years."

"So have we," Sora said. "And we haven't laid waste to the galaxy in the process. It was the Lanteans who unleashed the Replicators in the first place, and who woke the Wraith. Before they came — "

"Sateda fell before the Lanteans came," Cai said flatly. "They're not responsible for the Wraith doing what Wraith do."

"And are you happy that so many worlds have now met the same fate? The Lanteans don't know how to defeat the Wraith. All they've done is make things worse and interfere with our plans."

"And your plans involve Sateda?"

"We are so close to being able to use the technology of the Ancestors," Sora said. "To have their weapons in our own hands, not the hands of the Lanteans who claim to be here to protect us. Why should they care about any of us? They're here for their own purposes. They want what's in that museum, too."

Cai picked up one of the cups and drank deeply before he answered. "No offense," he said. "But if our choice is to be robbed of our treasures by the Genii or to sell them to the Lanteans, I would prefer to deal with the Lanteans. At least they didn't come as robbers demanding we hand over our wallets."

"More like vandals setting your house on fire," Sora said. "Did you hear about the Travellers' colony, the one destroyed in a moment when their gate exploded? It wasn't the only world where that happened."

"Wild rumors," Cai said. "People hear of many things that aren't true. If worlds have had their gates destroyed, there's no need to go looking for a cause other than the obvious. The Wraith Cull more deeply every year."

Sora gritted her teeth. She'd heard this too many times on too many worlds, people who blindly believed that the Lanteans could help them, save them, when how could they, and why should they? It was pure superstition; the Lanteans' blind luck in stumbling on the city of the Ancestors and having it answer to them wasn't a sign of either military genius or purity of heart. But try to tell a people like the Athosians, or what was left of them.

"The Wraith can't destroy a Stargate," she said.

Cai shook his head. "Because your people can't? I hope you're not looking for a convenient Stargate to experiment with, or a place to try out your — what are they called — 'nuclear bombs'?"

"I'm not going to talk to you about our weapons testing program. But we're aware of how valuable some of the things in this city are. If you just let us use them — "

"Now you want to make a trade? I'm sorry if I'm skeptical of your good intentions after you came among us with your rifles in hand."

"I'm not offering to trade," Sora said. "I'm saying that it's in the best interests of your people and of every human being to let us have all the weapons we can find to fight the Wraith, because it's not as if you can use them anymore."

"There will be a Satedan army again," Cai said.

"Who? Your army won't even come live in your settlement. Your great 'hero' Ronon is more a Lantean now than a Satedan — "

"All of our people are Satedan," Cai said. "Those of us who have returned, and those of us who never will. If you can't understand that, you don't understand very much about us."

"I don't need to understand much about you," Sora said.

Cai shook his head at her. "I can see that you've never been a trader," he said. "You may find when you don't get what you want by demanding it that you change your mind about that. Please enjoy our hospitality, if any of it suits you. I have other people I need to talk to."

Sora watched him go, trying not to feel that she'd handled that badly. If she'd made up to him, been soft and apologetic the way Dahlia wanted her to, he'd never have believed her. At least she'd tried honesty, not that it seemed to be worth much.

She hesitated, and then reached for one of the cups on the table. She was beginning to feel like a drink wouldn't be a bad idea.

By the time it seemed possible for John to get enough people back into the conference tent to formally adjourn the meeting for the evening, there didn't seem to be much point. The Genii had set up tents of their own, provoking glares but not arguments from the Satedans, and everyone was making serious inroads on the food and drink.

Cai's people had brought out oil lamps, and some of the open windows around the square cast more lamplight into the street.

Darkness softened the jagged shapes of the buildings against the sky, but it made the square seem like a fragile oasis of light in a big, dark desert. There were no distant lights at the outskirts of town, no moving headlights or lit lamps beyond the square. Just a big, dark ruin, empty of people the way no city on Earth stayed empty for long, no matter how bad the damage had been.

The square was anything but empty, though, and anything but quiet. Radim was talking intently to Teyla, who looked like her patience was being tested by whatever he was saying, although her polite smile didn't fade. Across the square, Ronon was apparently introducing Dahlia Radim to a Satedan woman who John thought he remembered as one of Cai's engineers. A good move, but he could probably use Radek, who would have more idea what they were talking about.

John looked around for him, and found him on the fringes of the crowd with a cup of whatever liquor Cai had broken out for the occasion in hand. There were still cups of the smoky tea set out, but they'd gone cold, and most people seemed to have moved on to the heavy drinking portion of the evening. That might be a good thing, or really not, but he expected they'd find out which.

"I think Ronon's trying to get Dalia Radim and some of Cai's people to bond over science," John said. "He could maybe use some backup in that department."

"Right," Radek said resignedly, draining the cup and setting it down. "Is there any sign that we're getting anywhere?"

"At least they're talking," John said. "We're going to have to sit down again in the morning and see if anybody's willing to bend at all, but maybe if they can start seeing each other as people, it'll make them a little more sympathetic to each other's problems."

"Yes, that is a theory," Radek said. He sounded as skeptical as John felt.

John ran a hand through his hair. He was pretty sure that by this point Elizabeth would have come up with some creative solution to the problem and figured out how to bully everyone into accepting it. Woolsey would have kept everyone at the conference table, on the theory that fatigue and boredom would eventually motivate them to actually negotiate. In hindsight, that might have been the way to go.

"Or maybe they're just going to grandstand at each other, but at least right now they're talking and not fighting," he said. As he said it, he wondered if that was true; he could hear rising voices, and when he looked up, one edge of the crowd seemed to be turning into a pitched argument between some of the Genii officers and what looked like about half of Yan's Satedan Band, with Caldwell in the middle of it trying to make sure they stayed bodily separated.

"Cool it off, people," Caldwell was saying sharply, but no one seemed very inclined to listen to him.

"Damn it," John said. "Come on, let's go break it up."

"I am sure they will be happy to listen to us," Radek said dryly, but he trailed John as he shouldered his way through the crowd.

"You want a fight, you can —"

"Back off, Satedan —"

"You and your whole regiment —"

"All right, settle down," John said when he was close enough that he thought anyone might listen to him.

"Oh, they'll settle down," one of the Satedans said, a little too loudly. One of Yan's Satedan Band, John's brain supplied, the young officer Ronon had been talking to earlier. "They like to talk, but they don't like to fight."

"Everybody knows Satedans like to fight," one of the young Genii officers said. "They just don't like to win."

Caldwell interposed himself as the Satedan took a step toward the man. "Let's not do this."

"Maybe you'd have gotten farther if you put men in the field instead of girls," one of the other Genii put in.

"You mean like Sora Tyrus?" John said. "Or maybe Teyla."

"I mean like these pretty little flowers," the Genii officer said. John wished he was more certain exactly how he ought to translate that. Any way you looked at it, it seemed a little rich for a bunch of guys most of whom stood half a head taller than the Genii they were squaring off with.

"I don't think anybody needs to be calling anybody else names," John said.

"You wouldn't last ten minutes in a fight," the Satedan officer said over his shoulder.

"Says the man hiding behind the Lanteans."

John was losing patience. "You two want to fight? You know what, fine, go beat the crap out of each other. And then it's over, all right? No saying 'somebody got a bruise and now it's a diplomatic incident'."

Caldwell gave him a look. "Sheppard—"

"A fair fight, no weapons. Call it sparring."

"More like giving lessons to children," the Genii officer said, but there seemed to be muttered agreement on both sides.

"All right," John said. He glanced across the square at Teyla. He was pretty sure she wasn't going to think this was a very good idea. "Let's get out of this crowd. I don't want this to turn into a general brawl."

"You are a crazy person," Radek said as they trailed the would-be combatants and their friends behind a row of buildings, following the light of the lamp one of them carried. "You know that, yes?"

"It'll get it out of their systems."

"Assuming they do not kill each other."

"Let's hope not," John said. He made sure the lantern was set high enough that it was unlikely to be knocked over — setting what was left of the city on fire probably would cause a diplomatic incident — and said, "Let's have some rules, here."

The Satedan officer gave him a look that reminded him of Ronon. "Why?"

"Because I don't want anybody put in the hospital."

"First one knocked down," Caldwell said. "The point's not to see how much damage you can do, the point's to see how well you can fight."

"Whatever," the Genii soldier said, glaring at the Satedan. "You probably won't get up after the first time anyway."

"Sure," the Satedan said.

John repressed the urge to roll his eyes. "You people have names?"

"Petros Dar," the Satedan said.

The Genii officer scowled at him. "Airth Gradon."

"Eat dirt," the Satedan said, and rushed him.

There was a clamor from the spectators, but they seemed willing to stay out of the fight, so John settled for shouldering people back if they looked like they were going to get in somebody's way. Both Dar and Gradon were good, but John thought Dar was better. Gradon looked more thrown by not having a weapon, and Dar had the reach on him, although he wasn't built like a brick wall the way Ronon was.

They circled each other, exchanging experimental kicks and punches that mostly didn't connect, and then Gradon closed the distance between them, not a good move in John's opinion. Dar grabbed for him, but Gradon managed a sharp uppercut that bloodied Dar's nose and drew whistles and shouted encouragement from his men.

Dar stepped back and to the side, a move that might have looked like a staggering recovery to Gradon but that John had learned from sparring with Ronon to associate with the ground coming up toward him fast. Before he thought Gradon knew what was happening, Dar kicked Gradon's feet out from under him and sent him sprawling.

Gradon came up mad, rolling to his feet and making as if to throw himself at Dar, but Caldwell grabbed him by the jacket at the same time that John stepped — if not happily — between the two would-be combatants. *Teyla's going to ask why I stepped out in front of a drunk soldier who was looking for somebody to punch,* he couldn't help thinking, *and I'm going to have to say that it sounded like a good idea at the time...*

"You agreed to the rules," Caldwell said. "Now this needs to be over."

"You heard him," John said. "Shake hands and make up."

"I expect they'd rather kiss and make up," Gradon said. "Or haven't you heard what they say about the Satedan Band — "

"You mean that we win fights?"

"I mean that you're a bunch of perverted — "

"I really don't give a damn what they say," Caldwell said, in a tone that cut through the general noise. "You had your fight, you lost, now let me suggest that you take it like a man and walk away. Otherwise, this is going to turn into a diplomatic incident, and I don't think either of your commanding officers are going to like that."

"Everybody break it up," John added, although it felt a little weak after that.

Gradon glared at the Satedans and then stormed off with the rest of his friends following. Dar scrubbed at his bleeding nose with his sleeve and said something under his breath that sounded a lot like speculation on whether anyone had ever bedded Gradon without being paid for it.

"Nice plan, Sheppard," Caldwell said as the Satedans also began heading back in the direction of other people, and probably of more to drink.

John shrugged. "At least they were talking?"

Caldwell shook his head. "That kind of talking we could do without."

"Well, that is the military for you," Radek said a little sharply, and suddenly John could see the conversational pit opening up but wasn't sure how to avoid it. Radek had been drinking, too, and he did have a temper, and if a member of his team was less than complimentary about the American military and Caldwell made the kind of remark in return that John was expecting, he didn't know what the hell he was supposed to say —

"Like anybody has time for that crap," Caldwell said instead. "The Genii are stuck in about 1950. They kept assuming Colonel Carter was somebody's secretary when she tried to meet with them."

"It's apparently cultural," Radek said with a more conciliatory shrug.

"I'm getting tired of cultural," Caldwell said. "Is there any way to get these people to come to terms?"

"We'll give it a try in the morning," John said.

Caldwell shook his head. "At this rate, everybody's going to be too hung over in the morning to make any sense."

"Well, if they're too hung over to endlessly repeat the same positions that they started with, we might actually get somewhere," John said.

He wondered what Woolsey would say to that theory. At this point, possibly that it was worth a try.

Teyla set her cup carefully aside, took a step backward so that she was outside the circles of light, sheltered by the shadows. Dahlia Radim had retreated to a tent some time ago, before the men started drinking, but the Satedan women were still present, though they were careful to stay together, or grouped with their men. Most of the Marines had been told to consider themselves on duty, and were following orders, sticking to the perimeter and avoiding the drinks. And then there was Sora. There was no mistaking her anger, for all that she seemed to have herself rigidly under control, it shrieked in the set of her shoulders, the tight smile and the hands clenched on whatever was nearest, cup or chair back or closed tight on themselves. She was dangerous, Teyla thought; perhaps the most dangerous person at this meeting, because her agenda ran counter to everyone else's, and she had no reason to stand aside. More than that, it was not in her nature to stand passive, and never had been.

Teyla scanned the crowd, thinning now as people began to retire, the Satedans to their houses, the others to the temporary camps. John had been wise to say that the Lanteans would be staying: there would be no complicated dialing procedures to betray the problem with the shield. Not all of the Genii were doing the same — she suspected that Ladon did not like to be out of touch with his government for too long — but enough were remaining that it didn't seem to be a slight.

Movement caught her attention, a shift of light and shadow at the edge of her vision, and she let her head turn, to see Sora sliding out of the lamplight. She waited, but the younger woman did not reappear. And that was not a good thing, she thought. Sora's camp lay in the opposite direction. She turned, looking for John, but he had disappeared somewhere, along with Colonel Caldwell. And Sora should not go unwatched.

One of the young Marines was standing off to the side, arms folded on the P90 clipped to his chest. He had been with Atlantis on the first mission, a skinny dark youth with his head shaved almost bare; he had filled out since then, grown his hair, gained weight to go with his rangy height, but he was still one of the ones she knew she could trust — more importantly, who would trust her, and not waste time with questions.

"Corporal Kneeland."

"Ma'am?" He didn't quite come to attention, but his stance shifted.

"Come with me, please," Teyla said. "Sora Tyrus has gone off in an — unexpected direction."

"Sora," he said, and she remembered he had been stranded on Manaria during the hurricane, had heard all about Sora's part in the attack on Atlantis. "Yes, ma'am."

Teyla glanced sidelong again, saw no one paying them any particular attention. "This way."

Outside the circle of lights, the ruined streets were very dark. Teyla paused in the shadow of a door, blinking as though that would make her eyes adjust faster, and Kneeland slipped a pair of IR goggles from his pocket.

"Do you want them, ma'am? I've only got one pair."

"You keep them," Teyla said. Her sight was clearing, with her back to the lights. Sora had stepped out of the light, and moved—left, she thought, left and back, and sure enough, there was a break in the wreckage. "This way," she said, pointing, and Kneeland followed, goggles in place. He wasn't as silent as Ronon would have been, but he moved with care and grace and she thought they might have a chance at catching Sora unaware.

Something moved ahead of them, and she lifted a fist. In the same instant, Kneeland breathed, "Ma'am."

Teyla nodded. They were in cover, of a sort, a pile of rubble that slanted halfway across the street. The person—Sora, it wouldn't be anyone else—was moving toward the corner of a building that jutted above the wreckage like a single tooth in an old woman's mouth. The Genii uniform blended well with the darkness, but her hands and face in profile were bare and white, and her movements were still angry, jerky and abrupt and noticeable in the dark. Teyla eased forward, peering over the edge of the rubble, and after a moment Kneeland joined her, holding his P90 away from his body to keep it from clattering against anything.

"Can you see what she's doing?" Teyla kept her voice a thread of sound, the just-above-a-whisper that carried only to the ears for which it was intended.

Kneeland edged past her, adjusting the goggles. "It looks like she's—climbing something? Maybe to some kind of platform?"

He shifted to bring the P90 to bear, and Teyla frowned into the darkness. They were too far from the Satedan settlement for this to be a firing point—and Sora had not been armed at the meeting, though, of course, she could have weapons stored in the broken tower. She turned to look over her shoulder, trying to imagine the sight lines in daylight. From the tower, you would probably have a view of the gate, as well as of the settlement's main square: an observation post, then, or most likely so.

"Is there anyone else present?" she asked.

"No, ma'am," Kneeland said. "Just her."

Teyla sat back on her heels, wondering what to do. John should be informed, and Cai—perhaps Ladon also, it would be a suitable embarrassment—but she did not want to leave Sora unwatched, nor was she sure radio traffic would go unheard—

There was a sudden crack, not very loud, but sharp and sudden. The tower moved, the stones tilting, and abruptly the whole thing tipped sideways in a rumble of stone and wood. There were a couple of smaller, sharper sounds, hard flat noises like a blow, and then silence.

"Holy crap!" Kneeland said, and started to his feet. "Ma'am, she's still in there—"

Damn the woman, Teyla thought. "Is she still alive, can you tell?"

"No—" Kneeland was scanning the wreckage, the goggles making him look like a monster from some fireside tale. "Wait, yes, ma'am, I can see her moving."

"Then we must help her," Teyla said firmly. "But be careful."

"Yes, ma'am," Kneeland said, and moved forward.

There was no point in concealment now. Teyla reached into her pocket, found the small flashlight she always carried, and let the beam play over the pile of rubble. Most of the wall had fallen outward into the street, stone and brick mingled with new wood—reinforcing beams, she guessed, for the observation post. And yes, it almost certainly had been precisely that: her light picked out the cylinder of a telescope, front lens missing, and the leg of its tripod jutted from among the stones.

Kneeland flicked on the light attached to his P90, joined its beam to hers. "Damn."

Teyla winced in sympathy. The building had had a cellar, and when the reinforcement gave way, at least part of the makeshift tower had fallen into that space. The air was hazed with dust, bright in the flashlight's beams, but nothing else moved. "Sora?"

"There." Kneeland had pushed the IR goggles up onto his forehead, swung the P90's light to focus on the edge of the gap. A pale hand clung to the edge of a beam, and then another reached up, scrabbled for purchase on the wood.

Without thinking, Teyla flung herself onto the ground, spreading her body to make herself as heavy as possible, and reached for the groping hand. "Here!"

Sora's hand closed on hers, and then released it as though she'd been burned. Teyla grabbed for her wrist instead, caught and held, feeling the younger woman's weight in her shoulders and back.

"Let go!" Sora glared up at her, face filthy and smeared with blood, swung her feet, groping for a toehold.

"I should," Teyla said. "Be still, and we will get you out."

Sora didn't answer, instead shifted her grip on the beam, reaching again for a foothold. Teyla gasped, feeling her fingers slip.

"Don't be stupid—"

"Ma'am!" Kneeland swung his light. "Look there!"

Teyla tried to turn her head, but the strain was too much. "What is it?"

"Something—explosives, I think." The light moved, flicking from spot to spot, but Teyla still couldn't see. Sora was twisting again, and it took all her strength to keep her grip. "God, ma'am, don't let her fall!"

Sora was abruptly still, staring blindly up at them. Teyla tightened her grip, digging her toes into the dirt.

"It's a trap," Kneeland said. He dropped to his knees at Teyla's side, slinging the P90 out of his way, and reached for Sora's other hand. "If she falls, she'll set the rest of it off."

For a second, Teyla thought Sora was going to let go, pull herself out of their hands and kill them all. She could see the thought in the younger woman's eyes, and saw the moment when it passed, and Sora wrapped her free hand around Kneeland's wrist. Together they hauled her up and out, dragged her gasping onto the pile of rubble. She looked terrible, Teyla thought, covered in dust and blood—but the blood was from her nose, and she moved easily enough as she dragged herself to a sitting position.

"So much for peaceful negotiations," she said.

"Hey, now." Kneeland had his P90 in hand again, was cautiously examining the pit.

"You cannot seriously think we did this," Teyla said.

Sora pressed the back of her hand against her upper lip, glaring, and said nothing.

"If we had done it," Teyla said, "it would have worked. That I promise you."

"And we would have used C4," Kneeland said. "That stuff isn't ours."

Teyla looked where the light pointed, saw a fist-sized sphere tied to a beam. She took out her flashlight again, found two more packages, and looked back at Sora.

"That is Genii explosive. And only your own people knew of this post. Can you tell me you have no enemies among your men?"

Sora took a deep breath, looking suddenly old and tired. "Not among my men," she said. She took her hand away, and sniffed hard as though deciding if the nosebleed had stopped. "This can't be."

In spite of everything, Teyla felt a thread of sympathy. She remembered Sora as a girl just coming into adolescence, eager for stories of the worlds beyond the Stargate. And that farmgirl was pretense, she reminded herself, a lie deliberately contrived to protect the Genii while they built their armies and their nuclear bombs.

"It's a trick," Sora said, without conviction. "You used our explosives to make it seem like our people did it."

"And how would we get your supplies?" Teyla asked. "We could have used a tiny bit of C4, and no one would ever have known that it wasn't just an accident."

Sora didn't answer, just looked away, wincing as though something pained her.

"Are you all right?" Kneeland asked. He kept the P90 ready, but reached one-handed for his pocket. "I've got a first aid kit —"

"I'm fine," Sora said. "It's just bruises."

"It is Ladon who has done this," Teyla said, sitting back on her heels. "The Chief would never —"

"You are an embarrassment to him." Teyla cut through the words as though she hadn't spoken, feeling the truth strike home. "A danger to his plans. This is his solution, an unfortunate accident that he can blame on your own carelessness."

"If Ladon Radim wanted to get rid of me, he'd have me arrested," Sora said. Her voice was bitter. "There's no one who'd bother stopping him now."

Kneeland shone his light into the cellar again, shook his head silently. Teyla said, "Do you wish to survive this?"

"That's unlikely," Sora said, with a thin smile.

"Survival and revenge," Teyla said.

"And how can you give me that?"

She had known that would appeal. Teyla said, "You have luckily survived a frightening accident. We came upon a collapsed building and heard you call — perhaps you strayed there seeking a short cut to your camp? A tragedy narrowly averted — it would be a shame if anything were to happen after you were so providentially rescued."

"And the revenge?" Sora asked.

"You survive."

Sora gave a bark of laughter that turned into a harsh cough. "And the Lanteans get what they wanted all along."

"It is past the point where you can influence that," Teyla said. That was what her father had called a trader's truth, not entirely a lie, but without much acquaintance with honesty. She had a flash of memory, flowers tumbling as a red-haired tomboy swung upside down from a tree branch, Tyrus scolding her down, too old to play like that — She put the thought firmly aside. "That is for Colonel Sheppard and Ushan Cai and Chief Ladon to work out among them. But you can live and know you are a thorn to his foot."

"Why not?" Sora said. She looked old again, drained. "Why the hell not?"

"Why not, indeed?" Teyla looked at her. "Can you walk?"

Sora nodded, and Kneeland offered a hand to pull her to her feet. She came up wincing, and Teyla gave her a wary look. It would do them no good to bring her back unconscious, she should walk into camp on her own two feet — And then Sora straightened, nodding. Kneeland kept one hand on her elbow, steadying her, as they started back to the gate square.

At least they'd gotten through the rest of the evening without another incident, though John was aware that the Satedan Band and some of the Genii were still muttering insults when they thought none of the authorities were listening. He hoped that meant they'd got the worst of it out of their system, and that there would be no further need for anybody to prove their manhood. He'd seen Yan talking to Dar, and thought he could rely on Yan to keep the peace. But, of course, they'd won. It was the Genii he probably needed to worry about.

At some point, the Satedans had cleared the long tables, except for a small tapped keg and a scattering of cups. He wished briefly he could believe it held beer, but it was too small to be anything but the harsh Satedan moonshine. He'd nursed a cup of it for about an hour before he'd been able to set it discreetly aside, but everyone else seemed to have been knocking it back pretty steadily. He kind of hoped they did all have hangovers in the morning...

"Colonel Sheppard."

John closed his eyes for a second, then stitched a smile on his face and turned to meet Radim. "Chief Ladon?"

He'd seen Radim drinking along with the others, matching his officers toast for toast, but it didn't seem to have affected him. "This sparring match—"

"Was very impressive," John said. "Your guy, Gradon, he throws a nice punch. I wouldn't bet against him—but of course there won't be a rematch."

An unwilling smile flickered across Radim's face, and was instantly suppressed. "I'd hoped we could ensure that, yes."

"I'm sure that won't be a problem," John began, and something moved at the edge of the light. He saw a Marine swivel toward it, P90 not quite raised, and a sober Genii reached reflexively for his sidearm, stopped himself at the last moment.

"Colonel Sheppard! And Chief Ladon! How fortunate you are here." That was Teyla's voice, and she came fully into the light, Corporal Kneeland behind her, supporting a battered-looking Sora. John caught his breath, hoping there hadn't been another fight, and Teyla kept talking, her voice raised just enough to carry, riding over any comment. "There has been an accident, a collapse of wreckage, but luckily Sora is unharmed."

"Lucky, indeed," Radim said. He sounded sour, and John gave him a glance. The Genii's face was impassive, and John wondered if he'd heard correctly after all. "And very fortunate that you were there to help."

"Yes," Sora said, with odd emphasis. "It was very fortunate indeed."

She looked like hell, John thought, blood on the front of her jacket, her vivid hair dulled with dust. She glared at Radim as though she blamed him, and abruptly the pieces clicked into place for John. Radim hinting at Woolsey's murder, his willingness to ignore Sora's near-insubordination, everything he'd done to get power... He opened his mouth to say something, and Teyla gave him a minatory look.

"I believe she is unharmed," Teyla said, "but I would like our medic to take a look at her. So that there can be no misunderstandings."

"We have a physician here ourselves," Radim said.

"We insist," John said. "Like Teyla said. No misunderstandings."

Radim shrugged. "If Sora wishes, I have no objection."

"I'm well enough," Sora said. Teyla's eyes narrowed, and the younger woman sighed. "But, yes, I suppose it would be wise."

Radim lifted his hand, and the blond aide hurried to his side. "Ambrus, if you'd go with Sora and—"

"Corporal Kneeland," Teyla said. She made no move to go with them, and Radim bowed.

"Then I think I should retire."

"I'd like a word before you go," John said. Radim paused, tipping his head in question, but John waited until he was sure the others were out of earshot. "I know what you did, or what you tried to do, there. Not a smart move."

Radim blinked once. "Frankly, I would have thought it would be to your advantage."

"It looks bad," John said. "Trying to get rid of the officer who was running this operation before she got caught? It makes it look like you have something big to hide. But. We want this deal to happen. You need a deal, the Satedans need a deal. Make it happen, and we don't have to go into what you might have been planning that you needed to cover up this way."

There was a little silence, and John hoped he hadn't completely screwed up whatever Teyla had been planning. Then, abruptly, Radim laughed. He looked momentarily younger, and genuinely amused. "That's not exactly easy to arrange, Colonel."

"I think you can handle it," John said.

"I — you'll accept an agreement to trade for what we need?"

"If the Satedans will," John said. "But I think that would work out."

"Then I expect we can reach an agreement," Radim said. "Good night, then."

"Good night," John said, and Teyla echoed him politely. He looked sideways at her, and saw that she was smiling.

"Your diplomatic technique is improving, John."

CHAPTER TWENTY
ZPM

IT WAS quiet in the lab, clevermen moving in careful choreography as they drew a newly formed cable from the wall. It was designed to mesh with the framework that held the ZPM, and Quicksilver adjusted the socket, eyeing the connector warily. The last three had failed catastrophically, and he was more than a bit tired of being splashed with molten cable… Salt tugged it forward, letting it wind around his off hand, so that he could examine the cable's mouth Quicksilver leaned closer himself. It wasn't his specialty, but he couldn't help wanting to see what things had changed. It looked like an adapted sucker, a leech-mouth lined in tiny sparks like diodes, and at his side Ember gave a shrug.

We won't know until we try.

Salt showed teeth in answer, and unwound the cable from his wrist. He led it into the frame, and it reached out hungrily, fastened and clung. Lights pulsed, data cascading down the monitor, and Salt lifted his head eagerly. And then there was a snap, and the cable shriveled back, trailing smoke. Salt caught it and another cleverman quickly smothered the flames.

How hard can this be? Quicksilver exclaimed. *How many times do you intend to try this?*

Until it works, Ember snapped, and Salt snarled in agreement.

Which will be when?

When it is done, Salt said, and Ember lifted his hand.

As you saw, we are nearly there. He had himself under tight control. *The next iteration should resolve the last compatibility issues.*

Salt turned away, carrying the damaged cable tenderly, and another cleverman came to join him, examining the connection.

It needs to be done, Quicksilver said. *I've given you everything I can —*

Quicksilver.

Quicksilver turned on his heel, his long coat flying. The blade in the doorway was a stranger, his mind bright and scattered like sunlight on glass, his hair bound back in an elaborate double club.

The queen requests your presence.

I am at her command, Quicksilver said. In spite of himself, he glanced at Ember, and the other cleverman nodded.

I will accompany you if you wish.

The queen wishes to speak to Quicksilver, Sunshard said. *Not to you.*

There was a moment when it might have tipped into violence—half the clevermen were Ember's own—but then Ember stiffly bowed his head.

So be it, Quicksilver said. *Stay and finish this.*

He followed Sunshard through the corridors as they wound slowly toward the heart of the hive. Bright Venture was a healthy ship again, and her crew was busy, blades leading teams of drones about their business, here and there a junior cleverman testing the tone of hull and bone. Rumor said they would need to Cull again soon, to supply all the men now working aboard, but Ember said the cells had seemed full enough. They passed through the large assembly room, where a quartet of drones waited in mindless patience, and the door of the zenana opened to them.

The inner chamber was in an uproar, the air hard with crowding thoughts. Quicksilver checked in the doorway, seeing the lords caught mid-quarrel, and Sunshard gave him a look that was like a shove.

My queen. The chief of the physical sciences, as you required.

Death swung to face him, skirts flying. Her hair gleamed in the shiplight, and her courtiers ducked their heads as though they were afraid to catch her eye. Even in her anger she was beautiful, Quicksilver thought, and made his own obeisance.

My queen.

So. Despite her temper, she paused to smile at him. *The very man we need.*

This is not his business. That was the youngest blade, Sky, his own anger barely in check, and Guide stirred in his corner.

My queen, I must agree. This is a matter for blades, not clevermen.

He is the one who gained entrance for us before, the Old One said. *It will be he who takes down their defenses this time as well. If he can.*

We need not risk it, Farseer said. *My queen, we have energy shields—thanks to Quicksilver, I fully acknowledge it—and we have installed them on nearly all our ships. Let us take a fleet against

Atlantis, not fiddle about with attacks through the Stargate.*

We have attacked Atlantis before, the Old One said. *Without success.*

Their ships were too strong for us, Noontide said. *And I believe they still will be. I remind you that these new shields require much power —*

We cannot delay, Sky said, and Farseer bared teeth at him.

Enough, Death said. *We have talked that to death, and I have given my decision. We will not attack the city from space until all our ships are ready, and Quicksilver has worked out this new power plant.*

Quicksilver looked warily at Death, afraid he knew exactly what they wanted from him, and she smiled again, laying her off hand on his shoulder. *We are on the knife's-edge, cleverman,* she said, and made the word a caress. Her touch was delicate, thrilling, and Quicksilver suppressed a shiver. *My Old One has proposed another attack, while we know their shield is compromised, and you, Quicksilver, have given us control of their computers. But Noontide believes they will have found a way to counter us, and Guide, who has fought the Lanteans more than any man, agrees with him.*

It has been my experience that the Lanteans cannot be taken the same way twice, Guide said, with a deferential bow.

Sky tossed back his hair. It fell almost to his waist, Quicksilver saw with envy, straight and silver and unbound. *Yet if we can weaken them further — we must try.*

You should lead it then, Farseer said. *For I will not.*

You will do as I bid you, Death said. *And I bid you depart my presence.*

Her tone was like the slap of a hand. Farseer flinched and bent his knee.*My queen —*

No more. Return when I summon you and not before.

For an instant, the room sang with Farseer's fear and anger, and then he had mastered himself. *As my queen commands,* he said, and turned away.

The drones opened the door for him, and the lords of the zenana drew aside from him as he passed. Death raked the room with her stare.

Do not doubt me, she said, soft now as silk, *for I am your queen.*

She let her gaze sweep the room a final time, daring them to defy her. *But we have more important matters. Quicksilver. You lowered their shields before. Can you do it a second time?*

Maybe, he began, but her eyes met his, and he could refuse her nothing. *Yes. Yes, I can.*

The camp looked pretty much like every other dig site William had ever worked in, a couple of tents rigged to shelter the equipment, and a makeshift kitchen where most of the crew had gathered in the morning chill, huddled close to the fire while a woman who had bound her braids up in a scarf dispensed cups of the hot mint-lemon-and-smoke-flavored tea. A second bucket had been set aside to cool, ready for the heat of the day, along with a box of MREs and a couple of smaller baskets of Satedan rations. William took his place in line, let her fill his travel mug—he'd already had a couple of offers to trade for it, would probably succumb one of these days—and ducked through the doorway into what had been the museum's loading area. The stairwell there was one of the less damaged, though the big elevator shaft was blocked by the wreckage of the car; it had taken them a full day of hard labor to shore up the walls and clear a passage, but he thought they might be just about ready to see what was in the catacombs.

The combat engineers had already gotten the generator going, and the lights rigged, and a thin Satedan woman was talking to one of them as they both peered dubiously into the opening. He could see Radek a little beyond them, checking the supports, and his steps slowed in spite of himself. Not that he was avoiding Zelenka, he told himself. It was just easier to gather his thoughts in relative quiet.

"So, today's the day, huh, doc?"

That was Corporal Sinclair, one of the engineers, a pottery cup of tea in one hand.

"If we're lucky," William answered.

"Say." Sinclair glanced over his shoulder, lowered his voice just a little. "You were at the meetings, right?"

"I was," William said, warily.

"What did Colonel Sheppard say to get the Genii to back down? I was on Atlantis the first time, and those little — those guys never seemed to give up."

"Damned if I know," William said. "I agree, Chief Ladon conceded much more quickly than I would have anticipated. But as to why?" He spread his free hand. "Your guess is as good as mine."

"Weird," Sinclair said, and William nodded in heartfelt agreement. It was extremely strange — and someday, he told himself, he would find out what really happened.

"There you are," Radek said, and came bustling over, brushing dirt from his hands. "I think we are ready to send someone down."

"I'll go," William said. For a moment, he thought Radek was going to protest, but then the scientist shrugged.

"I suppose that's best. It is your job."

"Yes," William said. He was already divesting himself of unnecessary gear, anything that might get caught climbing down through the floor, handed his tea absently to Sinclair. The engineer grinned, but didn't comment, and William checked his camera and light a final time. "Will you lower me, or do I need to climb?"

"We can lower you," one of the Satedans said. "No problem."

Radek nodded. "Yes, it will be safer that way." He paused. "You are clear on your location?"

"Yes," William said again. This stairwell had led into the Museum's largest storage area — where large incomplete fossils were stored before restoration, according to one of the women who had been married to a scholar and had spent a fair amount of time in the underground areas — but the map she had drawn for them showed a corridor that led to the room where the Ancient artifacts had been stored. If it was blocked, there was another way around — but perhaps they would be lucky this time.

He stepped into the harness, waited while Sinclair double-checked the buckles and the rope, and stepped to the edge of the opening. "All right."

"Go," Radek said, to the Satedans working the winch, and William felt the harness tighten as it took his weight. "All right. Stay in radio contact, please, and do not take chances."

I didn't know you cared. William swallowed that remark as thoroughly inappropriate, and adjusted his grip on the rope. "Ready."

"Now," one of the Satedans called, and William stepped gently into the empty air.

He let the light play ahead of him as he descended, grimacing as it picked out the signs of destruction. The floor was strewn with rubble, thick with brick dust, and something had fallen on a pile of crates, shattering the top tier and spilling their contents. He recognized pieces of armature, broken stone, shreds of some kind of packing material. None of that was a good sign. If the Satedans had been trying to move their best pieces to safety, there was no telling where the ZPM or the crystals had ended up.

As his feet touched the floor and the rope came slack, he swung his light in a wider arc, surveying the pile of crates. Teeth glinted among the shattered wood, the smallest as long as his hand, seemingly dozens of them poking from a bony snout. Tusks curled up from the lower jaw, the skull poking out of the wreckage like a dragon half buried in its hoard. He let out a sound somewhere between a yelp and a curse, and Radek's voice crackled in his ear.

"Are you all right?"

"Fine," William said. "I — stepped wrong." The rope slackened further, and he unclipped himself, watching as it slithered up and out of sight. "I think — " He switched on the camera as he spoke, panning slowly across the threatening skull — one of the incomplete fossils, presumably — and around the rest of the room. "It looks to me as though they'd started to pack things up to move them out of harm's way."

Radek's voice tightened. "Understood."

William let the camera linger a moment longer on a cracked black case that looked like plastic. More bones had spilled from it, along with another, weirdly crocodilian skull, and his fingers practically itched to examine it more closely. He compromised on a couple of close-ups, then switched off the camera and turned to look for the door.

There were more crates in the way, undamaged ones, and for an instant he hoped the passage might be clear. Then he came around the last crate, and his heart fell. The door was there, and open, too, but beyond it was a tangle of wood and plaster. He swore under his breath and moved closer, letting the light play slowly over the chaos.

At second glance, it wasn't quite as bad. The debris didn't look entirely structural, or at least there was only one large beam that looked as though it had come from the ceiling. The rest might have come from the furnishings, might have been shelves and boxes and packing materials. And artifacts, too; he winced at the glitter of broken crystal among the mess.

Still, there was a bit of a gap, and the camera's light seemed to show more open space beyond. He could probably fit through it easily enough, especially without a pack or any heavy gear — He curbed himself sternly. That was a stupid choice at the best of times, on Earth, say, on an ordinary dig somewhere in Western Europe. Here it was utter folly. He touched his radio instead. "Zelenka."

"Yes?"

"The door's partly blocked. I think I can get through without causing any more damage, but I'd like your opinion before I try it."

"Hell and damnation," Radek said, in Czech. There was a pause, and he went on in English. "Ronon and I will come down."

William lifted an eyebrow at that. He hadn't expected Ronon to be at the dig at all, much less to participate. Especially when he was easily the biggest person around, not at all the sort you'd normally want to have crawling around narrow spaces underground... But it was his planet, his homeworld, and that made a difference, too.

Ronon came down first, as though he was expecting attack, and Radek followed, muttering to himself in Czech. As he landed, his light caught the tusked skull, and he swore more loudly. Ronon turned, amazingly fast, reaching for his gun before he saw the skull and relaxed again.

"That's Tsuzhur. She used to be in the Great Hall."

"Is that her name or her species?" William asked, and Radek sighed loudly.

"Nickname," Ronon said. "Where's the door?"

William pointed, and followed as they ducked around the piles of crates. Radek studied the debris for a long moment, running his light up and down the one long beam, then examining the frame and the walls.

"Well," he said at last, and shrugged. "I think it is stable. I am smallest —"

"But I know what I'm doing," William said. He unbuckled his harness, not wanting it to catch on anything in the rubble, and Ronon gave him an appraising look.

"He should go," he said, and Radek shrugged again.

"As you wish."

William edged into the gap, turning sideways to scrape along what felt like a wall, then went to hands and knees to pull himself through the last low gap. There were sharp things in the debris, and he felt his trousers tear, felt something else jab into the heel of his hand. That he stopped to check, but there was no blood, and he crawled out at last into a larger space. A few rows of shelves were still intact, and several more had been tipped over, leaning against the wall like dominos. Crystal dust glittered on the bare tiles, but the shelves were mostly empty.

"Oh, damn," he said. He had known better, had known not to hope too much, but he never managed to be sensible about such things, and the barren shelves were like a blow. There had been a ZPM — here, in this room, according to the dataleaves; after everything they'd been through to get it, it seemed unfair to lose the prize.

He swung the light again, focusing more carefully. The tilted shelves were definitely empty, what had remained of their contents broken on the hard tiles, but there were still a couple of boxes in the closest upright shelves. They were made of the same black plastic as the broken cases in the fossil room, only intact, and he lifted the smaller one from its place. The latches had held, though the hinges felt weak, and he opened the lid with renewed hope.

It was an Ancient crystal, all right, long and narrow and pale gold, but a jagged crack ran all along one narrow face. He sighed, closed the lid again, and moved on. The next case had more crystals, dulled and chipped, obviously unusable.

"Lynn!" Radek's voice sounded in his ear. "What have you found?"

"Sorry." William stretched to take another case down from the top shelf. "There's not a lot left, I'm afraid. I did find a couple of crystals that look like the ones you wanted, but most of what I'm seeing is damaged."

There was a fractional pause, and then Radek said, "Keep looking." His voice was scrupulously neutral.

William worked his way down the row of shelves that were still upright, and was not particularly surprised when most of the cases turned out to contain only damaged crystals. One small box held what looked like a single Ancient data crystal, and he tucked it, box and all, into the pocket of his jacket. Not that it was likely to be that much help; what they needed right now was power, weapons, ways to defend the city, not random information.

"Nothing so far," he said into the radio, and Radek answered patiently enough.

"Understood."

William shone his light along the top of the tilted shelves, looking for anything that might have been caught between, that might have survived, and a pale object by his feet caught his eye. He swung the light down, his breath catching as he recognized the bones of a human hand. He let the light play further, picked out a sleeve and a shoulder, the fragments of a skull beneath a fallen case. A soldier, he guessed — the remains of the clothes looked like a uniform, complete with badges and what were probably rank stripes ringing the sleeve. And there was carrying case, almost invisible in the shadow of the tilted shelves, lying as though the soldier had dropped it when the crates fell on him. On her, he corrected, assessing the size of the hand. A woman, or a very young man. He wouldn't know for sure unless he could examine the rest of the skeleton.

He shook that thought away, pulled the case free. It was rounded at the corners, with an extra set of straps to keep the lid in place. He picked them loose, pried open the lid, and peered inside. Nestled in the padding was a narrow crystal pyramid, its jagged edges seamed with darker color. "Oh."

"Lynn!" Radek sounded distinctly out of patience, and William grimaced.

"Sorry. It's here. I have it."

"The ZPM?"

"Yes." William closed the lid, relieved that the case seemed solid, refastened the straps.

"Does it have power?"

"I don't know. It's not glowing, does that mean anything?"

"Not really."

"There isn't any obvious damage," William said. He looked back at the body, wondering if the Satedans had known what they had, if that was why she'd been trying to retrieve it, or if she'd just been trying to save one more piece of her people's past. And that was gross speculation. All he could say for certain was that she had died trying to get the artifact out of the Museum. "The case was undamaged, and it seemed to be well padded."

Radek sighed again. "We must get it out right away."

"All right," William said, and moved back to the debris-choked doorway.

It took them almost ten minutes to work out how to fit the case through the gap, Radek swearing in Czech the whole time, but at last it was through. William squatted against the wall, feeling the sweat trickling down his spine, and after a moment, Radek spoke in his ear.

"It is intact, at least. It is not at full power, but I can't tell any more than that until we get it out of here."

"Go," William said. "Ronon?"

"Yeah."

"I've also found a body."

There was a little silence. "Yeah?"

"It's mostly buried, but I can see sleeve marking — unit insignia, maybe, or rank? I'll photograph them, but do you want me to bring the actual sleeve end?"

This time the silence was longer, and William winced, hoping he hadn't inadvertently offended. The Air Force people he'd known, the Marines, they would have wanted that tangible memory, but maybe Satedans, the Satedan military, didn't work that way.

"Yeah," Ronon said. His voice was just a little hoarse. "That'd be good."

"Right," William said. He fished in his pocket for his knife, sawed carefully through the tough fabric just above the rings that looked like rank stripes, freed it gently from the skeleton. In spite of his care, he dislodged a couple of the smaller fingerbones, the tendons too far gone to hold them, and he nudged the bones back into place.

"Sorry," he said, softly, and turned back to the blocked door.

He worked his way through the gap, emerged gasping and sweating in the fossil room. Ronon extended a hand, hauled him to his feet, and William nodded in thanks.

"Here," he said, and held out the cut sleeve.

Ronon took it, held the scrap of cloth into the beam from his light. His face was shadowed, but William thought his voice was unnaturally controlled. "University Brigade. A corporal." He tucked it into his own pocket. "I'll give it to Cai."

William nodded, suppressing unworthy regret. He had the photos, he didn't need the actual artifact.

"What happened, could you tell?"

William shrugged. "A crate fell on her — from the size of the hand, I think it was a woman — and my guess would be that she was trying to rescue something from the shelves. The ZPM, it looks like."

Ronon nodded in turn. "Thanks."

"You're welcome."

Several people were looking over the edge of the hole, and William climbed back into his harness, let himself be hauled to the surface. Ronon came after, hand over hand up the rope, and looked at Radek, who had the ZPM lying on a worktable, cables snaking to it from his laptop.

"Well?"

"Well." Radek glared at both of them. "It is a ZPM, and it is intact and undamaged. But. There is only minimal power."

"How small is minimal?" Ronon asked.

"Too small," Radek said. "We might be able to power the shield for a few minutes. We might be able to launch drones. I will not know for certain exactly how much power is available until we go back to Atlantis, but it is not enough. Not enough at all."

"Bugger," William said.

CHAPTER TWENTY-ONE
Obstacles

"DR. KELLER?"

Jennifer pulled off her exam gloves and thumbed on her radio. "Keller here."

"Ma'am, you wanted me to tell you when Colonel Sheppard and his team returned," Airman Salawi said.

"I did, didn't I," Jennifer said. She felt the knot settle back in the pit of her stomach, the one she'd managed to distract herself from while checking out Dr. Altman's sore throat. "So how did it go with the Satedans and the Genii?"

"All right, I think?" Salawi said, in tones that suggested that she wasn't sure whether she was supposed to have been listening to whatever post-mission conversation had gone on in the control room. "No injuries to our people, anyway."

"Well, that's what we like from a diplomatic conference," Jennifer said, although given the Satedans and the Genii, it probably hadn't been a foregone conclusion.

"Yes, ma'am."

"I'm not in the Air Force," Jennifer pointed out. "You don't actually have to call me 'ma'am' all the time."

"Sorry, Dr. Keller."

"Don't worry about it," Jennifer said. She glanced at her computer screen again, wondering if she should run one more set of the simulations of Rodney's recovery. It wasn't as if using the same data and the same computer models was going to give her different results, but there was some part of her that stubbornly hoped that it would.

She picked up her laptop instead and headed up to Woolsey's office, which was now at least temporarily Sheppard's office. The first few times she'd had to make these kinds of reports, it had been in Elizabeth's office, sparely but beautifully decorated with the artifacts of half a dozen worlds. Woolsey's was more a stubborn little oasis of Earth, as if asserting his own personality over the space was his small act of rebellion against the weight of people's expectations.

It was hard to imagine what Sheppard would do with it if it turned out to be his office on a more permanent basis. He had an office of his own, but he was hardly ever in it, and as far as Jennifer could tell it wasn't much more than an oversized closet full of paperwork and spare clips of ammunition.

She paused for a moment outside the door of his office, then squared her shoulders and walked in. "Colonel Sheppard? If you've got a minute, there's something we need to talk about."

"Sure," Sheppard said. "Is there a problem?" He looked like he hoped the answer was no. "We just got in."

"I know," Jennifer said by way of apology. "But, yes, I think we may have a problem. You know we've been trying to figure out how the Wraith retrovirus works, so that we can reverse its effects."

"Yeah, and?"

Jennifer took a deep breath. "Here's the thing," she said. "All of our efforts to transform the Wraith completely into humans have involved essentially writing over the part of their DNA that comes from the Iratus bug with human DNA."

"I know that much."

"So, what we keep finding is that the Iratus bug's regenerative abilities — which are also present in the Wraith — make it very difficult to eradicate the Iratus bug DNA completely from someone's system. It was possible the time when you were transforming into a bug — "

Sheppard looked sour. "I try not to remember."

"Sorry," Jennifer said. "But that transformation left your body in such an unstable state that it was easy to get your body to reject the alien DNA. The Wraith combination of Iratus bug and human DNA is stable, and in some ways almost self-protective. If I didn't know better, I'd think that somebody had deliberately designed it that way."

"You may not be wrong," Sheppard said. "We know that the Wraith are pretty advanced at genetic engineering, given the way they grow their ships — "

"Yeah, I try not to remember that," Jennifer said.

"It would have been pretty cool to have our own hive ship," Sheppard said, and then, "Joking. That was a joke."

"Very funny," Jennifer said. "My point is, I think given a little more time I could work out how to transform a human permanently into a Wraith."

"If we wanted to do that," Sheppard said. "Which we don't, although being able to do it temporarily could be useful."

"It could be, if we could do it," Jennifer said. She was aware that she was talking around the point, as if as long as she didn't say it, it could stay hypothetical, an anxiety to keep her up at night rather than her best professional opinion. "The thing is, I've gone through about a hundred computer models, I've run simulation after simulation, and… I'm really sorry," she said. "But I don't think we can permanently reverse what the Wraith have done to Rodney. I just don't think it can be done."

She could see Sheppard's jaw tightening, see him glance away as if meeting her eyes would betray that he was upset. "I'm sorry," she said again uselessly. She was aware that she was doing the same thing, shoving her own feelings down under professional distance that left her cold, but she wished he'd say something. It would be easier to play the role of comforter than to watch Sheppard leashing whatever it was he felt about this before he'd meet her eyes.

"All right," Sheppard said, finally looking back at her. "What can you do?"

"Well," Jennifer said, trying to assemble her thoughts. "I'm hoping that we can come up with a way to temporarily suppress at least most of the Iratus bug DNA, something that would be safe to use as a long-term therapy. Like Carson's original retrovirus, but hopefully without global amnesia as a side effect."

"Yeah, that would be good," Sheppard said.

"I want to be really clear, though. I don't know that something like that will work. If not…" Jennifer let out a breath. "I think there's a pretty good chance that trying out the treatments that we've come up with will put so much strain on Rodney's system that he's either going to need to feed or… basically, or we're going to kill him."

"Well, Rodney feeding isn't really an option," Sheppard said. There was something off in his tone, though, and she wished that she had a better idea what was going on behind those eyes.

"No, it's not," Jennifer said. "Hopefully, we'll have enough warning if our treatments are making things worse that we can put him in stasis until we come up with something better."

"Right," Sheppard said. He let out a breath. "All right. What can I get you that'll help?"

Jennifer blinked. "I'm sorry?"

"You don't know how much I wish this was a problem that could be solved by going out and shooting something," Sheppard said. "There's probably going to be that part of the problem, and I'm really looking forward to that. But right now, my job is to make sure that you have whatever you need to do your job, so you can figure out a way to help Rodney."

"You mean, what would help short of having a Wraith bio-engineer tell me exactly what they did and what they think might fix it?"

"That's not out of the question," Sheppard said. "Todd still owes me one. More than one, the way I figure it." He looked her over. "How much time have you been spending on this outside of your scheduled work hours?"

Jennifer hoped that didn't mean she looked as strung out as she felt. "Nobody ever told me I had a schedule," she said.

"Very funny," Sheppard said. "How about we see if *Daedalus* or *Hammond* can spare one of their physicians to take over your office hours for a while? Because as much as I know we like to think around here that there are more than twenty-four hours in a day, I'm told that's not actually true."

"I don't know," Jennifer said. "Frankly, my office hours are the only time right now that I feel like I'm actually getting any results. At least I can fix sprained ankles and treat strep throat."

Sheppard shrugged. "It was just a thought."

"I'll think about it," Jennifer said. "And I'll let you know if I can think of anything else that would help."

"Okay," Sheppard said. He glanced around the office as if he still wasn't entirely comfortable being there. "We'll figure this out." Whatever else he might have said was cut off as an alarm sounded from the gateroom below.

"Unscheduled offworld activation!"

"So much for anybody getting more rest," Jennifer said under her breath as Sheppard headed for the door. At least the mechanical iris was in place.

John hurried into the control room, vaguely aware that Keller had abandoned him. Headed to the infirmary, he assumed, and turned his attention to the situation. Below in the gate room, Marines scrambled into position, weapons at the ready, and the new iris team kicked the generator from stand-by to full ready. Its whine filled the air, and Salawi had to raise her voice a little to be heard above the sound.

"No IDC, sir."

"Close the iris."

"Yes, sir."

The new bell sounded — yet another alarm, John thought — and the sergeant in charge of the iris team hauled back on the lever. Carter and Zelenka had had a long discussion about why it was simpler, and better than a button, something to do with failsafes and the gearing, but he hadn't been paying much attention, hoped only that it would be simple enough. And faster. The plates were moving, sliding against each other, intersecting to eclipse the event horizon, but it seemed to take forever for them to meet in the middle, the plates interlocking at last to form a spiky metal star. Behind it, the event horizon shimmered blue, casting watery shadows. Zelenka brushed past him and slid into the seat next to Salawi's, frowning as he touched his keyboard.

"No sign of any transmission," Salawi said, dubiously, and Zelenka spared her a crooked smile.

"We have seen that before, yes?"

"Sir," a Marine said, and John turned to take the P90 the young woman handed to him. Out of the corner of his eye, John saw Lorne lurch into the control room, P90 dangling from his chest harness. He put down his crutches, braced himself against the console, and tucked the P90 into firing position. John opened his mouth to order him away, but the radio sounded in his ear.

"Colonel Sheppard. What's going on?"

That was Caldwell on the command frequency, and John touched his radio. "We have an unscheduled gate activation. We've closed the iris."

There was a second of silence, and John could almost hear the unspoken questions. "Keep me informed," Caldwell said instead, and cut the connection.

Zelenka said something in Czech, and looked over his shoulder. "Colonel Sheppard. We are under attack. It's Rodney."

"Or someone using his codes," John said. He looked at Salawi. "Lock us down. And put me on citywide."

"Yes, sir." Her hands flew over the keyboard.

John waited for her nod, then took a breath. "This is Colonel Sheppard. We have an unscheduled gate activation and a computer intrusion. We are initiating a full lockdown immediately. Sheppard out."

In the gate room, he saw a flash of bronze hair as Colonel Carter moved to join the iris team. He saw her head tilt as she examined the interlocking plates, tilt again as she turned to speak to the sergeant in charge.

"Ty sráèi," Zelenka said, his hands working. He looked over his shoulder as the lights flickered. "Apparently Rodney had another bolthole." He turned back to his monitor, scowling through his glasses. "Ach, ty lstivý bastarde." He shook his head. "I have lost the shield."

If we had one, John thought. His hands tightened on the P90, and he made himself relax his grip. That'll teach me, he thought. Not five minutes ago, I was saying to Keller that I wanted to solve problems by shooting them. Remind me never to make dumb remarks like that again.

"And I have lost main power," Zelenka said. The lights flickered again, came back up. "Ale ano, mám ti! We are on back-up now." He peered at his screen. "And holding. He is locked out. Of that, at least."

The event horizon glowed behind the iris. John knew how the iris was supposed to work: it lay so close to the surface of the puddle that matter wasn't able to reintegrate, was destroyed before it could exit the system. Something thudded against the shield, and he flinched, bit his lip. Surely that wasn't — but the thud came again, and another, a series of blows like hail on asphalt, too dull for explosions, but each one a death. The gate's occluded light shivered, rippled and changed; John had lost count of how many hits the iris had taken, and the thuds kept coming. In the gate room, Carter was watching the plates, the Marines ready at her back, and still the iris rang dully. One of those thuds could be Rodney. John pushed the thought away. Rodney was working the computers, he told himself. He wouldn't come though until he knew he had Atlantis's systems under his control; Radek was giving him a hard fight, he'd be needed on the hive...

The sounds stopped. John took a breath, waiting for the wormhole to collapse, but it stayed open, reflecting blue against the gateroom walls. Carter looked up at him from her place beside the iris controls.

"Probe first," she said, sounding almost serene, "then explosives."

"Right," John said. The Wraith weren't stupid — and especially Rodney wasn't stupid, he'd figure out what they'd done, and try to blow open the gate.

There was a new sound from the gate, higher, harder. The probe, John thought. "Fall back!" he shouted. "Everybody into cover!"

Carter gave him a look at that — if the iris failed, it would take half the gate room with it, and they would be seriously screwed regardless — but the Marines scrambled obediently for their secondary positions. There was a long pause, the only sound the whine of the generator and the occasional click of keys, and then there was a huge and heavy whump, a sound so deep John felt it in the marrow of his bones. The iris shivered, and held. A minute passed, then another, and then the wormhole collapsed.

John took a deep breath and then another, feeling the tightness in his arms and shoulders, saw Lorne reach wincing for his crutches. He set his P90 aside, got the crutches under his arms, and hung there for a moment, breathing hard, before he straightened.

"Stand down," John called, and motioned to Salawi. "Citywide."

"Yes, sir."

"This is Colonel Sheppard. The city is secure. We are ending the lockdown. I repeat, the city is secure. Sheppard out." He drew a finger across his throat, and Salawi cut the broadcast. He looked at Lorne. "I wouldn't call this light duty, Major."

Lorne had the grace to look abashed. "Sorry, sir. But I was right here, and —"

John nodded. "Yeah. I know. Don't do it again." He looked around the control room. "Nice job, people. Very nice job."

Zelenka finished typing something, and swung away from his keyboard, the lights gleaming off his glasses. "And we are secure again."

"Good work with the iris, Radek," John said, and felt the words were ridiculously insufficient.

Zelenka gave a flick of a smile and lifted his eyebrows. "I would not like to do that every day. But, yes, it has held."

The iris unfolded with a soft hiss of metal on metal, and Carter came up the stairs, shaking her head. "That was interesting."

"Impressive," John said. "It sounded like they lost a few men there before they figured out what happened."

Carter nodded. "Sounded like it. Pity they won't try it again."

"For what it is worth," Zelenka said, "Rodney was not among them. He was trying to break into the system throughout the attack."

"Figures," John said, and didn't know exactly what to feel.

The wormhole collapsed, leaving the Stargate empty, the red hills of this barren world caught in its perfect circle. The air around it roiled in confusion and anger and above it all the long harsh shriek of the queen's loss. Quicksilver stared at the screen of his portable computer, baffled and furious. He should have known — should have guessed, anyway, even if the Lanteans had left the shield program intact and running to attract his attention. He should have insisted on sending a probe first, even if it would have given the Lanteans a few moments' warning…

Thirty men, Death cried. *And my blades.* She did not name Sky, who had led the second party, nor did she need to, and the circling blades flinched from her grief.

I knew we should send a probe, someone said, and the queen whirled, her skirts flying.

Who says that now?

There was no answer: the thought had been fleeting, involuntary, and no one dared claim the words.

Quicksilver ducked his head, scrolling back through the pages of data. If he could not save the dead, at least he could see how they had failed. Certainly someone had been though his programs, excised them from the Ancient systems — sometimes neatly, a hand he thought he should know, sometimes with equal skill but less precision — so that he had had to fall back on the last of his fail-safes, the one program he had been almost sure they would not find, and could not eradicate completely if they did.

You, Quicksilver, the Old One said, softly. *Was there no sign of this change?*

Quicksilver looked up, scowling. *If there had been, I would have told you so. Everything seems to be just as it was before — except, as

I told you they would, they'd found my first way in.*

We must attack at once, Farseer said, *and revenge our losses.*

It's still too far from any base of ours, Noontide said. *And Atlantis—this proves they're too strong to take on lightly."

Death looked at him coldly. *Do you call this a light choice, blade?*

Noontide bowed deeply. *I do not, my queen.*

A wise answer. Death lifted her head. *And it is I who will choose our next action.*

This one swore he could get us past their defenses. That was Flare, whose full brother had led the first wave. He raised his feeding hand—deadly insult—and pointed at Quicksilver. *He has betrayed us, my queen. Kill him now, tainted thing—*

Be silent, the queen hissed, the words a blow that drove Flare to one knee. She turned slowly. *What, then, is your explanation, Quicksilver?*

My queen. Quicksilver stared at his screen, not daring to meet her eyes. *The Lanteans must have built some kind of mechanical barrier for their Stargate—a moveable one, they couldn't afford to block it entirely. It is not tied into their computers, or I would have found the controls there.*

It withstood the most powerful explosive we had with us, Nighthaze said thoughtfully. He was a cleverman, a specialist in such things. *Perhaps something more powerful could breach this barrier?*

What I'd like to know, Farseer said, *is why this one didn't know of it?* He gestured toward Quicksilver, who lifted his head.

Because they didn't have it when I was there, he said. *That should be obvious.*

The Old One turned to survey the Stargate, tilting his head so that his thin braid slithered across the back of his coat. *I don't believe it's even possible. A moveable barrier for the gate? I cannot conceive it.*

Well, obviously it is possible, Quicksilver said. *And I know who did it. That has to be McKay's work—I'm sure of it, he's the only one of them clever enough to design such a thing, make it work within the wormhole's tolerances. And he's got an assistant, what's-his-name—he could build it for him. With guidance. And it's McKay who's locked me out—* He stopped, aware of a strange tension in the air around him. *What?*

You will not speak that name again, Death said. Her tone was even, her anger leashed, and all the more terrifying for it. The fingers of her feeding hand spread and flexed, and Quicksilver ducked his head. *That is my will and command, do you hear me? Never again.*

Quicksilver went to his knees under the force of her gaze. *Yes, my queen.*

Into the sudden silence, Guide said, mildly, *The Lanteans are quick to learn, my queen.* He did not say that he had said as much before, but everyone knew it. Death's eyes narrowed.

What, then, would you have us do?

Return to the hive, my queen, Guide said. *We have given the Lanteans more cause to fear us, and that will buy us time to reconnoiter, to plan a direct assault. They, on the other hand, must wonder every moment when we will next bombard this shield of theirs — and perhaps we should do just that, and keep them worrying. It is not an altogether worthless result.*

Death eyed him for a long moment, and then she had mastered herself *No. Not entirely. Very well. Let us go.*

Quicksilver hauled himself to his feet, his mind still ringing as though he'd been struck. He reached for his computer, hunching his shoulders as though that could hide him from the queen, but she turned to block his path. He froze, the computer still in his hands, and Death laid her feeding hand against his chest. Even through his coat, he could feel the prick of her claws, see the shift of muscles as she slowly tensed her fingers. She smiled.

Do not forget what I have told you, cleverman.

CHAPTER TWENTY-TWO
Allegiance

DICK straightened his notes and tried to look calm and confident in the face of the assembled IOA members. That would have been easier if they hadn't spent the last hour demanding that he explain one more time why they'd turned an Ancient warship over to the Genii. At this point, he felt they were well aware of his reasoning, and were taking the opportunity to air out their own personal soapboxes.

"The potential benefits of having an additional warship under the direct supervision of the IOA cannot be underestimated," Shen said. Her eyes were on the American committee head, Dale Strom, who was watching her with an expression of polite interest that revealed nothing. "To let such an opportunity slip through our fingers this way—"

"Personally, I'm more concerned about the effect of the Genii having the ship than I am about our losing it," Jean LaPierre said. "I'm not sure that arming an ally on whom we can't depend from moment to moment—"

"The Genii have been extremely helpful in many ways," Dick said firmly. "Certainly in our current search for Dr. McKay, their intelligence network is proving invaluable."

"Let's talk about how you came to lose Dr. McKay," Strom said. "Can we review the mission where he was captured, just so that it's fresh in all of our minds?"

"I'd be interested in hearing a little more about that myself," Roy Martin said. Martin was the new U.S. representative to the IOA, a former senator who O'Neill hadn't seemed particularly enthusiastic about. He had thinning white hair and a soft Southern drawl.

"Lifetime politician," O'Neill had said, in the same tone he'd have used to say convicted felon. "Never served in the armed forces. Retired a couple of years ago, and probably a big donor to the President's campaign." O'Neill had shaken his head as if to say what can you do? "You watch, he'll be Kinsey all over again."

Dick took a deep breath. "We received a distress call from our allies on New Athos. We believed they were under attack by the Wraith. We sent two teams through the Stargate to render assistance."

"Two teams," Nechayev said. "How many men?"

"Eight," Dick said. Somehow it sounded less adequate put that way. "Was that really enough to deal with a Culling?"

"Obviously not," Shen said. "I think the results speak for themselves."

"It wasn't a Culling," Dick said. "It was an ambush. When we arrived on New Athos, no one knew anything about the distress signal. Colonel Sheppard and his team were talking to the local leaders while Major Lorne's team guarded the gate. At that point, three Darts came through the Stargate. We believe their intention was to capture Dr. McKay."

"Bear with me, please," Martin said. "I'm new here. Why would they want to do that?"

"Presumably because of his scientific expertise," Dick said. "Dr. McKay also had extensive knowledge of Atlantis's defenses, including the city's computer security and its shields and weapons technology."

Shen folded her hand in front of her. "And what efforts did you make to recover Dr. McKay?"

"You've seen my report," Dick said. "Colonel Sheppard's team was very nearly successful in retrieving Dr. McKay, but they had to fall back when the *Hammond* began taking heavy damage."

"Not a very good trade, one of our warships for one scientist," Nechayev put in.

Dick met his eyes. "One with information that could give a dangerous strategic advantage to the Wraith."

"And given his access to that information, why was he sent on such a mission?" Shen said. "Why would you risk such a valuable asset on what was essentially a military maneuver?"

"Dr. McKay is an integral part of Colonel Sheppard's team," Dick began.

"He is a scientist," Shen said. "Surely responding to reports of a Wraith Culling does not require Atlantis's Chief of Sciences. I think it is a sign of dangerously misplaced priorities to send someone so valuable on a mission for which he lacks any professional training."

"He has over five years of experience in the field," Dick said.

"It doesn't seem to have done him much good," Aurelia Dixon-Smythe said. "And now that you've lost him, you say that he must be recovered at all costs. How many costs do you expect us to absorb?"

"It's a reasonable question," Strom said. "How much has losing Dr.

McKay cost us? Including your efforts to get him back."

"I would characterize those efforts as part of our normal operations," Dick said. "Which the IOA has already funded for the fiscal year."

"Are you saying your normal operations include your personnel getting kidnapped by the Wraith?" Martin asked, sounding almost curious.

"It's a risk that we understand to be part of our activities in the Pegasus Galaxy."

"A risk that could in many cases be avoided by better judgment in the authorization of missions," Shen said. "There is no sense in sending non-military personnel to respond to combat situations."

"We're not made of money, Mr. Woolsey," Strom said. "I understand that in the past, you've had a great deal to say about the need to weigh the costs and benefits of missions that involve substantial risk to American — or international — personnel."

"The benefit, in this case, involved keeping our allies from being slaughtered by the Wraith," Dick said.

"A handful of local hunter-gatherers," Shen said. "Who were not, as it turns out, in any danger. And in exchange, you have lost a valuable scientist, compromised Atlantis's security, and risked one of Earth's only battlecruisers."

Desai, who'd been listening quietly for some time with an expression that suggested he had a headache, spoke up mildly. "The Athosians are descended from an advanced technological society with a long history, now decimated by the Wraith," he said. "They have extensive trading contacts within the Pegasus Galaxy."

"We're not there as merchants," Shen said. "This is a scientific expedition, and its goals should not be compromised by ill-conceived military actions."

"I think the goals of the expedition have evolved," LaPierre said. "It's all very well to study Ancient technology, but keeping the Wraith from reaching Earth has to be a priority."

"Which losing Dr. McKay didn't help, either," Nechayev said.

"I frankly question whether either one requires funding a project of this magnitude," Dixon-Smythe said. "If Atlantis had remained on Earth, we could have studied the Ancient technology without further provoking the Wraith."

"So I advised," Shen said.

"If Atlantis had stayed on Earth, it would have been the property of the Americans," Nechayev said. "Do you really think they would have let you play with their toys?"

Strom cleared his throat. "There may have been a number of mis-understandings," he began.

"I think I understood very clearly that the American government claimed Atlantis as long as it remained within American territorial waters," Dick said. "As I recall, the IOA's position was that returning Atlantis to Pegasus under international jurisdiction was a preferable situation. It's not as if now we can bring it back."

"Because your ZPM was depleted in landing the city," Shen said. "How convenient for certain parties involved."

"If you're implying that I'm somehow misrepresenting our current power situation —" Dick began, stung.

"I am sure you are not," Shen said. "Just as I am sure that there is some malfunction preventing Atlantis from communicating with Earth."

"They could be having some technical difficulty," Dick said.

"Like what?" Martin asked.

"I don't know," Dick said. "I don't have any more information than you do about why Atlantis isn't dialing Earth, but I'm certain that Colonel Sheppard will be in touch as soon as he can."

Shen shook her head. "I wish I were as certain."

"You can't seriously be accusing me of... I'm not even sure what you're accusing me of," Dick said.

"Let me just say that I have serious doubts about whether the first loyalty of any of the leaders of the Atlantis expedition is to the IOA," Shen said. "It might well prove in your own best interests in the short term to have your operations in Atlantis proceed without our over-sight, but let me make this perfectly clear. In the long run, all you will accomplish is the end of the Atlantis project."

"If the IOA ceases to be interested in funding the Atlantis mission, I think there may be other options worth exploring," Desai said.

"Let's not get ahead of ourselves," Strom said. "Mr. Woolsey, I think we could all use some more information here. I'd like you to prepare some notes on your reasoning for assigning scientific personnel to field missions in Pegasus. I think we'd all be interested in hearing about your thinking there."

"I'd be interested in hearing from Atlantis," Dixon-Smythe said. "When do you think they might manage to dial in?"

"I don't know," Dick said. "I'm as eager to hear from them as you are." And I actually care about more than whether they've wasted any money, he thought but managed with an effort not to say.

"If they've all been killed by the Wraith, this is going to turn out to have been an incredible waste of time," Nechayev said.

"Not if the city of the Ancients is intact," Shen said.

"Now I think we really are getting ahead of ourselves," Martin said, his eyes on Dick as he spoke. "I don't think we should write off these men and women yet."

"Thank you," Dick said quietly.

"This meeting is adjourned," Strom said. "We'll be in touch to schedule the next session."

Martin lingered by the table as the others filed out, Shen and LaPierre already back to arguing in low tones. "I don't expect you to like me much, Mr. Woolsey," he said. "I wouldn't, if I were in your position."

"Your congressional record is impressive," Dick said.

"Like I said, I wouldn't like me much," Martin said. "I've actually read all those reports you submitted, which is more than I suspect you can say for a couple of other people who were just sitting here. I can't fault your commitment to your people."

"Thank you," Dick said again. It meant more to hear than he would once have believed it ever would.

"But Shen's got a point," Martin said. "You're supposed to be representing our interests out there. If not America's, then…" He waved a hand around the conference table. "And I can't help wondering if that's really what you're out there to do."

"I'm out there to represent Earth," Dick said.

"To represent Earth," Martin said. "That's a tall order."

"And yet someone's got to do it," Dick said. "In the Milky Way, that's the IOA and under their auspices, the Stargate program. In Pegasus, right now that's the Atlantis Expedition, because we're the ones who are out there. You sent us back to Pegasus, and so there we are." He shrugged. "I personally still believe that's for the best."

"Someone has got to do it," Martin said. "I think the question we're all asking right now is whether that ought to be you."

"I can't answer that question for you," Dick said. "I have only one question for you in return: who else would you prefer?"

"Personally, I'd rather have all our extraterrestrial operations back in the hands of the U.S. Air Force," Martin said. "With congressional oversight, of course. But I don't think that's going to fly anymore. Carter ruffled too many feathers."

"Colonel Carter did an exemplary job of defeating the Replicators," Dick said.

"On behalf of the Air Force," Martin said. "Or at least that's some people's feeling. Not to repeat every bit of the gossip that I've heard since taking this job — oh, about a week ago — but let's just say that the best thing that I've heard said about the situation was that Carter's Air Force through and through, and she wasn't about to let American interests take a back seat."

"What's the worst?" Dick said.

Martin shrugged. "That if we'd wanted O'Neill calling the shots in Atlantis, we would have hired him."

Dick wasn't sure what response he could profitably make to that. "What would you like to hear from me, Senator?"

"Whose side are you on, Mr. Woolsey? And don't say 'Earth'. I don't think it's possible for anyone to represent the interests of the entire planet."

Dick shook his head. "Then with all due respect, Senator, I'm not sure what there is left for me to say."

Martin considered him for a moment longer, and then turned away. "See you in the next round of hearings," he said. "You might want to give the question some more thought before then."

"As might you," Dick said. "I understand Shen is interested in the job."

Martin snorted. "And I understand it's good ice-skating weather in Hell this time of year." He picked up his briefcase and went out, closing the door behind him.

Dick gathered up his notes in the sudden quiet. None of them had proven to be of very much use. He resisted the urge to crumple them angrily into a ball, and put them away carefully instead.

It was all he could do at the moment on behalf of either Atlantis or Earth. He wished it didn't feel like doing so little in the face of what he could hardly believe anymore was a simple communications problem.

"I'm sure they're all right," he said aloud, hoping that would make it sound more like it could possibly be true.

Atlantis quieted down at night, but it was never silent. Besides the few people assigned to man the control room and monitor the city while it slept, there were always some who just weren't sleeping. Some of that was what on Sateda they'd called 'losing the sun'; when you spent too much time on planets where the day was different, it was easy to get day and night screwed up. Jet lag, they called it here, although Ronon had never entirely figured out why.

He thought some of it was just that as busy as they usually were, if people wanted time for themselves, they had to steal it at weird hours. John could usually be found after midnight doing pretty much anything but sleeping. John and Rodney played video games or played with toys like a couple of overgrown kids, although at the moment that was out.

John also hung around the gym if Ronon or Teyla were up, although he didn't seem as ready to spar with the Marines as he used to be. Ronon thought it wasn't even that he minded if some eighteen-year-old guy got the better of him so much as that he didn't think it looked great for a commander to get kicked around too often by his own men. He was a good fighter, and Ronon thought he'd finally shaken off the ache in his side that had bothered him for a while after he got impaled twice in a month, but still.

He wasn't in the gym, though, or in the TV lounge watching the new DVDs people had bought while they were on Earth, or out driving golf balls off the balcony into the icy waves. It was probably a little dark for golf, although John was apparently kind of fascinated with it since a giant tentacle had reached up out of the waves and snagged one of his golf balls a meter above the water. Or anyway so he claimed.

Ronon was heading back to his quarters when he nearly ran into John carrying McKay's cat with the same defensive expression he had sometimes when Teyla handed him Torren, as if daring anyone to say anything about it.

"Not again," Ronon said.

"I found him wandering around, and I hate to wake up Keller, so I figured I'd just keep him until morning."

"Better you than me," Ronon said. "What if he ruins your stuff?"

"I'll put him in the bathroom," John said. Ronon trailed him out of a sense that this ought to be entertaining. The cat flailed as John attempted to put him in the bathroom, and John hissed in pain, or maybe that was the cat hissing.

"Stupid cat," he muttered as the door shut.

"You're bleeding," Ronon pointed out, settling into a chair.

"I'm used to it," John said. The cat yowled from the other side of the door, making an impressive variety of noises. "He's not as bad as the Wraith." He sat down on the edge of the bed, fingering the scratches on his wrist. Ronon couldn't help noticing that the room looked neater than usual, as if John hadn't actually been spending very much time there. "So," he said.

"So, what?"

John shrugged. He looked tired, as if this was just one more thing added to a really long day at work. "I never really got a chance to ask," he said. "Are you okay with the way things went down on Sateda?"

"This works," Ronon said.

"Okay," John said after a moment, in a tone that invited more of an answer. Ronon thought about it, although he hadn't actually been hoping to talk about work at this point either.

"It would be better if the Satedans could keep the artifacts of the Ancestors," he said. "But right now we need a lot of supplies for rebuilding, and this stuff is valuable. It's better to make a good deal that means we get help rebuilding and Atlantis and the Genii get stuff that helps them fight the Wraith."

"We?" John asked, his voice carefully casual, and, okay, that wasn't entirely about work.

"I'm still Satedan," Ronon said. "I thought I could never go back. Now... maybe when I get done fighting the Wraith I could retire and have a house or something. Train the new Satedan army."

"Yeah, you could go home," John said, with a smile that didn't look happy at all. "That would be a good thing."

"When I get done fighting the Wraith," Ronon said. "I don't think that's going to be anytime soon. I'm not quitting the team."

"I wish there were more of one," John said. "Right now it's you and Teyla and Radek, and Radek keeps making it clear that he's only planning on doing this in the short term."

"In the long term, we get McKay back, and somebody else takes over Woolsey's job so you can go back on the team."

"Maybe even Woolsey," John said. "Or somebody. But not me."

"You're not doing too bad," Ronon said. "Nothing's blown up."

"Not exactly a really demanding standard there, but I see your point." He looked away, his eyes shadowed.

"So?"

"So what if it is me?"

"You try not to get stuff blown up," Ronon said.

"I can do that," John said. "It just isn't the same as being on the team." He still wasn't meeting Ronon's eyes. "And, I mean, I know that's just… sooner or later this happens, right? You get promoted or transferred or something, and people say they're going to write, but…"

"What are you talking about?"

"I mean, I'd still be here, but there'd be a new team, and…" John looked like he was struggling for words. "Just working with people isn't the same as having friends," he said finally.

Ronon looked at him for a long moment. "You think it's all about the team?"

"It's intense," John said. "You get to know people, and you spend all your time hanging out with them, they're your buddies, and then…" His mouth twisted in a sharp smile. "People move on."

"You suck, Sheppard," Ronon said.

John looked like he had no idea why Ronon's voice had gotten so sharp. "Okay."

He was tired of crap like this, tired of dealing with the ways that Earth people talked about things like friendship or loyalty and turned out to mean something entirely different, something he didn't understand and wasn't sure he wanted to. For a moment it was tempting to rethink Cai's offer to come back to Sateda. It would mean living with people who made sense again.

"You said we were friends," he said.

John shrugged one shoulder. "We are. So?"

John still looked like he didn't get it, and Ronon was tired of trying to explain things, but that was the choice; go home, where people understood things without endless explanations, or make the effort to live here.

"So what is this 'people move on' crap? Is that how it works for you? Because if so, I'm just saying, you do suck."

"No, I… " Ronon thought he was finally getting it that Ronon wasn't happy. "It's not like I want that to happen," John said after a moment.

"Then you think I suck."

"No," John said, not quite laughing. "I think stuff happens. People lose touch."

"People break up, too, but that doesn't mean you plan on it."

"I try not to," John said, but maybe that's what he was thinking, in the back of his mind, that this thing with Teyla wouldn't work out any better than being married had. That he wasn't going to hold onto his friends when he'd gone years without speaking to his own brother.

"You want me to say I'm going to be around when you get old? I'm going to be around when you get old," Ronon said. "Unless one of us gets killed first. If I end up living on Sateda and you don't come visit, I'll get Teyla to make you."

"She can be pretty scary," John said with a sideways smile. "So that would probably work."

It wasn't either an apology or a promise, not by Satedan standards, but Ronon suspected it might be by John's standards, and those were the ones he'd made up his mind to live with.

"If you don't want this job, fine," Ronon said. "But don't be stupid."

"Okay," John said. Behind the bathroom door, the angry yowling rose in pitch. "You think he wants water or something?"

"I think it wants blood," Ronon said. "You really let kids on Earth have these things as pets?"

"It can't really hurt you," John said. Ronon glanced down pointedly at John's wrist striped with deep scratches. "Much."

"We had dogs," Ronon said. "They were domesticated. They didn't attack anybody. Or if they did…" His fingers lingered on the stock of his pistol.

"You can't shoot McKay's cat," John said.

"I could stun it," Ronon offered. "Then you could get some sleep."

John shrugged. "I was going to just…"

"Go sleep in Teyla's room?"

"I didn't say that," John said, but he was smiling. "I should probably put water in there for the cat first, though."

"Yeah, have fun with that," Ronon said, standing up.

"You could help," John said.

"Or I could not."

"Some friend you are."

"Let me know if you want me to come back and stun it," Ronon said, and left smiling.

CHAPTER TWENTY-THREE
Divided Loyalties

QUICKSILVER rolled himself in the quilts that filled his nest, turning his back to the light so that it would seem as though he slept. Soon enough, Ember would be stirring, slipping away either to the lab where his team of clevermen were still working to create a stable interface for the ZPM, or, more likely, to confer with his commander. Quicksilver grudged neither, and only hoped it would be soon. He had managed to ignore Ember's story, Guide's hints, but the disastrous attack on Atlantis — and it was a disaster, no matter how good a face Guide tried to put on it — and the queen's reaction had wakened his fear again. Not that he could be McKay, that was impossible. The transformation had not worked with Lastlight, with Michael, and it was even less likely that the process could be made to work in reverse, from human to Wraith. Suppress Wraith DNA, yes, that made sense. If, as he suspected, there were connections between Wraith and human DNA somewhere in the distant past, then, yes, suppressing the genetic material that differed from the human norm would produce something more or less human — less, if one went by Michael. But to add genes, to change an unwilling human — that should be far too difficult.

Except that biology was not his specialty. Ember had spoken as though it was unthinkable: something immoral, disgusting, not something impossible. And the queen's reaction, the reaction of the entire zenana, had been profoundly wrong. When he added that to the hostility he still felt throughout the hive, Ardent's insults and the accusation of taint that dogged him — the possibilities were unsettling, to say the least. It was, surely, impossible. But he needed to be sure.

To distract himself, he began naming prime numbers, had reached 1531 before he heard the gentle stirring in the outer chamber. He kept still, heard the door open and close, and counted two hundred heartbeats before he unwound the quilts form his shoulders.

The lights brightened as he moved into the main room and settled himself at the computer console. Data spilled down the screen, updating the current experiments. He banished that with a gesture, and touched the keys to open Ember's accounts. If he was lucky, the other cleverman wouldn't enter the system at all, would be in Guide's quarters rather than the labs; even if he was going to the lab, it would take him time to get there, and Quicksilver only needed the account for a moment, a springboard to reach the ghost he had planted some time ago

He activated it, closing Ember's account behind him, and watched the subroutine leverage its privileges until it had wormed its way into the closed database where Dust had kept his data. The layers unfolded before him, data parting like curtains, and he touched keys to enter the search he had so carefully prepared. He would have time to let it run, Ember wouldn't be back for hours, no matter where he'd gone.

But the screen was already flashing results at him, a torrent of data that he scanned, scowling, and brought back to review more slowly. Yes, this was his own record, the care that Dust had taken of him since his rescue: injuries, surgery, notation spelling out a drug — the drug Ember still made for him — chemical names that meant very little to him. A tailored drug for hyperplasia, Ember had said, and he couldn't tell otherwise.

That was a dead end, unless he could somehow persuade one of the biologists to explain it to him. He tipped his head to one side — Nighthaze owed him a favor, certainly — but discarded the idea as too dangerous. But here was the record of his progress, from waking amnesiac from surgery, which had disappointed Dust, to the last entry two days before Dust's death. He winced at that memory, and the brief note of good progress and high expectation, and went back to the beginning. Maybe the reference to surgery would tell him more.

That file was shorter than he had expected, obviously edited down from something larger, perhaps notes dictated during the procedure itself. He frowned again, set a search to locate the original file, and focused his attention on the summary. Most of it had to do with work on his feeding hand, repairs and adjustments to the handmouth, and at the thought his fingers curled protectively. The Lanteans must have tried to change him, despite what Ember said, must have tried to keep him from feeding — no wonder any attempt to feed left him shaking, if the Lanteans had tried to maim him.

Except that wasn't what the file said. These were repairs to an earlier surgery, the one that wasn't recorded in this database — his search program flashed at him, confirming the lack of data. Surgery that had not been completely successful, that had required repair, rebuilding…

No. He would not, could not accept that. He had been injured — the Lanteans had tortured him, that was what had to have happened. He turned his feeding hand over slowly, studying the neat mouth that creased the palm. Were those scars, there at the corners? They couldn't be. Wraith did not bear such marks. He turned his hand palm down, seeing his ordinary, unremarkable claws, in need of tending, but otherwise perfectly normal. The heavy veins that carried the enzyme were taut to the touch, ready to serve. He turned his hand over again, laid his finger gently between the lips, and felt the feeding membrane pulse and swell, tugging at his own life. He was whole. It was just what Ember had said, he had suffered an injury of the mind — and perhaps more, perhaps Dust's surgery was to mend some further damage, perhaps not even from the Lanteans, but suffered in the escape he could not remember. He was Wraith, Dust's brother, Quicksilver.

And if he was not, if that were a lie… He made himself take a breath, his chest aching with something that was neither fear nor grief but some strange mixture of the two. If he were human, somehow transformed — he could not make himself go further.

The dark-haired queen of his dreams seemed to stand before him — a human queen, he realized for the first time, and there was a tired smile on her face. Rodney, she had called him — all the Lanteans had called him that, and tried to help him; they wouldn't keep up a pretense as long as they had, wouldn't try that lie when he stood before them armed, leading armed drones into their city. McKay, they had said. Rodney, we can help you…

No, he said, and hit the keys that would back him out of the database. *It isn't true. I am Quicksilver, chief among clevermen, Quicksilver, Dust's brother…* The words rang hollow.

Teyla stepped through the Stargate out into a warm morning on New Athos. She couldn't help feeling her fingers tightening around the grip of her P90, and wondered if she would ever be able to step out onto New Athos again without remembering the day they lost Rodney to the Wraith.

Beside her, Ronon seemed untroubled, although he had his pistol in his hand. He paced her as they walked toward the settlement, his feet crunching on the dry grass.

"You know, you're not going to be able to keep Sheppard and Kanaan from being in the same place forever," Ronon said.

"I cannot imagine what you mean," Teyla said.

Ronon shook his head. "Sure."

She had to admit to herself that she wasn't eager to bring John to New Athos yet, and told herself it was only because this thing between them was so new. Kanaan had teased her for that, back when they were friends, before they were lovers or whatever it was they were now. *Our Teyla, cautious only in love.* But now she supposed he would not call her "our Teyla" at all.

She tried not to let that sting, and to pretend that she had no doubts about how she would be received in the Athosian settlement. Probably better than she would have if she'd brought John, for all that he got along well with Halling and the others. She couldn't pretend it was for John's sake that she had asked Ronon to accompany her instead. It was for her own sake, selfishly, because she was not yet ready to hear "so this is the man of the Lanteans Teyla left us for."

It was untrue and unfair; she had left Athos to defend her people from the Wraith, and she hated the idea that people might think otherwise. It was also something no one had yet said. It was unfair to be angry at people for what she only feared they were thinking, and unfair to arrange always to visit without John as if she were ashamed of him, and unfair to drag Ronon into the tangled mess she had created.

"I am sorry for dragging you back here again," Teyla said, as that was the only part of the matter she felt she could remedy.

"It's not a problem," Ronon said. "I just think eventually they're going to run into each other. It's not like Sheppard's going to start a fight."

"No," Teyla said. "He will more likely be awkward and say nothing. And Kanaan will say nothing that would cause a scene." If she had been living in the settlement, they would have had to deal with this already. It would have been understood that both of them would find other partners eventually after they separated, and that they would both have to live with that or move on permanently. There was no room in such a small community for any other choice.

"So, there's no problem."

"There is not a problem," Teyla said. "I just… am not ready."

"Suit yourself," Ronon said.

She could see the settlement now, see people working and a couple of small children playing a game of tag at the outskirts of the camp. She heard Torren call "Mama!" before she saw him dashing toward her, and bent swiftly to gather him up in her arms when he reached her.

"Torren," she said, holding him close. "Come here and let me see you."

"We playing chase," he said, pointing to a pair of children who hung back, watching her. The older girl was Jaidie, her hair now grown out from a cropped baby cut into long braids down her back, but for a moment she couldn't call the younger boy's name to mind, until she realized she'd last seen him as a baby at the breast.

She smoothed Torren's unruly hair and touched his forehead, fighting the temptation to keep him caught tight in her arms so he could not run away. "Finish your game," she said. "I will be here all afternoon."

"Promise?" Torren said.

"I promise," Teyla said, and watched him return to his game, running giggling after the older children, who kept just ahead of him and called for him to come catch them.

"Teyla," Kanaan said, coming out to meet her. She braced herself and smiled.

"It is good to see you," she said.

"And you," Kanaan said. He looked awkward as well, as if not sure how they were to begin after the way they had last parted.

"Ronon, would you mind going to tell Halling we are here?" Teyla said. "And perhaps he will want to show you how the autumn plowing is coming along."

"Right," Ronon said, although he didn't look all that enthusiastic at the prospect of being proudly shown long rows of tilled earth. It was John who had always seemed surprisingly happy to be shown gardens or half-done weaving, John who had always been surrounded at once by a crowd of children who he didn't seem to have any real desire to fend off. She wished now that she had brought him, despite her defensiveness at what people might think; it would have been good to see John smile.

"Have you come to take Torren back to Atlantis?" Kanaan said. "You will have to give us some time for that. His things are spread all over the settlement."

"Not yet," Teyla said. "We do have a new iris now, a mechanical defense against the Wraith if they open a wormhole to Atlantis. It is good that we have it, because the Wraith have already attacked, attempting to lower our defenses as they did before." Her eyes were on Torren, who stumbled on the uneven furrows of the fallow field and then picked himself up again without crying. "If it is not too much trouble for you to keep him a few days longer…"

"It is no trouble," Kanaan said. "I would have him safe."

"So would I," Teyla said a little sharply. "But you know as well as do I that New Athos is not perfectly safe either."

"I do know it," Kanaan said. He hesitated, and then went on. "I think I have been unfair, when I know this must be a difficult time for you. I… admit I have been jealous, but that is a small matter beside what you must feel at such a time."

"It is true that we are very worried," Teyla said, feeling that was an easier topic than their feelings for each other. "I still hope that we will find Rodney soon."

"I do not know Dr. McKay well, but he is well-respected among the Lanteans, and has been your hunting partner for many years," Kanaan said. He smiled a little ruefully. "I can hardly object on the grounds that he is not good enough for you."

"What?" Teyla found herself momentarily at a loss for words.

"I spoke with him briefly, before he was captured. He did not speak of your love in so many words, but he gave me to understand…"

"Oh, no," Teyla said. "No, no. I think there has been some great misunderstanding. Rodney is a good friend. I care for him as if he were my own kinsman, but…"

"I must have misunderstood," Kanaan said after a moment. He looked as though he were at a loss for words now, and as if he would give anything not to have just made himself look like a fool. It was a way that they were alike, both of them all too conscious of their dignity.

"Kanaan," Teyla said. For a moment she was tempted to embrace him, relieved by how silly and normal this all was, two parted lovers making a great fuss over who they loved next as if it were of great consequence to everyone. She still held back, remembering against her will what actually was important. "The things you said when I was last here were not a misunderstanding."

"They were not," Kanaan said, reluctantly but without apology.

"It is not easy for me to come among my people and wonder if I will be seen as a stranger," Teyla said.

"You will never be a stranger," Kanaan said. "Believe me, if you had said to me five years ago that I would challenge your place as leader…"

"Is that what you want?" Teyla asked. He had never been an ambitious man in the time she had known him, content with his work and his family. But then she supposed he might have changed as much as she had in nearly six years, when they had spent most of that time apart.

"It may not matter what I want," Kanaan said. "The people look to me to protect them from the Wraith because I have the Gift. It does not matter how many times I say that I am not you."

"They have been content with Halling as leader in my place," Teyla said.

"Halling is a good man," Kanaan said. "But he has stood in your place these six years, and he is not sorry to have another strong voice to speak beside him in council. And more than that…" He hesitated. "He is a good man," he went on finally. "But he would like our lives to return to what they were when we lived on Athos."

"I think many people would like that," Teyla said.

"Wishing will not stop things from changing," Kanaan said. "How can we go back to a time before the Lanteans came? Or, for that matter, before the Ancestors themselves returned, only to turn their backs on us?" He shook his head. "Those things happened. Just as generations ago the cities of Athos fell. The survivors could not go on living as if they had not been destroyed."

"We chose not to try," Teyla said.

"And now we must make new choices," Kanaan said. "We must talk of what bargains we wish to make with the Lanteans, not just for a season but for many generations, and we must talk of what it means that the Ancestors were not as we had hoped."

"Many people do not want to talk about difficult things," Teyla said. "Or so Charin told me often enough when I was a child."

"You never held back from asking hard questions," Kanaan said. "But now you are gone, and someone else must ask them instead." He shook his head. "You know how few we are," he said.

"I know," she said, with an old familiar stab of grief for their childhood, when the questions had all seemed easier.

"We will have to find more people who wish to be Athosian, or we will be absorbed into someone else's people and disappear," Kanaan said. "It would be easy to be absorbed by the Lanteans. They are a generous people, and we have made ties of friendship with them. But the easy path is not always the best one."

"When we are so few, will you really say I am not one of you?" Teyla said.

"You are my kin," Kanaan said. "We will always be kin, now that we are bound by blood." He watched Torren, who had abandoned the game of chase and was making his way back toward them, dragging a stick behind him.

"But you still do not want me to speak in council."

"I still think you will speak for the Lanteans," Kanaan said. He smiled a little, a flash of spirit in his eyes as if they were still children playing their own game of chase. "Does that make us enemies, Teyla? I think you would be a bad one to have."

She shook her head at him, smiling just a little in return. "It does not," she said. "But I am still not happy about what has been decided."

"I did not expect you to be," Kanaan said. "There is no answer that will satisfy you and everyone else as well, and I cannot make there be one by wishing it."

"I know," she said, and then she did put her arms around him, bending her forehead to his. She felt awkward almost at once, too near not to be reminded of their ill-favored months together after Torren's birth, but when she drew away, she thought something had eased between them.

Torren came running toward her, then, and flung his arms around her neck. "My stick," he said, showing it off to her.

"It is a very nice stick," Teyla said. In the distance, she could see Ronon looking out over one of the fields at Halling's side. She suspected he was saying that it was a nice field.

"I have work to do," Kanaan said. "Find me when you are ready to leave."

"We will be here for a while," Teyla said, sitting down and drawing Torren into her lap, even though that meant dodging his stick.

"Go home now, Mama?" Torren asked, sprawling in her lap.

"You must stay here with Papa just a little while longer," Teyla said, stroking his hair, and hoping he would not ask her to promise that was true.

CHAPTER TWENTY-FOUR
Quicksilver's Test

WE MUST Cull soon, Bonewhite said.

Guide frowned at the screen. He had known this was coming, had hoped they could stave it off just a little longer. *How soon?*

Now, ideally, Bonewhite answered. There was a touch of rough humor in his thoughts. *But, knowing the situation — thirty-six hours. We will have to find a hunting ground, you know.*

I know. Death had devastated too many worlds, picked them clean and spoiled what remained. *Riath is near, and Arcola.*

I have sent scouts to both, Bonewhite answered. *Death has been there already. Arcola may serve us, but barely. I would like to hunt further.*

Guide nodded. *That would probably be wise.*

Will you join us? Bonewhite paused. *Our people grow restless, they worry we do not seek our own queen.*

Guide grimaced. That, too, he had expected, but it still sent a pulse of fear through him. He was not nearly ready to defy Death, had barely begun to find a few allies among his peers. The failure of this last attack had helped, made some of them reconsider his suggestions, but it was too soon yet to try to build on that. Part of him was glad of the excuse, of the chance to leave the zenana and its dangerous undercurrents, to deal only with the ordinary work of keeping the hive alive and fed. And, of course, to deal with his missing queen, the one who did not truly exist — yes, he would have to deal with that as well, and soon. They could not keep up the pretence forever; perhaps it was time to disclose that Steelflower had died tragically, her cruiser overwhelmed by another hive before she could summon Consort and hive to save her. Yes, perhaps it was time, and perhaps this would be the excuse he needed to make that adjustment. Of course, it would leave him at Death's mercy, but he was beginning to build his own alliance again — which brought his thoughts full circle. He suppressed a snarl, focused on the matter at hand.

I will seek leave of the queen, he said, *and join you if I may.*

The assembly room was empty except for the drone guards, and the doors of the inner chamber were closed, but he could feel the tension like a shout. The young blade who watched outside the door looked harried, and dipped his head more deeply than was proper, hiding his nervousness.

Is the queen within? Guide asked, though he could feel her presence.

*She is — *

The door slid back before the boy could finish his sentence, and Death beckoned impatiently from behind her throne. Guide made a cautious bow — it was not a good sign that he had not been summoned to this council — and joined the others. The door slid shut behind him, but not before he'd felt the young blade's relief. And that, too, was no good sign. A man so young should be lost in worship of a queen as strong as this, not afraid.

Most gracious queen, he murmured, burying his thoughts, and Death flicked a hand at him.

You come before I would have summoned you, Guide.

Then I crave your pardon, he answered. *I came only to beg your leave and favor.*

Oh?

My hive must Cull, he said. *And I would go with them.*

Do you not trust your shipmaster? Death asked.

Of course, my queen, Guide said, and permitted himself faint surprise. *But I am commander. It is my responsibility.*

My queen, Farseer said. *Since Guide is here, it would be as well to get his opinion.*

The Old One snarled at that, but Death gave the flick of a smile. "Perhaps so. After all, it was his idea.*

Guide bowed again, hiding a pang of fear. What had been his idea? *As my queen wishes.*

Nighthaze tells me he can make a stronger explosive than the one we used before, Death said. *And Quicksilver still can master the Lanteans' computers. You said it yourself, we should keep them in fear. Farseer has proposed that we attack again.*

Guide kept his head down, calming the surface of his mind. He didn't really want to see another attack on Atlantis, not when he was relying on them to be a counterpoise to Death, not when he might still be able to work with them, trade them McKay for concessions… *I believe it to be a wise choice, my queen.*

The Old One curled his lip. *It is a waste of time and effort. We should gather the fleet and attack them directly, not fritter away our resources on piecemeal attack.*

We don't have the strength. That was Mist, newly admitted to the zenana. Guide thought he had not meant to speak, but to his credit, once the words were formed, he lifted his head bravely. *My queen, our fleet is large, but it is not overwhelming. Not to face Atlantis. Four years ago, I was part of the first attack, and saw what their defenses are like. And they are stronger now.*

We have the new shields, a newcomer with a mind like the sound of water said, but he did not sound entirely confident.

They — I believe they will be of use, Mist said, *but I don't think it will be enough to overcome Atlantis.*

They escaped by trickery that time, the Old One said. *They pretended to be destroyed, and your queen was fool enough to believe it.*

Mist snarled, reaching for his weapon. *My queen was there, Old One — * He stopped himself in the nick of time, and Death turned slowly to face him.

What?

Mist went to his knees. *Forgive me, my queen…*

Death regarded him for a long moment, her feeding hand opening and closing at her side. *It is a pity you are not as clever as you are beautiful,* she said at last, and he sagged in relief.

Guide took a breath. He didn't really want Death attacking through the Stargate, but he liked the idea of an all-out attack on Atlantis even less. *Surely one need not preclude the other?* he asked. *It will take time to prepare and provision our fleet to take on the Lanteans, and Mist is right that there is still work to be done on both these new shields and on this ZPM. Why not continue the gate attacks in the meantime? And send a ship or two to investigate the city's defenses, so we are prepared for anything new the Lanteans may have devised.*

There was a whisper of agreement, sourceless but definite, and Death smiled. *You are a cautious counselor, Guide, but wise. Farseer, see it done.*

Farseer bowed. *I will arrange it, my queen.*

The Old One said, *As my queen wills. But is it necessary to keep the abomination alive? He grows dangerous — remember what he said about McKay. We should take the knowledge from him, and use it ourselves, not rely on such as him.*

Death shook her head. *No. Whatever else he may be, he knows his own hand, his own work, better than any man of ours could manage. And I am sure he still believes himself Quicksilver. I felt it in his mind. No, Old One, there is still use in that tool.*

As my queen wishes, the Old One said.

The tension had eased a little with the decision, and Guide bowed again. "Forgive me, my queen, if I'm importunate, but — my hive's needs grow stronger with every hour.*

Do not think I don't know your plan, Death said, and Guide fought down a surge of pure terror. *You will seek your Steelflower, and so be it. But you have made alliance in her name, and you know well what will happen if she dares question it.*

Yes, my queen. Guide folded himself almost double, his coat hissing against the floor. For a moment, there, he had thought himself undone.

Go, Death said. *Your cleverman, Ember. He will remain.* She smiled. *We have need of him to handle McKay, after all.*

As my queen commands, Guide said. He could only be grateful it had gone no worse.

The third cable was holding, winding around the ZPM in its cradle, the readouts pulsing steady blue. It wasn't yet stable enough to feed the power directly to the hive, but it was smoothing out with each new connection. Four more cables, Quicksilver thought, and the hive would be able to draw directly from it, rather than through the transformer that radiated heat in the far corner; six more, and it would be an easy transition, nothing to strain any of the systems.

And that left him with no distractions, while Ember's men worked, and he frowned at the power readings as though they told him something new. He could not forget what he had found in Dust's records, could not rid himself of that lingering fear. Suppose he were McKay, suppose he were human — everything he had been told would be false, Dust's care and kindness a lie, Ember's dry friendship manipulation. And all his work would be treachery, betrayal of the humans who had genuinely meant to help him...

He shied away from the thought, then made himself face it. If it were true, if he was McKay, and he was helping to destroy his own people — well, he'd have to stop. Somehow. Which was more easily said than done, considering that the queen had made it clear his life was in her hands, and that failure was unforgivable. And besides, there was still the chance that he was wrong, and that this was just some lingering symptom of having been held prisoner on Atlantis.

What he needed was proof — something that would tell him, one way or the other, whether he was Rodney McKay or Quicksilver. He tapped his claws on the console, oblivious to the other clevermen's wary glances. The humans had offered to help him, even when he'd led the strike force; the small human in the ZPM room could have shot him, and had chosen not to, at the risk of his own life, there-fore... Therefore the others would take even greater risks to rescue McKay. He was sure, though he could not have said how he knew it, that the small, untidy human who had cornered him in the ZPM room was no warrior, and if he had taken those chances — yes, the others, their queen and the consort, they would do more. And that was a test of sorts: if they were willing to risk their lives to save him, then it was likely he was indeed McKay.

However, that was not an entirely practical solution, not least because if he was wrong, he would also be dead. He had no illusions that the Lanteans would spare any Wraith, least of all a cleverman of his stature. So even if he had a way to confront them directly, he didn't dare. Maybe a message of some kind — except that if they responded, it would not only confirm his fears, but it would betray him to the Wraith as well. He glanced around the laboratory, see-ing his clevermen with new eyes: pale, lank-haired monsters, hands tipped with heavy claws — so must the humans see them, in the moments before they were fed upon.

A message, he reminded himself. Some kind of message. More specifically, some kind of safe response to a message. If he told them to meet him someplace? If they went, he would know. Except that it would be impossible for him to meet them, and if they didn't find him, queen and Consort would assume that it had been a trick, and he'd never get them to do it a second time, which ruled out rescue...

He had been listening with half his mind to the clevermen's conversation, and suddenly a fragment caught his attention. *What?*

Ember looked up from his own console, frowning slightly. *I told you this before, Quicksilver. These cables aren't easy to grow, we'll need to take on supplies soon, if we're to make the rest of them.*

Yes, yes, I heard that, Quicksilver said. *Where were you going to go?*

Ember looked at Salt, who said, *Gaffen is best. And we can Cull as well.*

Gaffen, Quicksilver said. *I thought you said somewhere else.* He ignored the exchange of glances, turned back to his console, and let another diagnostic cascade down his screen. When he was sure the others' attention was fixed on the new cable, he touched keys, called up information on the planet. It was unimportant except for its mineral salts, easily harvested from a thick ground cover that absorbed them into its woody stems; there was a human population, and, yes, a Stargate. He closed the window, his hands trembling, controlled his thoughts with an effort. If he could get a message into Atlantis's systems, tell the consort to look for him on Gaffen — not that he would meet them there, that was too much, but just to look — It might work. At least he would have the chance to see if the Lanteans had used the gate — and, yes, he was sure he could make himself part of the group that went to harvest the salts. That was easy. The rest… He tapped his fingers on the console again, mapping out the message in his head. Just a piece of code, tucked just here into Atlantis's systems — yes, if anyone knew him, that's where they'd look, and if they knew him, he was McKay. And if he was McKay, they would come looking. The Lanteans did not leave their own behind.

Of course, there was still the problem of gaining access to the systems, but he'd be willing to bet that Death would try throwing another bomb through the Stargate. Nighthaze had already been talking about bigger bombs, greater yield; she was bound to try it, and soon. He would be ready then.

The chance came sooner than he had expected, but he had finished his message. Or mostly finished it: the program was complete, hidden among the tools he used to access the Lanteans' computers. It could probably use further refinement, a few tweaks here and there — but there was no time, and it would have to do. For an instant, there was almost a voice in his mind, rough and urgent, but it was gone before he could grasp the memory. And then there was nothing but the work at hand.

Nighthaze was in charge of the clevermen this time, instead of Ember, and instead of the queen, the Old One brought them down to the planet, ordered the drones to guard the perimeter while Nighthaze and his men busied themselves with their new toy. It was a sphere almost a meter in diameter, its surface covered with knobs the size of a man's thumb-claw — touch-triggers, Quicksilver assumed, seeing how they held it in a suspension field. Sensible: if he could not find controls for the mechanical barrier — and he doubted there would be any in the computer — there was still a chance that the bomb might materialize close enough to trigger the explosion and destroy the barrier. He bent over his computer, readying his programs, and to his shock the Old One came to lean over his shoulder.

Well, cleverman. These are your weapons?

Quicksilver made himself focus on his screen, on the codes he entered one by one. *They are.* He could feel the Old One's sneer, and couldn't stop himself from adding, *At least mine work.*

The Old One moved to face him across the barrier of the computer, bared teeth in an unfriendly smile. *You had best hope they do.*

This time, Quicksilver curbed his response, and the Old One turned away, waving to the waiting blade. *Dial the gate!*

The symbols circled and flashed, and the gate lit, the vortex stabbing out into the sultry air, and settling to the rippling pool of blue. Quicksilver touched the keys that dispatched his first transmission, was not surprised when his first probe was refused. And the second, and the third… The bomb hung heavy in its frame, the other clevermen watching over their shoulders as he wrestled with the distant system, matching minds against whoever had the watch in the Ancients' city. And then he found the weakness, a small, deliberate flaw in a piece of code, and his program slipped past the defenses, lodged itself in a corner of the system.

I'm in! he exclaimed, and Nighthaze turned to signal his men. *No, wait! No, no, no, I'm just into the system, I don't have control yet. I'll tell you when I do.*

He thought Nighthaze snarled at that, but he couldn't be bothered to look, all his attention focused on the screen. Shield control — he didn't dare overlook it, just in case the Lanteans were using it and the mechanical barrier — shield control and the environmental systems, let them worry about what he was doing there, that would draw their attention —

And if he was McKay, he was attacking his own people. He hesitated, fingers still for an instant. If he really was McKay, he couldn't go much further; if he was truly Quicksilver, he should do more, bring the systems into greater disarray before Nighthaze launched his bomb. But if he was Quicksilver, there would be other chances. He took a breath, and launched his message, watching it sink into the mass of Atlantis's code.

Now, he said, and Nighthaze lowered his hand. The team of clevermen urged the bomb forward, still held in its field, shoved it forward into the event horizon. Quicksilver counted seconds, saw his screen go blank as the explosion killed his transmission, looked up to see the wormhole still serene within the gate. The attack had failed.

Shut down the gate, the Old One said, his anger leashed but evident, and Nighthaze shook his head.

Perhaps it gave them a headache, at least.

You find this amusing? the Old One asked, and the cleverman ducked his head.

Of course not, lord. Forgive me.

Quicksilver hunched his own shoulders, hoping to draw as little attention as possible as he disconnected his own computer. At least his message was away. He would know soon enough what was true.

CHAPTER TWENTY-FIVE
Out of Time

THE SKY outside the gate room windows was almost clear, just a few high clouds streaking the morning sky. For once, John thought, it wasn't a tease. The meteorologists swore the weather would continue to clear and the temperatures would be comfortably above freezing. Not only that, they hadn't had an unscheduled gate activation in over seventy-two hours, not since the Wraith tried their bigger bomb, and, while he didn't really think that the Wraith had given up, it was nice to catch a break now and then.

He looked around the control room, savoring the quiet. Lynn was doing something at the console they reserved for research, one of the botanists leaning over his shoulder and frowning at the screen. Working the Ancient database, John guessed — that was one place Lynn had made himself pretty much indispensable now that Rodney was gone… He flinched at the thought. They would get him back, he told himself, though the words were starting to feel a little hollow. They had to get him back, or the IOA would send a team out hunting, and John didn't think he could be part of that. And even if they did find him, figure out a way to rescue him, then what? Keller wasn't confident she could get him back, return him physically to his old self. Maybe not even mentally, and then all they could do was kill him, because a Wraith with Rodney's knowledge, Rodney's skill… It would be far too dangerous to let him live, even if there wasn't the problem of feeding him. And that was maybe not the worst-case scenario. If he'd been too transformed to be changed back, then Rodney was, to all intents and purposes, dead already. John could kill him then, if he had to, one more Wraith who happened to look strangely like a lost friend. He could live with that if he had to.

No, worst-case would be getting him part way back, to where he knew himself, knew what he'd done, to where he was really Rodney again, and then not to be able to complete the physical transformation. Then you'd have Rodney, but Rodney unable to eat, Rodney who was going to starve if he didn't feed, didn't steal his life from his friends. He couldn't see Rodney being willing to live like that — wouldn't want to live like that himself, terrified that the hunger would take over, drive him to something worse than simple murder. But if it were Rodney who had to feed or die—

He shied away from the thought, refused to let it form. It wouldn't come to that. Keller was smart as hell and so was Carson, not to mention that Carson knew more about Wraith-human hybrids than anyone else in two galaxies. And if for some reason they needed more help, John was prepared to go straight to Todd on this one. Todd owed him, owed him big time, and he was prepared to see that the debt was paid.

And it wouldn't come to that, he repeated. Get Rodney's brain back to normal, and he'd be the one solving his own problem, bitching all the while. A pigeon swooped past the window, a fat shape against the bright sky. It was obviously enjoying the good weather, too, John thought. It was the first one he'd seen in a while, though the maintenance crews' reports made it clear the colony wasn't exactly diminishing. Maybe they could put Rodney on the whole 'alien life-forms' problem, not that there seemed to be much of a local ecosystem to interfere with. It would be worth it just for the look on his face.

He glanced down into the gate room again, automatically noting the Marines beside the Stargate, the sergeant less than an arm's length from the control lever even while he looked at something one of the kids was showing him on his phone. In the control room, Banks was frankly reading what looked like an old copy of Cosmo, and Airman Salawi looked to be studying something distinctly non-regulation on her laptop. Even Zelenka seemed to be checking the schedule for movie night rather than running another diagnostic. It was almost—peaceful, John thought, and winced as his mind formed the word. That was the worst thing you could say, guaranteed to bring trouble. He could hear Rodney's voice in his head—*oh, come on, Sheppard, you don't really believe that superstitious crap, do you?*—and Salawi straightened at her console.

"Dr. Zelenka?"

Zelenka closed his file, slid down the bank of consoles to look over her shoulder. Everything seemed to be moving in slow motion, John thought, as though they were underwater again, waiting for the windows to collapse on them...

"Yes," Zelenka said, softly, sadly. "I see it. Can you increase — yes, good."

Salawi gave him a quick, scared look, and turned back to her controls. Zelenka turned to face the upper row of consoles where John was standing, and John knew what he was going to say before he opened his mouth.

"Colonel Sheppard. Our long range sensors have picked up a Wraith cruiser just exiting hyperspace."

See? John said, to Rodney's memory, and braced himself against the rail. "What's it doing?"

"Nothing, at the moment," Zelenka said. All along the row of consoles, the signs of leisure had vanished. Lynn and the botanist were closing windows, clearing the console for the defense team; on the gate room floor, the phone had disappeared, and somehow all the Marines were back in full body armor.

Zelenka touched keys, frowning through his glasses. "I think — I believe it is scanning, though at very low power."

"It doesn't know we're here?" John said, dubiously.

"Or it is merely here to test our defenses," Zelenka said. "It is at the very edge of our sensors' capability. Salawi did well to pick out the anomaly."

"Dr. Zelenka," Salawi said. "A second window just opened. It's a hive ship."

Zelenka said something pithy in Czech. "It is moving to join the cruiser. They are both scanning now, I think."

That made 'testing the defenses' seem unpleasantly likely, and John bit his lip, considering his options. "Put the city on standby," he said, to Banks, "and get me colonels Carter and Caldwell."

"Yes, sir," Banks said.

It didn't take long for the colonels to reach the control room, but even so, most of the key personnel had found their way in ahead of them. Teyla had appeared, silent and competent, shaking her head when John asked if she could sense the Wraith. Ronon was skulking in the background, not as quiet as Teyla, but with enough discretion that John could pretend he hadn't noticed him, and Lorne was leaning on his crutches at the end of the consoles. That, at least, John could do something about, and as he crossed to meet the approaching colonels, he said, "Sit down before you fall down, Major."

Lorne gave him a look at that, but did as he was told.

"Colonel," John said, to both of them. "We've got a situation."

"So I heard," Caldwell said.

Carter nodded. "How far out?" She was already heading for the sensor station, and the others fell in behind her.

"They are just inside the orbit of the last planet," Zelenka said. "So, perhaps — five hours out, maybe four at their best speed? But right now they are just lurking."

"Lurking?" John said.

"And probably scanning." Zelenka shook his head at the screens. "I cannot be sure about that. They are using very low power. But neither ship is approaching the city as yet."

"What the hell do they want?" Caldwell murmured. John assumed the question was rhetorical, but Carter looked over her shoulder.

"My guess is they're scouting. Unless they're Todd's, but I'd expect him to have contacted us by now."

"We can't let them get close enough to tell that we don't have a shield," John said. It might be obvious, but he figured somebody had to say it. "Otherwise — "

"Otherwise Death sends her fleet and we're well and truly screwed," Caldwell said. "On the other hand, I'm not eager to take on a hive ship and a cruiser with just *Daedalus* and *Hammond* unless we have to."

"It is one of the smaller ones," Zelenka put in, sounding almost apologetic. "And the cruiser is of the kind that does not carry Darts."

"They're still just sitting there," Carter said. She straightened. "Colonel, I'm inclined to ignore them unless they decide to make a closer pass. From their current position, there's no way they can determine that we don't have shields, and it's far enough out that we might not have picked them up."

John nodded, though every instinct was screaming to get to the chair, to be ready to defend the city. "Dr. Zelenka. You said we had a little power in that ZPM. How much is a little?"

"Not enough." Zelenka spun his chair away from the console and looked up at them. The light glinted from his glasses, hiding his eyes. "You could probably fire drones, one, maybe two. Perhaps — in one simulation, perhaps as many as five. But the shield... it would only hold for a minute or so, which would hardly do us any good."

Not even as a bluff, John thought. He said, "OK, shield's out, but we might have drones. That's something."

"I'd rather it didn't come to that," Caldwell said.

Carter nodded. "If we have to fight, I think we're better off intercepting them well before they get to the planet. Outside of Dart range, if we can manage."

"But then the 302s don't have a fallback option," Caldwell said. "I'd rather take them at the next orbit."

Carter reached for a secondary console, brought up a schematic of the solar system. The Wraith ships glowed malevolent orange just inside the orbit of the outermost planet, the cruiser a little ahead of the hive. "There's a lot of debris," she said. "That's harder on us than it is on the Darts. We'd be better off meeting them closer in."

Caldwell's lips tightened, the expression that John had learned meant that he agreed and didn't want to admit it. "Well, if we go after them, we won't have any options anyway. We'll have to kill them both. We can't risk either of them sending word back to Death that we're vulnerable."

"Colonel Sheppard." Zelenka's voice was suddenly tense. "The ships are moving."

Of course they are, John thought. "Course?"

New lines appeared on the screen as he spoke, tracing a pair of gentle curves that ended at the planet.

"They are heading right for us," Zelenka said.

"Right," Caldwell said. He looked at Carter. "That settles that."

Carter nodded again. "Yes." She touched the screen. "If they continue on the present course, and we intercept here—"

"We've got a pretty good chance of stopping them well before their Darts can reach the city," Caldwell said. He looked at John. "Sheppard, you're going to need to be in the chair."

"I'm needed right here," John said. It was his city, his command. "Sir."

"You're the one with the gene," Caldwell said.

"Beckett—" John stopped, shook his head. Caldwell was right, he was needed in the chair—there was no way Beckett could handle the drones delicately enough to conserve their power. "Yes, sir." He looked at Zelenka. "How long do we have?"

"At their current speed—" Zelenka touched keys, frowned at the results. "Ha, they have increased power just a little, but they are still not at anything approaching their full speed. Seven hours, maybe a little less? I believe they may only be scanning."

"We can't take the chance," Caldwell said again. "Colonel Carter, I suggest you get the *Hammond* ready for launch. I'll do the same with *Daedalus*. Colonel Sheppard — do what you can to protect the city."

Which wasn't much, John thought. But they'd do what they could. "Yes, sir," he said, and his salute was almost accurate.

Sam lay flat on her back in her narrow bunk in the *Hammond's* cabin, lights dimmed, the soft sound of the ventilators filling the air. They were about as ready as they were going to be, last minute repairs and work-arounds finished an hour ago. Now there was nothing left but the waiting, to see if the Wraith ships were going to come any further into the system. The hive had slowed again three hours ago, and the cruiser had come a little further, matching its trajectory to one of the larger pieces of debris that filled the middle orbit, remains of a planet that had failed to form. Right now, its course would keep it far enough out that they could afford not to react. And that would be very much the best option, but she somehow doubted it would happen. The Wraith would keep scanning, would make a very thorough scan, but eventually they would move to attack.

She wanted to be in the control room, watching the ships' slow progress, listening as Atlantis reported the faint brush of scanner beams, but she knew there was nothing she could do that Franklin and Alvarez wouldn't. She'd sent all but the duty crew to eat and sleep, to get what rest they could before the fighting started, and it behooved her to set the example — not to mention that the younger members of *Hammond's* crew were more likely actually to get some rest if they knew she was sleeping, too. Or trying to.

Jack would have slept. She'd seen him do it in the most unlikely conditions, switch off brain and body and fall instantly asleep. Special Forces training, maybe, or maybe it was just Jack. She'd never had the gift, any more than Daniel had, though at least she wasn't pacing up and down pretending to study some random object or translate some obscure Ancient stele. He probably wasn't pretending, either, any more than Jack was, though she did wonder sometimes how he'd managed to unearth quite so much erotic poetry. She smiled at the ceiling. Actually, considering all the things she was careful not to notice on the *Hammond's* computers, she didn't wonder at all. Porn seemed to be a universal human habit. Of course, for the first years, Teal'c hadn't needed to sleep at all, so he'd been the one to watch while the rest of them flaked out. She could hear the soothing rumble of his voice. *I will take the watch, O'Neill*, he'd say, and they'd all feel better, even at the worst of times. Probably Teal'c had felt better, too, knowing he was in control of at least that much.

She turned her head. She couldn't make out the details of the pictures stuck to the metal walls, but she knew the images by heart anyway. She'd done what she had to, updated her emails, done what she could to make things better. Not that there was any guarantee that they'd be sent, not if the *Hammond* was destroyed, but she turned her thoughts from that with the ease of long practice. There were letters at the SGC as well, just in case, and Mitchell would take care of them. She'd done everything she could, and now it was just waiting. And sleep, if she could manage it.

"Colonel Carter." Franklin's voice snapped her upright, reaching for the intercom. "The Wraith are moving, ma'am."

"On my way."

The bridge was purposeful chaos, engineers muttering over the shield generators, Lieutenant Chandler, her best helmsman, in conversation with Atlantis and his counterpart on the *Daedalus*. Carter ignored them — she'd be told if her input was required — and focused instead on the display on the main screen.

"What have we got?" she asked.

"The cruiser's picked up speed," Franklin said. "And the hive with it. They've stopped scanning, and their projected course brings them into the system over the city. It looks like they're planning a hit and run."

Damn. Sam studied the projected course lines, the relative velocities, but she couldn't see anything else it could mean. "Put me through to Atlantis."

"Yes, ma'am." An airman in a short braid that made her look twelve touched keys on her console. "You're through."

"Colonel Sheppard," Sam said.

"Yeah, we see it," Sheppard answered. "I'm recommending you and *Daedalus* launch now."

It didn't take them long to get to the intercept point, enough time to get shields ready, enough time to have a brief conversation with Caldwell about tactics — not that they needed it, exactly, except to choose their targets; it was pretty clear what they'd have to do, and the best way to do it — enough time to be at the peak of readiness without tipping over into nerves and repetition. The Wraith changed course to meet them, the cruiser picking up speed, the hive turning to avoid their pincer movement. Pawn moves, Sam thought, gambit offered, and as briskly refused. Pretty much what they'd expected.

"Railguns are ready," Franklin said. "Shields at 100%."

"Thank you," Sam answered. On the screen, *Daedalus* rolled left, swooping down and away in a curve that should split the hive's fire. Lieutenant Chandler pitched the *Hammond* into a mirroring turn, up and over the cruiser as she rolled to meet them. "Pick your targets and fire at will."

There was a heartbeat's pause, the cruiser swinging away, *Hammond* turning to match, railguns firing. Blue fire sparked from the cruiser, impact dissipated by what looked like an energy shield; the *Hammond* shuddered as the first shots struck her own shields, but a quick glance showed them steady.

"What the hell was that?" Franklin demanded. His hands were already busy on his controls. "It looked like —"

"Ma'am," Jarrett said, from comm, "*Daedalus* reports the hive is shielded."

"It looks like it's similar to Asgard shielding," the duty engineer said. "I'm trying — OK, yes, I've got a read on the shield frequency —"

McKay, Sam thought. This had to be McKay's work. The cruiser rolled, Chandler turning to present a narrow target. Both ships fired, shields flaring. "What kind of power is it drawing?"

"A lot," the engineer answered. "They're slower than I'd expect."

Sam nodded. That made sense. The problem with Wraith technology was that it lacked a power source sufficient to run both energy shields and hyperdrives; until now, they'd always preferred to rely on the living hull regenerating itself. But if McKay had figured out a way to do both — and that was probably why he'd stolen the ZPM in the first place — No, there were still limits to what the Wraith power plants could do.

"Forward shields at ninety-two percent," Franklin said.

"Their shields won't hold," Sam said, with more confidence than she felt. "Keep hitting them hard."

The *Hammond* rolled up and over, swooping down on the cruiser as it passed *Daedalus*, trying for a shot to support the hive. Fire bloomed on *Daedalus's* shields, and then *Hammond* struck, railguns hitting the cruiser's shields just beyond the curve of the bow. The cruiser staggered slightly, recovered, and rolled away. Chandler kept the *Hammond* on their tail, and the forward shields recorded more impacts.

"Their aft shields are down," the engineer said.

"Missiles," Sam said, and Ellefson answered from the weapons console.

"Missiles away."

"Direct hit!" someone said, and in the screen the cruiser shuddered and pitched, starting to roll as atmosphere vented from a massive breach. "They've lost power, losing life support — it looks like they're beaming survivors out."

That evened things up a little, Sam thought. And it proved these new shields weren't as good as the Asgard-based design. "Leave the cruiser," she said. "Go for the hive."

"Ma'am!" That was Jarrett, her voice high but under control. "*Daedalus* reports they've taken a hit to their maneuver engines. They're launching 302s to cover."

Sam's mouth tightened. Two against one had been good odds, meant they could tag team the hive, save their shields while running down its defenses, but this... Was what it was, she told herself, and frowned at the tac display.

"Ma'am, the hive's launching Darts," Jarrett said.

"Hive's coming around for another try at *Daedalus*," Franklin said.

Chandler was already altering course to compensate, interposing *Hammond* between the hive and the drifting *Daedalus*, forcing the Wraith ship to bank away. Sam saw the railguns fire, a steady pulse of blue, saw a couple of secondary explosions near the hive's stern before they flashed away. A stream of Darts flickered past, fire too light to do damage yet, but every hit depleting their own shields. She could hear the 302 chatter in the background, forced herself not to pay attention until she had to.

"Take her on the left flank," Sam said. That would force the hive further away from the *Daedalus* as she turned to answer, even if it would mean *Hammond* would take a few more solid hits on the forward shields. They would hold through this pass, she was sure, and then they should show her their tail, try to get her to chase.

"Yes, ma'am," Chandler said, and *Hammond* rotated around her own center, diving in for the attack. The hive rolled away, maybe a little sluggish this time, maybe the power shortages kicking in, and the railguns stitched fire along her back, lighting up her shields. The hive's guns answered, and even with the inertial dampeners, Sam felt the *Hammond* shudder under her.

"Forward shields at sixty percent," Franklin said. "Ventral shields at seventy-five."

"Let's see if she'll chase us," Sam said, and leaned forward in her chair.

CHAPTER TWENTY-SIX
Daedalus and Hammond

THE 302s streamed out of *Daedalus's* bay, the big rocket engine kicking Mel back in her chair before the internal dampeners fully compensated. And that was worrisome, but there wasn't time to think about that. Blue Flight formed up on her in loose echelon, Gold Flight following suit on Dwaine Grant's 302 — there never was and never would be a 'Red Leader' on Caldwell's ship, and as always that made her think of Sheppard and grin behind her oxygen mask. She settled herself into the controls, the thought vanishing as the HUD winked into focus. The cruiser was drifting away, all systems dead, nothing more than space junk. That was a good sign: these new energy shields couldn't handle their energy weapons. They were ahead of the Darts, the first flight just clearing the hive, the *Hammond* working the far side to keep them from launching anything from the opposite bay. And that was something, a chance they didn't always get, though it didn't do much to offset the damage to *Daedalus*.

"Blue Flight, Gold Flight, this is Blue Leader," she said. "Gold Flight, Blue Two, Blue Five, engage the Darts. Blue Three, Blue Four, with me. Our target is the hive."

The first wave of Darts was closing, spreading out like pellets from a shotgun. The 302s drove toward them, spreading a little to match. Symbols flashed on the HUD, counting down to optimum range, and she pulled up and right as a Dart flashed toward her, spitting blue fire. She turned her roll into a half-loop, caught the first Dart's wingman in her crosshairs. She fired, saw the bolts clip the Dart's wing, send it spinning and sparking, but curbed the instinct to pursue.

"No shield!" she called. "Darts are not shielded!"

Behind her, Gold Flight was mixing it up with the Darts; at the edge of the display, she could see someone break off after a couple of Darts that had gotten through. *Daedalus's* thrusters flared, trying to turn their narrowest profile, but she put it all from her mind with practiced ease. The hive swelled in her screen, the weird pebbly surface dark against the stars, and her computer shrieked a warning. Enemy at four o'clock, rising from under the cruiser's belly. A bolt of fire slashed past her, and another clipped her shields. Everything was still green, and she rolled over and down, risking the belly shot to get him chasing. Sure enough, he followed, and she came up on his tail, cannons firing. The Dart exploded, sparks and debris flying, and she dove beneath the expanding cloud, stitching shots along the hive's spine. Something fired back at her, and she pulled up and away, proximity alarms chattering briefly.

Another Dart dove at her, a companion following; she took their fire, shield warning chiming, and lined up her shots, first one, then the other exploding in a flash of fire. She passed through the edge of the second fireball, pulled up again to check her instruments. All systems green, shields still at ninety percent.

The *Hammond* swung on its axis, coming in for another pass. A Dart flashed past, and she fired, knew she'd missed anything vital.

"I've lost engines!" Blue Three's voice was high and tight, cutting through the static. "Going in — "

Sure enough, the 302 was arrowing toward the hive's stern, trailing debris, engines dark.

"Thrusters," Blue Four called, "hit the thrusters — "

Mel hit the emergency channel. "*Hammond*! 302 in trouble, can you beam the pilot — ?"

EM crackle drowned her words, drowned any answer, and Blue Three hit hard, erupting in a ball of flame and smoke. Blue Four screamed a curse. Mel flinched, and then she realized what she'd seen.

"*Hammond*, this is Blue Leader. The hive's aft shields are down. I repeat, the hive's aft shields are down."

"Roger that, Blue Leader," the *Hammond's* comm officer said. "Pull back — "

The rest of the words were lost in static, but Mel was already switching to her command channel. "Blue Four, fall back. Rejoin Gold Flight." She spun the 302 as she spoke, clearing the hive. She hoped to hell *Hammond* had managed to get Rob, but there was no time to think about it. She hit the throttle, steadying onto the fastest closing course for the melee surrounding the *Daedalus*.

The hive swung to meet the *Hammond's* dive, more sluggish than before, but all guns firing.

"Forward shields at forty percent," Franklin said.

"Stay with her, lieutenant," Sam said. This was what she'd been hoping for, that the Wraith power plant wouldn't be able to handle the demand, that they'd compromise either shields or maneuvering. She'd assumed they would give up shields first, but if they wanted to sacrifice maneuverability, that was fine with her. The gap in the shield was easy to spot, a smoking scar on the dark hull, a pit where the emitter had been. The hive pulled up, slower, but still dangerous, and Chandler spun the *Hammond*, fighting for the shot.

"Missiles," Sam said, and the weapons officer confirmed. She heard the thump of their release, and in the same moment the shields flared blue under a barrage of shots. Something shorted on the secondary environmental console, and an airman grabbed the nearest fire extinguisher, sprayed foam. For an instant, the air was thick with the smell of burning wire and the stink of the foam, and then the ventilators cleared it. The hive was firing short now, trying to kill the missiles; she saw one explode prematurely, and then another, but the third struck home.

"Forward shields at twenty-five percent," Franklin reported.

Chandler was already looping away, turning to present their aft shields to the hive. The railguns flashed again as they turned, but the hits were minimal, caught by the hive's remaining shields.

"The hive's lost hyperdrive," Franklin said. He bent closer over his console. "They're venting atmosphere aft — no, that's sealed now." He glanced over his shoulder. "Our rear shields are at fifty percent."

"Anything from *Daedalus*?" Sam asked.

"No, ma'am. She's still not underway."

And if Steven could do anything to help, he would, Sam thought. Darts flashed past, a 302 in pursuit: Hocken's wing doing what she could in support, and the *Hammond* shivered again as a shot struck a failing shield.

"Ventral shield at twenty-five percent," Franklin said.

Chandler pitched the ship into a tight corkscrew, trying to keep the good shields toward the hive. He was gaining ground, too, putting a little distance between the ships, attenuating the hive's fire — buying time, Sam thought. The *Hammond* wouldn't win a straight slugfest, was already getting close to the point where she'd need to break and run — but the hive was still vulnerable. If they could get a decent shot at the unshielded stern —

"Get us one more good shot, lieutenant," she said.

"Yes, ma'am," Chandler said, and *Hammond* turned on its axis, trying again for the stern shot. The ship shuddered, the ventral shields taking fire as they rolled past, and red lights flashed on Sam's console, warning of damage in the empty 302 bays. Harmless for now, she thought, and concentrated on the hive as it dodged and turned. Chandler matched it, but the hive's guns were striking home, the shield warnings flashing.

"Forward shield at ten percent," Franklin said. "Ventral shields at minimum."

"One good shot," Sam said.

The railguns were still firing, groping for the target, and Ellefson launched another missile salvo for good measure. For an instant the hive loomed in the screen, and then Chandler broke away, rolling to catch the return fire on the dorsal shield.

"The hive's shields are down," Franklin said. "We've lost ventral shields, forward shields holding at eight percent. Rear shields at twenty percent."

They needed to get clear, Sam thought — well, they needed *Daedalus's* support, but that wasn't happening. But they couldn't let the hive get close enough to see that Atlantis was undefended. And they couldn't afford to lose the *Hammond*, either. The hive was turning, a little faster now that the shields were down, all its power channeled to the engines, and Chandler drove past its nose, turning again to put the dorsal shields between it and them. The railguns were firing, shots solid on the hive's leading edge, but the hive's guns were still intact. The *Hammond* rocked as a blast hit somewhere aft, and an alarm shrilled for an instant before the duty engineer slapped it to silence.

"Hull breach in compartment C14. I'm rerouting shields."

"Good," Sam said. She looked at her screen again, looking for another way out. "The cruiser," she said. "Lieutenant, put the cruiser between us and the hive."

"Yes, ma'am," Chandler said, and pitched *Hammond* into a tight turn. The hive followed, wallowing, and Franklin looked over his shoulder.

Sam forced a smile she didn't entirely feel. "Let's play dodge'em."

Caldwell watched the *Hammond* drawing the hive ship away from *Daedalus*, getting a little more maneuvering room every time she broke away in a tight turn the hive ship apparently couldn't quite follow. It bought him some breathing room, but it also meant he couldn't bring *Daedalus's* weapons to bear on anything but Darts that unwarily ventured under his guns.

"Sub-light engines are still not on line," Meyers said, as if he had any doubt about why she wasn't closing the distance.

"I can see that," Caldwell said. He resisted the urge to tell Meyers to take evasive action, since she was obviously already doing that to the extent that she could. Two Darts streaked across the forward viewscreen, with 302s in pursuit. Marks's hand twitched on the weapons controls, but he held his fire, his shot fouled by the 302s.

"Dr. Novak, we need those sub-light engines," Caldwell said, raising his voice to carry over the comm system. "Can you give me anything?"

"I'm trying!" Novak said from down in Engineering. "They're just not responding. We're trying to re-route power around damaged components, but I think the ignition system itself may be shot. I'm just not sure I can get this back online without doing major repairs."

"Do what you can," Caldwell said. "Right now pretty much all we can do up here is watch."

"I know," Novak said unhappily. He suspected she was wishing Hermiod was here muttering to himself in Asgard and coming up with some improbably fast fix for their problems. At the moment, so was he.

He could see Sam maneuvering to keep *Hammond* behind the derelict cruiser, getting off shots from her railguns whenever she could bring them to bear. The last thing she probably wanted at this point was a full-on exchange of fire, but the hive kept maneuvering for one, trying to get clear of the cruiser's bulk.

At least its shields were down. He hadn't even had time to think about that yet, except as an immediate tactical problem, but he was aware that the bigger problem was looming. The main advantage they had over the Wraith was that ships equipped with Asgard or Ancient shield generators could take more punishment than the fragile hives.

If they'd lost that advantage…

Two more Darts streaked into view, arrowing straight toward the viewscreen, apparently on a kamikaze run for the bridge.

"I've got them," Marks said. Meyers' hands were moving swiftly over her console, playing with the maneuvering thrusters to get them a slightly better angle. Caldwell's hands tightened on the arms of his chair, but he resisted the urge to backseat drive.

"Fire at will," Caldwell said, and Marks waited another endless few seconds, then fired, two bursts from the forward rail guns that splintered both Darts well clear of the *Daedalus's* hull.

"Forward shields at seventy-five percent," Marks reported. "Rear shields back up at twenty-five percent."

"We're in better shape than they are," Caldwell said. He hated to leave himself even more of a sitting duck, but the *Hammond* was clearly having trouble extricating herself from her standoff with the hive ship. "Blue Leader, *Hammond* could use some help."

"Copy that, *Daedalus*," Hocken said crisply, and then, startled, "*Daedalus*, I have multiple Wraith Darts breaking away in formation."

"Confirmed," Meyers said.

Either they were pulling back to support the hive ship, or, worse, planning to make an exploratory run on Atlantis. The first would be bad news; the second, a disaster.

"We're in pursuit," Hocken said.

"Copy that, Blue Leader," Caldwell said, wishing grimly there were anything he could do besides sit and wait.

CHAPTER TWENTY-SEVEN
Over Atlantis

JOHN stretched out in the control chair, feeling it come alive under him as he leaned back, lighting up and warming up under his hands. As always, it felt easy to sink into its enhanced perceptions, the world lighting up around him, showing him the airspace around Atlantis, the bright spots of jumpers launching and then dimming as they cloaked. There was more information there when he thought about it, wind speed and direction as much a feeling as a visual display, the wider sweep of the solar system sharpening as he reached for a broader view.

Some part of him was restless, though, thinking of too many other places he needed to be. He itched to be up in the control room, to know where all the security teams were and what they were doing. The chair responded, obligingly building him a map of the city with life signs readings included, and John willed it firmly out of existence. It wouldn't tell him anything he wanted to know.

Lorne was up in the control room, coordinating the security teams, checking in with Teyla to make sure she was ready to alert them if she sensed Wraith in the city. Lorne wasn't up in a jumper because he had to be in the control room. John wasn't either place because he had to be in the chair. He took a deep breath and let it out, willing himself to let it go.

He relaxed deeper into the interface, the view from the long-range sensors coming up for him as he thought about it, easy and clear. The Wraith cruiser was drifting, clearly disabled. *Hammond* was engaged with the hive ship, and while they were too far out for the sensors to pick up individual Darts or 302s, the energy signature surrounding the two ships suggested a melee in progress.

Daedalus wasn't coming up to support *Hammond*, clearly damaged. Still, they were holding the hive ship off. There was no way it was in close enough to be able to tell that Atlantis's shields were down. Two battlecruisers on one hive ship wasn't bad odds, even with one of them stationary. He wished he could see what the Darts and 302s were doing, and met the soft resistance of the interface when he asked for something beyond its capabilities, which he always imagined as apologetic.

That's okay, he told it. *We'll just sit tight.*

Something was changing, though, something subtly shifting in the pattern of the fight, and then the display lit up with the first warning of incoming Darts, still well out from the planet but heading for it fast. He heard the crackle of his radio activating as if it came from a long way away, the words seeming painfully slow.

"Sir, Daedalus reports Darts breaking off and heading for the city," Lorne said. "302s are in pursuit."

"I see them," John said. "Tell the jumper pilots to stay out of the way. Fire drones if necessary, but do not engage at close quarters."

"Yes, sir," Lorne said. The jumpers were well-matched with Darts in the hands of an experienced combat pilot, but they had too few of those right now. Pilots unused to tactical speeds flying invisible ships sounded like a recipe for somebody crashing into one of their own 302s.

John could have done it. He'd played tag with Darts in a jumper plenty of times before, keeping them off Atlantis while dodging between towers at top speed. He'd never tried it in a 302, but there was some part of him that wished he was out there in one, tearing toward the city fast enough that even with the inertial dampeners the acceleration pressed him into his seat, thinking about nothing but finding his targets and sticking to them until he could blow them out of the sky—

He could feel the weapons system responding, readying drones. *Not yet*, he told it, or told himself, whichever was the best way of thinking about it. He couldn't afford to waste power until he was sure he needed it. He had to let this play out a little while longer. They were approaching the atmosphere, the 302s not quite matching the Darts' speed but harassing them whenever they came into range, trying to force them into evasive maneuvers that would cut their speed.

One of the city's built-in subroutines informed him in a flicker of images and Ancient, in which John had by now developed a useful vocabulary of phrases like 'WARNING: CRITICAL FAILURE', that the city's shields should now be raised in response to incoming enemy craft, but that current power levels were insufficient to sustain shields for more than twelve seconds at maximum strength.

So let's not. They might need those twelve seconds, but they didn't need them yet.

The 302s were still harrying the Darts as they hit the atmosphere and began pulling up, leveling off to make a run on the city. One of them wasn't slowing its descent, though, on course for the city at suicidal speeds.

If it pulled out of the dive and shed speed at the last minute before it hit, it might only take out the central tower. If it hit them like a missile from orbit —

The 302s weren't going to be fast enough either way. John launched a single drone, sailing it up along the projected path of the Dart, guiding it until the drone acquired the target on its own. It slammed itself into the Dart like a magnet, the Dart blossoming into fire as it hit. Some of the debris could still strike the city, and he thought about raising the shield, but — Twelve seconds.

He forced himself to wait as the rest of the Darts dove on Atlantis, with the 302s streaking in behind them.

Mel swore as the HUD flashed red and orange, jammed her throttle all the way open. They were too slow, only three of them anyway, Blue Four still tangled with the Darts around the *Daedalus*, but they were what Atlantis had. She cursed again, seeing one dive toward the city, flung her 302 into a turn to pursue, but another Dart's energy beam flashed past her wing, slammed against her aft shields. She dove away, spinning, saw Blue Two slide past her, weapons blazing, pressed her own firing stud as another Dart slid through the crosshairs. It wasn't a clean hit, but the Dart went spinning, pilot or systems unable to compensate. She flipped the 302 up and over, turning back toward Atlantis, but a drone flickered on her HUD, and the diving Dart vanished in a cloud of flame.

Another one was trying the same attack — maybe not a suicide run, it was slower, and she pitched the 302 into a steeper dive to intercept it. Warnings chattered on her console, the shields hazed with the fires of re-entry, and then she leveled out, lining up on the Dart. Fire control refused to operate, the 302's skin too hot still, and she shoved the throttle forward again, ready to ram if the Dart kept its course for Atlantis. The Dart's pilot peeled away, and she followed, trying to stay on his tail until the computer would let her shoot again. Energy beams flashed past her cockpit, and the 302 rocked to impacts on the right wing. Shields were at seventy-five percent and holding — and at last the weapons light went green. She pressed the firing stud, and the Dart erupted in a cloud of smoke.

The HUD was showing another one behind her. She cork-screwed up and around, clawing for altitude, and the Dart broke away, making another run for the city. He'd caught her wrong-footed, but Blue Five was on him; she let him go, rolling over to circle the city. They probably had jumpers out, cloaked, and she hoped they had the sense to stay out of the way.

Another Dart was coming in, lower this time, leveling out as though it planned to strafe the towers. She pitched the 302 over, but it was faster than she'd thought, slipped past the intercept point before she could fire. She swore, followed it between two towers, not daring to fire for fear of hitting one of the buildings. But she was on its tail, tight in its slipstream, and the pilot was too busy trying to shake her to complete his attack. He curved around the main tower, and she followed. Just a little more, just a fraction — but he banked hard again, keeping himself close to the buildings. If he got time to signal, the hive would know the city was undefended —

And then the moment came, the clear shot she'd been waiting for, and she took it, energy beams sizzling across the gap between the ships. The Dart blew in an instant, the sound barely audible over the roar of her own engines, and she pulled up into a tight spiral, scanning the HUD. Two Darts left, she thought, and in the same instant saw twin explosions.

"Blue Flight, Blue Leader," she said. "Nice shooting."

"Blue Leader, this is Atlantis." She didn't know the voice, only that it wasn't Sheppard's. "We show all Darts destroyed. No further waves incoming."

"Thanks, Atlantis," she said. "You need us to stick around?"

"Negative, Blue Leader. It looks like *Hammond* could use some help."

Mel glanced at her HUD again, pressed the toggle to select the larger picture. *Daedalus* was still dead in the water, no more than a few thousand meters from where they'd left her. *Hammond* had come closer to the planet, the hive in pursuit. From the numbers on the screen, she was taking a pounding.

"Colonel Carter would appreciate any distraction you can provide," Atlantis continued.

Crap. "Roger that," Mel said. "Blue Flight, Blue Leader. We're going after the hive."

Lorne switched over to long-range sensors for a moment as the 302s peeled away, just to see that *Hammond* was apparently still holding her own, but he didn't have the luxury of sitting and watching. It hadn't sounded good up there, Colonel Carter's voice too deadly calm as she requested assistance, but there was nothing he could do about that at the moment.

"Teyla, what have we got?"

"I do not sense the Wraith," Teyla said over the radio. "We are continuing our security sweep, but I do not think any Wraith are within the city."

"There are no signs that any Wraith beamed off of the Darts," Radek said from his station behind Lorne. "At least we may not have that problem to worry about at the moment."

"That's one," Lorne said. They had plenty of other problems. He wrestled with his chair for a moment, trying to find some way to sit close enough to the console that didn't involve running his bad leg into it every time he turned to look at somebody, and decided there wasn't one.

"I have damage reports coming in," Salawi said. "Some windows broken by debris, some minor structural damage. No reports of casualties yet."

"We need to get everybody clear of any damaged areas," Lorne said. "We don't want a building falling on anybody."

"No, that would be bad," Radek agreed absently. He shook his head. "The hive has sustained damage, but it is still perfectly capable of attacking the city."

"It hasn't got a lot of other choice, unless it can get its hyperdrive engines back online," Lorne said. "Where else are they going to go?"

"What's going on up there?" Ronon said over the radio.

"Security teams, please stay in position," Lorne said as a city-wide announcement rather than answering Ronon directly. "The incoming Darts have been destroyed, but there are probably going to be more. If you're not on a security team, and you're not evacuating an area of the city that's taken structural damage, please stay where you are and keep the radio chatter to a minimum."

Beside him, Banks was giving a quick account of the space battle so far over her radio. Probably to Ronon, who didn't have any reason to need to know at the moment other than being frustrated by not knowing, but Lorne didn't know that for sure, so he let it go.

"This is Sheppard," Colonel Sheppard said over the radio. "Get some of the security teams up to the gateroom. I don't know if *Hammond* can hold off that hive ship forever, and if they get here, they're going to want to bring in reinforcements."

"Yes, sir," Lorne said. "Ronon's team, Captain Cadman's team, fall back to the gateroom to protect the Stargate. Dr. Zelenka—"

"Yes, I am locking down the dialing computer," Radek said without looking up from his console. "There is no telling how long that will hold them if they gain access to the main computer system, but since it is not likely that they have Rodney with them, maybe at least a little while."

"Let's hope a little while is all we need," Lorne said.

"Personally I am still hoping that the Wraith do not invade the city," Radek said. "Call me an optimist."

"Me, too," Lorne said, and not just because he suspected that getting into a firefight with the Wraith when he couldn't walk without crutches was going to end badly. If the Wraith made it to the city, it was probably going to be because they'd lost *Hammond*. Colonel Carter would do everything in her power to stop them, and if that wasn't enough…

He pulled up long-range sensors again, hoping Hocken and her 302s were enough to turn the tide. If they could get in a few solid hits on the hive, take out its power generation or its sublight engines, that would do it.

Below in the gateroom, Ronon had arrived and was directing the security already stationed there into a different formation as his own team took up their positions. Lorne didn't argue with that; Ronon was the one who was going to be down there in a position to see what was happening if the Wraith beamed troops in.

"We're in position," Ronon said over the radio.

"I have nothing incoming yet," Radek said.

"Come on," Lorne said under his breath, watching the

Hammond trying to evade the hive ship as it rolled out from behind the cover of the cruiser, firing as it came.

Sam scowled at the engineering console, wishing she could will it into better readings. The ventral shield was fluctuating wildly, an emitter on the verge of blowing out; the other shields were all below thirty percent and falling. Hyperdrive was still good, not that it would be much help at the moment, and she touched keys, transferring its power to the maneuver engines and the weapons array. The duty engineer gave her a wild look—she was the junior, red flecks of burns on her face and neck from the same explosion that had sent Harting to the infirmary—but her voice was steady enough.

"Should I re-route power to the shields, too, ma'am?"

"No," Sam answered. "You'll blow the ventral emitter. When it goes—yes, do it then. But not before."

"Yes, ma'am," the sergeant answered and Sam pushed past a repair team to take her place behind the chair. The air was hazed with smoke, life support starved for power and running at about forty percent, but that would hold them a little longer.

"Anything from *Daedalus*?" she asked quietly, and Franklin shook his head.

"No, ma'am. Atlantis reports the 302s are on the way—"

Another explosion rocked the bridge, and lights flared red on the pilot's console. Chandler winced, hands racing, and the lights faded. "Colonel, we've lost main controls. I've switched to auxiliary."

"Understood," Sam said. She did, that was the problem. They had to stop the hive, destroy it somehow, or it would come down on Atlantis like a ton of bricks, and that would be the end of everything. They had McKay, and were making use of his knowledge, and the next stop would be the Milky Way—

She shoved that thought back down into the box where she kept those things, focused on the immediate tactical problem. *Daedalus* was out of the picture; the 302s could harass, but they'd have to be beyond lucky to do the hive any serious damage. And the cruiser was no longer any real protection.

"Get me Atlantis," she said, and Jarrett touched keys.

"Yes, ma'am."

"Atlantis, this is *Hammond*," Sam said. "We'll be in beaming range of the city in about four minutes. I'll be sending off injured and non-essential personnel as soon as we're in range."

Franklin looked over his shoulder at that, but she ignored him. Lorne's voice was perfectly calm, even though he must have understood the implications as well as Franklin had.

"Copy that, *Hammond*. The infirmary will be standing by."

"Thank you, Atlantis," Sam said. "*Hammond* out." The ship rocked again, and another panel shorted out. Sam flinched as a spray of sparks hit her shoulder, slapped at her coveralls to be sure nothing caught. An airman came running, extinguisher in hand, and the air was thick with the hiss and stink of foam.

"Ma'am?" Franklin said, warily, and Sam forced a tired smile.

"You heard me, Major. As soon as we're in range, start evacuating the wounded and any non-essentials."

"Yes, ma'am," Franklin said, and bent over his console. They'd had the procedure in place for a long time, though she'd hoped never to use it. A moment later, the three-toned klaxon began to sound, and she knew that the beam-out protocol was underway.

And that was all she could do for them, for now. She turned her attention back to the tactical display, where the hive was just rolling free of the cruiser. Chandler pitched *Hammond* up and away, and the hive's beams went wide. A 302 zoomed past, and then another, diving toward the hive — heading for the damaged stern — but the hive's gunners were good, and the 302s broke off, looking for another angle.

"We're in range of the city, ma'am," Franklin said.

Sam nodded. "Commence the beam-out."

"Yes, ma'am."

Lights flickered on her console as the Asgard beams activated. At least there was still plenty of power for that, diverted from the unneeded hyperdrive. At the top of the screen, numbers flickered and changed — *Daedalus*, underway at last? She caught her breath, and then hope died. No, not yet; she could expect no help there.

"Damn it," Chandler said, and she braced herself. In the screen, the hive had turned head on, forward guns flaring; an instant later, the forward screens flashed blue, and alarms sounded across her boards.

"Hull breach in A12," Jarrett reported. "Bulkheads are holding."

"We've lost the ventral emitter," the engineer said.

"Reroute power to the rest of the shields," Sam said, and ducked as an overhead cable blew in a shower of sparks. She ran her hands quickly over her head, not feeling any flame, and Chandler looked up from his console, fear naked in his face.

"We've lost main maneuvering."

"Go to auxiliary," Sam said.

"Yes, ma'am," Chandler said. "Ma'am, they're — OK, I've got auxiliary, but only sixty percent."

"Forward shields are at twenty percent and falling," Franklin said.

Sam took a deep breath. "Get our people off the ship," she said. There was a protocol for that, too, though it was another one she'd hoped never to use. "Beam them to Atlantis."

"Everyone?" Franklin asked warily, his hands poised above the controls.

"It's time for Plan Z," Sam said, and somehow achieved a smile. Franklin swallowed hard, but matched her.

"Yes, ma'am. Plan Z it is."

Sam slid back into her seat, shutting out the noise of the alarms and the voices on the intercom. Plan Z was the act of last resort, the hail Mary pass, the absolute last chance — the sort of thing only the SGC would think of, she'd heard an engineer grumble, and at the time, she'd taken it as a compliment. Now it didn't look so good, but it was all she had. Beam the crew away, that was step one, then aim the *Hammond* for the hive and set the engines to overload. As long as someone stayed with her to the last possible moment, matching the hive's evasive maneuvers, the explosion should take out the hive.

Air shimmered in the control room, half the crew beamed away, and Franklin looked up from his console. "All but priority crew are safe in Atlantis, ma'am. Permission to stay aboard —"

"Denied," Sam said briskly. The ship rocked again.

"Forward shields at ten percent," Chandler said.

"Go," Sam said. "That's an order, people."

Franklin's face tightened, and for a crazy instant she wanted to ruffle his hair and tell him that he was a good guy even if he was a gossip. Instead, she reached for the controls. "I'll be right behind you, Major," she said, and beamed them away.

The bridge stank of smoke and foam as she moved to Chandler's console, typing in the commands that swung the *Hammond* stern-on to the hive, putting the best shield and the bulk of the ship between her and the hive. Autopilot was still working, more or less, and she engaged the docking system, overriding safeties to convince the system to home in on the hive. Satisfied it would hold for a little longer, she turned to the engineering console, and stopped short. The panels were blown, smoking; there was no way she could create an overload from there. She blinked once, then reached for an overhead panel, pulling down a tray of crystals. Maybe if she rearranged them here —

The first crystal exploded, showering her with sparks. It set off a chain reaction, a line of popping flames that ended at the beam controls. No way to set the overload — and no way to get off the ship now, either, but that wasn't important. Sam took a deep breath, moved to check the tactical display. *Hammond* was still closing on the hive, sluggish but inexorable, and that would have to be enough. *Sorry, Jack*, she thought, and turned her attention to the pilot's console. They were still closing, three minutes to impact. The hive was firing steadily, *Hammond's* shields faltering, failing, alarms sounding as aft sections vented to space.

And then the hive rolled, thrusters flaring. The tac screen brightened, showing *Daedalus* closing, all guns firing. *Hammond's* autopilot fired thrusters, too, trying to match the hive's maneuver, and Sam ran to the weapons console. There was still power to the railguns, and more in life support. She moved with frantic speed, diverting every scrap of power to the guns, glancing over her shoulder at the main tac screen. The hive was turning, showing its already-damaged stern.

Come on, she thought, working the railguns' controls. Come on, turn... And then the hive was in her sights, and she slammed her fists down on the firing controls. The railguns fired, and she counted five heavy pulses before the power gave out entirely. Life support was gone, too; the depressurization alarm had been sounding for a while, and now the inertial dampeners were off-line. In the screen, the hive ship exploded, glorious as fireworks. Without inertial dampening, she was as good as dead, but at least she'd seen it go —

The air shimmered, and she was suddenly on the bridge of the *Daedalus*, blinking in the sudden normal air. She took a breath, hoping she didn't look as shaken as she felt, and Caldwell swung to face her.

"Nice shooting, Colonel."

"Thanks," Sam said. She realized with pleasure that her voice was steady. "Very nice timing, too."

CHAPTER TWENTY-EIGHT
Last Chance

JOHN looked around the table, wishing the coffee would kick in. He'd managed to shower and shave, but he'd been up well into the early hours of the morning reading the various reports, and he was still kind of surprised they'd done as well as they had. From the look of the faces around the table, he thought the others might be feeling much the same way.

The door of the briefing room slid open to admit Colonel Carter. She looked as though she hadn't slept since they'd managed to wrestle the *Hammond* down safely onto the West Pier — probably hadn't, John thought, and nodded a greeting.

"Sorry," Carter said, generally, and reached for the coffee.

Caldwell slid his chair aside to make room for her, and Keller looked up with a wincing smile. Might as well start there, John thought, and took a breath.

"Dr. Keller. How are the injured doing?"

She gave him another nervous smile, glanced down at her tablet. "Actually, not badly. We've got six people with moderately severe burns, all of whom I believe can be successfully treated here. Dr. Flecha has a broken shoulder from falling debris, but everyone else has been treated and released. That includes those of *Hammond's* crew that were beamed to the city during the fight."

That was unexpectedly good news, John thought. "Speaking of damage to the city — "

Zelenka looked over the top of his glasses. "We have been lucky there, too. The three smaller towers on the Northwest Pier took structural damage, and I have placed them off limits until we can shore up the supports, but that is the worst of it. I have a team resurfacing the hole on the South Pier, the area that we use as an auxiliary landing pad for the jumpers, but they expect to be done by nightfall. The rest is broken glass and blown fuses."

Repairing the landing pad wouldn't be much fun in this weather, John thought. The wind was strong out of the south, dropping the apparent temperatures below freezing again. But it was better than he'd expected. "Keep me posted."

"Yes, I will do that." Zelenka frowned at his tablet, made a note of something there. "I have also put every available person to help with the repairs to the *Hammond*, and there will be more, Colonel Carter, as soon as our repairs are in place."

"Which I appreciate," Carter said. "Very much. There's a lot of work to be done."

"Which brings us to the bigger issue," Caldwell said. "The Wraith have got an energy shield. And I think we all know where they got it."

That was the elephant in the room, pirouetting in a tutu in the middle of the table. John bit his lip, not sure what to say that wouldn't make things worse, and Carter looked up from her coffee.

"They've got a shield," she said, seriously, "but it's not a very efficient one. I don't know about you, Steven, but it seemed to me that when the shield was up, the hive was significantly less maneuverable."

Caldwell gave a reluctant nod. "I'll agree with that. And I'll agree that it's not effective as ours. But it's still something they didn't have before they got McKay."

There was another little silence, and then Zelenka said, "It is possible that they have reverse-engineered it on their own. The Wraith have always been very quick to react to our technology, to counter anything we have done."

"Do you really think that's likely?" Caldwell asked.

"They've done it before," John said.

Carter wrapped both hands around her coffee mug. "I hate to say it, but I think this is McKay," she said. "Or at least information obtained from him one way or another. The Wraith never had enough power to make energy shields practical — and still don't — so the decision to try it seems to have had to come from outside."

"I am not sure I entirely agree," Zelenka said. "They are well aware that energy shields are more effective. Perhaps they have decided it is worth the power drain."

"Rodney McKay has already led an attack on this base," Caldwell said. "Why wouldn't he go ahead and develop shields, too?"

"This may be why he took the ZPM," Carter said.

Zelenka sighed. "That makes sense. And if he has it..."

There was a depressed pause, everyone thinking about the attack on Earth, the super-hive powered by stolen ZPMs. John took a breath.

"McKay doesn't know who he is. He thinks he's a Wraith, that's pretty obvious, so he's not going to think he knows a lot of things. And he hasn't told them how to get to Earth, or they'd be there already."

"Hasn't told them yet," Caldwell said. "Colonel Sheppard, I know he's your friend, but we're going to have to face facts here. Leaving McKay in their hands is increasingly dangerous."

"So we get him back," John said. "I'm open to suggestions, Colonel."

Caldwell's face darkened, and Carter said, "I think this discussion is premature, given our current resources. Right now, I'm more concerned about getting the *Hammond* spaceworthy again."

Caldwell nodded, and after a moment, John copied him. "OK," he said. "If that's everything?"

"There is one small matter," Zelenka said. "But it does not concern everyone."

"OK," John said again, and pushed himself to his feet. The others filed out. Carter paused in the doorway, seeming about to say something, but then she thought better of it, and turned away.

"So," John said. "What's up, Radek?"

"First, there is the Wraith cruiser," Zelenka answered. "It is in an unstable orbit around the planet, so at some point we may need to send a jumper up to finish it off. Otherwise, it will make an uncontrolled reentry, and, although the chances of it hitting something important —"

"Like us?" John asked.

Zelenka smiled. "Yes, like us — are fairly small, still we may not wish to take the risk."

John bit his lip, considering. The jumpers had plenty of drones, but at the moment, he didn't want to waste anything. "How long before we have to do something about it?"

"Several weeks," Zelenka answered. "Perhaps longer. I will run more exact calculations today."

"Good." John paused. "And second?"

"Second—" Zelenka grimaced. "Second, I think Mrs. Miller and I need a word with you privately."

That did not sound good. "All right," John said, warily, and started for his office.

Jeannie Miller was waiting in the control room, pretending to look out over the city, swept bare now of snow by the steady wind. She turned at their approach, her face lightening, and John waved her ahead of them into the office. The door closed softly behind them, and John leaned on the edge of Woolsey's desk.

"OK," he said. "What's going on?"

The others exchanged glances, and then Jeannie drew a breath. "It's Rodney," she said. "I think he's left us a message."

"What?" John winced at his near-shout, and Zelenka nodded.

"I agree. You know that we have been finding and deleting pieces of Rodney's code after each attack."

"Meredith's been trying to set up new backdoors," Jeannie interjected.

"And so after the last time, we found another subroutine that had burrowed in," Zelenka said. "But this one was different."

"It's a code we used to use when we were kids," Jeannie said. "Something only Meredith would remember." She reached into her pocket, pulled out a slip of paper and handed it across. "He wants to meet you."

John took the scrap, smoothed it carefully twice before he could bring himself to look. *For John Sheppard*, it read, in Jeannie's neat printing, *I'm on Gaffen. Help me. Rodney McKay.*

"You're sure it's him," he said, and both of them nodded.

"It is McKay's hand, no question," Zelenka said.

"He must have remembered who he is," Jeannie said. Her eyes were bleak. "We have to help him, John."

It took Ronon and Teyla a few minutes to get up to John's office. Time enough to think about what he was about to ask them to do, and about whether he was entirely sure it was a good idea. There was something about sitting behind that desk that made it seem harder to tell what the right answers were.

"What's going on?" Ronon said, stepping back in the doorway to let Teyla come in before him.

"Shut the door," John said. Ronon raised his eyebrows but shut the door.

"Are we in trouble?" Ronon asked.

John frowned. "For what?"

"That just usually means somebody's in trouble."

"Somebody sent us a coded message," John said, laying it down on the table in front of him. "It says it's from Rodney."

Both Teyla and Ronon glanced down at the paper, as if needing to see even that much concrete evidence for themselves.

"So, we go get him," Ronon said after a moment.

Teyla shook her head immediately. "We must take time to think," she said. "We could very well be walking into a trap."

And of course she was all too aware of the possibility, having walked into Michael's trap herself intending to rescue Kanaan. He didn't think she'd ever be quite as quick to throw herself into danger again. They'd all been younger five years ago, and more fearless, if probably not as smart.

"We still have to go," Ronon said.

"I agree that we must," Teyla said before John could. "But we must think of the fact that it may not truly be a call for help."

"Believe me, I am," John said. "We'll take a Marine team for backup, but we need to act fast. If he was able to send a coded message through the gate, he must have at least radio equipment with him. That suggests a Wraith scouting party or something like that, and they may not hang around the area for long."

Teyla looked at him a little too perceptively. "What do colonels Caldwell and Carter say?"

"I haven't asked them," John said. He looked from her to Ronon, knowing the one he really had to convince here was himself. "I don't know what Colonel Carter would say, but Colonel Caldwell thinks that it's time to eliminate Rodney as a threat. I'm not ready to do that yet, not if he's remembered who he is and is trying to escape."

"Nor am I," Teyla said. "I think that changes the situation."

"I don't think Caldwell's going to see it that way," John said. "But he's senior to me and Carter both. If he really wants to arm-wrestle over who's in command in Atlantis, we're going to have a problem."

"Mr. Woolsey left you in command," Teyla said.

"That's the way I see it," John said. "It's my responsibility to make a decision, and I'm making one. But if we have to have an argument over whose responsibility it is right now, we could be losing our last chance to get Rodney back."

And with Caldwell and Carter both on station, it wasn't like he was leaving Atlantis undefended if this went badly. Carter had certainly done a fine job when she was in command, and as many times as he'd clashed with Caldwell over the years, John did at least trust him to take care of the city if he wasn't around.

Ronon shrugged. "You're in charge of Atlantis. We work for you, not for the Air Force. It's not a problem for us."

"All right," John said. It wasn't exactly disobeying a direct order. They hadn't gotten the orders yet, although he knew they would as soon as they got back in contact with Earth, as soon as he reported in. And he'd do it, if there wasn't any other way, but not without trying one more time. If that didn't work, if this was a trap, then he'd do what he had to do and try to live with it.

It was the best decision he knew to make, the best he could do for Rodney and for everybody who was screwed by the way the Wraith were using Rodney, for everybody who was also going to be screwed if they didn't get Rodney back to saving their asses on a regular basis. The best he could do for Atlantis. He'd think about whether it was the best he could do for the Air Force later.

"Let's go get Rodney," he said.

Stay in touch...
Follow us on Twitter
@StargateNovels

Find us on Facebook at
facebook.com/StargateNovels

Sign up for our newsletter
at StargateNovels.com

THANKS!

STARGÅTE
SG·1.

STARGATE
ATLÅNTIS™

Original novels based on the hit
TV shows **STARGATE SG-1** and
STARGATE ATLANTIS

Available as e-books from leading online
retailers

Paperback editions available from
Amazon and IngramSpark

If you liked this book, please tell your
friends and leave a review on a
bookstore website. Thanks!